PANCHO II

PANCHO II
A NOVEL OF MEXICO
A PREQUEL & A SEQUEL

DON ERIC CARROLL

Copyright © 2018 Don Eric Carroll
The moral right of the author has been asserted.

Apart from any fair dealing for the purposes of research or private study, or criticism or review, as permitted under the Copyright, Designs and Patents Act 1988, this publication may only be reproduced, stored or transmitted, in any form or by any means, with the prior permission in writing of the publishers, or in the case of reprographic reproduction in accordance with the terms of licences issued by the Copyright Licensing Agency. Enquiries concerning reproduction outside those terms should be sent to the publishers.

This is a work of fiction. Names, characters, businesses, places, events and incidents are either the products of the author's imagination or used in a fictitious manner. Any resemblance to actual persons, living or dead, or actual events is purely coincidental.

Matador
9 Priory Business Park,
Wistow Road, Kibworth Beauchamp,
Leicestershire. LE8 0RX
Tel: 0116 279 2299
Email: books@troubador.co.uk
Web: www.troubador.co.uk/matador
Twitter: @matadorbooks

ISBN 978 1789014 907

British Library Cataloguing in Publication Data.
A catalogue record for this book is available from the British Library.

Printed and bound by CPI Group (UK) Ltd, Croydon, CR0 4YY
Typeset in 11pt Baskerville by Troubador Publishing Ltd, Leicester, UK

Matador is an imprint of Troubador Publishing Ltd

In loving memory of the
Two Dannys in my life
Brother Danny (1945-2011)
Nephew Danny (1970-2013)

BY THE SAME AUTHOR

"Feast Of Expectancy"
"The Painter"
"From Dust To Flowers"
"Pancho"

PRAISE FOR **PANCHO**

Matador 2016 (ISBN 978-1-78589-365-0)

"… A revelation
The writing is superb, with words
just flying off the page.
It is witty, emotional, wonderfully
descriptive, sensitive to both the
characters and the terrain.
In short it is a triumph!"
Pashtpaws
Breakaway Reviewers

ABOUT THE AUTHOR

Don Eric Carroll left school at 14 and joined the RAF as a Boy Entrant, serving for fifteen years. Since then, he has been a professional chef, a College lecturer in Bermuda, poet and traveller, amateur photographer and muralist, a ranchero in Mexico, bartender, EFL teacher, and a VSO Volunteer in Egypt. Now long retired don Eric is utilising time editing and redrafting a string of stories he wrote in earlier years.

BY WAY OF AN EXPLANATION

The character Pancho was created in the late 1970's when I lived in the State of Guanajuato, Mexico. He featured in a novel I wrote, titled "The Scorpion's Last Day". Sample manuscript chapters sent to London publishing houses were rejected outright, mistaking my novel for a Western. Some twenty years later I resuscitated certain portions, the remainder getting binned. From the surviving pieces I produced a narrative prose poem, titled "From Dust To Flowers" (Publisher: Ros Ruadh 1998).

PANCHO, published October 2016, dealt with a long hot dry summer on Mexico's central plateau. PANCHO II deals with a winter and spring (a prequel), and autumn (a sequel).

Thus, as "From Dust To Flowers" tells of A Day In The Life Of Rural Mexico, the two PANCHOs formulate ... A Year In The Life Of Rural Mexico, the full story set in the late 1950's.

Like the first volume I have adapted portions of my narrative prose poem, and readily admit to the fact that some of this second volume involving the eponymous character Pancho, is autobiographical. All the same, what might be true reality and what possibly is pure fiction, the author regretfully refrains from ascertaining any form of enlightenment for the reader.

THE
PREQUEL

THE
CRUSADES

BOOK I
WINTER

PART ONE

1
A Quiet Commune

*I*t was a memorable and pleasant *Natividad* at the Ramos homestead this year. Late summer and early autumn had yielded a fairly bountiful harvest, in marked contrast to the previous year when the entire region had suffered a hard and debilitating drought.

What joy for the family as they surveyed towering mounds of pumpkins, lovingly collected during long clear sunny days, stacked now against the walls of the inner courtyard. And there were crate upon crate of luscious peaches and apricots, huge baskets of string beans, gunny sacks of corncobs, and a golden hill of shucked corn sat in majesty in the cornstore. As *mamá*– or *doña* María – had said at the time, the husks shucked from these cobs, thrown in a barrel, would make excellent fuel for the winter fires.

The family was equally successful with their apple orchard and small field of alfalfa. They had even grown a little wheat, winnowed under deep-blue cloudfree skies, over on traditional threshing grounds behind the stable and the pig-pens. Chaff and dust had floated as firesmoke for days on end over the yard and outbuildings, like a dusting of icing sugar.

Even now in late December the weather was fine each day, though there was a sharp crisp cold at this time of the year in the valley, situated as it is on Mexico's central plateau and some several thousand metres above sea level, making the air fresh but thin and raw.

What was different this time during the festive Christmas days was the presence of a special guest. None other than the family's good friend of long-standing, the old *ranchero* Francisco Medina Ramírez, more familiarly known to all in the valley and beyond as – Pancho.

He was adequately accommodated in his own small snug room squatted between a cornstore and a chicken-house. He had arrived mid-morning of

Christmas Eve, awkwardly grasping in one hand a generous bunch of royal-red poinsettias, roots dripping wet soil, which the oldster promptly handed over to mamá, at the same time planting a kiss upon her broad cheek.

On Christmas Day morning the ranchero raised his old hide early. Gave a hurried *"Buenos días, María"* to mamá, who was lost in billowing smoke as she built up a woodfire under the kitchen lean-to.

"I'm off to the river," he added gravelly in his morning voice to the smoky wraith that was mamá, and carried on gimp-wise out of the yard.

He soon left behind a copse of beefwood and mesquite, following a track alongside a field of winter alfalfa stretching down to the river – which was more in the order of a modest stream.

To many folk for long distances around the well-known figure of Pancho was immediately recognisable, because of the old man's shape and the way he walked. He reminded people of a rough-hewn rock; sort of square-like with the edges chipped off. Keg-chested and with broad chunky shoulders, all in all a physical powerhouse. Walking on short bandy legs – the legs of a horseman, which in truth he was – and moving with a peculiar gait, swaying and rocking from side to side, like an old Spanish caravel caught in a turbulent sea swell.

Down as far as the river he went gimping along.

Not having washed back at the farm he would do so here, he decided. He hunkered down at the water's edge, quickly glanced around and saw at once that he was alone, and removed his *sombrero* – he always felt naked when it was off his head. The low morning sun struck on an amazing thatch of spiked ginger-red hair on his scalp.

With cupped hands like pan-sized ladles he splashed water over his face and partly down his front as well, gasping and spluttering at the biting coldness of the river water. He shook his head as a dog would and, well satisfied, speedily replaced his sombrero over wet, communion-wine-red hair.

Time being his own the old man idled by the riverside for a while, hunkered on his heels in the habitual manner of a Mexican horseman, and gazed interestedly about him. Across the river a few cornfields to the right lay the *pueblo* of San Angelo, temporarily lulled into peace by the early morning stillness. A slight mist, cold and vaporous, still clung to the valley's floor, but visibly shredding and breaking up with every minute's passing and the sun's inching movement upward, gaining in strength.

He was feeling happy and satisfied with himself. When an old man is happy and content, he is yet young, he was thinking complacently.

There were sounds now, he at last realised, the kind of sounds he was so familiar with, that at first he wasn't aware of them. A rustling of dry grass behind him as a fresh whispering wind probed the valley's length; a cock crowing in the pueblo, and another; and coots sounding alarums as they invaded one another's territory. There were other birds too, chirruping and chittering in stands of *carrizos* just a little distance away on the river's south bank.

Quietness moved in once more in a soothing wave and Pancho gave a sigh of contentment, though totally unaware he had done so. It was a countryman's uninhibited appreciation of God's innumerable creations on display for him to feast on. He believed that it was the Maker's breath that gave air to feed all living things; His hand that shaped the curves of hill and valley; put the roundness in a bird's breast and sweetness in its calling voice, and coloured the green in the fields and dropped nourishment in the soil.

Soon enough the chapel bell started up, pealing joyously and vigorously on this Christmas morn. And dogs began to bark and a *burro* loudly snorted and brayed; and there were shrieks and shouts of children, all of this clamour emanating from the pueblo.

Two thoughts arrived at once in the old man's head:

It is Christmas Day and María is this very moment cooking breakfast, or at least she ought to be.

He rose then, stretched himself like a large jungle cat, and headed back to the farmstead, working up a healthy appetite. He seemed to be back with the family in hardly no time at all.

Feeling hungry!

2

Family Gathering

Everybody was now up and about, alive and thrilled, sounding not unlike a crowd in a town *plaza*. The excitable family chatter and savoury cooking aromas hit Pancho full in the face the moment he entered the main courtyard. There was the plum plump homely figure of mamá, as usual bustling by the woodfire range which was burning merrily. Helping mamá with the breakfast preparations was her eldest daughter Cristina, a good-looking girl but prone to appear solemn and serious of mien at times.

And there were the two younger girls, dancing and skipping about the yard, laughing and prattling away between themselves; Ruth, almost into her teens, a lovely girl obviously destined to become a dusky beauty; and little Julia, seven going on seventeen, a pretty creature of precocious bent, high spirits and gay nature.

Lastly, there was young Juan, a sturdy handsome boy of thirteen and mamá's most favoured offspring. He was sat on a three-legged stool by a large wooden table where the family ate all their meals. Slumped by his side like a scruffy pile of old rugs was his dog Salté, a great shaggy hound that rarely left his master on his own day or night, at least not if he could help it.

The girls wore their best festive frocks of white muslin, draped to the ankles and hemmed with fine embroidery. Underneath this finery they wore thigh-length woollen leggings, feet snugly tucked into fur-lined ankle boots to keep the cold at bay. Around their shoulders and hanging to the waist, each had on a gaily multi-coloured sarape of thick homespun wool. And in their hair was tied a cardinal-red ribbon, heightening their long blue-black tresses.

And *papá*? Don Antonio was not to be seen, no doubt still in his room and poring over pages of *The Lives of the Saints*, with a magnifying-glass, as his eyesight was poor and he had long needed a proper pair of reading spectacles.

Julia was first to spot the old ranchero and dashed to him at once on light limbs and calling "Oh Pancho! *¡Feliz Navidad!*"

He bent to her and, as her down-soft lips touched his cheek and her honeyed breath caressed his face, he felt that he could eat her up for breakfast right there and without a qualm. Indeed, with his long-sweeping moustache and a livid scar running down one side of his dark swarthy face, he looked altogether only too capable of devouring the child, like the mythological Greek god Cronus. Pancho however was a soft bighearted good-natured soul with a decided sense of humour. Ever smiling and jovial, possessing kindly blue eyes, even a stranger would instantly take to him and which was often the case.

These characteristics of the old ranchero were unusual, because the typical rural Mexican is dour, solemn and somewhat sedate, taking life quite seriously; he is generally introvert and can indulge in long almost sulky silences.

Not so Pancho.

After his solitary walk and quiet commune with the delights of nature, his senses reeled with the atmosphere he now found himself in. The sounds of clattering pots and dishes, the spitting, crackling fire, girls' laughter, and mamá humming *Albur de Amor* to herself. Not forgetting the homely smells of woodsmoke, fresh-baked corncakes, panfried eggs and beans and *tostados*, all mingling and teasing his nostrils.

"Look at what I bought for mamá," piped Julia eagerly, tugging at Pancho's *poncho* and pointing to her mother.

"What is it, my rose-flower?" he asked, then turned to mamá. "What have you got there, María? – Ah, I see it!" as mamá showed off a corn-yellow poppy pinned to her hair. She put a hand to the back of her head and seductively gyrated ample hips to sultry effect.

"It's artificial," Julia informed him, as if that was the flower's chief value and attraction.

"What a temptress you are, María," grinned Pancho, eyeing the coy lady's motions, "you'd tempt the skin off a *coyote*, so you would."

"It'll last and last forever," Julia burbled on, "because it's artificial, you see."

"Which is the least we can say for your mamá," quipped the old man.

"Do you like it then?" teased mamá with mock coyness.

"The flower or the shaking peach tree?" responded Pancho.

"In my young days, I'll have you know … " began mamá.

"*Claro*, I think I do remember," he laughed, turning now to Juan. "And what have you got here, Juanito?"

"It's a Swiss army knife," said the boy with some measure of pride, "from mamá and papá. It's got lots of different - *¿Como se llama?* – What's its name? – different blades and devices. Here, look at this. It's a bottle-opener. That one there is for removing stones from a horse's hoof."

"Hmm … useful eh, *muchacho*? And what might this be then, a screwdriver or something is it?"

"It'll be ready in a moment!" called mamá from under the kitchen lean-to, face red with exertions at the cooking-fire.

"*¡Bueno, María!*" roared back Pancho in a tone husky and gravelled, his notably early morning voice.

"No," returned Juan, "that's a corkscrew."

"Hmm, a cork screw," but the old ranchero was none the wiser.

"For taking corks from wine bottles."

"Ah *sí*, for the Communion I suppose."

"This one here – "

"See what I've got, Pancho!" cut in Julia. "From Rutí. Rutí bought it for me, a colouring book and lots of coloured crayons. Do you like them?"

"*Ay que caray*, my sunflower, I must admit that I do."

"I can give you a crayon if you like, what colour would you like?"

"No my precious, you keep them, you'll need them all, I'm bound to say."

Meanwhile, three females were competing for space around the kitchen fire. Ruth was making a rather botched job of the tostados, Cristina dished up black beans and mamá fried fresh-laid eggs. Julia skipped over to join them.

"Can we give it to him now, mamá?"

"Rutí, you're burning the tostados again."

"*Ay* Cristina, I never get it right, do I?"

"Give who what, *niña*, what are you on about?"

"The *present*, mamá."

"Oh that. Later on my sweet. Can't you see I've got my hands full here?"

Mamá was indeed fully occupied, with one hand saucing eggs for *huevos rancheros*, the other sprinkling on chopped raw onion and sprigs of coriander, her final touch to a classic Mexican dish.

"Shall I go and get it, mamá?" pressed the little one.

"Get what?"

"You know, the *present*!"

"I told you, later. Now get from under my feet, *por favor*, go sit down."

"I'm putting the beans on the table," announced Cristina.

"I've burnt the tostados, mamá!" wailed Ruth.

"Never mind, *muchacha*, and that's enough for now I think," sighed mamá.

"Where's papá?" Julia wanted to know.

"It all smells bueno!" Pancho called over.

"It's ready too," mamá said, "so sit yourselves. *¡Andale!* Juanito, go and get your papá – Sit, Pancho, right there if you please."

"A man always knows his place, María."

"And yours is over there, see, *¡Chihuahuas!*" threatening him with a spatula.

"Here, next to me," invited Julia, wriggling her bottom on the bench-seat.

The old man did as he was told with some alacrity. Don Antonio made his appearance at last, and Juan quickly threw a sarape over the parrot's cage, to curb the bird's habitual throwing out of abuse at everyone when at the family table.

3

Breaking the Fast

They were all now seated, except for mamá, who hardly ever sat down with them for a meal but constantly fussed about between table and kitchen fire, ensuring that the family tucked into the prepared food, topping up plates and dishes as and when needed. She would eat later, alone and in repose, as she always did.

Don Antonio glanced briefly at everybody about him, then lowered his head and intoned a prayer of thanks for this special day. He motioned a sign of the cross and the family did likewise, but not exactly with the same decorum or sense of devotion. They proceeded without a moment's hesitation to break their fast, mouths open to chatter as much as to put food there to eat.

"You've given me two eggs, I only wanted one."

"Just get it down your neck!"

"That's your second helping in one go."

"Pass the tostados, por favor."

"A clever brain is not all that important if you have feelings," the old man was telling Ruth.

"Well, Pancho, how was your walk this morning? I saw you set off."

"*Bueno, compadre, gracias.*"

"Are you warm enough, niña?" enquired mamá.

"Until this very moment," Pancho was now telling Juan, "- right now – every bit of your life is in the past."

"Sí, mamá," returned Julia. Her mother thought the child was coming on with a slight cold.

Even though the gathering were sitting out in the open air it was surprisingly snug and cosy in the courtyard, enclosed as it was on four sides by the outbuildings and stable, which kept the wind in check. Earlier that morning Cristina had strewn cornstraw over the hard-trodden ground, covering it completely and somehow making the yard appear smaller. The yard cock and half-a-dozen hens were everywhere kicking up the straw, grubbing for what they could find underneath. It also managed to draw the two yard-cats from the warmth of the hearth to play in the straw, though they were long out of kittenhood.

Around the homestead buildings the wind coldly stirred, occasional predatory gusts stealing into the courtyard and lifting the cornstraw. These buildings surrounding the family gathering were rather old and shabby, knitted and tacked on, one to another in hardstone, mortar and adobe brick.

The old ranchero was into reminiscing mode: "I remember one Christmas a few years back," he was yarning to his listeners, "and I was on don Roberto's *hacienda* – naturally, hmm. Well, late on Christmas Eve don Fernando rolls in on his wagon with a one-day-old foal tied up in the back."

"Who is don Fernando?" asked Julia.

"Shush, niña!" admonished mamá, "and let him get on with his story."

"Only, listen to this," Pancho pressed on. "In the middle of the night he comes, this don Fernando – He owns a small horse ranch west of don Roberto's land – " in an aside to Julia, "and it was a good thing I was there, because the man was almost weeping.

"'¡*Oye*, Pancho!' he calls to me, 'I've got a foal here and my roan mare died giving birth to it, and my sister's sick in town. I must get over to see her. Can you take care of this foal until I get back from town?'

"'¡*Caracoles!*' says I, 'one man's favour is another man's saviour. We can put it in with the old chestnut mare.'

"Hmm, and that's what we did, and it *was* a lucky thing I was there. *Uuy*, I stayed the night in the stable, with the foal and the old chestnut mare, for it was a damn sight warmer than my own draughty place."

"You should take better care of yourself," said mamá, "and light a fire so as to keep warm."

"Well, María, I searched my pockets but found no common sense there."

"You need to take care, I say."

"Hush, mamá!" said Julia, "and let him get on with his story."

Mamá took a quick look at Pancho and the pair of them simultaneously burst into laughter.

"What's so funny?" Julia begged to know.

"Go on then," urged Juan, eager to hear more, "what happened next?"

"Ay que caray, where was I?" Pancho simmered down. "Well, you wouldn't credit it but that old chestnut mare and the fresh-born foal took to one another like natural mother and daughter. Hmm, the chestnut mare was all over the young one, licking her silly. So I left them to it, so I did.

"The next morning – and by the grace of God it's Christmas Day, you understand – there's such a commotion going on around that particular stable … and it's our Julian. You know Julian, not exactly the full *peso* and forever tripping over things like a brainless *burrito*."

"Poor Julian," sighed Ruth with feeling.

"A little charity wouldn't come amiss," mamá scolded her guest, "and you yourself trip over things – drunk or sober."

"Oh don't get me wrong, María. I love Julian like a son, and it's not his fault that he has no wits to speak of."

"Anyway – if I may go on – our Julian is dashing here and there and bawling at the top of his voice.

"'It's a miracle! It's a miracle!'

"I get myself from behind the stable door and says to him:

"'What's the big noise for then, Julian? *¿Que paso, muchacho?* And what's this miracle you're mouthing off about, eh?'

"And Julian looks at me as if he's just witnessed the Transfiguration.

"'*Señor* Pancho,' he manages to spit out, 'the old chestnut mare – she has just *foaled*!'"

Pancho and mamá again spluttered into laughter. The tale even elicited a modest smile from the usually dour don Antonio.

The old ranchero snapped a piece of tostado, crisp and biscuit-like, its scorched corn aroma attacking his food-sensitive nostrils. He used the piece as a scoop to pick up the egg and its sauce from his dish. Chewed a moment, a bit noisily like a horse crunching grain, and cast a swift glance at mamá who had been carefully eyeing him the while.

"*¡Ay que rico!*" he spat out with satisfaction, and shovelled up more egg and rich sauce, popped in the tostado too, reached for another one.

"You like my huevos rancheros then?" asked mamá, broadly smiling.

"If you're fishing for compliments, María, then you've already hooked me. No doubt about it, this is excellent!"

"A woman's touch you see," she responded, pleased with herself. "You can't beat a woman's touch in these matters – Julia! Wipe your face, niña, you're dribbling!"

"As they say," continued Pancho conversationally, "a stomach will never quarrel with good food."

"There are more corncakes later," sniffled Julia, wiping her little oval face with a grubby handkerchief. "They're still baking, aren't they, mamá?"

"Oh ¡Chihuahuas! My blessed corncakes! And I almost forgot them. Better look at them right now," mamá said in a gasp, and fled to her cooking range.

"There is no pork until you have killed the pig – or *burnt* it," mumbled the old man unclearly.

"*Frijoles* here as well, Pancho," sang Ruth, "which you must try next."

"Black beans, que bueno, I love them, Rutí. Life without beans – "

"Real ranchero's food," grinned Juan.

"Sí Juanito, it gives you strength to handle a horse … and women too," the oldster added in a lower tone.

"Ha! I heard that. So you need beans to get the upper hand with us females, is it? You sinner!" mamá laid into him. She never missed a nuance that was within earshot. "Well, Francisco Ramírez, we womenfolk only need a tongue in our heads to twist you round our little fingers."

"Oh I agree with you there, María. I've always maintained that a woman's strength is assuredly in her tongue. Which explains why many of us males are sometimes slightly hard of hearing," and the old ranchero pounded a fist on the table, roaring with laughter.

Juan grinned at this sally, at the same time surreptitiously passing bits of food under the table to his faithful though ravenous canine companion. Salté was part wolfhound part sheepdog and part something else that no one could ever determine. Luckily for the Ramos family – and their neighbours too – the dog was, in spite of its formidable size and ferocious-looking aspect, it was in truth an amicable mild-natured creature. Slavishly attentive to its one acknowledged master, young Juan, whom it adored beyond measure.

"They've made a beautiful *nacimiento* in the pueblo," Cristina informed the group at the table.

"And what - ?" began Pancho, face screwed with curiosity. "What's a nacimiento if I might ask?"

"Oh Pancho, you miserable pagan!" tut-tutted mamá. "You rancheros know about nothing except your blessed horses and getting *Borracho* on mezcal."

"Drunk? Me? No, never ... but a nacimiento I ask you! Never heard of such a thing."

He busied himself shovelling beans into his mouth as Cristina kindly explained:

"It's a clay model of Bethlehem, a - ¿Como se llama? – a replica in clay. And there's a stable where Jesus was born – "

"You know about that I presume?" interjected mamá.

"You presume correctly, my dove."

" – The new *maestro* at the school made most of it. It's very good."

"More huevos, *papacito*?"

"Sí, gracias, María."

"I made the sheep," put in Julia, "five little sheep – "

"Little!" scoffed Juan. "Why, they were as big as the cattle."

"So? They were corn-fed, my sheep," retorted the child with unconscious wit.

"I thought the cattle were supposed to be camels," mamá threw in, "on account of the lumps on their backs."

"Ay, mamá!" fretted Ruth, "I made those cattle."

"Well, I saw one that was about as delicate as a short-leggety donkey."

"They do make good camels though, Rutí," said Juan, a little more tactfully this time around, "for the Magi did arrive at Bethlehem on camels – or so I always thought."

"On camels as small as sheep ... " muttered Pancho *sotto voce*, and it was as well perhaps that no one caught this remark. "So where is this – this nacimiento, then?" he asked, in trying to cover up for his gaff.

"At the chapel entrance of course," Cristina told him, "where it's put every Christmas time. You'll see it tonight anyway."

"I will?"

"Sí, we're off to the midnight mass tonight," said Ruth. "Aren't we, papá?"

"That is so, God willing," don Antonio smiled over the table at his favourite one.

"Here you are," butted in mamá, "corncakes, hot and fresh."

"With none burnt," observed Ruth.

"You are coming too, aren't you, Pancho?" enquired Juan.

"I expect you'll find me there, sí, *amiguito*."

"And we shall hope and pray that the ceiling doesn't come crashing down over our heads," drawled mamá with one raised eyebrow. "When did *you* last see the inside of a church, Pancho?"

The old reprobate grinned a Mephistophelian grin and said, "The whole range is my church, María, and I pray wherever I find myself."

"I just wonder if I should excuse you."

"Forgive a man his faults, Maria – though they may be many – and they will go of their own accord."

"If you sit next to me in chapel," chirruped Julia, "the ceiling will never fall on us both – because I'm too good, eh, mamá?"

"I shall pray for us all," mamá returned cryptically, passing round a full platter of steaming golden corncakes.

4
The Christmas Gift

Julia cleared a space for herself at the table, soon absorbed in the pleasant task of crayoning in her colouring-book, her present from Ruth. It was usual in these times to give gifts on Christmas Day, an influence filtered down from the United States of America – the *norteamericanos*. No doubt the elders remembered the old traditional day, January 6th, called *Día de Santos Reyes*, when *regalas* – or gifts – were given to the children. For it was on this day that the Magi presented their gifts to the Infant Jesus. Nor was it customary for adults to exchange gifts, but this too was falling by the wayside, because Julia began again to pester her mother about a present set aside for a certain adult person.

"Alright, alright, niña, run and fetch it, ándale," mamá finally gave in to her, and the child was off in a flash.

Moments later she tripped out from papá's room, laden with a large oblong parcel tied with red ribbon which she carried tight to her chest using both hands.

She thrust the package out to the astonished ranchero.

"It's for you!" she announced with a beaming smile. "¡Feliz Navidad!"

"For me?" said Pancho, all agape, and turned to mamá for confirmation.

"Open it, then," was her immediate response.

"Claro … clear enough …right … " said the old man uncertainly and a shade self-consciously, and his great spatula paws fumbled with red ribbon and wrapping paper, to reveal a long cardboard box.

He sat gazing at the box.

"Open it!" urged Julia breathlessly.

"Sí … " said Pancho, in barely a whisper. He lifted off the lid. "Ahh … " he breathed, eyes widened at the sight of the softest whitest tissue paper he had ever seen.

"Well, are you going to open it or shall we wait for the Easter festivities?" prompted mamá in sarcastic tone.

"It is open," he declared, "as you can plainly see."

"Take the paper off, Pancho," said Ruth. "You have to remove the paper."

"See what's under it!" Julia panted out.

The old ranchero did as he was told.

"¡Ay-ay que caray!" he gasped, at last seeing the real contents of the package. He pulled out a fine pair of handsomely tooled light-tan León calf-leather boots. "These ... are for ... for me?" he croaked haltingly, holding up the boots, one in each fist, for everybody to view. "How ... how did you know my size? – If they are my size, they might not be my size," glancing at mamá. And two tears welled up in his kindly, blue eyes, like sap seeping from a tree trunk.

"We measured your feet," giggled Julia, "that time after the peach-picking when you were fast asleep in the stable."

"And borracho," added Juan with a grin.

"¡Borracho!" roared the ranchero, suddenly regaining normal level of voice. "Why, I've not gotten drunk since ... since –"

"The day before yesterday, or maybe yesterday, I shouldn't wonder," cut in mamá. "Now, aren't you going to try the boots on? You can see we're waiting."

Pancho was still holding the boots at arm's length, admiring them. He placed them carefully on the ground, and began to slip his feet from worn, scuffed, filthy horseman's riding boots.

"He really ought to wear them with stockings," suggested Cristina, casting a meaningful look at her father.

"Socks!" Julia burst out. "He needs socks. Pancho, you need socks, don't you know!"

"Stockings, my precious one," mamá corrected her. "Stockings are what he wants," and she too gave a significant glance at papá.

"Something like this?" said don Antonio, suddenly producing from under his arm a small soft package, passing it down to Pancho. The old man opened it at once and found a pair of red knee-length woollen stockings.

"Ay, papá," said Ruth with a quick adoring glance at her father, "you think of everything."

Pancho pulled on the stockings and began stomping on the straw-strewn ground, gazing down at his fire-red woolly feet.

"Well, we can see that *they* fit," said mamá pointedly, "now try on the boots."

The ranchero sat down again and picked up a boot, buried his face in the top of it, inhaling the satisfying smell of new calf leather.

"Oh, ¡Chihuahuas!" cried mamá, fast losing patience, "they're not for eating, get them on your feet, for goodness sake!"

And Pancho did as he was told.

"Well, and how do I look?" he asked moments later, up on his feet once more, arms out wide like a fairground impresario.

"*¡Wapo!* Handsome!" said Juan with open admiration.

"Well, come on, let's see you walk in them," ordered Cristina.

"Okay, claro," and the ranchero turned on his heels and almost toppled over. The boot-heels gave him extra height and he tottered unsteadily like a little girl walking in her mother's high-heeled shoes.

"Oh the Saints preserve us, my friend," said don Antonio, trying to master a grin, "you look as if – Oh, what is it now? – you look like – "

"I know, I know," gruffed the old man, turning round to face them, "like I've gone and peed myself, is it?" which started the females off giggling.

" – like a hobbled mule, I was about to say," smiled don Antonio.

Mamá thought this side-slicingly hilarious. "He'll be alright," she said dryly, "once he learns how to walk again. You haven't been at my tequila, have you Pancho, you rascal?" which prompted him to throw her a knowing wink.

Then:

"Shush, everybody! … Listen … " murmured Cristina.

5

A Small Rural Service

"They're coming," Ruth said.

"Who are?" asked Julia.

"And about time too," mamá said.

Everyone listened to the sounds of shuffling feet and a rustling in the long grass of the outer yard, with a gentle murmuring of many voices. The voices were those of the people from the *pueblito*, a community of some eight or nine families who lived a short distance southwest of the farm, many of whom had their own fields but did much extra work for don Antonio's larger land when the seasons demanded it.

Mamá had done her bit for the morning and did it splendidly, for the Christmas breakfast had proved munificent. Now it was don Antonio's turn in his capacity as a *rezandero* – or lay preacher – to give a modest service for the pueblito families.

So in they came, filing into the courtyard quietly and politely, their conversation now abated. And the moment they started coming in, the retarded winter sun cleared the tree-tops in the orchard and shone directly on them, almost as if they had so timed it.

There was Florencino, blind since a boy, who wove baskets and ran the tiniest of *tiendas* selling Fanta orange juice and Chiclet chewing gum as well as other cheap, everyday sundry items. With him were his wife and three sparkle-eyed children.

In strode Pancho's friend and fellow ranchero, young cross-eyed Cándido. The two men exchanged grins but nothing was said between them, as this was supposed to be a solemn occasion.

Next, in trooped an inordinate number of children of all sizes and age, one after the other and filling up one side of the yard. The boys, hair wet and slicked down over brows in well-washed smart fashion, tended to herd together. Thus the girls, left on their own, also became a separate entity. Dressed up in their best frocks, colours rather faded and material on the worn side, but nevertheless the girls were no less pretty for it. They stood about in their groups, shyly and solemnly.

The women too congregated within one party, murmuring softly among themselves and searching out their offspring for any possible signs of misbehaviour. While the men banded together, glancing around somewhat nervously and self-consciously, some embarrassed in obviously new sarapes wrapped around their shoulders.

And as the whole crowd milled about in the yard, their feet kicked up the cornstraw and the straw gave off a slight dung odour, a homely country smell, reassuring everybody there.

Don Antonio had in the meantime gone straight to his room, or rather his and mamá's shared bedroom, which would serve as a tiny chapel. At the far wall between two single beds was a miniature shrine to the Virgin of Guadalupe. Here, don Antonio lit several candles of pleasant-smelling beeswax.

At a signal from mamá the adults began quietly filing into the room, kneeling where they could, shoulder intimately bunched against shoulder. The children then came forward and knelt in the cornstraw outside, taking space around the room's entrance.

Pancho was a short snippet tardy and ended up outside with the young ones. He found himself next to Julia who turned to him and gave an impish wink.

The simple country-style service commenced without further ado. Don Antonio's voice was strong in prayer and it carried over the heads of the worshippers in the yard. Plain words, like a kind of sustenance for these poor people of the land, strengthening faith and cleansing the soul.

The old ranchero's thoughts had slipped into another sphere, his mind pondering on things not of a devotional nature, but on practical matters to do with horses and the training of them, and so on.

'I'll need to worm that roan colt again, I suppose, and fix that broken saddle of mine,' he was thinking, his swarthy, range-hardened face incongruously lit as though with religious awe and reverence.

6
More Gifts

A time later with the service over the children dispersed about the yard, and the elders came out to join them. Mamá appeared, carrying a large cardboard carton which she placed on the kitchen table.

She was about to distribute gifts for the children. The elders were of course paid earlier for their labours on the Ramos farm, but most of these youngsters had also worked in the fields and orchards all the year long. They too had been paid for their efforts, but mamá was going to reward them extra with a gift for each child.

The biggest ones came first, knowing the procedure, bobbing and curtseying as mamá made the sign of the cross and blessed each one, handing out the presents. Then the smaller ones came forward; again, ever so shyly or solemnly or otherwise – depending on individual personality – and one or two of the little boys, faces fresh-scrubbed and apple-red, grinned cheekily up at her. There was however with them all an inner excitement that could barely be contained.

That done, the whole community quit the yard, after thanking their hosts and with parting shots of festive felicitations. Going back the way they had come, the young ones now chattering more freely, their gifts tightly clutched to chests, to be opened in the freedom of the pueblito homes.

And as the entire party swished its way through tall dry grasses it sounded not unlike a distant shore with long waves gently rolling in, or an ascending murmur of winter birds in low flight.

"Mamá, can we go and play in the pueblito?" asked Ruth courteously, perhaps still moved by her father's Christmas service.

"Sí, you can all go, so I can get some work done around here."

"Oh gracias, mamá."

"On one condition though," mamá checked her, "don't go anywhere near that mad dog of Cándido's, any of you. I don't trust that beast. ¿Claro?"

"Sí, mamá. Ready, Julia? Cristina! Juan! Come on, we're off to the pueblito."

"Not me," said Cristina stiffly, "I too have things to do."

"*Un momento* – wait a minute," said Pancho, glancing at mamá and giving her a crafty grin and wink, "I have something for the muchachas – and muchacho," nodding to Juan.

"You have?" piped Julia eagerly, eyes lighting up with a seasonal festive sparkle.

Mamá's offspring excitedly gathered around the old man as he rummaged under his sarape, delving into a pocket on his denim vest.

"Right, hands out!" he rumbled portentously. "Just one hand will do, Julia, my peach blossom," the youngsters closing in on him as a crowd, showing rounded eyes and fired up with anticipation; panting a little, their breath fresh and clean as good mountain air; the winter coolness burning their faces, colouring the cheeks.

There was a metallic clinking and quick flash of silver as the old ranchero counted three large coins into each outstretched hand.

"Silver dollars!" cried Juan with delighted surprise. "Mexican silver dollars!"

"I'll look after that silver for you all," said mamá decidedly, "till you come back. And *muchas gracias*, Francisco," she added with a warm smile at a now shy-faced old man.

She stretched on tiptoe to kiss him on the brow, and he happily breathed in her smell of spices and woodsmoke and corn dough.

"It's *in* the giving that means more to me than *what* I'm giving," he quietly murmured.

He beamed contentedly.

And perhaps a little wistfully or woefully too. For he had given away in value almost a year's pay in wages. Mamá gazed fondly at him; such a gesture, she thought, typified the good soul and generosity of our own señor Francisco Medina Ramírez.

PART TWO

PART TWO

7

River Crossings

*I*t was into early February; in fact the day of the Candelaria Feast, and old Pancho had not worn his new boots since he tried them on at Christmastide. He was saving them, he informed his fellow rancheros on don Roberto's hacienda, saving them for a special occasion.

Each day he would take the boots out from their original cardboard box and sensually sniff at them, like a dog sniffing at a marking spot. And like a dog, it seemed that by sniffing he perhaps expected the boots to impart some pertinent knowledge to him. The truth of the matter was, as he must have well known, was that he simply enjoyed that delicious smell of fresh leather, as a smoker would enjoy the smoke of his own *cigarro*. With a satisfied air he'd return the boots to the box and put the box away.

The nearest thing to a special occasion he had mentioned was to be on the following day. Orders from his boss don Roberto, who entrusted him with the task of performing a certain errand of importance in the nearest town, a town known as San Stefan.

This planned trip he initially viewed with slight trepidation, as an inexperienced rider might feel when confronted with the prospect of breaking in a wild spirited stallion. In Pancho's case it was solely because he hadn't hardly stepped foot in a town for many years – he was a man of the open range and long wide horizons. He had a deep-seated aversion to towns in general. To be cooped up in the labyrinth streets of a town made him shudder at the thought of it.

This task would normally have fallen on don Roberto's youngest son, but he was needed on the ranch at that particular time. And it was to the residence of the *haciendado's* middle son Alexandro that Pancho would be bound.

The next day dawned clear and bright and the old ranchero soon set off on his way. Without a mount! Not even his own white rawboned mare, Macha. This was because of a temporary quarantine order which had been slapped on don Roberto's hacienda; on his horses, on his cattle, on all the livestock. A precautionary measure because of a disease scare, the scare spreading faster than any supposed disease.

Such was the situation. So Pancho had therefore to travel on his own two pins, as he grumblingly told everyone.

In order to reach the town he had first to cover several miles of open country, with no roads but only goat tracks, and one or two rivers to cross. Which would lead him to the main north-south highway, where, southbound, the traveller would ultimately land himself in San Stefan. Young Juan Ramos was near to giving his friend a lift on a buckboard tilt-cart, but learned it was required for work on the farm on the same day.

So the old man took to footing it across rough terrain. Wrapped in a warm wool sarape, wearing his new boots, faithful saddlebags slung over one shoulder, and a large water canteen strapped to his waist. The canteen contained not water as to be expected but mezcal, to fortify him during what he reckoned a tedious journey – by foot!

He clumped on under an azure blue winter sky. The sun gave little heat but its brilliance lit the landscape with such clarity that it banished shadow and any dullness of colour. The land sparkled and shone back which evidently geared him into a better frame of mind.

A time later he reached the first river which was wide but fairly shallow. Normally, he would have ploughed straight on through it, but not today, not in his new boots. He sat at the bank and began to pull off his precious boots. A few paces downriver some women were washing clothes, bare brown arms going like pistons as they scrubbed away, arm muscles like fat wriggling snakes as they rinsed and wrung out the garments. No pretty ones, thought Pancho, eyeing them over. Pairs of black beady eyes strayed his way in curiosity. Two of the younger women giggled between themselves, maybe because he was removing his boots to cross the river. He waved to them cheerily, then paid some attention to his canteen. He gulped a generous swig, smacked his lips, clapped the top back on and got to his feet.

As he waded through the shallow waters with pants rolled up to his knees, he heard high-pitched laughter issuing from the women at the bankside, arms pointing at his bright red stockings.

Damn! he thought, should have taken them off as well. On reaching the other side he peeled off the soaked stockings, slipped into his boots, and carried on walking or rather gimping in his inimitable way. The stockings were laid one across each shoulder to dry in the sun and desiccated air.

He felt good to be on the move, though he would of course have preferred a mount as a ranchero should, instead of clumping along in booted feet like an infantry soldier. So, in wishing for four legs to take him on his journey, he knew he had to contend with only two – and short ones at that – but infinitely better he supposed than no legs at all. And in that mind frame he quickly glanced down at his own two legs as though to reassure himself that he was in fact still in full possession of them, and in reasonable working order.

Reaching a slight rise in the lay of the land Pancho scanned westward, then eastward, to their furthest limits. The sharp clarity of the winter air and the full power of midmorning light seemed to bring the ranges of hills and mountains nearer to him. Directly ahead he could distinctly make out the town of San Stefan, though still a fair distance away, nestled against a hill and spilling out a little way over the plain in front of him. He saw it almost as a painter would see it; the way the clear cerulean blue of sky fitted so perfectly flush like broad brush strokes against the rim of the far mountain range; and how greens and browns and ochre-yellows oozed in to the flat rooftops of the town dwellings, pouring down between slim towers and goblet shaped cupolas of the churches, sliding along tall ancient walls of buildings, seemingly rubbing gently against them with their colours and light and strong dark shades. So near it appeared to the old man, yet with a deal of travelling time to reach it, by foot and then later by *autobus* when he hit the highway.

After covering some distance from the river and deciding that the stockings must now be dry, he paused to retrieve them.

But the stockings were not there.

A wind had taken them some while ago. He back-tracked for a stretch and soon realised that they were gone for good. With a forced philosophical shrug he continued on with his journey.

8

Two Boys and a Skeleton

He presently arrived at a dry watercourse where he saw, climbing in and out of a gully, a small herd of goats and two tousle-headed boys. The youngsters, evidently in charge of these goats, could not have been more than eight years of age apiece.

At this moment they appeared fully preoccupied with poking carrizo sticks between two rocks deep in the gully. Something or other interested them there, observed the old ranchero. They started guiltily and stared wide-eyed at the villainous looking stranger gazing down on them.

"¡*Hola, muchachos!*" he greeted them, breaking into a warm friendly smile which at once had the effect of putting the boys at ease. If anyone looked more like a bandito it was surely this hombre with a scar running down one side of his weather-wrecked face. "What are you digging at there, found gold or what is it, eh?"

"It's a skeleton, señor," squeaked one of the boys.

"Looks like a coyote, señor," cried the other.

The little goatherd shyly put a hand up to his face, peeked through dirty fingers at the old man.

"Ah, sí, and what makes you think you've found a coyote?" rasped Pancho, stepping partly down into the gully, mindful of his new boots scraping against rock.

He reached the youngsters, towered over them. They smelled of sour goat's milk and straw and dust.

"Sure it's a coyote, señor," said the squeaker.

"Here, señor, here's its head – its skull," said the other boy, holding it up on the end of his stick.

The old man laughed. "Why, muchachos," he gravelled, "that was no coyote. That was a dog."

"Just a dog!" chorused the boys with obvious disappointment.

"Sí, my little friends," smiled the ranchero, "and let that be a lesson to you. When you go to a peach tree you expect to pick peaches, right? And you won't find peaches on a pecan tree."

"¿Que que?" queried the boys, not understanding the homily.

The old man hawked and spat in the dust at his feet. "You reckoned it was a coyote, as that takes your fancy more than a dog would, hmm?" he went on.

"Sí, señor," squeaked the one who squeaked.

"And you also thought that maybe I was a bad hombre, is it? I saw how you took a fright at first sight of me."

He smiled kindly, almost beatifically, down on the two little urchins. A really friendly fashion kind of smile, though they perhaps hardly saw it that way at first.

"We're not frightened now," murmured the other boy bravely, though somewhat bashfully.

"That's alright then and I'm happy for it," returned Pancho with his smile, "but don't trust every stranger who comes your way. If you need to know the true worth of honesty in a man, look into his eyes. You look him right in the eye and you can almost read him like a book."

The younglings shyly blinked basalt-black button eyes and gazed up at him and closely scrutinized him, seeing now only a kindly old man with twinkling sea-blue eyes. He saw in them a perfect innocence and trust and openness. He also noted their dirt-grimed hands and faces, much in need of a good wash, to be sure, he inwardly opined.

The two little ones dropped their gaze, stared down at their bare, dusty feet, shuffling them and kicking pebbles in embarrassed, silent agitation.

Pancho clambered further into the gully and scanned more carefully over the canine remains lying between rocks. "A lame old dog that came here to die," he said quietly.

"¿Señor?"

"Give me your stick, muchacho – you can keep the skull. Do you see the teeth in them jaws? Worn down grinders if ever I did see. An old dog that was, no doubt of it."

"You said it was lame as well, señor, how could you know that?"

Pancho pointed the stick and said, "See that foreleg bone there? Must have fractured at some stage when it was alive. Hmm, and knitted together again but crookedly as you can see for yourselves."

The two innocents gazed winsomely back at this rough-hewn old man, sliding and kicking their feet in the dust.

Pancho glanced up. "Your goats are wandering off all over the place. Better get to them, have a roundup."

The three climbed out the gully.

"Now, muchachos, if you work your way over there a bit," advised the old ranchero, pointing with the carrizo to where he had walked from," you'll find decent grazing grass and juicy plants for these animals of yours."

A sort of companionability was fast developing between him and these young goatherds. But it was time to move on.

He returned the reed cane to the squeaker. "And I best be on my way – this way. ¡*Adios!*"

The old man abruptly set off.

He had barely covered a dozen paces when he heard, "¡Oye, señor!" and turned. "I like your boots!" came the cry, called over in a ringing voice.

Pancho laughed, raised a hand in acknowledgement of the compliment, and spun round on his heels to continue on his way.

9
Pancho Meets a Friend

After a time he approached the second river, narrower than the first, deep and silent running. A track led him to a bridge of sorts, consisting of two heavy tree trunks spanning the river's width, and resting only a hand's length above its surface. He crossed it without any show of acrobatics, but his feet were beginning to hurt in the stiff new boots. He strode on with a slight limp, still following the track.

A short distance ahead was a man leading a burro by its halter, heading directly towards him. He could not distinguish the other's features, for the sun was full in his face. He stopped and shaded his eyes with one hand.

"Is it you, Pancho?" smiled the man, almost coming abreast of him.

"Why, it's Florencino!" said Pancho with surprised pleasure. "¡Que va, hombre! How did you know it was me?"

It was the same Florencino who lived in the pueblito near the Ramos farmstead, the blind man who weaved baskets and ran a tiny tienda. He had recognised the old ranchero before the other had realised who it was.

"I was downwind of you, Pancho," the blind man smiled, "and knew you by your smell."

"*Újule, amigo*, do I smell as strongly as that?"

"No, no!" laughed Florencino, "but we all have our own smell you understand, and being sightless gives you a good nose for it. You may have the eyes of a hawk, Pancho, but I have the nose of a hound and the ears of a bat – Whoa, you awkward carcass!" as the burro stomped its hooves and jibbed at its bridle as though desperate to move on.

"Eyes of a hawk indeed," echoed the old man. "That was surely in my younger days. Why, twice already this morning I've gone stumbling into damned bushes – thorny ones! But what are you about and where have you been? Que paso, my friend?"

The blind man rubbed at his jaw. "I've come from the hot springs spa where I left my wife and eldest girl, to sell the baskets we've made this week. I say 'we' because all the muchachas give me a hand."

"Well, amigo, I don't usually see you in these parts."

"That's a good one!" laughed old Pancho, "saying you don't usually *see* me. You should be on the wireless with your talent, if you catch my drift."

"Oh that," Florencino dismissed it with a grin. "My sight," he went on light-heartedly, "is the play of the wind and the tone of a sound. It's the touch and feel of things and the smells I smell – Steady there, you beast!" addressing the donkey. "For instance, I can smell water hereabouts and I know it's that river over yonder," pointing uncannily to the river Pancho had crossed moments before.

"My compañero," said the ranchero with evident admiration, "You can see better than I ever can, ay que caray."

"Are you heading for San Stefan?"

"That's right. A job for don Roberto - ¡Uuy! What's up with him?" growled the old man, indicating the restless burro. "Why is he jibbing about so, eh?"

"I don't know, *compadre*, he's been like that the best of this day."

"I'll take a look at him," said Pancho. "Hold his head a moment, Florencino," and he felt at the animal's underbelly. "Think I know what his problem is," he grinned. "Give me your stick, amigo," and the blind man handed it over.

The old ranchero hawked heavily and spat on the tip of the stick. He spread the thick saliva over the stick end with a finger. Then he carefully inserted the lubricated end into the beast's back passage. He wiggled it about a bit and gently withdrew it.

A moment later a long expulsion of steaming dung dropped from the donkey.

"That should lighten his load," he quipped. "He was only a bit tight, bunged up like, that's all it was. He'll be okay now I reckon."

"I can only guess what you did, Pancho, but I smell the result of it and thank you very much. I wondered what was wrong with him this morning."

"*De nada,* my friend, it was nothing. You can always rely on me to get to the *bottom* of things. Well, compadre," rasped Pancho, taking the blind man's hand and gently squeezing it in the Mexican manner, "I'll be on my way, so it's *hasta luego*."

"Adiós, Pancho, and good luck in town. May God go with you," and Florencino gave a tug of the halter that signalled his beast to move on.

The old ranchero stood a moment in admiration, amazed at the other's independence and ability to cope with a life in darkness. Whereas he had stumbled and crashed about and got himself stuck in gorse-brush, Florencino stepped swiftly and nimbly and accurately over the rugged terrain, unhesitatingly missing gorse-brush, cactus, thick shrubbery - just about every obstacle daring to challenge his blindness.

Reaching the tree trunk bridge spanning the river, the blind man unerringly stepped on it and stick-tapped his way over. Pancho could only shake his head in wonderment. Then he too plodded on, limping a little, and new boots losing their sheen in spumes of dust.

10

A Restorative Spa

Pancho at long last reached the highway, at a spot which formed a terminal for autobuses journeying to and from San Stefan. There was a mini-market here of makeshift stalls set up in a rough square of waste ground barely off the highway. The stalls sold mainly local produce of the land and large clay pots in vivid colours.

Here was Florencino's little booth where his wife and daughter sold their reed baskets. And as always where people gathered there was also a *taco* stand. The reason this small community existed here in the first place was not only on account of the autobus terminal, but because the place boasted a mineral water spa. A subterranean hot spring ran through here, its beneficent waters at exactly the temperature a human body could readily tolerate without getting scalded.

The old ranchero came limping in with huge bunion-size blisters on his heels. This was through walking in boots without stockings, boots moreover that were new and not broken in. He wished he could have ridden the distance on his white mare Macha, but the creature was not only confined to her stable on account of the local quarantine order, as already mentioned, but Macha also suffered a slightly lame foreleg. Pancho felt as constricted and lame as his mount.

He paid the required five *centavos* entrance fee to an attendant and limped into the spa building to undress. He soon obtained a cubicle and gingerly tiptoed in. It was like a dimly lit cave with sides and roof squared off. The walls were roughly white-washed, the wash having a lurid turquoise tint to it. The water too had a greenish look to it but looked inviting enough. He found himself sharing the space with another man and two boys. There the four of them stood, stark pale-fleshed naked, at the water's edge.

Old Pancho was not in the least abashed over his mother nakedness, and stepped down into the pool, the others following his example. They sat in it as though about to take a bath, soaking themselves in its refreshing velvety warmth.

After ten minutes or so the two boys clambered out, padding to the door and closing it after them. Now there were only the two men left, and Pancho immediately struck up a conversation with the other.

"I'm on my way to town," he informed the man in his usual gritty tone of voice, "for don Roberto."

"And who might don Roberto be?" asked the other, not much interested either way.

Pancho was somewhat crestfallen, assuming the fellow must surely know the renowned don Roberto. "He owns the big horse ranch past San Angelo way. I'm doing an errand for him in town."

"Ah, sí," responded the man with the same disinterest. "I was there myself last week."

"Last week!" parroted Pancho. "Uuy, the last time I was there the town mayor was José-Cruz Argüello."

"José-Cruz Argüello!" ejaculated the other in astonishment. "Újule, hombre, that must be twelve or thirteen years ago."

"As long ago as that, is it?" said Pancho blandly. "How time rushes on, *muy rapido*, without you even knowing it."

The stranger condescended to take an interest and asked him if he had perhaps been working in the United States for such a length of time.

"No, no, but here and there you know," said Pancho, "up and down the country – for don Roberto you see."

The other man had apparently exhausted his social skills or lost interest once more, for he turned and moved away from Pancho, thereby cutting dead any further possible discourse between them.

Presently, the man rose and took his leave without a word of farewell. The old ranchero was not perturbed at this. He revelled in the comfort and restorative powers these waters afforded him. The pain and discomfort seemed to seep away; he wriggled his toes, tried to recall with some complacency the hurt he had earlier felt. The waters even soothed the aches and prickles of pain which greater maturity generally inflicts on a body.

Well satisfied with his soaking and sousing he got up to leave.

He swiftly dressed in the changing-room, not knowing if an autobus was due at any moment. Then he noticed a pair of long socks hanging on a peg in the wall opposite him. Quality socks in good condition, possibly new, he supposed. Had his companion in the cubicle left them there, forgotten to pick them up? Should he run with them and find the man? What if they are not his after all? Besides, he reasoned with a hint of craftiness, had not the hombre uncivilly clamped up and said not another word to him?

Pancho was of course a true-blood Mexican and here was an opportunity not to be missed. 'The Lord provides,' he thought with false or faulty piousness, 'on those who peel their eyes and keep them so. In life's travails we look for some enlightenment; well, enlightenment is there … waiting for you – in the guise of a nice handy pair of socks,' he thought with equally fake piety. 'Get the best out of life before it takes it from you.'

He pulled on the socks without further deliberation, and slipped into his boots.

How splendid he felt after that stint in the miraculously healing spring waters. He was like a new and younger man in vigorous good health. His feet seemed in such top condition that he danced an impromptu jig in the middle of the room. As he was happily prancing around twinkle-toed, the attendant chose that moment to open the door and pop in his head. He stared open-mouthed at the old man's antics.

Pancho saw him and at once ceased his lively footwork. "Que va, hombre, damned fine tonic that spring water!" he gushed cheerfully, by way of an excuse for the eccentric behaviour.

"Sí, señor," the attendant responded, and promptly withdrew his head.

After his brief exuberant spurt of dancing, the old ranchero continued on out of the building with a youthful springy lope.

An autobus rumbled noisily and dustily into the square, at the exact moment Pancho jauntily emerged into the glorious sunshine.

11

The Autobus

The autobus was an ancient wreck of a vehicle. It had no glass in its windows, but three parallel lined wooden bars ran each side of the coach body, horizontally across the windows, presumably there to prevent passengers from tumbling out.

It took a few minutes in disgorging passengers, who were encumbered with wares bought in town : iron pans and plastic buckets – one man and his wife struggled to manoeuvre a deep zinc bath off the bus. Another man was pulling at a lead attached to a stubborn goat that apparently wished to stay aboard. With their belongings these people would disperse over the countryside to their various tiny pueblitos.

There were many people waiting to board – suddenly appearing as if from nowhere – and this they now did, Pancho discovering himself at the outer fringe of the crowd clambering aboard.

The bus soon filled up.

The old ranchero noted a number of young ones, including a babe-in-arms, so it would not be a quiet journey, he guessed. A kid goat was held by someone – presumably why the other goat was reluctant to disembark; they had wanted to get acquainted – while another fellow had a fighting bantam cock under one arm, the cock's long cruel claws sheathed in leather pouches and tightly tied at the shanks.

The cranky old bus set off at last and tore along the *auto* road with a terrific clattering din. As with most vehicles in Mexico, its muffler was missing, or rather deliberately removed so as to economize on petrol consumption; at least that was the general idea behind it. It might also have been removed so as to make a noisy racket, a point of *machismo* to suit male sensibilities.

There were on this bus, as on many buses in the country, apart from a driver and passengers, a ticket-man and a ticket-man's assistant. A foreign visitor taking a bus may perhaps wonder why such an overly-manned crew was required for conveying people from one point to another, and particularly why it was necessary for the ticket-man to have the support of an assistant. But labour is cheap here, and there is also another worthy consideration.

If that same visitor were to be seated in this vehicle, he would realise a moment later at least one aspect of the assistant ticket-man's true role. That moment came of a sudden when the bus violently swerved to avoid hitting a mule and cart hogging the road centre ahead. The ticket-man lurched and was about to topple over, but his assistant was right behind him and promptly reached out to grab him and hold in an upright position.

Throughout the bus journey the assistant stayed glued to his superior, ready at any moment to ensure that his senior partner never met the floorboards except by his feet; thereby, the assistant showed proof enough of his usefulness and dedication to duty, and was an undeniable asset to the bus company – which, rightly, considered 'superfluous' a nasty word.

Another notable feature of this modest though essential mode of transport, is the sellers.

Usually, nimble boys and youths who leap aboard at one stop to sell their wares and get off at the next stop, their 'beat' as it were. Filling the aisle, these young entrepreneurs are pressured between stops to sell as much as they can of what is displayed on their shallow presentation trays – their mobile, miniature shops – confections and bottled drinks, near-warm tacos with various fillings, and suchlike delicacies to tempt the hungry traveller. One may find among them a sombrero-seller, wearing a half-dozen or so sombreros stacked on his head and a sombrero in each hand. Another might be a dispenser of cheap religious trinkets; crucifixes on chains and rosary beads, grasped dangling in one hand, and generally thrust in the face of a potential customer.

The seasoned traveller to Mexico's hinterland will readily tell you what an interesting experience it is to ride a rural bus across the country. There would naturally be the gay nonstop chatter of children or cry of an infant. You are sure to hear the clucking of poultry, or a grunt and squeal of a hog.

The adult passengers, however, are invariably sedate and decorous, talking quietly among themselves.

As will be revealed, it was not to be the case on this particular autobus.

No, not with Pancho on board.

12

Conversations and Conviviality

As soon as he found out that the old man sitting next to him was a retired ranchero, the pair got along like a burning barn, Pancho's gravelled rasping voice and occasional rips of roaring laughter dominating the bus's interior at intermittent stretches of its journey.

"So you work for young Roberto?" wheezed the old-timer horseman, a small-built fellow; wizened, shrivelled and spindle-shanked. "Well, do you?" he pushed testily.

"No, no, hombre, that's the eldest muchacho you speak of. In fact, I'm going to see his brother in San Stefan. I work for his papá, don Roberto."

"That's who I mean, young Roberto."

"Why, he's older than I am."

"You're not old," countered the retired ranchero relic.

Pancho glanced askance at his frail-framed neighbour, noting myriad lines and wrinkles on a gaunt, drawn face; scraggly-bearded, wispy locks of grey hair escaping from under a well-worn but still smart sombrero. And this little old man, in an oversized sheepskin jacket with a huge collar, looked to him not unlike a tortoise peeping out from its carapace.

"No, I suppose not," Pancho agreed, "not by your standards, amigo."

Pancho became aware of his water canteen lying on his lap. Feeling a shade religious today, he was ready for communion with his canteen of tequila – or was it mezcal? he tried to recall. Either way it made not a whit of difference.

He offered it to the ancient who eyed it with some distaste.

"No, señor, gracias," he said.

"It's hard liquor, hombre," said Pancho. "Mezcal, I think, haven't yet checked."

"Ah, gracias, señor," and the old one eagerly snatched the canteen, expertly unscrewed the cap and put the neck of the canteen to ready lips, drinking heartily.

It was passed back. And the one baby aboard, a row in front on Pancho's right, began to bawl with gusto. He was about to reach his canteen out to the infant's mother, but the woman, knowing a better remedy, hefted out a melon-sized breast from her dress and held it for the infant to suckle. It ceased its noise at once, guggling contentedly at this more natural, more appropriate form of sustenance.

Pancho shrugged and pulled a swig at his canteen. "There," he rumbled, "we're both satisfied, eh, niño!" eyeing a breast with a baby stuck to it.

As though the little infant's cries had been a signal, the women in the bus began removing cloths from *tule* baskets set on their knees. All manner of eatables were then distributed to family members and strangers alike. *Tacos* and *tortas* and cold *tamales*, *enchiladas*, chicken pieces, raw chillies.

Even Pancho had something to eat in his saddlebags; some of mamá's culinary delights which were prepared and brought round to him by mamá herself the evening before. She had also given him advice on how to behave at the house of don Alexandro; not to spit on the floor, as one example. The last thing she had told him was to put a razor to his scruffy face and have a decent shave for a change. The food however was given with her love and blessings. He shared this fare with his newly-acquired friend, also a fat señora and her two kids sitting on his right, across the aisle.

The conviviality and good cheer were infectious, spreading the length of the foodstall-smelling bus. The floor was soon littered with orange peel, melon rinds, chicken bones, and scraps of tortillas. The kid goat was having a field-day, roaming the aisle and vacuuming everything in its path, including paper wrappers smelling of the food they had covered.

Pancho was now passing his canteen of mezcal to all and sundry, clumping up and down the aisle, showing off his new boots, exchanging pleasantries and banter with fellow travellers. The driver, a man of consequence everybody recognized, was not left out in receiving a share of food and Pancho's mezcal. And it must be understood that, contrary to what one would reasonably assume, his driving was remarkably improved in performance; as compared, it may be added, to his normal alcohol-free driving skills, which were hardly to be commended by any standards.

The tired, overheated engine of the bus coughed and gears grated as it took a sharp incline in a narrow pass of living rock, a deep shadow falling on it. Next moment the bus was chugging into open country of low scrub and pale purple-hued maguey. And the sun shone strongly into the vehicle. Pancho glanced out his window, saw the sun burning blue the sky, and also thought he espied a lone hawk on the wing.

"You know," opened up the retired ranchero to his companion, who had now at last returned to his seat, after distributing mezcal to most of the men on the bus, as a medic would give out blood transfusions at a disaster area, "you know, that Roberto owes me a debt."

"Don Roberto?" Pancho was unpleasantly taken aback at this remark, knowing his boss for an upright and honest person – a *caballero*!

"The very same, sí, hombre, a matter of forty-five pesos he owed me – and still does – for a horse I sold him. A grand filly it was too."

"Wait a moment," Pancho was seeing a glimmer of light in the stable, "forty-five pesos you say, for a young filly?"

"The very same, sí, as I just told you, last part payment it was, which he never did pay."

Pancho saw the light now, clear and bright. "Why, I remember that. He sent Cándido, who works with me, sent him to go and pay it."

"Was he by any chance a young, squint-eyed hombre?" wanted to know the old man.

"That's him, that's Cándido," Pancho replied with a smile.

"I seem to remember a squint-eyed young fellow coming to my *casa*. In a real bad way he was at the time. Got himself mixed up in a fight in the local town, so he told me, and lost all his money on gambling in the bargain."

"Lost all *your* money, my friend, and I reckon I know what you're going to say next," grinned Pancho, delight plain on his face.

"Anyways," the old one continued on, "one of my muchachas patched up his hurts – for he was in a real sad and sorry state I can tell you – and we put him up for the night under our roof.

"We rattled on about this and that, because I took to him right off. And I remember telling him about my grandson's twelfth birthday, which was soon coming up at the time, and I couldn't think what to get the boy for a present. And this queer-eyed hombre gives me a few suggestions, but I wasn't keen on his ideas, as I recall. Pretty queer ideas too, as I recall.

"He left our house the very next morning, and I was honestly sorry to see him go. He charmed my daughters, so he did. I haven't seen him since."

"Well, compadre, I've got news for you. ¡Caracoles! So I have," said Pancho, grinning all over his face. "This Cándido fellow – a good friend of mine and who works with me as I say – he told me about it. How he lost the money gambling and the rest of it, hmm. I says to him : 'Cándido, you pay that money to the hombre you should have paid in the first place' – that's *you*, my friend!" – nudging him in the ribs – "'You pay him *pronto* or you're no friend of mine.' That's what I said to him. And the next day I see him with a whopping great parcel, wrapped up and tied with string. Well, I could see by the shape of it that it's a guitar wrapped up there – "

"A guitar, you say?"

"Hold your horses, hombre, if you will. Sí, a guitar it was. 'What are you doing with that, muchacho?' I says to him. 'That's your new guitar, isn't it?' 'Sí, it's my guitar,' says Cándido, 'and I'm sending it to that hombre I owe money to.' 'Why,' I says to him, 'you paid a lot more than forty-five pesos for that guitar.'

"And that was the truth of it, for it took Cándido the better part of a year to save up for it. 'I know that,' he says to me, 'but right now I'm in a hurry to pay that debt, and I don't have any smaller change. I'm sending this to him as payment.'

"You hear that!" laughed Pancho, nudging the other.

"Sí," smiled the old man, "and I remember the day it came to me in the post. I did wonder where the hell it had come from. But there was a note with it, to be sure. Something on the lines of 'Hope you can make good use of this special gift. Muchas gracias'. It was signed too, though I'm damned if I could make it out … somebody-or-other Alvarez, I think it was."

"That's him!" beamed Pancho, well pleased. "Cándido Alvarez! My friend and co-worker."

"Well, do you know I somehow never connected this – this cock-eyed young fellow with the guitar. Though I did make good use of it, oh sí, I certainly did. It made an excellent present for my grandson's twelfth birthday, sí, and – " It finally got through to the old man the significance of what he had just uttered. "Why, ¡Carambas!" he broke into a delighted smile of surprise. "That Roberto doesn't owe me a single *centavo*."

"Damn right he doesn't," laughed Pancho, "and Cándido paid his debt as well, every bit of it. Not only your forty-five pesos worth, but also for your good daughter's care of him, and your hospitality in putting him up for a night.

"You see, that guitar was easily worth a hundred and forty pesos – "

"Does he want it back, then?" interjected the other.

"No, no, rest easy, amigo. It was a deed well done and a fellow's honour kept intact, and Cándido kept his. You know, life often comes to a crossroad of sorts at times, when you either have to move aside or move on. Young Cándido came to his crossroad and he moved on. It was a noble gesture on Cándido's part, if I may so say.

"*Ay que bueno, amigo*, but it's a small world after all, wouldn't you say?"

And the two oldsters, one senior by a fair number of years, laughed together as companionably as though they had known each other most of their lives.

"Uuy, speaking of presents and special gifts," Pancho set off again apace, "and this concerns that very same Cándido, but a while back when he was a real young buck. We were visiting on don Fernando's horse ranch – "

"I know don Fernando!" butted in the old horseman excitedly.

" – Sí, on his horse ranch one time, riding together like, a social call you might say, because I've known don Fernando since the biblical flood. And Cándido, young as he was then, fell madly for a very pretty, very fetching *señorita* who lived nearby or thereabouts – "

"I knew don Fernando too, knew him a long time too," the old one again interrupted. "Why, he was at my second daughter's wedding. But, *perdónome* – excuse me."

"Though he wasn't getting very far with this señorita – like me with this story, hmm. At any rate, she says to him one day, she says : 'Cándido, if you can give me a gift before the sun goes down, I'll walk with you to the river – without a chaperon.'

"'Pancho,' he says to me later, 'where the devil can I find a gift of any kind out here on this godforsaken range?' 'Well, muchacho,' I tell him, 'you can pick some wildflowers, there're plenty hereabouts, and make her a present of them, eh?' 'No,' says he, stubborn young mule, 'she expects something better than a bunch of wild flowers.' '¡Uuy!' I explode, 'please yourself then, but flowers always did and always will find a path to a woman's heart.

"For all that though, he took no heed of my little bit of wisdom …"

13

A Mobile Bar

Pancho gazed out the window and saw that the sun was as high as it could be for this time of the year. He watched as a cart with a starveling bullock between its shafts, trundled along a track on the rise of a hill tacked with spreading thorn trees. Dust followed the cart, drifting in streams like a smokescreen.

"And so?" prompted the older man.

"Well, that same day, much later in the day it was," Pancho pressed on, "a good wind got up strong and you couldn't see for thick dust. In that blinding blast of dust something slapped right into Cándido's face, and the wind held it there. He tore it from his face, and – well, can you guess what it was?" – At this the retired ranchero nodded in the negative – "It was a red silk bandanna. *Muy bonita* it was, and new as if bought that same day.

"So Cándido, with God's providence, had his gift after all to give to his pretty señorita. Well, old fellow, didn't that muchacha look a treat as she strutted around wearing the bandanna as a *rebozo* about her head.

"But you see, as you always find in life, there was a catch in it. What Cándido didn't know – nor the lovely señorita for that matter – what they didn't know, though most everybody else did, was this : That there red silk bandanna had belonged to the boss himself, don Fernando. And when his wife happened to see the bandanna wrapped about the head of this chit of a girl – well, ay caray, there was a hell of a storm let loose, I can tell you. The old *doña* drubbed poor don Fernando, and drubbed him good and silly with the base-end of a cast-iron frying pan," and Pancho let loose his own storm of roaring laughter.

"And the señorita, what happened to her?" wanted to know the retired ranchero, smiling at the other's tale, because he personally knew two of the characters involved.

"I'm right pleased you asked me that. Why, my friend, that was Laura and she's been Cándido's good and faithful wife these past six or seven years."

When Pancho's store of mezcal was depleted, there was a lull as it were in the babble of chatter and merriment. Then a ranchero type sitting in a rear seat, suddenly on an impulse produced a full bottle of tequila, intended as a gift for a relative in town. Once the bottle was broached however there was no time or space for misgivings, and it was freely passed back and forth among the adult male passengers.

The revelry seemed to increase more than ever.

Pancho was up from his seat once again and gave a highly commendable rendition of '*Sentimiento y Dolor*', long a favourite of his. Later, as the autobus finally reached the outskirts of San Stefan town, with the younger males undoubtedly intoxicated to a near high degree, falling about in the aisle or onto ample laps of fat señoras, the entire body of people lustily sang a Mariachi tune – the infant baby on board bawled too, but it had nothing to do with Mariachi melodies.

The tired old bus turned slanting off the road and screeched to a jarring halt, jolting everyone inside. The spontaneous camaraderie was at an end.

Presently, Pancho alighted, stepped into a smoking powder of dust by a wayside shrine marking the boundary of the town's municipal limits. There was the usual confusion and chaos at the tiny bus station, with swirling, milling masses of people, handling baggage and other belongings, children shrilly calling for their parents and vice versa. And among them pushed and pressed the ubiquitous hawkers and hustlers and street food vendors, adding to a tumult and disorder that generally prevails at such scenes. The bus roared away, coughing black fumes from its exhaust, ready perhaps for a hard-earned rest and refit at the town depot.

For a moment or so Pancho stood uncertainly, as wearied travellers do when trying to get their bearings on arrival at an unfamiliar place. He could see, as the crowds thinned out and dust began to clear and settle, the steep, sloped streets of this old Spanish Colonial town, with its tumbled tiers of buildings stepping crookedly up the hillside. He vaguely remembered it from a long way back in time.

He had finally decided on which route he should begin, and set off on his way, when he felt a tap on his shoulder. 'Beggars are pestering me already', he thought, swinging sharp round.

Standing there was the ticket-man's assistant from the bus he had journeyed on.

"Señor," the young man said politely, "you left this on the autobus," holding up the ranchero's water canteen.

He thanked the man and took the canteen from him.

"Why, uuy, it's full!" said Pancho in surprise.

"Sí, señor," the youngster smiled. "I took it myself to that *pulquería* – you see it, over there? – and took the liberty of having it filled for you. With the compliments of myself and some of our passengers."

Pancho was deeply touched. Beggars begging indeed! He ought to have known better.

He clapped a spade-square hand on the other's shoulder and thanked him once more, with greater sincerity. The young man grinned a little deprecatingly, turned on his heel, and was soon lost among the people of the township.

Out of some instinctive curiosity – he simply had to make sure – the old ranchero unscrewed the cap, put the canteen to his nose, and sniffed.

"What the - !" he exclaimed to himself in astonishment. "Where did he get this from then, and why?"

The canteen did not contain the cheap fermented drink called *pulque*, as he had supposed. It was full to the neck with first grade eighty per cent proof mezcal!

The happenings that most excite or please are invariably those not anticipated, he mused.

He set off on his way once more, grinning broadly.

PART THREE

PART THREE

14

Townscape I

*P*ancho climbed up a steep cobblestoned street, gaze wandering to left and right and at all around him with bemusement and curiosity. To his country-fed eyes the streets appeared long and the buildings tall, intruding on his eye-space, as he would put it to himself. So many blessed places where folk lived, he observed with some incredulity, and places as well for prayer or for pleasure.

He walked right in the middle of the street, as a countryman would. That is, until a taxicab coming up behind him, loudly honked him aside. He leapt to the high, narrow flag-stoned sidewalk with surprising agility, and stared in wonder at the vehicle as it passed him. Painted a light peppermint-green with a cream top, he had never seen the like before.

The driver stopped and poked his head out the window.

"Where to?" he shouted, in what seemed to the ranchero a belligerent tone.

'Well, never mind that.' Pancho increased his pace, listing from side to side. 'What luck I'm having today,' he thought happily, 'only five minutes in town and this fellow is offering me a lift, and I don't know him from Abraham the Hebrew.'

"Where to?" the man repeated, as Pancho reached the vehicle.

"The *casa* of don Alexandro," said the country horseman, smiling.

The driver, his face hard as slate-stone and almost the same slate-stone colour, gave him a sardonic look, said, "Have an address, does he, this don Whoever?"

"Ah, sí, amigo, number fifteen *Calzada de la Luz.*"

"Get in!" the driver ordered curtly, "I can take you there for two pesos."

Two pesos!

The old ranchero was thunderstruck. It dawned on him at last that this was not a private vehicle but one you hired and paid a fare for. He thanked the man and hurriedly waved him on. He did not feel that he was being in any way parsimonious, but knew very well he could get to Alexandro's residence on his own two pins for hardly a quarter centavo's worth of boot leather, as he saw it. Besides, he was in no particular hurry.

The driver, plainly disgruntled at losing a cab fare without even trying, deliberately revved up his engine with noisy crescendo and spurted on, blasting out black exhaust fumes into the pedestrian's face.

The old ranchero reached the brow of the hill where this particular street ended, and turned right, remembering in his head and now following implicit directions given by don Roberto Senior back at the hacienda.

He was intrigued over the variety of things a town this size offers, as for instance in this second street he was negotiating, with its myriad shops and bars and workplaces. In this one block alone on his left, which began with a pulquería at the first corner and a cantina at the furthest end, he saw that there were sandwiched in-between : a silversmith, a cobbler and a candle-maker, a baker (of *bolillos*), a tinsmith who made lamps and lanterns, a potter, tailor, knife-grinder, carpenter and coppersmith, draper, ironmonger, another tinsmith making the exact same product as the first; and in one tiny cubbyhole of a place, sombrely lit, a wizened old señora had set herself up as a *curandera* – or herbalist. This ancient crone lanced boils and treated blisters, mixed herbal concoctions to cure warts, corns and other unwanted excrescences.

At the precise moment Pancho passed her small premises, gaping in with the curiosity of a country yokel at a fair, she was attending a client with a gooseberry of a blister nestled alongside a septic corn on the sole of one foot. As Pancho's quick but nosey glance swept over the scene, in went a long lance at the base of the blister bubble next to the infected corn, and out came a mighty spurt of pus which shot across the narrow room and hit the wall. The old man gulped in astonishment, and speedily went on his way.

After a spell of trudging the streets, he at last reached the hub of the town; that is to say, the main plaza, known locally as *la plaza principal*, with its square *jardín* or garden. In its centre stood an ornate stone and iron-railed bandstand which the locals called *el kiosco* or 'the kiosk'.

At this moment it was crammed with a boy's brigade of musicians toting cumbersome brass instruments, drums and cymbals, rendering a popular tune with irregular discordant abandon. All the same, as Pancho realised, these young amateur players were in fact in competition at the same time with a Mariachi band playing loudly and furiously only a stone's throw away outside a cantina.

The walkways of the jardín were almost tunnelled by overhanging branches of mature evergreen trees, mostly laurel, festooned with strings of coloured light-bulbs and bunting, after the recent *fiesta de la Candelaria*. On Pancho's right loomed the exotic façade of *la parroquia*, the town's main church, an edifice noted for its eccentric architecture. Originally designed by an Indian stonemason who drew his plans and inspiration, according to local legend, from a picture postcard showing a frontal view of some European cathedral. The parroquia's frontage was a spectacular mock-Baroque-Gothic confection, heavily whitewashed and gleaming like a freshly iced wedding cake. From the side and rear elevations it appeared more similar to a city cinema or a dancehall.

The old ranchero was beginning to recognise aspects of the town. Facing the jardín on three sides stood solid two-storey 17th and 18th century mansion houses in remarkably good condition. At street level they had been converted into shops and banks and cantinas. The north and south sides were colonnaded, to the extent of covering the wider plaza walkways. Large thick flagstones of the sidewalks were worn concave with centuries of use. At the lower east side stood municipal buildings, which included a police station and gaol cells.

There were many people wandering rather aimlessly by the first-floor shops and in the jardín, even though it was well into the *siesta* hour. Pancho juggled himself among the townsfolk, nodding to and greeting anyone bold enough to make eye contact, all total strangers of course, eventually wending his way to the southeast corner of the plaza.

Here he paused for a while, like a regular idle town loiterer, wondering if he should make a right turning or cross over to go straight on. He stood patiently at the plaza corner, waiting for don Roberto's directions to come to the fore in his mind, jumbled as it was at present with the relative novelty of what he was experiencing in this boisterous, colourful town.

Idling there at the street corner, like a traffic island with people flowing around him, he gazed to the right nearside street where a handsome light-brown bitch dog lay indolently in the gutter, with a pup-dog at her tail.

It was a scene close to the horseman's heart, for he held a high regard for animals. He knew that they played their roles with a sure integrity, always themselves, never pretending to be anything else. It was this which impressed him about dumb creatures, more than humans ever could. At times he much preferred the company of animals to people – socially gregarious as he indubitably was – because animals could be relied upon to go by their own basic instincts and behave in the expected manner of their breed or species.

He watched the antics of the puppy-dog with quiet amusement, as the little chubby animal worried its mother's bushy tail. It took the tail between its jaws, yanking to right and left and softly growling. It lolloped on clumsy, un-coordinated legs to face the mother and see what response it may have caused.

The bitch lay there on her belly, head above fore-paws, tongue out and happily grinning, tail thumping in the gutter and raising dust. The pup made as if to run off on its unsure limbs, did a spirited turnaround with ears flapping like flags, went again for the enticing tail, wrangling and worrying it. It repeated this process, a comical expression on its appealing little face as it cocked a head in front of the grownup, in search of some sort of a reaction to its strenuous mischievous efforts. The mother lay comfortably and unconcernedly in the gutter, content in simply staying still.

Go across and straight on from here, the ranchero navigator presently realised.

He crossed the main plaza street at the intersection and started down another thoroughfare, heading due east, as he reckoned it. He was into the new street when he heard a sharp, terrifying yelp.

Swinging round in an instance, he saw the brown bitch-dog under a pickup truck which was slowly cruising along the street by the plaza. With careful, deliberate slowness, the driver caused the left front and rear wheels of his vehicle to run over the dog, crushing its ribcage and mashing its internal organs. The driver was a young, heavyset man with bloated, peach-pink cheeks, and wearing the type of high-crowned straw sombrero favoured by the younger set. He smirked with relish at what he had just done so intentionally.

"Oye, you! You fat pig's turd! You blind-eyed bat!" volcanically roared Pancho in his fury. The driver poked his fat head out the cab window to spit contemptuously at the other's harmless, pointless invective. He increased speed and was soon lost behind other traffic.

The old ranchero stood in the middle of the street, shaking a fist at the fast disappearing truck.

"You donkey's arse! You fat useless turd! " he bellowed, as people began to stop and stare at him.

Realising the futility of shouting at mere exhaust fumes, he ceased at once. But inside he was seething with anger.

There was nothing he could do for the handsome bitch-dog, he clearly saw, the poor creature expiring before he could reach it. Nor was it feasible to get near to it, because the puppy-dog snarled and growled at him. Pancho shook his head at the pup with something of genuine sorrow, then turned and continued on eastwards as before.

An hour later the puppy was still there, quietly whimpering, nestled by its dead mother's mangled body. The *policia* eventually came and took the dead dog away to be disposed of. The pup was put down and also disposed of.

It was perhaps just as well that the old ranchero never learned of this outcome.

15

Townscape II

There was something about this town that gradually seeped into the old man's consciousness, after negotiating a few more streets. It was something vaguely familiar which he remembered from his last visit so long back in time.

Three things in fact. One was the ever constant ringing of bells in the numerous churches scattered throughout. And the even more monotonous crowing of cocks. It seemed to him that there was a cock in every home yard and garden. When one started up others would follow suit, right across the town. On a by no means lesser scale was a proliferate number of dogs barking their lungs out, usually from the flat rooftops of the dwellings. They barked for one reason only, deliberately held on the rooftops in a permanent semi-starved condition, to serve their purpose as effective guard-dogs.

Pancho was now in a poorer part of town, following his feet down a steep and narrow cobblestoned alleyway, new boots squeaking like a horse saddle, heels ringing hollowly on the hard cobblestones.

He could see ahead a trio of young street urchins sauntering along toward him. Though ragged and dirty, Pancho couldn't help but notice their appealingly cherubic and slightly mischievous faces.

Upon reaching him one of them piped, "¡Hola!" to which he readily responded, wearing a smile on his dark weather-worn face.

The little scruffy ragamuffins tittered among themselves and ran back down to where they had started, did a quick turnaround, and capered up towards him once again.

"¡Hola!" another greeted him this time, a girl, and the old man made reply as before, beaming benignly on these small-fry rascals with their audacity in making fun of him, which he didn't mind in the slightest.

A quick suppressed giggling among the small group, and off they pelted back down the alleyway, only to repeat the process as they returned tramping in unison up toward him. A different tactic was now used:

"What's your name?" asked the third member, small head cocked to one side like a robin's.

"Pancho Villa!" boomed the old man, still grinning down on them.

"Ooo!" the little scamps chorused, and shot off like startled starlings, once more in the same direction as before, halting further down to swing round. Being streetwise, they knew exactly how far they could go with this stranger, as they marched abreast one last time, merely to nod politely as they passed by and carrying on without comment.

Pancho continued on himself, bouncing off the stone cobbles in his loud leather boots. He had not covered more than a few paces when he heard a cry behind him.

"¡Oye, hombre!"

He swung his head round.

"¡Hola, Pancho Villa! ¡Hola, Pancho Villa!" chanted the merry band of cheeky rapscallions from halfway up the alleyway. Laughing with glee they flew like hawks to the street at the top.

The old man shook his head, a big amused smile spreading over his face.

16

Don Alexandro's Casa

Pancho now reached an intersection, a much wider street laid before him, in a clearly wealthier *barrio* or neighbourhood. 'This must be Calzada de la Luz,' he correctly surmised. He turned on to it and found number fifteen less than twenty paces further along, on the left-hand side. He faced a massive antique wooden door set in a long and high, mustard-stuccoed wall. Under the number was a burnished brass plaque with the legend *La Fiesta* embossed on it. This was indeed his final destination.

He rapped his knuckles hard on the door, then saw a bell-pull, so gave that a yank as well for good measure, and waited a moment. At eye-height a panel cut into the door opened inward and a weather-bronzed face appeared in the square aperture.

"Sí, señor?" said the face filling the open square.

"*Buenas tardes,*" bawled the old ranchero expansively. "Francisco Ramírez, come to see don Alexandro."

"Don Alexandro is not here, señor," said the man on the other side of the door.

"Hmm, probably still working at the bank, I suppose. But doña Alexandra, she's in, isn't she?"

"Sí, señor, doña Alexandra is here. *Un momento, por favor,*" and the man closed the panel, shot some bolts and rattled chains, finally swung the heavy door wide open.

Pancho stared inside, fancied it looked like the Garden of Eden. It was a large square courtyard, with rooms facing onto it on two sides, and countless exotic plants filling every available space. In the centre of the garden was a *palapa* set in an oblong of marble tiles, with neat thatching on its roof. To one side stood a barbeque grill, brick-built, its exterior covered in glazed tiling. Around the palapa and running zig-zag fashion to various focus spots in the garden, were red brick pathways.

"Come in, señor, come in, ándale," invited the man with a friendly smile. "I'm José, the gardener."

"Well, José, I reckon I must congratulate you," said Pancho with warmth. "Don't think I've seen anything that looks so … so muy bonita."

"Gracias, señor, muchas gracias," responded the gardener, slightly flustered, perhaps a little embarrassed over the compliment. "Doña Alexandra is keen on her garden and keeps me busy, I can tell you. I'll take you to her right away, if you'll follow me, señor, this way, if you please …"

"Is that you, José? Has someone arrived? Who is it?" modulated an educated female voice from behind a tight cluster of potted palms."

"Oh, I see who it is," she went on, coming into sight. "Francisco! Well, Francisco Ramírez, this is a delightful surprise, though we have been expecting you these last few days."

Playing her famed gracious hostess role, doña Alexandra, a tall, lithesome woman of thirty-five years or so, good-looking with a carefully coiffured modern hairstyle, dramatically swept an arm before her, and said:

"Do come in and make yourself comfortable, Francisco, you must be fairly exhausted from your travels – I know I would find it tiresome and tedious. Did you have any difficulties finding us? But you are here at least, and that's a blessing – Thank you, José," in a curt aside to the outdoor staff member, "no security problem – as yet – for this is Francisco from papá's hacienda. You can finish trimming the corner rose-bush for me, if you would – Please come this way, Francisco," returning to her guest like someone juggling balls. "Oh, do mind the high step! I even forget myself sometimes … " as the old ranchero was beginning to wonder if the lady ever stopped to catch her breath.

He stepped into another world.

Should he have removed his boots at the French windows? To hell with that, he decided, wait till she says something first. Gazing around in wonderment he was reminded of the interior of a cathedral, so high was the ceiling, and almost snatched off his sombrero as a mark of piety.

Doña Alexandra, on a permanent basis it would appear, kept arrangements of plants and flowers in every room of the house – even the toilet. So it was that at all times the rooms emanated mixed richly exotic scents to tantalise one's senses – even in the toilet!

Sprays and purls and flushes of bright colours in beds and coats of lush greenery, scattered and cluttering what space they could grab. It was, to every intent and purpose, a living indoor garden. In fact, to the old man, this main room in which he stood, daring not to make a wrong move, rather more resembled a jungle. He wouldn't in the least be taken by surprise were he to suddenly come face-to-face with a snake – or even a small monkey.

Doña Alexandra was, as earlier hinted at, an elegant woman who looked younger than her years; always wore expensive makeup, always 'young' and fashionable in her dress, enhanced by her height. Old Pancho knew her well enough, knew her to be a lady of taste and quiet refinement, amiable in a mild way but with a certain tendency to aloofness, even haughtiness at times, as he had learned from previous contacts with her on don Roberto's ranch.

She airily waved a hand about the enormous room, as though to say that this was his for the moment to use and to enjoy. It was artfully and tastefully furnished, aspects quite lost on the rough ranchero, though he did for the sake of politeness put on an expression of appreciation.

"Oh, Francisco, you're like a horse with a burr under its saddle-blanket, as dear papá would put it," exclaimed his hostess with a flutter of long, slim arms. "Please, do take a seat," she invited with an awkward smile.

Pancho always seemed to manage, whenever as a guest at someone's home, and with the unerring instinct of the accident-prone, he somehow always found the flimsiest chair on which to park his generously broad backside, as he sat himself now on a delicate reed-cane chair that could barely contain his considerable bulk and weight.

"Can I get Cuca to fix you some *huevos rancheros*?" smiled his hostess kindly, believing this to be the horseman's staple diet, along with black beans and tortillas. "You must surely be hungry after that trying journey."

"Sure, gracias, Alexandra," the old man accepted cheerfully. "Plenty of 'huevos' if you please, but easy on the 'rancheros'," he joked, which fell flat as a tortilla.

"So Cuca is still with you, eh?" he gravelled on. "And, ay que caray, there she is herself! ¡Hola, Cuca! Que pasa, my old girl?" as a severe-looking señora as skinny as a stick poked her head out the kitchen entrance across the room.

Cuca had been cook and housekeeper for don Alexandro ever since he could remember. She and her sister had worked as housemaids to don

Roberto Senior back in the old days when his wife was still alive. Cuca had followed Alexandro to San Stefan when he had married and took up residence here on Calzada de la Luz.

The moment she saw who she knew as an old life-loving reprobate of a ranchero, Cuca's habitual visage of severity collapsed as she grinned with delight at sight of him.

"Merciful heavens, if it isn't Pancho himself!" she exclaimed, "and what on earth are you doing in town, might I ask, smelling as usual of dust and dung, you ruffian!"

"On business for the don – Roberto," beamed Pancho importantly, getting up from the reed chair and politely bowing a fraction, inclining his head, in the true gallant manner of a ranchero, and which he well knew would flatter the dried-up old broomstick.

"Small wonder then the church bells have been ringing like mad things all this day long," she continued, critically eyeing the ranchero for any signs of recent aging. But he was as spry and in robust good health as ever; only she was getting older by the minute was the sad realisation. "Pancho Ramírez himself in town, of all places! Would any sane person believe it? Well, I'll say it, it's surely a chilli in the fruit-bowl!"

Cuca turned to her employer, straightening her face to how it ought to look in a respectable household, and said, "I'll make something up for him, doña Alexandra. I know exactly what he likes and plenty of it too. Just give me five minutes or so, and we'll fix him alright."

"Thank you, Cuca," smiled the other, "and if you will make a little lemon-grass tea for me, there's a dear."

The cook/housekeeper disappeared into the kitchen, after giving Pancho a sly wink on the side, and feeling as though she'd just tossed off a generous measure of tonic.

"So where is our young Alexandro?" asked Pancho in polite tones, dropping down heavily onto the creaking cane chair.

"He's still at school, Francisco, practicing in the school play today, so I believe," referring to her ten-year-old son.

"Ah sí, the muchacho, but I meant your other half, Alexandra."

"Oh, *Alexandro* ... He should have arrived by now, at this time," glancing at an expensive ladies dress watch on her wrist, "but as usual the bank is keeping him busy. As General Manager of the main bank in town," she went on with an air of superiority, patting the hair on the back of her head, as though to emphasize her point. "As General Manager his various high responsibilities weigh heavily upon him, as you can appreciate. He is so very conscientious in his work, as you may realise ... "

"Why, I do, Alexandra, I do indeed," agreed the old man, playing up to her. "It's a big responsibility right enough. Újule, I mean it's bad enough worrying about your own money – if you have any – without caring over other people's cash as well.

"Still, we live in better times and banks don't get robbed as they used to, not with the modern safes they have these days to protect the banknotes. So there's a worry our Alexandro can safely put away along with the pesos. What he need only think on is the correct counting of the cash coming in, down to the last centavo, eh?"

He hawked then and was about to spit on the floor but caught himself in time, recalling doña María's admonition only the day before. This was no hard-trodden dirt floor, as he glanced down at the beautiful polish of parquetry, with a scattering of thick-pile expensive-looking rugs. He gulped, swallowed, showed a martyr's face.

"Please, Francisco, don't speak of bank robberies," implored his hostess in distressful tones, "not in a banker's own home indeed, it can only bring bad luck."

"Ah, perdónome, Alexandra, I guess I wasn't thinking straight. A shootout at San Stefan's major bank is out of the realms of possibility in these modern civilised times, to be sure, and – sí, I'll just shut up and say no more, but look around to admire these pretty pictures you have hanging here on the walls."

"I'll see how Cuca is doing with the food," said his hostess with some relief, and left her guest to it.

The old ranchero stared incomprehensively at a Braque reproduction, title at the bottom of the frame stating *Man with a Guitar.*

He screwed up his face with distaste. 'If that's a guitar,' he thought, 'then I'm a squashed square melon.'

The picture frame though, he contended, was worth admiring. He moved on to the next picture frame.

17

Don Alexandro

A short time later the boy Alexandro II arrived home from school. Though only a tender child of ten he appeared much older; large and thickset, taking after his father, who strode in shortly after him. The boy was off to his room to do his homework, while his mother excused herself to superintend the cooking of *comida*, leaving the two men to get acquainted with any follow-up news, sure to be plentiful.

Don Alexandro senior wore steel-rimmed spectacles, and with his stout figure finely clothed in a smart pin-striped suit, he was every inch a bank manager, or could be taken for a successful businessman or even an able administrator. In fact he was competent enough in all three spheres of enterprise.

And he was as different from his younger brother Jorge and older brother Roberto as a cart-mule is from two wild stallions. Pancho knew the three brothers since they were boys, and had taught them to ride, though almost failing with Alexandro. This middle son of don Roberto's was not cut out to be a horseman. From the start he was destined for a desk job, which he had welcomed with open arms and some relief. While his two siblings, who were more like their father, were exactly attuned to ranch work and horses.

"Well, Pancho, and how is papá?" enquired the young don Alexandro, plunking himself heavily into a wide-berthed easy-chair, a complacent though cheery smile on his business executive face.

"He's faring well is the grand old boss, I warrant," returned the other, "and sends felicitations to your little family. Those sales went through like a dream of course, so I suppose you know why I'm here, eh?"

"You have brought the money, then?" a slight gleam in the young man's eye.

"Sí, Alexandro, I have at that, as you'd expect. Every bit of it in cash and in cheques."

Pancho raised himself with a near leap from the rickety cane chair. He shucked up his *camisa* and unclipped a wide leather money-belt wrapped round his waist.

The bank manager was utterly appalled. "Good Lord! Pancho, why didn't you come straight to the bank with that?"

"Your papá said I was to give you this here in the privacy of your home. This end clip is mine, by the by, or rather belongs to María and Antonio Ramos. They want me to get one or two items while I'm in town."

"Good gracious, you might have been robbed on your way here, do you realise that?"

The old man gave a dismissive grunt. "If anyone had fancied his chances of putting paws around my middle," he growled with menace, "he would have copped a fistful of knuckles right between the eyes. Besides, I have a loaded pistol in my saddlebag – "

"Good God! Pancho, you've come into San Stefan with a firearm? Who do you think you are, Pancho Villa! You're lucky the policia didn't latch on to you. All the same, you should have come immediately to me at the bank. Fortunately, I have a wall safe, so I can at least put it away for safety and security's sake – and peace of mind. Phew!"

"A wall safe. Well, there's an innovation for you, Alexandro. I don't imagine anyone could make off with that, eh? Not without getting a hernia with the effort," and the old ranchero handed him the money-belt packed fat with cheques and banknotes.

After checking the contents of the money-belt don Alexandro put it all away in his safe and locked it. He fell weightily into the easy-chair once again and, with a somewhat speculative eye on his guest, immediately opened up on a subject most close to his heart.

"Speaking of ready cash," he began suavely, "and seeing that you're here in town, I take this opportunity to say that I wouldn't mind in the least were you to use advantage of my position at the bank – not to mention our long-enduring friendship – hellfire, you're practically family.

"What I mean to say is, old fellow, for you to thrust forward while the power is on, as we would term it at the office. Meaning exactly, would you by any chance be interested in a small loan? With generous terms of course, which goes without saying. It can be arranged quite easily too, you know. No problems there as I see it, you being such a friend and practically family."

The old man's own perspicacity, with regard to Alexandro's possible motives, convinced him to reject outright whatever the young banker was prepared to offer him. No, impecuniosity was more in Pancho's line. Financial considerations of any kind were of no interest to him. There had never been so much as one iota of avarice in his makeup, and, apart from that, he didn't care being poor or near it and saw no shame or regrets either.

"I'll keep that well in mind, but no, Alexandro, gracias," he smiled affably. "It's good of you to suggest such a thing and I appreciate your intentions, but I'm done with that sort of business – no offence meant, amigo – but I've been bitten before, you understand, hmm."

"What do you mean?" asked the banker, who was offended all the same and deeply so.

"Well, a long stretch back a so-called friend gave me a loan for something or other – I can't remember what exactly, but that's of no matter. Only a tiny loan it was, a piddling little sum to be sure. And the very next day this hombre is asking me to repay the loan. Pestered me and moaned about it, so I was forced to let him have it back, without having made use of it. 'Here, hombre,' I said to him, 'you can have it back, for what use it was to me in so little a time.' That's what I told him, the money-lender, the centavo-counting tail-end taco. Which settled the whole matter of loans for me and never bothered about money since. Hmm."

"At any rate you can be assured, Pancho, we simply don't operate in the manner you've just described. Not at our bank. Proper terms of agreement are drawn up and strictly adhered to. Contracts are binding, controlled and safeguarded by rules of our banking fiscal laws.

"As you know, you can always rely on me in matters of finance," don Alexandro said smoothly, "and you'll be welcome in our bank. Most welcome. You and I go back a long way and I trust you implicitly, as I do my own father, and … Well, you let me know whenever you're ready, to consider taking out a loan, or perhaps investing your money, or anything of that nature. I'm here to help you, old fellow," he added expansively.

He waited for an answer, any kind of response, but old Pancho was at first unforthcoming.

Then, at last, he fired off his guns:

"Gracias again, Alexandro. But I'm really not much interested, so you must forget it, compañero," he told the other, rather offhandedly. "Money, uuy. Who needs money? I have my life and my health. I don't need money, but I have need of my life and health.

"There are three things important to us in our lives, young friend," he went on in more kindly tones, "for they are what we are : blood and bone and breath. Anything else are merely accessories … In any case I'm careful with my own money, always have been. A centavo saves a peso, as wise folk will tell you, and that's how it is," he informed the banker in a now altered tack-sharp tone.

Don Alexandro gazed at the old ranchero for a long moment, scratched his head, perhaps accepting defeat, and said with warm urbanity:

"How was your journey here today, Pancho? The quarantine is still on at papá's place, I suppose? Are they still running that fine spa baths setup at your end of the highroad?" and other lines of polite inquiry utterly remote from the world of banking and finance.

18

Comida at the Casa

A time later Pancho found himself alone in the spacious lounge. Don Alexandro had excused himself to work on some papers in his study. The boy was still presumably hiding in his room, as the old man figured it, and doña Alexandra glided from room to room, attending to her many precious plants with a dainty watering-can and a pair of sharp secateurs.

So old Pancho was left to entertain himself, sitting on the reed-cane chair which creaked and groaned if he as much as batted an eyelid. He wondered what sort of family life this was supposed to be, unfavourably comparing it with that of his friends, the Ramos family. These thoughts were soon dismissed from his mind; instead, he ached to be in the kitchen so as to chat awhile with Cuca.

This situation seemed to last for a long time, until Cuca began making loud noises in the kitchen, indicating to her mistress that *comida* was almost ready.

"Alexandro!" called doña Alexandra shrilly.

"Sí!" returned the father and son duet from their respective rooms.

"Wash your hands, please, we are going to eat."

"¡Sí!" sang Alexandro senior and junior, the elder going to the main bathroom, the younger making for the out-yard tap.

"Be seated here, Francisco, if you will," offered the hostess with a pleasant hostess smile, pointing out another possibly unstable reed-backed chair at the head of a highly polished dining table set in an alcove of the room.

"Alexandro!" she called again, with an imperative note to it, as Cuca emerged from her kitchen, bearing a tray of hot dishes.

"¡Sí!" piped a small voice from the out-yard, and another of a deep base quality sounding from the bathroom doorway.

"It is already on the table," pressured doña Alexandra. "Alexandro, are you there?"

"Coming!" called back Alexandro the husband.

"I'm here!" said Alexandro the son.

Pancho listened to this neat family rigmarole with mounting amusement.

When they were at last seated, don Alexandro mumbled a quick grace and everyone crossed themselves; they then began tucking in to dishes of hot food set out on mats on the gleaming table. Doña Alexandra kept glancing questioningly at the sombrero still stuck firmly on the old ranchero's head, while he blithely regaled them with what he considered anecdotes of interest.

"… He had the longest pointed ears . . ," he was saying in loud tones, as if he imagined he was out on the range, "…the longest sharp pointed ears I'd ever seen on a fellow, and I asked him, 'Are you some kind of satyr or by any chance related to Satan?'

"'We are all members of the human race,' he told me, ears twitching like a jackrabbit's, 'we are all the same sort of people here.' Then he shot a glance over at Gerardo – and you know how ugly Gerardo is – and realised straight off that there certainly must be some exceptions!" the old man breaking into a rumbling laugh, sounding like an expensive car engine in tip-top condition.

Doña Alexandra smiled at her guest; a wan, weak smile, it must be noted, as though she found it a tremendous effort to smile at all.

The host introduced Pancho to chilled San Miguel beer, served from an apparently brand new refrigerator, for which he instantly acquired a taste, and amazed that something could be so cool and refreshing. After downing three bottles of the stuff, drinking it as a man would drink water after a full day in a desert, he began burping his appreciation.

Not the polite burping one usually expects, showing one's enjoyment of the fare; no, not by any token. Among a higher class of people, a discreet, decorous, gentle *burp* is considered sufficient to convey appreciation of food at mealtimes – a point of politeness always readily acceptable in Mexican households. Be that as it may, but among the poorer classes the host/hostess would sink into huffy mode if a good wholesome meal was not recognised and celebrated with a ripping, window-rattling thunderous *BELCH*!

Pancho's praises were mighty resounding cavernous belching which reverberated around the walls of the dining alcove and out into the street.

Don Alexandro was drinking almost at the same pace, and soon loudly guffawing at Pancho's funny anecdotes. He evidently forgot his middle-class status as a straight and sober bank manager, but was once again the impudent young man of his rancho days. His wife sat through it all with puckered mouth, as if she had tasted the tartness of unripe plums.

While Cuca, lounging idly by the kitchen entranceway, usually with a severe and disapproving look on her face, was widely grinning like a monkey finding nuts. She was in fact stitched up with suppressed laughter half the time, as she listened in on Pancho's non-stop gabbling about the old days on the hacienda when Alexandro was a mere stripling. Cuca had never enjoyed herself so much since her own days on don Roberto's ranch, when she used often to meet and talk with this rogue and rascal, Pancho.

The boy, Alexandro junior, stolidly and steadfastly ploughed his way through everything that was put before him, shovelling food into his face like coal into a furnace; or, as Cuca once succinctly expressed it, like dropping grain into a bottomless silo. To old Pancho, glancing over at odd moments and watching with wonder, the youngster seemed to be attacking his food with consummate greed, energy and relish, as if he'd lived a month on bread and water.

"And do you remember that time, Alexandro, when you dipped your hand in that apple-barrel?" Pancho was now recalling an old favourite happening. "You put your hand right into the barrel and lifted out a dead rat.

"'Look, papá,' you says, 'there was a dead rat in this barrel, and here it is!'

"'So!' your old man said, 'that don Antonio is selling me rats in a barrel, is he?' And you said, 'But, papá, there was only this one I found.'

"'Is that so?' your father said. 'In which case, you run to the Ramos farm and ask don Antonio where the hell are the rest of the rats from this barrel.'

"'That's very funny,' you dare to tell him, 'but this rat has spoilt the whole barrel.'

"'That's alright,' said your papá, 'you can give the apples to the pigs. Apples go well with pork, I always say… Now, if you drop your hand in that other barrel over there,' he said, 'you won't find anything other than black molasses. Go on, dip your hand in, muchacho, and I bet ten pesos to a centavo that you'll come up with black molasses.'

"'Should I really?' you says. 'Sure!' your papá said, face solemn and true, 'and if you come up with molasses you can lick it off, and there's a treat for you.'

"So you dunked your hand in the barrel, and when you lifted it out, uuy, you looked about ready to burst into tears.

"'Papá!' you screamed fit to wake the dead, 'this is manure! Liquid manure!'

"'Ah, so it is,' your dear father said again most solemnly, 'in which case, I advise you not to lick it off – and that's ten pesos I owe you, son.'

"And when your mamá came into the yard – She was still alive then, Lord bless her soul – well, she took one look at you, one hand holding a dead rat by its tail and the other thick with cattle-muck, and she bawled you out something fierce. 'Phew! You stink to high heaven!' 'But it's alright, mamá,' you says to her, 'we're only sorting out the apples and the molasses!'"

The old ranchero threw back his head and bellowed with laughter, nearly falling off his chair.

"You must forgive me, Alexandra, ignorant rough ranchero that I am," he said to the hostess cum martyr, with a threat of tears in her eyes. "I know I shouldn't raise such subjects at your dining table, at least not in front of the muchacho – " – Who was still greedily gobbling his grub like a running favourite in a fast-eating competition – " – we don't want to put him off his food, now do we?" and he once more fell into a merry fit of laughter, don Alexandro looking on with a rueful smile and beer-glazed eyes.

While the boy was oblivious of everything except eating, far and away absorbed in filling his little fat face at the fastest possible rate, with, as Pancho saw it, a seemingly vacuous sawdust-headedness.

19

Night-time Rest

Later in the evening, in the en-suite guest-room, Pancho pottered about in some bewilderment. He looked in the bathroom, finding it so immaculately clean and clinical that he dare not step foot in it. He found his way outside in the garden, to enjoy a most satisfying pee against a rare South American bush plant, the pride and joy of doña Alexandra – though he was not to know that.

He was about to scurry hurriedly back indoors, as the temperature had dropped a noticeable few degrees, when he was arrested in mid-step by an unusual sight.

He saw a man over on his left, a man standing perfectly still by a pecan tree. The man was completely naked and staring fixedly straight at Pancho. The old ranchero was transfixed, he tried to speak but no words came, for he could hardly believe what he was seeing.

What the devil was the fellow doing there? he thought perplexedly, standing by that pecan tree with not a stitch of clothing on. How odd and complex town life could be, he reasoned to himself; there are events and happenings quite beyond the comprehension of simple, honest country folk like himself.

Then a sliver of moon peeped from behind a cloud and the faint moon-glow shone fully on the nude figure by the pecan tree. And Pancho gave a sudden sigh of relief, as he could now plainly see that he was looking at a piece of stone statuary.

He returned to the room allocated to him, got between crisp clean sheets of a double-size bed which was his alone, wondering if he should have first removed his pants and stockings. He had of course seen fit to take off his boots, he knew that much at least – he wasn't a barbarian. His sombrero however remained jammed tight, stitched to his scalp – he was after all a rough and rugged ranchero.

I haven't blown out the lamp, he next thought with vexation, and just how was he to put that damn thing out? he asked himself, staring up at a light-bulb under its fancy shade in the centre of the ceiling. Then he recalled that this was one of those automatic things you switched off.

He saw the switch by the bedroom door. He lumbered out from his bed to put out the light. The electric glare momentarily cut his night vision, but the moon sliver shining palely through the window gave him sufficient light to see by without crashing into furniture. He got back into bed.

For a time he tossed and turned in the big soft bed, unaccustomed to such softness. Outside, over the town, church bells rang sporadically, dogs barked and howled, and cocks crowed – before their time – a massive and annoying discordant symphony.

"Dogs! Bells! Chickens!" darkly muttered the old man. "That's all you get in towns!"

Then he heard another altogether different sound, though quite mistaken by his ears, of a taxicab backfiring in a nearby street. Somebody out hunting, he surmised, taking the sharp *c-crack!* to be that of a rifle shot.

In another part of the house, the master bedroom, doña Alexandra was speaking to her husband:

"Alexandro?"

"Yes, my dear, what is it?"

"I'd like you to go and check on Francisco, to see that everything is alright."

Don Alexandro wanted to know why.

"Well," doña Alexandra continued, "he's not exactly used to our town life, as we know plainly enough already. I would like to know and would rest easier to know if he's okay. That is all. Would you, my sweet? Just a quick, discreet check."

"Sure, alright, I can do that small thing, it shouldn't take a moment," and don Alexandro clambered out from his bed, threw on a dressing gown and padded on slippered feet to the guest bedroom.

Moments later he was back, shivering with cold. "Brr, but it's cold," he whispered. "Come here, let me warm myself … Ah, that's better!"

A full minute passed. Then: "Well, my sweet?" she asked. "Is everything alright with him? Is Francisco comfortable enough?"

"Oh, he's fine. Sleeping like a babe. You wouldn't credit it, my dear, but the old fellow is fast asleep *on the floor*, head resting on of all things his saddlebag. Ah, that Pancho fellow, eh!"

PART FOUR

20

Mexican 'Walkabout'

*P*ancho walked the wintercold streets, his boot-heels ringing on the coldstoned cobbles, noticing a clutch of kids cheekily catcalling passers-by, including himself – not that he minded at all.

In fact the streets were filling up with people, going about their business; mostly women, as the old ranchero observed, probably off to shop at the *mercado* – or market – indicated to him by the baskets they carried, and having that air of firm purpose and knowing of their wants and needs usually seen on the faces of female shoppers.

He stopped at a corner tienda and on some impulse, and without any conscious thought of the matter, he went in and purchased two largish bags of assorted sweets, dropped them in his saddlebag. Satisfied with that little transaction, he continued on his way.

Ahead of him he saw a man urinating against a wall (not unusual in the small towns). The man swivelled his head to right and left, face eager with intent not to miss anything of possible interest, while he stood there emptying his bladder.

The pisser nodded to the old man in a familiar way, as if he had known him for years.

"¡Buenas diaz, señor!" came the greeting, as the man leaned with one arm against the stuccoed, rubblestone wall.

"Buenas diaz, hombre."

"Going far?"

"Already done it."

"You a ranchero?"

"Sí, sí."

"Thought as much, you look the type. Me, I work for the water authority, mess about with sumps and pumps and suchlike. Pipes is all it is. Pipes."

"The waterworks, eh? Que bueno." How appropriate, thought Pancho, and continued on, a smile on his face.

Anymore like him, he was thinking, and I'd have to get me a pair of water-wings.

As he strode leisurely, almost cavalierly, along the cobbled street – he was by now slightly adjusted to town life – he glanced down admiringly at his new boots, and murmuring to himself, quoted a few words of '*Love's Dream*', from *Song of Solomon*:

"'I will rise now and go about the city, in the streets and in the squares.'"

The old ranchero carried on by until he reached another poor barrio similar to the one of the previous day. But this one was more open. Line's of one-storey, flat-roofed houses faced on to a large expanse of dusty, waste-strewn spare ground. The dwellings were untidy-looking, poorly built of red soft-brick and concrete, with out-yards and high walls.

About this wasteland square a surprising number of children were playing. Scores of them, it seemed to the old man, although one would not readily think so by ear alone, for most played quietly, particularly the girls. And in spite of the apparent air of poverty permeating the area, these street children were not ragged by any means, as he could see, but decently togged out, which gave him some sense of satisfaction. He was well aware that Mexican parents generally take good care of their offspring, no matter how poor they may be.

On the other hand, as Pancho quietly observed, though these kids were chirpy and in fine health, a few irregularities were in evidence. One boy had a harelip. Another older boy limped, simply because he had a leg a little shorter than the other. And there was a girl, a pretty creature of twelve years or so, who was blind with cataracts.

He looked on at this school-yardish crowd of youngsters, marvelling at their boundless energy and inventiveness: playing marbles and leapfrog and spinning top, bowling old car tyres and playing hoopla with bicycle wheels. Toddlers chased chickens and puppy dogs, or threw balloons in the air and ran after them with squeals of delight. Two boys with catapults were slinging stone shots at a line of tin cans; they would have shot at bottles too, only they were returnable and therefore of value.

One boy, proud owner of a single roller-skate, scooted along the pavement as one would use a skate-board in a later time. A couple of girls played 'jacks' with the vertebrae bones of a long dead street dog. Another girl, with a clothes-line skipping-rope, skipped along nonstop on the sidewalk, moving forward a step at each skip, covering an entire street length with untiring verve.

This wasteland plot of ground would soon be used for more housing, as the town was near bursting at the seams with growing families. In one corner of the square was direct evidence of its fate: heaps of building materials; bricks, mounds of sand, bags of cement, a cement mixer and a great untidy clutter of wooden scaffolding.

A group of boys had made a crusading castle of this material. One of the boys stood atop a pile of bricks, his mother's aluminium colander fixed firmly on his head, striking a brave and manly pose as a stalwart defender of the faith, the courageous commander of the garrison. While his worthy knights steadfastly repelled murderous, devilish hordes of Saracens – three grubby-cheeked urchins scaling the 'ramparts' of the sand-pile, wielding their scimitars, made from wooden battens wrapped in silverfoil, 'blades' flashing in the sun.

No, Pancho may have thought wrong there concerning the boys on the sand-pile; maybe ... (his creative mind re-innovating). . maybe they were Santa Anna's troops storming the Alamo. Sí, that was more like it, he realised patriotically.

As far as the old man could make out, there appeared to be no bicycles or expensive toys of any kind to be seen. And yet there was no question of a deprived childhood to be witnessed here. The youngsters 'made-do' with what they had and what they could improvise with. Not a single girl possessed a doll. Indeed, as Pancho saw, there actually was no need, not with so many babies and little ones around to cuddle and coddle. Ten and eleven-year-old girls, with well-developed maternal instincts, carried infants in their arms or held tottering toddlers by the hand. These surrogate mothers took their responsibilities with serious, grownup attentiveness.

Such a group was parked in another corner of the spare ground, having a 'tea-party'. A ragged rebozo was spread out on the earth, on which were laid tiny plastic cups and plates. The 'hostess' plucked petals from a wildflower, sharing them out to her 'guests'. Pancho smiled as he gimped by them, these 'ladies' eating flower-petals as though they were dainty *petit fours*.

The old man reflected on what he was witnessing here.

Here are the children of the day, he mused.

Their mothers and fathers had played the same sort of games in these same streets many years before, and probably their parents too. Where those houses now stood, had not the area once been a wooded hillock?

Would the children of those earlier times have played hide-and-seek and stolen their first kiss? He imagined bare brown feet treading a woodland glade, through passion-flower or maybe sweet goldenrod, and kids picking windfall pecan nuts.

The cries and laughter of these present youngsters of the day must echo down from long years past. These young ones can't be any different from those of their distant forebears.

As Pancho plainly saw it, children are no different at any time or at any place. Children are what they are … simply children.

21

A Children's Story

Pancho went on his way, and hadn't gone far when three boys rushed up to him. So, I've been discovered, he thought, as the three crowded round him.

"Are you the new gas-man, señor?" piped one of them.

"He's a bandit, I'll bet," cried another bolder little fellow, round-faced and chipmunk-cheeked. "You can see he's one of those *desperados*, best watch him."

"What's your name?" wanted to know the third boy, with shining, intelligent eyes.

The old ranchero told them, and for some unknown reason he could not fathom why, they exchanged amused glances.

"I'm called Francisco as well," said the third boy, letting the old man know now why they appeared tickled. "This is my friend Pablito," pointing to the bold one with wide, fat cheeks.

"I'm called Ernesto," said the boy who had first spoken, a squint-eyed Cándido-type little urchin, smiling an equally charming, heart-melting Cándido-style smile.

"Are you a bandit, señor?" asked young Pablito brazenly.

"Do I look like one, then?" countered Pancho with a grin.

"Oh sí, señor, you do," said Pablito, following the old man's eyes down to his feet – the little fellow was wearing odd socks – and odd *huaraches*.

"Well, some might think so, and we can all think exactly what we please with no force to stop us thinking what we think. But what I am is no secret, I don't suppose," and he told them.

"A ranchero!" gasped Ernesto.

"He says he's a ranchero," said little Francisco, disbelieving.

"A ranchero! ¡Újule!" said Pablito, fully believing.

"Where's your horse?" enquired the intelligent-looking one, Ernesto, who had thick unruly hair which kept dropping and filling his squint eyes.

"Did you fall off it?" wanted to know the old man's namesake, who had a scar on his left cheek, just as the elder Francisco did too.

"It's strange you should say that," responded the ranchero, in warm and friendly conversational tones, "for it's truly what happened – well nearly so I dare to say, because I didn't really tipple off my mount. No, the horse threw me, you understand, hmm," he white-lied on. "A grey charger he was, with a mane as white as snowblossom, and a creature full of guts and mettle. A warrior horse to be sure, and you wouldn't find another like him, not if you started searching this moment and kept at it for a year …"

The three boys were hooked by the tale, eyes wide as they gazed up at this new character come so unexpectedly into their young lives.

"Uuy, muchachos," he went on, "he threw me like I said, the very devil he was, then galloped off like a raging wind. Away toward the *Sierra Madre Occidental*, that western *cordillera* far, far from here. That was a week ago when it happened, and I haven't seen his hide since."

A tiny slip of a girl approached this male gathering. She glanced up shyly at the old man, gave him such the sweetest kind of smile, it cut him to the heart. Other youngsters had stopped at their pursuits and skipped over, as neighbourhood kids will always take notice if there's a stranger in their midst.

"So how do you manage, then?" asked Pablito, fat cheeks mobile, putting Pancho accurately in mind of a chipmunk.

"I have my own two pins – only the two, mind - as you can see, and there's something to be said for walking awhile …" inwardly shuddering when he recalled his blistered feet of the day before.

"Now that charger, the one that unsaddled and sent me flying, reminds me of another horse I had some time ago," Pancho pattered on apace, as his audience grew, children trotting over from all corners, gathering round him. "This horse of mine was a fine black stallion of Spanish stock and named *Don Carlos*. He played much the same trick as the grey, tossed me neatly from the saddle. Then off he charged as if in a race. This was after sundown, mind you, and away *Don Carlos* went into the night.

"He galloped on through that night and part of the next day, and no one could catch that beast, so fast was he. He travelled far south, my precious black stallion, keeping to open country, finally reaching the coast at Veracruz, and night had fallen once again …

"That stallion of mine jumped aboard a ship in the harbour, a ship bound for some distant land. No one saw him leap aboard either, because the crew were drinking in the quayside cantinas. And the next day the ship set sail over the seas.

"The captain of the vessel, a bit of a horse-fancier by the by, discovered my stallion soon enough, and took care of him during the voyage. At the end of it the ship arrived in a strange and what you might say a magical kind of country – "

"Ooo!" came an appreciative response to this further development.

"Sí, sí, I tell the truth. And *Don Carlos* was off like a shot as soon as the ship docked in harbour. He flew at speed into the heart of this strange new land …"

"Ooo!"

"Sí, of a certainty. Well, you wouldn't credit it but it happened to be a land where flowers grow as big as trees. There were fields of sugar candy and orchards of toffee-apple trees. In the air were the lovely smells of vanilla and mint and caramel. And it was harvest time, with the muchachos of the countryside busy gathering it in: mushrooms made of meringue and marshmallow was one crop of interest."

"I believe it!" cried a girl at the rear of the small crowd. It was the blind child. "I've seen such things in my dreams," she added with a shy smile, blushing like a prize red rose.

"That's right, muchacha," said the old man kindly, recognising the girl, "I knew someone would know of what I'm saying. What you see in the mind's eye is as much a world as this real one around you."

"So, señor, what happened to *Don Carlos*?" asked the diminutive Francisco.

"Why, he liked the place so much he decided to stay. I mean for a horse it was as good a place as any. Mind you, he did get fat and lazy with the fancy living he enjoyed there. Which goes to prove that a lot of a good thing is not really good after all."

"But how do you know what happened to him, in that foreign land?" fat cheeks Pablito pressed him for an answer.

Sharp little fellow, that one, he'll go far, thought the old man.

"Glad you raised the subject, my little friend. You see, seven sea-birds flew in from the sea and told me so," Pancho informed the child with a straight and convincingly honest face.

"Seven sea-birds!" exclaimed Ernesto, pushing stray strands of hair from his eyes. "How was that, then?"

"A bird from each of the seven seas," was the old man's swift response, to the amusement of his young audience. "And to prove they had visited this foreign place, they each brought back some of the local stuff made or grown there. Here now, I have some of this special stuff right here, I do believe, *un momento* …" as he unslung his saddlebags from his shoulder.

Keen, expectant faces stared as he lifted out the two bags of sweets which instinct earlier on had prompted him to purchase.

The old storyteller noted at once when the sweets materialised that the former shyness of these youngsters – if indeed they had at all been shy – simply evaporated. They tittered and giggled, adazzle with excitement, hugely pleased with this generous stranger who had of a sudden popped into their world.

With the ready assistance of Pablito, Ernesto and little Francisco, the sweets were shared out equally among the happy, contented kids of this poor barrio. A rather nondescript place, completely lost and unknown to the outer world at large.

22

Meeting an Englishman

Later in the day, Pancho's meanderings about town eventually led him to its centre, and in the jardín he sat himself on a wrought iron bench, so as to watch the world go by for a spell.

At the other end of the bench was a blond-haired young man, obviously a foreigner he reasoned, absorbedly sketching the parroquia on a drawing-pad. He glanced up at the Mexican and flashed him a warm smile.

"Buenas tardes, señor," he said in careful Spanish.

"Buenas tardes," beamed back Pancho. "What are you drawing there, the church is it?" he inquired in his own tongue.

"Er … Que, señor?"

"*¿No habla español?*"

"*Poco, señor, pocito.*"

"That is okay," said Pancho, breaking into English, "I've worked with *gringos* before and picked up a bit of the gringo lingo."

"Oh, I'm not a gringo, señor," smiled the young man. "I'm English, not American."

"Ah, an English man. That's bueno – as we say."

"I'm from the north. North of England, that is. Your English is splendid, by the way."

The old ranchero's command of English was in fact fairly fluent, but he was not prepared to let on to this young Englishman, at least not for the present.

"I speak it good?" grinned the Mexican.

"You speak it *well*, señor."

"Ah, you correct me, that is well."

"That is *good*!" laughed the Englishman.

Said Pancho: "I'll pick it up again soon and speak it as I used to. So you the artist then, is it?"

"Of a sort you might say."

"And you come to Mexico to make picture of our church here."

"That and other things, yes. I'm in the country on a six-month visa. I've been here nearly a month already, in this town. I'll probably spend most of my time here, as I like the place, the people especially."

"That is well – I mean that is good!" Pancho corrected himself, and they laughed together. "So you like our country, eh? *Mexico*."

"Like it? I love it!" enthused the young man. "I don't think I've ever felt so happy. I could live here quite comfortably. So different from anything else I've experienced."

"What's your name?" the old man asked him suddenly.

"Oh, I'm sorry, forgetting my manners. Matt's the name, Matt Conners."

Pancho politely introduced himself, and the two rose from the seat and formally shook hands. They sat down again, nearer to each other.

"Well – Matt, did you say?" and the other nodded. "Is that English name?"

"Yes, it's short for Matthew."

"Ah, Matthew of the gospels. But you are not a tax-gatherer, eh?"

"Hellfire, no!"

"Tell me about yourself, please. It is interesting to talk with an English man. Are you married? Do you have any childrens?"

"No!" exclaimed Conners in mock alarm. "I don't intend marrying for some time yet. I'm still fairly young, you know. After my schooling I went on to college and trained as a designer. Industrial design, actually. Then I got called up."

"Called up?"

"Conscription, you know, military service. I had two years of it."

"Ah sí, the army, is it?"

"The Royal Navy actually. I wanted to see the world. After my national service I became a freelance illustrator, for book and magazine companies. I once did some work for an advertising firm, and that's how I ended up in New York, then San Francisco, and now here in Mexico – though this is a holiday period for me."

"A traveller of the seasons."

"A seasoned traveller, yes, I suppose you're right. But, you know, creative writing is my main passion these days. I want to write a novel; that would really satisfy me."

"You could maybe write a book about Mexico," Pancho suggested with a smile.

Conners thought that a possibility, if he spent enough time here. He was looking for someplace where he could hide out awhile and get on with some solid writing. He openly admitted to the old Mexican that he craved recognition, wanted to be known for his creativity.

"That's what I'm working on," and the young would-be-author sat back with hands behind his head, gazing complacently at the sky and thinking of an uplifted success-filled future, maybe tantalising close …

Said Pancho, "I once giving some thought – "

"Gave," the Englishman helped him.

"Thank you. Gave some thought to this – how do you say? – this fortune and fame business," went on the old man in his rough, gravelled tones. "Look at fame. Now, imagine, you're a famous mariachi man or maybe a bullfighter. And a hundred-thousand people know you. Strangers, each and everyone. They know you but you don't know these people, any of them. What good is it to you?

"And look at fortune. You have much pesos – sorry, many pesos in the bank. So many you can't count them. You wouldn't have the time to count your many pesos. No need to work anymore, there's truth in that. What good is it to you? What about your life? What can you do?"

"I know, but – "

Pancho steam-rolled on, telling his English friend about an American film actor he had known, who told him that fame gets you the best seat in a restaurant, and that fortune is not having to worry over a waiter's bill. The actor had also admitted to Pancho that he had enjoyed happier days when he was young and poor and unknown.

"Who was this film actor?" Conners perked up with interest.

"Well, a time back there was much filming in this state – cowboy films they were."

"They filmed here?" Conners' eyes gleamed.

"The Hollywood people. They filmed right here in this town – and on don Roberto's land as well."

"Who's don Roberto?"

The old man explained about his boss and friend of long standing, and how he owned many horses and several hundred head of long-horned steers, which the movie crews filmed for their western pictures.

"They're coming again this year, late summer," Pancho went on. "The don told me. This film actor hombre I met a long while ago. I can't remember his name. I was his friend. We were like – how you say it? – like a house burning. And uuy, he was a big hombre, a very big man."

"Good lord! It wasn't John Wayne by any chance, was it?" asked Conners excitedly.

"I've heard that name I'm sure. But the film people didn't call the big man by that name. No, they called him … Now, what did they call him? Was it Luke? No, it wasn't Luke … I have it! It was *Duke*. They called him Duke."

"That's it! That's him!" cried Conners jubilantly. "That's John Wayne, the famous film star. Made lots of Westerns. I'll be blowed! Duke is his old nickname, you see. Can you remember any more about him?"

"Very friendly hombre. Smoked many *cigarros*, liked to eat big beefsteaks, played cards most nights. We talked and we drank the tequilas many times."

"Were you ever in the movies, Pancho? The westerns, I mean."

The old ranchero reckoned he might have been caught on film when he rode with the herds on the locations.

"I never got rich or famous like that Duke fellow. We all looked up to him, and not just because he was so tall. Sí, a good man he was – for a gringo!" giving Conners a quick friendly nudge in the ribs.

They carried on chatting for some time, evidently enjoying each other's company. Later, Conners had to break it up because of his commitments.

"It's been marvellous talking to you," he told old Pancho warmly, "and I was thinking, maybe you'd like to go to *Los Dos Durangos* this evening. Say about eight. I can meet you here in the jardín if you like. 'Durangos' is up that street there," pointing beyond the parroquia. "It's essentially a bar, and they have Mariachi music some nights, and sometimes Peruvian! Tonight it's probably Marlowe and his small ensemble, kind of noisy but interesting – Marlowe's a cracking pianist. Do you like music?"

"I like Mariachi for sure, and the ranchero stuff, *corridos* and *norteñas*," the old man thinking of his favourite song: *Sentimiento y Dolor*.

"You'll love Marlowe. Trouble is he drinks too much; a bottle of brandy a day. I'd be surprised if he lasts out the season – And I've got to be off," added Conners, glancing at his watch.

"Ah, you are going, amigo. Where is it you go?"

"The *Instituto*. I'm teaching there, a temp. job to keep me in ciggies and beer."

"Ah, a teacher. What is it you teaching?"

"Drawing classes, you know, illustrating, stuff like that."

The two got to their feet, an aging Mexican ranchero and a young English artist, making an incongruous pair, yet as compatible as tequila and salt. They shook hands again Mexican fashion, and each went his own way.

23

Los Dos Durangos I

Pancho was there in the jardín at the appointed hour, Conners already waiting for him by the bench they had occupied earlier in the day. Church bells were ringing over the town, the entire populace it seemed out promenading on this chilly but windless evening.

Young señoritas, well wrapped up in woollen shawls, strolled in pairs or threes around the outer perimeter of the plaza square, gaily gossiping and occasionally throwing quick enquiring glances at the young bucks, also in small groups, ambling along somewhat self-consciously on the outside, which is called the *paseo*, moving contrariwise as tradition demands.

Conners and Pancho pushed their way through thick throngs of gay folk, and soon left the busy plaza behind them.

They reached Conner's 'watering-hole' – as he put it – in no time at all. Los Dos Durangos took up half the space of an 18th century building, and the two entered through a stone-arched carriageway which led to an inner courtyard. A fountain which did not function took a central position in the stone-paved courtyard. Alfresco tables and chairs – not used in months – and large potted plants jostled for room among beer crates and barrels.

Conners led his friend to a doorway on the right, which opened into the main bar-room. Long and high-ceilinged, with ship-size timber rafters running across the room. The ancient walls were at least two feet thick.

Pancho gazed about him, took in the rough, heavyweight wooden tables set in lines, with benches alongside. To one side stood the bar itself, with a short U-shaped counter. Opposite was a dais or stage raised a foot from a flag-stoned floor. On the stage was cluttered an old piano, a set of drums, two speakers and a microphone. The room was candle-lit, candles fixed in sconces along the walls, and stuck in bottles, two to each table.

Conners liked the place, because to him it seemed to possess a peculiarly archaic and enchanting quality of atmosphere. If one ignored the musician's paraphernalia on the stage, it could be a tavern of two hundred years ago. There was always a pleasant ambience about it, he felt, a place in which to mentally lose one's self, forcefully compelled to drop the barriers of social constraint, and simply have a good time.

Oddly, this establishment also appealed to Pancho, sensed it the instant he stepped inside. He too felt sure of enjoying an excellent convivial evening within these white-washed, solid walls.

At this moment the place was only half-full, of foreigners mainly, except for a few locals and the Mexican bar-tender; a pop-eyed, thick-moustached man named Gabriel.

A group of young men of Conner's acquaintance signalled and beckoned him over. He introduced Pancho to his American friends lounging against a wall by the bar. The old ranchero waved a friendly hand and inclined his head in respect for these foreign visitors. They returned the greeting with typically American openness.

Except for one, that is. He was a tall, lanky individual with pale, washed-out eyes, glaring at him with evident hostility. The man was named Harry.

"So you're the Mex who reckons he knows John Wayne," he sneered offensively. "I've met *wetbacks* like you before an' you're usually just full of crap. How can the likes of you know a great American movie star! An' that's a statement, bub, not a question," breaking into a braying laugh, which reminded the ranchero of a *burro* – a donkey.

"Hey, steady on there, Harry," warned Conners, hackles rising, "that was bloody well uncalled for!"

Pancho had heard of the term 'wetback' and what it indicated, knew it as a deliberate insult. He could easily have laughed it off as only the high spirits of young bucks. All the same he realised that his own country was belittled by such a rude and offensive remark.

This thought ran through his mind in milliseconds, as he clenched hands. And, inevitably, in a further fraction of a second an iron-hard fist slammed into the man called Harry, square between those wishy-washy eyes. As the back of his head rebounded off the wall, the same fist drove with lightning speed and hit him full in the mouth. Harry slumped to the floor, cross-eyed and mouth bloodied, not knowing what had hit him.

"Crikey! That was bloody neatly done, Pancho!" gushed Conners in open admiration, "and he certainly asked for it," the ranchero wryly grinning at the Englishman, and his surprised friends, who were in total agreement.

The Mexican horseman bent to lift the hapless Harry up off the floor.

"You okay, hombre?" he grated, though his tone was friendly. "Too much of the tequilas maybe, eh?"

"Yeah, I reckon …" mumbled Harry, holding a blood-stained hanky to his lower lip, groggy on his feet, shaking his head to clear it. The gangly fellow stared at this Mexican with something approaching respect, and not a little fear and wariness.

For the remainder of the evening the old ranchero was accorded abundant respect by the foreigners and locals alike. Though it was not entirely on account of that swift, neat feat of fightmanship, but also his enormous capacity in holding his liquor, his entertaining singing, and a singular show of skill and dexterity.

This last happened later in the evening, when Los Dos Durangos was jam-packed with people, when he was well into his cups, surrounded by a posse of fascinated, admiring foreigners.

"I want to salute you, Matthew," he declared to the Englishman in rough, husky tones, with near-inebriated bonhomie, "to salute you, your country, and your people!"

With that he lifted his sombrero and held it high above his head, loudly shouting the Mexican horseman's salutation:

"¡AHUA!"

He dropped the sombrero to chest height, holding its brim, and skimmed it in an ascending trajectory a clear sixteen feet across the room, where it snagged in amazing true precision on a peg in the wall opposite, and swung there like a pendulum. There was an immediate burst of applause from the roomful of revellers.

"Bloody hells-bells!" cried Conners, "that was pretty neat!"

"Any kind of a Mexican can throw things," grinned the ranchero, "but it's usually knives."

And he swiftly stalked across the room to retrieve his sombrero, as he felt positively naked without it.

24

Los Dos Durangos II

The evening drew on apace.

On the stage two plump-featured locals with battered guitars were banging out popular songs of the day, Pancho sometimes joining in, his booming voice filling the room.

At one point, he jumped onstage and asked the musician duo if they knew *Sentimiento y Dolor*. Nodding affirmatively with eagerness, they were willing enough to make a trio to share the limelight.

Pancho took control of the proceedings: "Bueno, we can start with that, after a count of three, sí?"

And he opened up for all his worth, pushing aside the superfluous microphone, and certainly not in the least suffering from stage-fright.

He sang a few robust, foot-tapping tunes as the room filled even more with ready revellers; some inspired to clap and bang on the tables, beers and tequilas bouncing on the tabletops. A few really let themselves go, by clambering up onto the benches and tables, stomping feet on thick solid wood.

At last, the old ranchero threw up his arms in mock despair, for he felt fair worn out. He stepped offstage amid raucous cheering, one or two making a rush to the bar in order to buy him a drink.

"Oh, Pancho," Conners tugged at his sleeve, the pair getting shoved and jostled by the crowd, "I'd like you to meet Benji, a good friend of mine. Benji, this is the Mexican chap I mentioned to you, the ranchero."

"Hi there," smiled the man Benji. "Pleased to meet you, a genuine kind of horseman no less, that's sizzling great."

The old man could not but grin with amusement at this owl-eyed, mild-mannered eccentric type, who would later meet his own wit and whimsy measure for measure.

Benji was dressed from shoulders to ankles in flowing orange robes, a cap of sorts fitted tightly to the crown of his head and down the back of his neck.

"Benji is the Dalai Lama tonight," explained Conners with a grin. "The other night he was Lawrence of Arabia. And what were you supposed to be when I saw you last week, Benji, dressed in black?"

"The President of the United States," returned the other in even tones.

"That was it," Conners confirmed, "at the time of your Civil War."

"Thereabouts," said Benji mildly. "I was waiting for some damn-fool screwball to maybe assassinate me – Would you like a tequila, friend Pancho? I can get you one."

"No, gracias, amigo. Look, I have plenty tequilas here."

"Something to eat, then. I'm starving. They got what are called pizzas here. How about a pizza? Or a piece of a pizza? I'll go get us a pizza, so stay right there – keep an eye on my drink, Matt," and he glided off in his ludicrous, stage-prop robes.

"Old Benji does go on, and has you wondering if he's right in the head," Conners confessed in a confidential aside. "I heard that he went through some terrible experiences in Korea when he served there as a medic with the army. But his heart's in the right place and he does no harm."

He went on to say that the veteran was on some kind of disability pension, enough to survive on, and, without a doubt, it was cheaper living for him down here in Mexico.

"We all love our Benji, you know," concluded Conners on a wistful note, perhaps envying the veteran's war experiences, horrific though they may have been.

To the regulars in the bar Benji may have appeared an odd character, but to the old ranchero, who intuitively understood the man, thought him a fine human being and sound as a peach at picking time.

"A man who has maybe suffered many sorrows," Pancho put in. "And, well – Ah, Benji, the food! Gracias, amigo," as the mild man in robes handed him a pizza on a wooden platter, the first pizza Pancho had ever seen. "Have a tequila, see here, I have so many. Take a tequila!"

"Thanks, friend Pancho … As they say in these parts: ¡Salud!" smiled Benji gently, and turned to Conners. "Hey, Matt, where's Marlowe tonight? Is he under the table again? I could listen to a spate of his kind of music right now."

He turned back to Pancho, said, "This mariachi stuff can tire your feet. I like the music of your country, friend, but it's strictly for nimble feet which I ain't got – Oh oh, here's your buddy heading over, wearisome Harry. Time to make my exit. Check you guys later. Just great meeting you, friend Pancho, and go easy on that tequila, it's dynamite," and Benji disappeared in the crowd.

He need not have concerned himself over Harry, however, because he was leaving. The gangly fellow had a headache, he told Conners aggrievedly, a pained expression on his now somewhat battered face.

"Care what you say to people, hombre," Pancho said with affability, "to have no aches in the head, eh?" the wisdom of these words acknowledged by a nod and a smile which came out as a grimace.

The American left them abruptly without a further word.

"I must sit with this lot," said Pancho presently, juggling his pizza and glasses of tequila.

More drinks appeared before him, enough to make him lose count. He found a table and the folk already there gladly made room for him and Conners. Benji later showed up again, after seeing Harry leave the premises, and he joined them at their crowded table. No one seemed to mind being squashed up against one another.

"I could do with some chilli or something for this," said Pancho, poking at his pizza.

"What kind?" asked don Tito, the owner, popping up from nowhere, or so it seemed. "Jalapeño? Habañero?"

"Whatever. Whatever you've got, I'm not fussed, amigo."

"I'll get you some," offered a hanger-on, who dashed off to the kitchen in the hope of scrounging a few hot ones.

"There're bits of sausage on mine," observed Benji a little sourly. "Looks like pork-meat to me. Do you think it morally correct, friend Pancho, to kill a pig merely to have sliced pork sausage on your pizza?"

"Well, amigo," returned the ranchero with a grin, "you can't kill just part of a pig."

"No, you have to go the whole hog!" threw in Conners laughingly.

At that moment a young Mexican girl approached the table, and seeing the old man, said, "Señor, please to accept this small gift with the compliments of don Tito," handing a bottle of rancher's mezcal to him.

Don Tito peeped in from the doorway, face beaming with mischievous delight. Pancho was getting to like the little fellow.

"Gracias, muchacha," he mumbled, embarrassed, "but why is this?"

"You have brought good business to our bar, señor, and it is … it is appreciated," the girl smiled, and quickly tripped off back to the kitchen.

"Well, I'll be blowed!" Conners exclaimed, "Compliments of don Tito no less. He's the owner, did I tell you?"

"And if he's a Mexican," voiced old Pancho, "then I'm a horse's halter."

"That's clever of you, he definitely isn't Mexican. Tito's from Peru."

"Hmm, here's what I've been waiting for," boomed the old man, when the hanger-on returned from his errand. "This is what I like. Gracias, amigo," and he began tossing small red chillies into his mouth.

"Pancho, you'll burn your guts out!" cried Conners, aghast.

"Each to his own culture, I say, each to his own cuisine," declared Benji benignly. "Chilli makes a marked improvement on this here pizza – But what's that dead animal lying at the bottom of that there bottle of hooch, friend Pancho?"

"Ah, sí, that is *el gusano*, the maguey worm."

"Ye gods, a bloody worm! In your mezcal?" crowed Conners.

"Sí, amigo, it is tradition. The worm goes with the drink, as the worm is always found on the maguey plant. Mezcal is made from the maguey. It is considered a great honour to have el gusano in your glass - ¡Oye, señorita!" he called to a passing waitress, who came to him in an instant, as though programmed to do so, and listened to his quick whispered instructions.

"One moment," he winked at Conners, as the girl hurried to the bar.

She returned shortly with another mezcal bottle, almost empty, but with a fat worm wallowing in a finger measure of liquor. She also had a salt shaker and a dish of lemon wedges.

"Gracias, señorita," as the old ranchero took the bottle from her, the salt and lemons placed almost ceremoniously before him.

"Now señor Pancho," he drawled, "will show you gringos how we Mexicans drink mezcal, ¡uuy!"

The air was thick with bluely cigarette smoke and animated chatter, the cheery smiling faces of the imbibers shining pinky-red in a mellow glow of candlelight. Alerted to what was going on, they bunched round Pancho's table, as he poured the mezcal into a fresh shot glass.

The worm plopped in too, sinking to the bottom.

He next shook a tiny shower of salt onto the crotch of one hand, between thumb and forefinger, and picked up his full glass with the same hand.

The wily ranchero shot a swift glance at his audience, no doubt in order to see that he had their undivided attention. He dipped his head and licked the salt, threw back his head and drained the glass in one swallow. Smacking lips in satisfaction, the empty glass was slammed down hard on the wood table, and taking a wedge of lemon he sucked on it as a baby would suckle a teat.

He then tossed the peel to the floor, sucked in his breath, and gave an almighty bloodcurdling Mexican yell –

"*¡AHUA!*"

"Bravo, Pancho!" called over Gabriel the bartender, others taking up the cry. Gabriel was selling mezcal for the remainder of the evening.

There were no takers among the tourists, however, in emulating the ranchero in downing a pickled, fat, slug-like maguey worm.

25

A "Pick-Up" Truck

Quite in an early hour of the morning found the old ranchero wending his way on unsteady feet through the deserted narrow streets of the town, stopping at one point to pee against a wall.

It was while he was relieving himself that the policia picked him up on their regular round of gathering in drunkards. Three burly men, with carbines slung over shoulders, handcuffed Pancho and hustled him onto the back-end of an open truck. Two other inebriates were already huddled behind the cab.

The complimentary bottle of mezcal, which the old man had tucked away in his saddlebag, was soon discovered and, as a routine procedure, instantly confiscated.

The truck cruised along a few more streets, bagged another hapless drunk, and finally ended outside the police station facing onto the plaza. Pancho and his fellow inebriates were pushed into a stone cell at the rear of the station, where they were to sleep on a cold damp concrete floor for the rest of the night.

Before oblivion in sleep began, the jailed inmates – and a few night-duty policia – were subjected to a soulful and poignant rendition of *Sentimiento y Dolor* by the tequila/mezcal soaked ranchero reprobate. Singing full-throatedly with deep feeling, as if he were by the campfire on the ranch with his trusty compañeros; notably Cándido, Gerardo, José and Emilio.

At a later though still ungodly hour, the revellers of the night before were roused from their drunken stupor and bundled back on the truck, with a guard to take care of each one of them. The vehicle roared off, shattering the early morning quietness and setting dogs barking and burros braying.

On the very same street where 'Los Dos Durangos' is located, the truck halted and Pancho was dropped off with his own personal guard.

The handcuffs were removed and a long stiff broom shoved in his paws.

It was by way of a penance, by order of the municipality, to sweep the entire street. The guard paid him scant attention, too preoccupied in yawning, scratching and stretching and adapting with little grace to the unremitting early morning hour.

But all in all, reflected the philosophical horseman, cheerfully following the gutter with his sweeping broom, it had proved an interesting and satisfying night out in town.

PART FIVE

PART FIVE

26

Cantina Companion

After the policia had finally released him, Pancho headed straight for the jardín, which at this early hour was completely deserted. He laid himself down on one of the iron benches, and there he slept undisturbed for a further two hours.

Upon waking he felt remarkably refreshed and his own vigorous self again. Though he was desperately hungry.

He made for a hot foodstall he spotted on the south side of the plaza, of the type that is popular late at night and early in the morning. The starving old man ordered and ate a couple of tamales in quick succession, gobbling them like a dog at his bowl. He ordered two more, demolished them in no time, and two more after that. And as he stood there by the stall, wolfing down the food, he joked with the tamale-seller, whose first customer he was this pleasant, sharp bright morning.

Replete with good hot sustenance, Pancho was off to tramp the streets of the town. He saw no point in returning to don Alexandro's house, for the simple reason he had finished business there, and he had his saddlebags and canteen with him.

He was his own man, which was how he liked it. All the same, the town's attractions were beginning to wear thin, and he still felt a tad intimidated and hemmed in by the buildings. The old man stumped on in an easterly direction, on the impulse of his instincts.

Presently, the pavements ended and the buildings parted to reveal a blessed expanse of earth and sky. This is more like it, he thought happily. He seemed in need to see the lay of the land and to look up at a big wide sky, to rest range-rider eyes on a far distant horizon. Sheer bliss!

Blue-grey clouds were rolling toward town, a threat of rain in them, though not to detract from the old man's enjoyment. He could hear bird calls and a soft rustling in the grasses, as a young, precocious breeze came up with the approaching darkened clouds. Realising that he would have to find shelter someplace, he sighed, and the clouds tumbled on nearer. A too short spell out here, reluctantly turning back now to the streets of the town.

Rain began as soon as he hit the first cobbled street, coming down at an angle. A determined flurry of rain beat against him, aided by a strong, mature wind which had sprung from nowhere. The rain was *hard*. Large drops now bouncing like beans off the sidewalk, flattening the crown of the ranchero's sombrero.

It occurred to him that it was not just hard rain, there was something else too: Hailstones! How extraordinary. *Like damn steel ball-bearings*, was his implacable view of matters, as hailstones and fat globules of rainwater continued exploding on him, thrashing the cobbled road stones and flat housetops. Rainwater rested on his moustache like a thick glaze of varnish.

The town appeared different in this wet state, the old man noted; kind of dreary and forlorn. He was not to know that it was as it had always been for centuries past; old and neglected and frowzy.

All its bad points were exposed by rainfall: water freely gushing from the roof gutters, shooting like miniature waterfalls on the narrow sidewalks. It streamed down the steep streets, flooding the level areas, filling potholes, and bringing out a stink of sewage and decay. Rats scurried out from holes in doorways and walls, running with brazen abandon along the pavements. Hardly a soul to be seen hereabouts, Pancho observed.

Only the normally clear bright Mexican sunshine had kept this town looking alive, healthy and presentable.

He hurried on in the hope of soon finding some form of shelter. And there at the next street, right on its corner, was a little, humble-imaged cantina.

What luck!

The old ranchero could not have wished for anything better. A quick restorative drink or two in there till these rainclouds pass over, he reasoned exultantly, and he would be – well, as right as rain.

Crashing through Western saloon-type swing-doors, raindrops falling from him, he shook himself as a wet dog would, sending a small shower about the place.

He swiftly took in his surrounds, keen blue eyes sweeping the room; rather a sad and dingy den, he saw, dimly lit and smelling of cheap alcohol, tobacco and urine. Naturally, he had seen far worse in his time. It was rainproof which was what mattered, and on top of that was an added incentive to obtaining a shot or two of his favourite tipple in here; a choice indeed of tequila or mezcal – or even a glass of pulque, should he so desire. After the onslaught of rain, this was pure heaven.

He found two customers in the room, well separated by at least three tables, and the barkeeper himself behind a makeshift, modest counter. The old ranchero's eyes were drawn to the man at a table in front of him. There was something vaguely familiar about this fellow. Not someone Pancho might have known in the past – he didn't know him from Noah - but a person representative of something with which he was familiar.

In short, the man appeared every inch a ranchero type, all the indications apparent: his leanness, his weathered swarthy face with the alert eyes, his manner of dress, even the way he was sitting by the table. There was only one defect to tell Pancho he might be amiss in his assumption. Two fingers were missing from the man's right hand. It would be difficult indeed to handle a horse with such a disability. But then, maybe he had once been a ranchero at some time, the old man reassessed his figuring.

The stranger was openly amiable enough – a telling trait – and with a slight inclination of his head and friendly expression on his face, Pancho was made welcome to join him. And this he did.

The two began chatting without any awkward preliminaries.

"So you're one of don Roberto's men, hey?" said Pancho's new drinking companion a short time into their conversation. "And to think I was myself a ranchero – "

"Ahh! I thought as much," cut in the old man with evident satisfaction over his own perceptive deducing.

"Oh sí, for many years, up in Sonora it was … Ah, so you know it? … Born and bred there you say? … Well, que bueno! A fellow of a northern State just like myself … And, well, misfortune jumped in as it were, as you can see, two fingers gone from this hand of mine. Lost them in a stupid knife fight in a cantina, ayí. It was my own fault I dare to say and got what was coming to me – and it came with a vengeance. Such misfortune! But then, such stupidity as well."

After a pause, the man went on:

"What's your name again? I know you already told me, but it didn't stick – Oh sí, that's it, Francisco. My younger brother goes by the same name. Only, back home we call him Pancho – Is that they damn church bells ringing again! They hardly stop their clatter in this no-horse town. Then, sometimes you see I gets a ringing in my ears. Can never fathom that. It may just be my imagination playing the devil.

"Well, uuy, I shouldn't wonder at that, the drinking I get through these past lousy times … "

The ex-ranchero began to tell of his personal history, without any apparent rancour, without self-pity, but with a peculiarly preoccupied air of indifference, as though he was not speaking about himself but of someone else entirely.

"And in Sonora," he went on, "my brother still lives there by the by, with two fine sons. Want to be bullfighters, the little cocky rascals. So they used to let on to their uncle – that's me.

"So my ranching days ended there when I lost two fingers. Lost my job in the bargain. Lost my spirit too I guess and lost some pride as well. But that's how it was. That's what life throws at you at times.

"Well now, why be angry with life's lot when it's so much easier to be happy? You smile at that, hey?"

"The human condition," said Pancho, now slipping into philosophical mode, "will let you know that you can be happy or you can be unhappy. Fate has all the answers, it is up to us to have the questions – the right ones."

"That is so, amigo, you never said a truer word. At any rate they were good to me, considering. The ranch owners I speak of, they paid me off handsomely, that they did.

"Well, you're only young one time around, isn't that so? The Good Lord provides … Sí, when you're young and wild and want to take on the world. 'He cometh forth like a flower, and is cut down …' as the good Bible tells us.

"What's that you said, Francisco, what I do now? Oh uuy, a fine job of work it is I do now …"

27

The Ex-Ranchero's Tale

At one of the cheap metal tables in a corner was slumped the other customer. A frail-looking man no more than forty years but appearing far older, because of a lifetime of dissipation which had ravaged and aged him.

Curiously – to Pancho, who had been observing the fellow – he wore a black patch over one eye, giving him a villainous, piratical aspect. His face however was grey-yellow, a ghastly pallor, like one who has risen from the dead. Pancho repeatedly glanced his way with objective interest.

The man stirred himself, got up from his seat with the stiff, jerky marionette movements of a drunk trying to appear sober. He staggered to the wall, rested a hand against it, and fumbled with his flies with the other. He pissed like a horse, long and gushingly against the wall, dark urine running and foaming away along a channel – cut specifically for that sole purpose – at his huarache-clad feet.

He then did up his flies fumblingly again, and returned jerkily to his chair. Casting his one good eye at the barkeeper, he held up a hand as a signal for another drink; although, as Pancho had noted, it was clearly evident that he was already into his shot-glass, as the old ranchero would have expressed it.

The drink was duly served and the patch-eyed man was left alone as before. He held his glass with two cupped hands as if to protect it. Nursing his drink so possessively, he nevertheless gave no sign of interest in anything else or anyone in the room, but simply gazed one-eyed and abstractedly into vacant space, lost in his own liquor-sodden world.

Pancho's drinking partner continued his monologue :

"Oh sí, San Stefan and the living I have here. Well, the pay is poor, you understand, though it keeps me from begging – Have you seen the number of beggars in the streets of this town? It's a damned disgrace, something wrong there somehow ...

"As I was saying, it's a caretaker that I am, or you might say a watchman – at the *Instituto*. You'll find me there most every night in my little hut by the gateway entrance.

"There you see it plain as a branding-iron, then. There went my pride, there dived my dignity, and to hell with it, I dare to say ...

"Sometimes I get in a bit of extra work in the daytime, weeding the grounds and suchlike – stuff I can still manage to do without making a damned fool of myself. Better than begging, isn't it?"

Of a sudden the ex-ranchero totally changed his tone and became near maudlin with it.

"Only, I can't hold a rein or handle a rope anymore," he complained miserably. "Well, you can form your own opinion on that score – No, no, let me tell you! Do I miss my ranchero days? Does the sun rise every day? Sure I damn and blast miss it – my compañeros, the horses ... Uuy, the freedom of it!" – His mood changed once again, this time to cheerful enthusiasm - "To be free as pollen riding the wind on the backs of bees. To sit your saddle from sunup to sunset. To know the back of a horse's ear like the back of your hand. Smell his animal sweat and hear him fart once in a while." He smiled at Pancho. "You understand what I'm saying, you've been there yourself – you're still there!

"Újule, that's the way of it – I see your glass is sitting empty, Francisco. Allow me the honour, if you will - *¡Oye, amigo!*" he shouted over to the bartender, "*Sí, por favor, otre vez, dos tequilas - ¡Muy rapido y gracias!*

"Where was I, Francisco? Where is it you're staying in town? You have relatives here perhaps – Oh, no relatives ... Ahh, don Alexandro ... One of don Roberto's sons, and I never knew that – Ah, the tequilas are here.

"Gracias, amigo ... Salt? ... You're welcome ... ¡Salud! ... Bueno, the ranchero's own tipple, hey? And I've been throwing them back all these years as a damned caretaker, pretending to be somebody that I'm not anymore. I drink tequila, but I taste bitter water. My 'days are as grass : as a flower of the field, so do I flourish ...'

"It's as well, I guess, for what real use am I? In another month I'll be fifty-five. My ranching days seem a lifetime away. Remember how it was in the old days, Francisco? ... Ayí, they were hard times sure enough but good times all the same. We were young then, amigo, and that's what makes all the difference."

The ex-ranchero became introspective, stared up at the ceiling for a moment as if his future thoughts were hiding there in the cracks, waiting to be discovered and voiced.

"You know," he started up afresh in flat, level tones, "thirty years ago I worked on a ranch in Chihuahua – Ahh! You know Chihuahua! – I worked for – you may have known him – I was ranch foreman, young as I was, for don Julio Madrazo ... So you have heard of him! I reckoned you might, on account of his reputation and the God-awful things that hombre got up to in them days ... "

The puke-faced drunk with the eye-patch suddenly sighed heavily, said something incoherent to no one in particular. He slumped forward, sprawled over the small tabletop. His glass was empty. He appeared to be asleep, or even comatose; so still with not a movement, not a twitch about him. Pancho, glancing once again his way, guessed he was in a drunken stupor; he had seen it often enough before. He gave a shrug of dismissal, turned eyes and attention on his drinking companion.

The ranchero-that-was-no-more rambled on:

"This Julio Madrazo was the point of a machete and the edge of it. He was dust in your eye and a slap in your face – in short, a mean and vicious hombre. Terribly hard on his own herdsmen, whipped them often for hardly a reason worth his while, and ... "

The ex-ranchero stopped his tale in mid-sentence. He struggled to speak further. How could he describe it to this friendly stranger? The cruel whippings and general harsh treatment this Madrazo meted out to his own workers. He'd had enough drinks in him, he realised, not to hold back now but give the full awful story, though finding it upsetting to relate.

"Listen, just listen to this," he started up once more in a firmer tone of voice, with an inner conviction to see this through to its bitter end. "You wouldn't credit this but one time Madrazo staked a man – barely a man, for he was only seventeen or thereabouts – staked him to corral fencing on his ranch. Then he tore the camisa from the muchacho's back. Slashed at him with his whip, till that poor young one's back was raw and blooded, till he passed out from his hurts.

"For some silly, unimportant wrong. He liked it, you see, Madrazo, he enjoyed inflicting pain on people. And animals! He'd slit the throat of a hog and sniff at its life-blood, feel it running over his hands. ¡*Loco!*

"Madrazo was like that for years, a crazed maniac of a hombre. Then a first-born son arrived, and a sudden change came over him. He quietened down some and spent time in his stables and corrals, taking good care of his horses. There were no more whippings and such after that boy came into his life. He changed for the better, seemed much of a miracle to the hands. But we could never trust him, those of us who knew his old ways. Ayí, not me for sure, nor those unlucky ones who'd felt his whip and could show their scars to prove it. No, they trusted him even less, and rightly so.

"And two or three years went by and Madrazo had mended his ways by all accounts. Two of my compañeros, Pedro and Ferdinand, who had suffered terrible whippings in the past – well, they'd been away them two years or so, and didn't know that Madrazo had changed.

"'So you're back, then?' I says to them. 'Sí, we're back, and here we are,' they said to me. Any rate, I couldn't help but notice a shifty look about those two. Up to no good, that was the truth of it, up to no good!

"They'd planned on getting rid of don Julio Madrazo, that was their game. I left the ranch soon after they had returned, so I couldn't know what happened exactly.

"But the stories afterwards were always the same …

"Pedro and Ferdinand – long dead by the by, shot down by the federales – they took and tied Madrazo, when they were on a short cattle-run over the desert areas. Just the three of them on that run, as it happened – or maybe planned that way.

"Uuy, they had him tied like a pig for slaughter, staked out naked on the ground in some Godforsaken place. Staked the man over an anthill. They lit a fire then and boiled a can of water. And threw the lot over him. Oh, he screamed alright, long and hard, so it was said. With the sun beating down on him for extra measure.

"Those two hombres waited half a day for the blisters to bubble up, then cut them open with a knife, red and raw and wet, see?

"And Madrazo – may the Mother of Christ have pity on his soul – screamed and strained in his agony. No one heard him out there in that desert wasteland…"

The remainder of the story became legend, and little changed in the telling:

Inevitably, the ants soon started up on him; the large, red aggressive type found in certain desert parts. They practically smothered the victim in their numbers, ferociously attacking his quivering, agonised body; tearing at his skin and raw flesh, making off with pieces of him. It was reasoned that his mind had gone eventually, and by nightfall still screaming like a female.

By morning of the following day, Julio Madrazo had lost his sight. Presumably, a predatory bird had plucked out his eyes; either that or the ants had taken them, bit by little bit. By the end of that same day he was a mass of raw pulp, although, amazingly, still alive. Screaming silently at that stage, as the ants were in his throat.

Ironically, it wasn't the ants that finished him off – though they did apparently eat him clean afterwards till his bones shone white. It was a scorpion that got him on that second night of his agony. It must have crept out from the brushwood Ferdinand or Pedro had stacked by the campfire.

The scorpion got itself in a tussle with the ants, and in its confusion jabbed its stinger in Madrazo's side and pumped its deadly poison in him, putting the final end to him at last …

That was how the story went, though how anyone knew of that final ending was anyone's guess – and guessing it must have been. As it was, the rumours were the same, the story was always the same, to fall into legend.

"And the muchacho? The son of Julio Madrazo?" the ex-ranchero concluded. "He turned out just like his old man used to be, so folks told me. As a kid he was sweet as ripe fruit, then something or other came over him too, and he changed from fruit-juice to coyote piss.

"Sí, in my little hut at the Instituto gate, I've often thought of those days and the crazed Madrazo and his terrible end – What is it, Francisco? What are you looking at? – Oh, him!"

28

The Patch-Eyed Baker's Tale

The patch-eyed drunk was coming out of his stupor, lolling back against the metalled chair, one bleary eye roaming over the place, as though unsure of where he might be. He pushed back the chair, metal legs screeching. Then he laboriously pulled himself up on unsteady legs, staggered a few steps and fell flat on his face, arms locked under him.

Pancho was there in an instant to assist the hapless fellow, his companion right behind him. Together they heaved the man, half carried him to their own table.

They had him safely seated, and Pancho glanced over to the bar.

"Oye, my friend, do you have any coffee?"

"I can fix coffee, if need be," returned the bartender disapprovingly.

"Make it hot, black and strong, pronto then, por favor."

The barman looked at him. The old ranchero, with his rugged, leathern features, his downward running cheek scar, the blazing blue-fired eyes, was not to be ignored.

"Coming right up, señor, or soon will be."

Pancho returned to his seat, with a cautious weather eye on the drunkard. His companion also retook his seat.

"Újule, hombre," gravelled the old man, "are you yet in the land of the living, or what is it? How're you feeling? Pretty rotten, at a fair guess. There's coffee on its way and it may do you a power of good, I'm thinking."

"Gracias, s-señor," slurred Patch-Eye. "I must have lost my balance and took a tumble, or something like."

"You're likely to lose more than your balance the rate you go at with the hard stuff," Pancho chided him mildly.

Moments passed, the three of them sitting in silence, listening to rainfall hitting the shutters of a nearside window. Pancho and his companion felt it tactful not to touch their drinks; instead, gazed at the drunk with interest.

The barkeeper approached presently with the coffee, a surly look on his face – a barman unused to serving *beverages* in his saloon. He ungraciously slammed the pot on the table, but no offence was taken there, as the men knew he would have done the same had it been tequila.

Patch-Eye gulped greedily at the hot mug of coffee, burning his tongue, his one good eye watering.

"Who're you, then?" he asked the old man with some interest, coming round to some recognizable form of life.

"He's a *ranchero*, hombre," said Pancho's companion.

"A ranchero, is it?" said the drunk. "I thought they'd all died out," and sipped his coffee, taking his time.

"There're still a few of us at it," grinned the old ranchero, thinking of his compañeros: Cándido, Gerardo, José, Emilio. And this fellow, who appeared to be sobering up pretty fast.

"Well, I'm a townsman myself, have been all my life – lived right here in this town all my life. A baker by trade, that's me, though I don't have my own business, you follow – could have done at one time, but you know how bad luck can get in your way, when you think you're on the up-and-up. Trouble and strife is always there for those that ask for it – and for those that don't.

"No-o, I work for – But that's of no matter, I work for somebody else in my case …"

Hmm, a baker, thought Pancho. That would explain the pale, pasty face; the man probably sleeps out the daylight sunshine hours.

The patch-eyed baker hedged about and shuffled his feet, taking delicate sips of his coffee, and coming alive a bit, to Pancho's satisfaction.

"I'm there after midnight or thereabouts, to start my shift," the baker continued on conversationally, his speech now noticeably clearer and articulate; all of which, surmised the old man, was put on as a show to prove his worth as a decent, sober fellow.

"The dough's already mixed by the time I get there. For the *bolillos*, if you follow me. Had its first *proving*, you see, as we say in the trade. When I start I have to get it all *knocked* back – "

"I bet you've knocked a few back in your time, eh?" broke in Pancho with a friendly grin.

"Ahh, I knew you wouldn't understand that," said the baker. "No, when I say I *knock it back*, I mean *kneading* the dough, as they say in the trade. I'll try not to be too technical, but it stretches the gluten in the flour, if you can follow my pattern."

The man grinned to himself, pleased to impart small snippets of his knowledge and know-how as a baker of bread.

"And the sweat's pouring off me and dropping in the dough, which does no harm – in fact it's beneficial for the dough mix, a bit of salt, gives it taste you see. Though I do add proper salt as well.

"Then I let it *stand* for a while, to prove over again. To rise, the yeast, you catch what I'm saying? It needs warmth, lots of warmth with no draughts coming in through open doors. Draughts is bad for it, sinks the dough, puts the yeast back to sleep, and it's a devil getting it to rise again – to *activate* that yeast.

"No problem in the summer, like. Plenty of heat then, by God! The hot air in that bakery has you swimming in your own sweat, so it does. But in winter time like now you have to be especially careful of cold draughts sinking your dough."

The baker cast his one good eye over his newfound companions, to assess whether their interest was sufficient enough for him to carry on.

He carried on:

"So I'm making bolillos. Well, after the second proving's done I knock it back once more – quite a rigmarole, wouldn't you say? Next, I cut it into manageable chunks, like. I roll it out like a long fat sausage, each chunk, and cut it into even pieces, each one bolillo size – Cut-cut-cut! Like that you see, a long row of them, if you get the idea.

"¡Sí! Then I roll them by hand into shape, one in each hand on a warm wooden table near the ovens. In the palms of my hands, the dough round and warm and soft – much like fondling the breasts of a señorita. Roll them, applying just the right pressure, hard at first, then easing off like, as they come up full and nicely shaped."

With the evident pride of an accomplished tradesman, the patch-eyed baker continued disclosing his trade secrets to the outdoor, open-range ranchero types listening respectfully at their table. How another quick deft roll would produce the recognisable bolillo shape. From that stage the process continued by being placed onto lightly greased baking sheets, and proved one final time. A slight scoring on top of each and a brush with milk or beaten egg. ¡Vamónos! Banged into the baking ovens, as he expressed it, and down go the doors, not too fast lest a draught is caused, which could prove disastrous.

"I can sit on my backside for a while then, as the bread is baking. Early batches usually take twelve minutes right to the second, but by the third or fourth batch they're only taking eleven or even ten minutes by the clock. Funny thing, but that's how it is.

"It's nice and warm and cosy in the bakery at this time of the year. Sí, I've a good job there I reckon, taking things into account. No, I'm better off where I am, baking them little loaves. Three-thousand a night I bake, three-thousand a shift I do.

"And what's the price of a bolillo these days? Why, the boss can hardly hold up with his costs of flour and yeast and fuel, not to mention the mortgage payments on the premises. No, I'm glad I only work for him, earning a weekly wage, like. Wouldn't do to own the place, I'd wager. Too much of a worry. A millstone it would be! Hey-oh, you'd need one of them for milling flour, wouldn't you say!" he said jestingly, fully alive now.

"And you, hombre," he said, addressing Pancho's drinking partner, "what do you do, then? You a ranchero as well, is it? You sure look the sort to me at least. A ranchero too, are you?"

29

A Dear Loss

Pancho left the cantina soon after the one-eyed baker's tale – he assumed Patch-Eye only had the one eye. The rain had ceased, he was relieved to see; the clouds white and fluffed, sun shining brilliantly, as it does after a fall of rain, sparkling the wet streets. After the darker rainclouds had pushed on and away, the sky appeared a fragile kind of blue, like oriental porcelain.

His priority now was to purchase those goods requested by the Ramos family, then board a bus and get the hell back into some decent countryside.

He strode along a street near the *mercado*, where a beggar had strategically stationed himself, sitting with his back against the side wall of a church. The man raised a hand in supplication on hearing the heavy, booted tread near him.

The old ranchero stopped, giving a greeting and searching in his pocket for a few centavos. He felt a hand of coins and stooped to drop them in the man's upturned sombrero in front of him.

As the coins clinked into the hat, so did the old ranchero's money-clip clink, as it fell from his pants back pocket onto the pavement. Completely unaware, he went on his way.

The beggar squatting on the sidewalk, evidently purblind with developing cataracts, nevertheless spotted the money-clip lying there so invitingly directly before him. He waited a breathless moment – sucking in his breath as though there wasn't much of it around – peering myopically to right and left of him, then reached out with his stick and hooked the enticingly fat money-clip. What a haul!

He hastily stuffed it in his own pocket, got to his feet, and stick-tapped away as hurriedly as prudence would allow, in the opposite direction of his unknowing benefactor.

In an ironmonger's shop close to the town centre, Pancho discovered his loss. He delved and rummaged in his pockets and saddlebags half-a-dozen times over, before resigning himself to the sorry truth that he had lost the money, all of it. He roundly cursed his own person for sheer negligence on his part; he could hardly blame anyone else.

What to do now? He wondered worriedly. Approach Alexandro at the bank and beg for a loan? No, his pride would never countenance such a drastic measure as that; an appalling and not to say embarrassing move without question.

So, what then?

After cooling his heels and attempting to simmer down a bit on a bench in the jardín – (He now regarded the jardín as his own personal garden) – it suddenly occurred to him that he would have to, out of sheer necessity, sell his new boots in a shoe-shop he had noticed by the mercado. He had nothing else of any real value, to sell, that is.

The old man began to sweat when another thought crept with venom into his mind: How was he to explain all this to the Ramos family? To say that he was still 'keeping' the boots only for special occasions, and buy another identical pair when he later had sufficient funds? It seemed the only solution to this dire dilemma. Though bad and uncivil indeed to lie to his dear friends, he realised with sadness and misgiving. The decision was made however and he hurried on now to the mercado area.

There was no problem at the shoe-shop, the proprietor generously offering him a fairly decent price for the boots. With a small amount of the 'blood-money', as the old man took it to be, he bought a cheap pair of *huaraches* and slipped his feet into them. How short in stature he now felt on leaving the shoe-shop, as his car-tyre, rubber-clad feet slapped the sidewalk like that of an ordinary poor *peon*.

The money also fortunately covered the price of the merchandise he had been commissioned to buy for María and don Antonio, with barely enough left over for his autobus-fare.

So he was all set up at last.

¡Uuy! he thought with flooded relief coursing through him, now let me get the hell out of this town!

30

An Opportune Meeting...

At a bend in the road, narrowed where it ran through a copse of laurel trees, the autobus slowed down, then came to an unscheduled halt. The road ahead was apparently blocked. On one side was slewed a beat-up old Chevrolet, on the other a mule with an overturned cart. Fruit and vegetables lay scattered about the road, and a small crowd had gathered, where moments before there had been no one.

Pancho flip-flop slapped to the front of the bus to see what the trouble might be. He saw an irate market-gardener jumping up and down and shaking a fist in a passion of fury, and kicking about his own vegetables.

The object of his anger was none other than the Englishman acquaintance Conners. Pancho recognised the young man and got off the bus. Others too began clambering off, to help upright the cart which was blocking half of the roadway. The mule, now unharnessed, took this rare opportunity to crop dry, dusty grass by the roadside.

"Pancho! Hells bells, what a turn-up!" cried Conners, on seeing his Mexican friend. "Can you help me out of this mess?" he implored, desperation in his eyes. "My Spanish doesn't stretch to this sort of situation."

"What happened then, amigo?" asked the old man at once. "I can see well enough the result of it. You're in trouble here – Hold on, hombre!" he snapped suddenly at the fruit-and-vegetable man, who had only a moment ago told him to mind his own business and why was he meddling in other people's affairs?

The man had un-redeeming ugly features, reminding the old man of his ranchero compañero Gerardo, who was considered by all who knew him as top league when it came to any degree of ugliness.

"It was my own fault, Pancho," admitted Conners with a cracked and rueful grin. "For a time while I was driving must have thought I was back in England, and didn't realise I was on the wrong side of the bloody road. Not until I met up with this waggon and donkey – or mule, whatever it is. The road's wet and I swerved and he did the same, this fellow here, and I must have caught the hub of the cartwheel and tossed it over on its side.

"But what the hell is this man trying to tell me? Thought he was going to kill me at first. God Almighty! It's a bloody good job you showed your face here, Pancho. Please, have a word with him, will you? I'm willing to pay for damages, tell him – Hell, I won five-hundred pesos at cards last night!" he announced eagerly, though he was, as old Pancho could see, still evidently distraught.

"*Con calma, hombre,*" he soothed the young man, "I'll speak to him. We can soon sort this out."

"Thank God for that! And thanks a lot, my friend," burbled Conners with gratitude and relief.

Pancho conferred with the much maligned vegetable merchant, while the other bus passengers and locals helped reload the upset produce back into the cart now back on its wheels and parked offside the road.

"Go on! Help yourselves!" ranted the vegetable man, breaking off the talk with the old man and not fully understanding what was happening, wildly gesticulating to express his anger. "I'm a ruined man anyway so what does it matter! Go ahead, help yourselves!"

The old ranchero tried to calm him down, speaking quietly so only the other could hear. Moments later he turned to Conners.

"The hombre here says he held seventy-five pesos worth of goods in his cart."

"Is that all it is?" Conners almost laughed outright.

"It's a lot of money to him, amigo … " returned the old man in severe, reprimanding tones.

"Oh, I'm sure it is. But tell him, Pancho, if you please, tell him I'll pay it here and now. In fact, you can tell him I'll pay another twenty-five over the top, as compensation for all the trouble and time wasted I've caused."

The young man smiled a little smugly, and further explained, "I'm flushed anyhow, after my luck in the card games. Would you let him know, then? One hundred pesos in cash."

"I'll tell him," agreed Pancho, smiling too in forgiveness for the other's earlier thoughtless remark.

The merchant was mollified when two crisp fifty-peso banknotes were thrust into his hand. As a further bonus out of the blue, a later inspection showed that hardly any damage, or rather none whatsoever, had occurred to his precious produce. He could still carry on to town and sell this lot, fresh and unbruised, and make a double whammy, by the devil!

Sí, thought the fruit-and-veg man, let the damn gringos hit his cart every time they care to – it's good for business! Clear profit!

"Phew! That was a close one, Pancho," said the Englishman, smiling in his relief. "You've bloody well saved my life, no less. How can I repay you? What can I do for you? I'm dead serious, y'know, I mean it. Can I buy you a dinner in town? A week of dinners – and tequilas. I owe you so much. Just tell me what I can do for you, absolutely anything you desire; that is, within reason. So, what do you say, my dear Mexican friend, how can I help you in return?"

The old man was about to dismiss the idea outright, then gave it a second thought. He gazed at the Englishman a long moment, somewhat circumspectly, maybe a smidgen speculatively.

Here then was a wide open opportunity not to be dismissed nor ignored; here was a redemption of sorts, though of miniscule and modest means.

He made up his mind, and came out with it:

"Matthew, there is something you can do for me, after thinking on it. Two things, as a matter of fact."

"Whatever. You name them, by all means," said Conners expectantly.

"Well, first off, you can give me a ride in that tank of yours – Where did you get that beat-up crate from? Did you buy that thing?"

"No, of course not," laughed Conners. "It belongs to Gabriel, y'know, the barman at Durangos. He's letting me borrow it for a couple of days, so I can tour around the country and see some more of Mexico.

"So, where do you want a lift to?"

"Ah sí, to the mineral spa on this highway is where I want to go. But before you take me there – if this is agreeable with you?"

"It most assuredly is, though hardly a way of paying you in return for saving my skin."

"Ay well, I did say two things, right? I also want you to take me first into town."

"Back to San Stefan? Where you've just come from?"

"That is so, sí, amigo, I have left something of mine there …"

"Okay. Let's go then. Jump in the old banger, and I'll run you to town."

"That's better than being run *out* of town," grinned Pancho. "You don't mind at all?"

"Not at all, at all, as the Irish say."

Before they could set off however, Pancho needed to pick up his saddlebags and other stuff still left on the autobus.

Conners drove his friend back to the town in the battered, cranky old Chevrolet. Straight to the shoe-shop near the mercado, where Pancho had earlier sold his own pair of boots. He quickly repurchased them, thanks to Conner's financial assistance (there was a sting in it after all, wryly realised the Englishman), pulled them on in the shop, leaving the hated huaraches for the shopkeeper to resell. The old man was relieved that his boots had not been sold, as he originally feared. His pride, dignity and standing as a ranchero rushed like adrenalin back to him, restored him to his normal self.

While the shopkeeper eyed him askance, probably thinking the oldster was in his dotage or mentally deranged – he couldn't decide which – selling his boots and buying them back again, in the space of an hour or less.

The pair left the streets of the town once more, Conners taking his friend to the mineral waters spa. There they parted, after a deal of embracing and back-slapping.

Pancho set off along the trackway which would lead him into open country. Where life was delightfully simple and totally without any sort of complication, or at least that was how he figured it, and exulted in it.

Conners, feeling somehow bereft and out-of-sorts, drove wistfully back to the old Colonial town.

He would love to have spent more time with that wonderful old man, that real-life, wide-alive Mexican ranchero …

31

...And Yet Another

"Oye, señor Ramírez!" piped a boyish voice. "Pancho! It's me, Juan! Over here!"

It was indeed young Juan Ramos, in the shade of a tree with the farmstead tilt-cart, his chestnut bay Chapulín between the shafts. The boy had only moments ago delivered a great pile of pumpkins to a wholesaler.

Pancho hurried on to the cart.

"¡Hola, Juanito!" he bawled happily, carrying a grin fit to slice his face in half. "Thank the Lord and the Saints you're here, amiguito. I didn't fancy that long walk to San Angelo and beyond. ¡Uuy! No-o, my favoured compañero, I couldn't tackle that today, even though it is nice to see some blessed space and countryside again, and not have some damned truck blaring his horn in your earhole and driving halfway up your backside," the old man merrily chuntered away, throwing saddlebags, canteen, and doña María's packages into the empty cart.

He clambered onto the buckboard seat, like a pirate boarding a treasure ship. The old ranchero relieved Juan of the horse's reins, at the same time giving the boy a hearty Mexican *abrazo*, almost squeezing the breath out of him.

"Well, mi compañero, let us away, eh? *¡Vamónos!*"

"You seem fairly keen to be off, Pancho," smiled Juan in amusement, "like you couldn't get out of town quick enough. You're not by any chance in trouble with the policia, are you?"

"No, Juanito, nothing like that. Though I did at one stage make their acquaintance – socially, you understand," giving a knowing wink. "Let's say I'm more than eager to be off and on my way. So let's get on, eh, muchacho?

"Yarrh! Chapulín, ay-yarrh, you lovely horsey creature!"

And they were off at a smart and spanking pace, raising a mighty cloud of dust, leaving the roadway and 'so-called-civilisation' safely behind them.

"By the way, Pancho," said the boy a few moments later, "the other day I happened to find these. They look very much like yours. Are they yours?"

Juan held up the old ranchero's missing pair of red woollen stockings.

"You found them! Merciful heavens!" laughed Pancho. "Ay que bueno, Juanito, the Saints are with us today and no mistake I'll own, hmm."

"But, Pancho, how on earth did you come to lose them?"

"Why, they blew off me, you see. They blew clean away, they did. And I nearly lost my boots in the bargain too, though they did find me again in no time worth mentioning – and that's another story, also not worth mentioning.

"Ay caray, Juanito, look at this land around us! Isn't it just sweet and beautiful, eh? My *El Dorado*, without a doubt – Yarrh! Yarrh! Come on then, Chapulín, show us what you're capable of, or do you want a taste of this here whip, is it? No-o, it's not oatmeal flavoured either, this here whip – As if I would! – " turning his happy face to the boy at his side.

"Look alive there, you handsome chestnut one. Yarrh! Ay-Yarrh!"

And the handsome chestnut one took them deeper into the familiar silent, lonesome, empty countryside, away from streets and roads and traffic, away from clanging church bells, barking dogs and crowds of noisy folk about at every turn.

The old ranchero began to breathe more freely at last, like a beast returning to its true habitat after wandering off out of it. He sniffed the air as though it held intoxicating aromas, and to him that is exactly how it was.

And he had ached to see a wide blue skyscape.

Young Juan showed a dazed, puzzled expression on his face, trying hard to figure in his confused mind just how his old friend's stockings had *blown clean away*. And nearly lost his boots as well …! He wondered why the old man should come out with such absurd remarks. What was wrong with him? Had something extraordinary happened in town? *Something* must have, the boy was convinced of that.

"Ah, Juanito," burst out Pancho, suddenly thinking at that moment of the ex-ranchero and the patch-eyed baker he'd met in that town cantina;

of Cuca and the Alexandros, the blind street beggar; and all those wonderfully contented barrio kids, enjoying their young lives in the midst of poverty.

"Our humanity," he continued with deep feeling. "Our humanity! Our own downfall, our very own saviour. It is our biggest flaw. It's our biggest asset!"

And the horse-and-cart carried them on into wild and rugged terrain.

BOOK II
SPRING

PART SIX

32

Air of Spring

Spring arrived in the valley of San Angelo like a carnival of nature, with mother Earth fully awakened and bedecked in new green finery. It was a time when everything appeared to have acquired a fresh coat of paint, as it were, a burnishing of bright colours, as fruit orchards blossomed, the peach and apricot and apple trees in wholesome regal bloom.

A silent explosive display when spring breezes took hold of the petals, pink and white, and tossed them in the air to fall like snowflakes.

The signature of spring was in its sultry seductiveness, in its sights and sounds and smells.

It was a time when even the animals knew all about it, as they do, naturally, this coming of spring, and they reacted to it accordingly and got on with it, moving and meeting and mating, fulfilling renewed appetites.

And the music began to be played again on the old, wind-up Victrola in the pueblo, rippling through the valley, drifting over the fields in melodious waves. It heightened the spirits of campesinos at their daily toil, put a jauntiness in every step and a meaningful smile on work-worn faces.

The sunsplashing light filled these first spring days, as they merrily danced on. The air was charged with the power of this light, that all green things may grow, every leaf and stem and grass-blade.

There was a spice and tang of fresh young herbage, and sweet sounds in the windsong woodland glades. The quickening leaves of trees, caught by wind and sunlight, waved and flashed like tinsel and glitter.

And above all this miraculous new growth, fine rolling clouds, puffballs of cotton, herds of them grazing in a vast plain of sky.

And Cristina Ramos was in serious, fully committed love for the first time in her young teenage life.

33

Spring Romance I

Summer rages and autumn withers, winter sleeps in a chilled torpor. But spring awakens with the lovers. And these two lovers loved as certain as the coming of the season.

Even as they filled their eyes with one another, the buds of spring shot out to leaves, leaf-green and leaf-spanning, taking tree space in the wood by *Sancho's Elbow*, where the lovers lay on the slipped leaf of yesteryear, fast to the soil beneath and of the soil, when Time ate into itself; making way for spring green, sapped in the bud that turns to leaf.

The trees surrounding this couple seemed tall in the world that was theirs alone, and the noon hour of their meeting was an hour of splendid stillness, for the day-wind had by now finally died. Theirs was a place of young lush grass, a secret glade that was for this spring season only; well hid by trees in full leaf and a spreading vernal froth of bush and shrub.

They felt they could stay there in the green, in the glade, to grow with the grass, to be silent as the stones, and let their minds grow old, before and beyond possible failings of their young bodies. To have their day in every hour, for all the hours of every day.

He saw in her that first bloom of beauty that becomes a girl … when she becomes a woman. Her face is a flower and sweeter than fruit. Fiery-eyed, she glanced at him in return, eyelids fluttering like bird wings, lips curved like folded flower petals, or so she herself wanted ardently to believe, because spring changes everything, was her thought on it.

He looked her way once again, and admired a beauty that was not quite there; it was a kind of beauty that shone purely from a happy radiance. And so she was in his love-smitten eyes as beautiful as she herself could ever hope to be, and maybe that was more than enough … for them both.

His sigh and her sigh made one sound, as of high grasses stroked by wind, with a warm breath of noon still upon them. She threw back her hair with one hand, spread fingers scissoring long full strands. It was a natural feminine movement which gladdened and moved him. And once more they sighed, breathing in the scented grasses which the high noon sun had stirred in a dreamlight air.

They laughed often for no apparent reason – simply joyful at being alive and in love – and gazed at each other for long intense moments, their eyes black, penetrating, expressive.

He caressed her cheek with a rough, calloused finger, marvelled at her softness; she responded with short intakes of breath, breasts heaving and swelling with a girl's pride. A low soughing wind arrived from nowhere to lift the hair from her brow, and the young man saw a sheen of moisture there on her brow, like velvet. He touched her brow and traced a line across the slight dampness, feeling, sensing soft velvet.

The lovers sat with backs against the bark of a beefwood tree, faces in leaf shadow, dappled sunlight dancing about their feet, like light on the surface of water.

Faces close together, eyes intently locked on each other. Her breath was clean and fresh, reminding him of apples and lemon-grass and peppermint. Her cheeks, as he tenderly gazed at her, were round and rosy like a peach, with even the bloom of fine-like hair of a peach.

Cristina got to her feet.

"Where are you going?" he asked sullenly.

To act sullen before your girl was considered manly and appropriate, done solely to impress, as he saw it; and would not in the least think it at all immature.

"No, it's alright," she whispered – whispering being her response to his sullenness. "It's just that – well, I spotted something over there – There, you see it?"

"See what?" the boy asked quietly. "What am I supposed to be seeing? What do you see? Do you want something? I can get it for you. Tell me!" his eyes smouldering, and feeling an odd prickle of jealousy.

"It's alright I say, it's only a flower I see and want to pick. But it's for me to pick, not you … not you. Stay here."

"You won't run off?" he asked with a high degree of sullenness. "You don't want to leave yet, do you? Say it!"

"No, no, it's only the flower, I want it. Wait here, and don't watch me, will you? I don't want you following me with those feasting eyes, else I'll feel awkward or embarrassed, or worse still, foolish. Don't make a fool of me, say you won't!"

"Of course not. What do you take me for? Go! Go get your flower, and find one for me."

"A flower for you!" Cristina laughed, and a certain tension that had slowly accumulated between them suddenly broke, like a wave upon a shore; and they relaxed, like receding tidal waters.

Cristina padded silently through thick grass in her bare feet, while her young man arched his back against the tree, gazing over the glade with his sullen expression. Too sun-lazy to think of any matter, too empty-minded to think at all.

Only to feel, effortlessly feel the power of this spring day coming on with new life …

When the señorita returned to the privacy of her room at the Ramos homestead later in the day, she dragged her old hardcloth schoolbag from under her bed. She unclipped the side pocket and reached in for a small leather-bound notebook, a Christmas gift from her sister Ruth. She found a pen and began to write, speedily and surely, already knowing exactly what she needed to put down.

Cristina wanted to express her present emotions in the form of a free verse poem; about a flower in full bloom which tells that it is spring, how it nods one way to give the direction of a wind, and of dewdrops on the petals indicating that it is morning. Finalised by stating in simple words that there is much in the world of a flower.

34

Spring Romance II

April flowers embraced the light of another day, the halcyon hours of this green season, when love and youth and beauty are in motion. Cristina's own shifting moods, from one moment of a deep brooding to another of a kind of ecstatic reverie, bore plainly the signs of a girl in love.

As her beau stood there beside her, the sun fully on his figure, she cherished even his shadow cast across the ground, and in that shadow she saw sweet herbs and tiny wildflowers among the grass and stones. The afternoon light was bright, the air soft, and breezes that were accommodatingly gentle.

"Do you really like me?" she said of a sudden in a small voice.

"Are you asking *me*?"

"Oh, I'm talking to the tree now, am I?" her voice tone pitched on a higher plaintive note.

The young man – merely a boy as yet – glanced up at the branches over their heads, then dropped his gaze on the girl once more, and said:

"The tree is saying nothing."

"And you, are you as dumb as that tree?"

"No, I can tell you anything, anything you might want to know. Do you want to know something?"

"No, it's not important."

He grinned at her. "What isn't?"

"It doesn't really matter, you see, and why should I care anyway? I … well, there was something … "

"Sí, what is it?" still grinning, rather superciliously.

"I wanted to know, I mean to say – Well, do you really like me or don't you?"

He considered a moment, deliberately holding back, losing the grin and putting on a pained expression. Then said, "No, I don't like you and I suppose I never did. Sí, I can say that for certain."

Cristina pulled a face and pummelled the boy's manly chest. "We're quits, then!" she declared in mock anger.

"No, you're wrong there," he smiled now, showing strong white teeth, and the girl's heart skipped a beat at sight of them. "I don't like you," he confirmed in a low voice, carefully enunciating each word, "as I've already told you. But there is something else, you see … "

"Yes?" expectant and eager to know.

"Oh, sí, it's true that I don't like you and never will, and that's a pity, isn't it? What you honestly want to know is this – *I love you!*"

Cristina broke into a gay, triumphant smile. "I knew it," she said.

"Then why did you ask?"

"Because I needed to know from you, that's why. I needed you to tell me. So let me hear you again, tell me now, quickly!"

"I love you, love you, love you!"

Cristina's triumph was crowned with joy, and the first pink-flushed blush of love burned her cheeks. They continued to gaze at each other in the tranquil, green-cloaked glade, with its carpet of grass and wildflowers, its sun-dappled shade, and a litter of white, early season butterflies flitting wind-tossed and winking in the sunlight.

She spoke again presently, lowly, almost in a whisper:

"Do you remember that first time, Javier, that first day I ever saw you all those years ago?" – It wasn't that long ago at all, though Cristina imagined it to be so, time being slow for growing youngsters - "In the street of the pueblo, by old señora Guzman's hut.

"You were standing there on your own and crying out your heart, tears streaming down your dirty face. Your mamá had slapped you hard for something or other, I can't imagine what. And oh my, what an ugly mug you showed because of your crying. Screwed up and wrinkled and red as a ripe tomato!"

He screwed up his face now in a perfect scowl, obviously embarrassed over what he was hearing and ought to have been forgotten.

"Crying quietly you were all the same, not bawling or anything, not shaking about like some little muchachos do. And standing so still, like a stone post planted in the earth.

"Do you remember it, Javier? You saw me then, that first time, and I was on my own as well, walking your way, to visit old Santos it was – that was it, to give him some fruit from our orchard. And I gave you a look as if to say what a silly stupid creature you are, crying like a baby and face wrinkled like your grandpapá.

"Then it was that you saw me, Javier. You stopped your crying just like that, like turning off a tap. You looked my way. You stared and stared at me, Javier. As if you'd never set eyes on a little muchacha before. By the time I reached to near where you stood, it was a wonder your poor eyes didn't pop right out with your rude staring.

"Oh, Javier! What did you do next, can you remember? No, you were only a silly little muchacho who'd been smacked and had a cry over the pain and humiliation of it – it's humiliation that males can't take, isn't it? Men and boys … such strange creatures when you don't know them, such children when you do …

"But what was it you did, Javier, that turned me over, slapped me too with the shock of it, a sort of feeling that I was not to know what had hit me with such force?

"You *smiled*, Javier! You smiled at me, and it was like the sun coming from behind a cloud, a sudden brightening of light. Your lovely white teeth flashed and your eyes were so beautiful. Your whole face became very handsome and like no one else I'd ever seen before. You were a little prince, Javier, even in the ragged camisa and dirty pants you wore at the time.

"Do you remember it? And what happened after? Yes, I smiled back, shyly-like I suppose then, and walked on past you.

"It was nearly a year before I saw you again … "

A butterfly fluttered nearby, its wings waving like tiny bunting, sailing with a breeze, flitting from one spring-warm air current to another, finally and surprisingly alighting on the senorita's skirt. It was poised there, wings outspread, perhaps realising that this was no flower. Its wings joined then, and the attractive-looking insect remained motionless.

The lovers watched it intently, not moving, hardly daring to breathe, waiting for it to make a move, any move. In their silent waiting they heard a lazy hum of flies in the glade, and music from the old phonograph in the pueblo, floating over them, as familiar as the sound of insects.

Becoming stiff with tension in the waiting, Cristina relaxed her limbs, and the butterfly was off into the space of air once more, winging raggedly through the glade and losing itself in sunrays streaming in from beyond the trees.

"You had changed a lot in that one year," she went on. "You'd grown tall and big, I barely recognised you at first. You were with that Esperanza girl, you remember, and I was very upset at the time. Yet I had no claims on you, and it was a long while before I even knew your name.

"Then afterwards I used to see you nearly all the time, and I'd lost interest in you for some reason, don't know what or why.

"But when I saw you with that Esperanza, my heart jumped and filled my throat. I wanted to disappear into the ground. Stupid me, what I'd really wanted was to see you alone in a quiet corner of the pueblo, crying as you did before. Then for you to see me appear! That's how I imagined it. That burst of sunshine again when you couldn't help but smile at me, and in that same cute, little muchacho way. Just like the first time; a special, wonderful little boy smile … "

Cristina looked away, at the trees that formed the glade, her mind's eye focused on a dusty pueblo street, where a dirty, tousle-headed youngster stood on his own, like a stone plinth … smiling his devastating smile.

She glanced at the position of the sun between trees, said in almost sorrowful tones:

"It's getting late. I must go, Javier. Mamá will be wondering. I should have picked some lemon-grass – though I can still get some on the way home.

"So, Javier, until tomorrow then?" and she stooped to kiss him chastely on the cheek. She swiftly turned on bare feet and broke at once into a sprint. Like a wood-sprite, Cristina flew from the glade and into full glaring sun-flooded light.

The music from the pueblo followed her. And no regret is felt at the dying of the day, she thought dreamily and happily, for night is quickly done in sleep and in dream, and a new day is born, as packed with promise as any you may find in the time of spring – composing the gist of a new poem in her head.

The young man remained in the glade for a while, with his back against a tree and lost, too, in his own thoughts. Did he suspect that her lovely looks and sweet señorita's voice would eventually be stolen by time? Never known again? Just as the wildflowers about him will fade and be gone, their beauty nothing more than a memory.

He shrugged and set off for the pueblo.

A time later, Cristina skipped into the Ramos courtyard like a child, face flushed and radiant.

"You're late for comida," said mamá from woodsmoke swirling about the kitchen fire, and not failing to notice the rose-blushed cheeks of her eldest daughter.

"I'm not hungry, mamá," trilled Cristina gaily, and tripped on to her room.

"Living on love, I suppose," mamá muttered to herself.

In her room, Cristina went straight for her old schoolbag, lifting out her notebook. And in a mood of suppressed joy she began to write. The putting down of words in lines of poetry gave the young lover a sense of self-purity; a delicious, complacent chasteness.

35

Romance Questioned

The quick-song throat of spring, like a fast-winged bird in flight, sang and rushed from one glorious day to the next. From the Ramos orchards the heady perfume of peach and apple blossom drifted over the homestead in the still morning air of a mid-April day. There was a fresh scent of flowers, a sharp tang of wild herbs. Above, in the vast expanse of blue, foamy pillow clouds, white as doves, serenely sailed the sky.

Mamá was peeling and chopping vegetables by the fire under a kitchen lean-to, while someone stood nearby watching her.

It was the old ranchero, Pancho.

"Well, María, if you don't mind my saying so," he voiced huskily, "but you have a face today like a blank stone wall – if you don't mind me putting it so. What's the matter? I know there's *something* the matter. This isn't like you, is it, eh?"

"Oh, don't mind me," mamá attempted to laugh it off. "It's just our Cristina I'm worried over. I suppose you know she's seeing one of the Lopez boys. I can't quite put my finger on it, and I don't know exactly what it is, but there's something about that family, and that muchacho, Javier. I feel uneasy in my mind, that's all," and mamá set to peeling onions with untoward concentration, head down and failing to look Pancho's way.

"Hmm, maybe you're right, María, but if you think on it, there's none of us who's perfect, is there? Look at me. No, don't look at me. I'm only perfect at being imperfect. Besides, why stew over these things, it gets you nowhere. Life is life, and it surely never is and never was perfect. You see –

"Why, María, my flower, you're crying!"

"No I'm not then, I'm laughing!" spluttered mamá, "but I'm crying too, but only because of these onions. They're very strong, these onions, the small ones usually are, I find."

Mamá twinkled moist eyes at the old man.

"Ay que caray, I thought you were crying with distress, and that wouldn't be your style, I warrant."

"You can be a dear soul when you want to be, Francisco," murmured mamá with feeling, calling him by his proper Christian name in a moment of confiding intimacy, "and a precious good friend as well."

"All the same, my instincts tell me nothing good or fine will come of this – this liaison."

"So that's what you call it," gruffed the old ranchero, "and I thought it was simply a young señorita in love – or maybe infatuated – with her young man in this blessed springtime season."

"Look, María, the coyote courts a coyote and not some prairie-dog, and likely those two love-birds are well suited after all, like sandals to your feet and eggs in a nest."

"I can't agree with you there, dear soul," mamá persisted in her thinking, "and I never did or could trust anyone of that Lopez family."

Pancho made a face at this. "Who knows but it just may blow over with time, as these things do. They're young and the young can be fickle. It's springtime, don't forget. The sap in the stem is near to bursting, and the wild passions of youth are soon spent, I can tell you. Uuy, these young bucks are like honeybees, they take their fill of nectar from one flower, then buzz on to another."

With that over, the old man lifted a boot and busied himself by scraping off dried mud from the instep, using one of mamá's kitchen knives.

Mamá was not yet finished. "And what if she should get herself pregnant by him, like that poor Carmelita?" she asked suddenly and pointedly, lifting her head. Her eyes were red-rimmed and wet with onion fumes, speaking now as if the dreaded deed was already done.

Pancho pulled his face again, of a reassuring nature, and said, "I don't think it would ever come to that, not for a moment, forget the very notion. Ay que caray, the muchacha has been too well brought up. Cristina is good and sensible and always was, from being a little one as Julia is now. She can take care of herself – you ought to know that, María."

"All the same," mamá sighed, almost giving in, "I can't help feeling some concern over it."

"We're only young once, we only have the one time around, and *our* time is near enough done, on that score at any rate. Don't lay into her like you have been doing. Give that good daughter of yours a chance. Ease off a bit. As the saying has it: 'Even the warmth of a candle will give greater comfort than a forest fire' -

"Are any of these corncakes going spare? They look real tasteful and tempting. Can I try one?"

36

Love Speaks Volumes

Through the trees they could see three old men passing by the river at *Sancho's Elbow*, frail backs bent with long and weary toil. When a day begins by ticking away its moments, this is not the place, this is not the time for bent old men, for the ticking time is almost spent for them. Certain it is that time consumes itself in a kind of triumph over the decaying of flesh.

And time it would seem ticks not at all for youth, with their hopes and desires loose on the windway, lost in bird-chatter and the present hour; following dreams through blue daysky, on to midnight castles, blacknight seas, and an apricot dawn, to another day ticking away. Though not for the supple flesh of the younghearts, with time to spin out their dreams through the daylong hours, and beyond the day at dip of sundown.

She kissed his work-roughened hand and tasted his malesalt, and leaning against his hard, hairless chest she caught the smell of the stable and the field.

"Oh, where are you at, Javier?" she whispered lamentedly. "Don't you want to speak words to shake the world with? Is your heart so dry and dull? Have you no soft words for me? You can make of me your lover, but can you make of me a woman?

"Your hands are rough, but they can be gentle too, I know. Caress me as you used to do. Show your love. Tell me! Tell me that you love me like that first time. When your voice went strange and husky and your eyes seemed as deep as wells. A serious one you were then, Javier. And all I wanted was your dear smile …

"I had to demand a smile from you, like ordering a melon in the market. Oh, my own love, you can be so dull and stubborn at times, you mule! Well, if you want to be like that, dull and dumb as some field-burro, then go ahead and do it, and see if I care …

"But I do care, my own, I care a lot and that's the pain of it …

"I expect too much, I suppose. I want to be romantic. I want to be a vulnerable muchacha, for you to protect. To sweep me off my feet, take me far away. Wouldn't you wish to leave the pueblo some day? No, I guess not, for you'd miss your sisters – and your many friends. The others like you so much, don't they? Look up to you because you are big and strong … yet only seventeen.

"With the smile of a prince. A smile that shatters me every time I see it."

Cristina paused as a waffling wind softly whistled in the woodland around them. There was a deep drone of insects, and the phonograph music from the pueblo sifted through a green cloud of trees marking the glade.

"I shall love you always, Javier," she went on liltingly. "You must know that. You'll be my very own. Lean and strong and dependable. You'll stay handsome as you are and keep those beautiful teeth, your wide straight mouth, that gives such a devastating smile I love so much.

"I shall give you lots of children of course – You wouldn't mind that? – and I'd be a good mother to them, as mamá is to us at home. You will be a fine father, a loving caring husband. Shall it be so, do you think? I think so, at any rate.

"Oh, Javier, can you see it? Will it come true? We don't ask for much, do we? Not really. Still, we must wait, for good things come to those who wait. I'll be waiting for you, my precious, because I love you so …"

The youth stooped to her then, so close, and she looked up at him, her eyes large and moist with emotion, gazing appealingly straight at him. Their lips touched, a touch as light as chaff, like a cloud touching a mountaintop, a dawn-eyed sun touching a dreamscape … Thus her romantic, poetic mind whirled deliciously.

A sudden warm breeze tugged teasingly at her long hair, crickets clicked in the drier grasses under the sun, and the merry sound of a folk *corrido* came over from the pueblo.

37

Spring Romance: Finale

"I want you to go to market this morning," mamá told Cristina one day in late April.

Within the hour she was walking along a narrow dusty by-lane leading to the plaza in the pueblo. The lane was enclosed on each side by adobe walls, tight-clustered pipe organ cacti, thorn bushes and wattled fencing. The lane then broadened out, with side-alleys and yards opening on the sides.

Ahead, she saw a group of young people, mostly girls she knew, crowding round someone – she couldn't see who. They were evidently taken up by something or other, going by the laughter and shrieking.

It was the boy, or rather the young man, Javier, who was the cause of the present merriment; the centre of attraction for the impressionable young females.

Cristina saw and recognised him at last, hurried her steps, and was about to call him. But his name was caught in her throat.

She stopped dead in her tracks, as she watched him place an arm possessively, almost arrogantly, around the waist of one of the young señoritas.

It was Cristina's dear friend, a long favourite companion, her closest confidant. The girl turned her face to him, to Javier, and impulsively kissed him fully on the mouth. He swung his youthful handsome head and saw Cristina down the lane, dust clouding her ankles.

He grinned at her inanely; perhaps a little awkwardly, shamefacedly, but also with an air that was meant to say, 'Well, what is to be done when a pretty señorita goes for you like that?'

Cristina spun instantly on her heels, stormed quickly away from such an awful, humiliating scene, with all those girls that she knew just looking at her, without pity it would seem, but with a certain malicious glee on their faces. It was too horrendous for her to endure, and couldn't get away from them fast enough.

She went back the way she had come, breaking into a run. Her sandalled feet slapped down on hard-trodden ground, almost blind with tears streaming down her face.

She ran all the way home, ignoring mamá and her sister Ruth in the main courtyard, to the sanctity of her room. Mamá was not in the least put out over the fact that Cristina had returned empty-handed from the pueblo, but she was concerned over her daughter's obvious distressed state.

Hours later, with eyes red and swollen and still slightly filmed over with salty tear stain, Cristina began to write in her precious notebook; furiously, with a female fighter's fiery determination.

Cristina wrote now in an entirely different vein to heretofore.

PART SEVEN

PART SEVEN

38

The Pueblito

It was a high noon in early May in the pueblito situated near the Ramos farmstead.

Siesta time.

Everyone resting in their rude adobe huts; apart from the children, that is, who played quietly in the shade of a large beefwood tree in the centre of the space bordered by the homesteads.

These are the same folk who had attended don Antonio's modest celebratory service on Christmas Day.

The huts formed a rough square looking on to a dusty compound, the entire settlement enclosed by wattle fencing and dense growths of cacti. About the compound freely roamed domestic animals; goats and pigs and burros, scrawny chickens and guinea-fowl, and a couple of mangy-looking dogs.

The huts were not as rude-appearing as one might imagine, all the same, because they were adorned with hanging pots of plants and flowers. This riot of rich, flamboyant colour formed a marked contrast to the dull grey-beige of the adobe walls. Each dwelling on front and sides was splashed with the bright gay colours of many varieties of flowers. Here, by a darkened doorway, was a burst of crimson and violet and mauve, and there below a window-opening, a cascade of lilac and citron-yellow against a backdrop of creeping green foliage. On another wall a tumbling of white like a cataract, from trembling pale-green fern. From the lintel of one door, a dripping of ruby and russet, a woven twist of sun-dried chillies, and plaited strings of brown button onions.

At the foot of the wattled fencing and stretching around the perimeter of the pueblito lay a narrow border of cultivation, watered from a nearby well. It contained flowers and tender vegetables such as lettuce and spinach and kale. There were also herbs for kitchen and medicinal use. A gradation of light and dark greens; jade-green, bottle-green and blue-green. This profusion of delectable eatables was a tempting treasure-house for the animals enclosed in the compound, the goats in particular, so it was necessary some time ago for the erection of wire fencing, to deny them access.

There were other telling signs of spring about the pueblito grounds: bald pink piglets rooting in a patch of mud; frisky kid-goats gambolling, butting heads against one another; and a chuckle of chickens scratching and kicking at straw, fluffy yellow chicks closely following the mother hens.

Into this relative paradise rode the ranchero Pancho, on his white rawboned mare Macha, and had in tow the chestnut bay Chapulín, Juan Ramos' horse, saddled-up but with no rider.

As the old man dismounted and tied the horse reins to fencing, the first person he recognised was Julia, rushing to him.

"Oh, Pancho, so you've come!"

"Didn't I say I would?" he smiled on her cheerfully. "How is my little cornflower - ¡Uuy! That mad dog of Cándido's, where is it?"

"It's alright, it's chained up, you'll be safe," laughed the child, taking his hand and leading him deeper into the compound.

By now, the youngsters had ceased their playing and shyly made way for him under the big tree. One girl smilingly offered him the only available seat, a stool, which he accepted with a gallant show of graciousness as befitting a true horseman.

"¡Hola, muchachas!" he greeted them jovially, eyeing them with a paternal-like scrutiny.

Satisfied with what he saw, he parked himself, for a moment silent in the shadow of the beefwood tree. The children gathered before him, in sitting or squatting positions, young limbs scuffed and scarred and dust-caked. Beyond them were the various animals, docile in the stillness of this near noon hour. The dwellings too were quiet, as though quite empty of humanity, yet a body or two rested in each one of them.

The sun was not in the least excessive with its heat; it was a springtime sun, mild and gentle – benevolent. The compound seemed a world unto itself, and the old ranchero felt comfortable there.

"Well, my little ones," he rasped huskily, "I expect you've all been good and decently-behaved since I was last here – though I don't expect too much, mind. Hmm."

The smaller ones squidged bare brown toes in warm soft dust, describing arcs with the big toe. But their attention was wholly taken in the main by the presence of the old man - the one who told them stories - and who now looked over them with kindly blue eyes.

"Our Gabriel was throwing stones at the chickens," piped up one whistle-blower, the culprit in question squirming hotly under a dirty face; smarting a bit, he scowled at his tell-tale sister.

"Ah, was he now?"

"But papá warmed his backside for it."

"Ah, did he now?"

"And he's stopped throwing stones at chickens."

"Ah, has he now?"

"He throws stones at the goats now."

"Ah … 'Woe to the rebellious children, said the lord,' and those are the very words you'll find in *Isaiah* – do you follow, Gabriel?"

Responded the boy, a mite shamefacedly, "I was only getting the goats along, to move them."

"Try using a stick next time to shift your goats. Wave a stick about and they'll soon catch on and move of their own accord."

"Are you going to tell us a story?" asked Julia spiritedly.

"I might at that, my meadow-flower, if that's what you want and you'd all care to listen," returned the old man, crinkling his face into a smile.

"We'll listen," said Julia in a sweet voice, and Pancho detected a hint of coyness too, which was to be expected from this precocious one.

Julia flicked her head to one side, a mannerism of hers, and settled down, hands clasped beneath her knees. The others quit their fidgeting and gazed at the storyteller with rapt expectancy. Pancho ploughed straight into his tale:

"Well, once in a time of long ago in the hot dry desert of Chihuahua, under a rock of golden-yellow sandstone, there lived two little scorpions…"

The youngsters listened large-eyed and open-mouthed. They *Ahh'd* and *Ohh'd* and sometimes crumbled into titters, as the old man rasped and rambled on. At the end of it they chuckled, delighted with the tale.

"Now, with your permission," he grated, getting to his feet, "I need to pay a call on my friend, Florencino," and stumped off across the sun-painted compound, boots kicking up the dust.

39

Blind Florencino

He found his blind friend absorbed in his usual task of basket-weaving, assisted by ten-year-old daughter Carmen. Florencino was sitting on a three-legged stool at the threshold of his hut.

Pancho's keen doglike nose sense twitched at the pleasant smell of finished baskets hanging on hooks just above his head, a kind of carpentry workshop smell – shavings, sawdust and glue – as he imagined it.

Florencino was of slight build, almost childlike in fact, and childlike in manner too. He was a gentle soul. His blindness had given him an innocence and sweetness of character, of a kind rarely to be found among the sighted.

"Florencino! Buenas tardes, amigo. ¿Que paso?" the old man greeted him robustly, and somewhat loudly – the sighted, too, seemed to deem it necessary to shout to a blind person, as though the blindness also affected their hearing!

"Pancho, my dear friend, buenas tardes – and welcome! I did hear you earlier, and Carmen here told me it was you come to visit our rather modest pueblito. Honoured we are, at any rate. I trust God is with you – Muchacha, a stool for our guest, quickly now!"

"No, it's alright, compadre, let me stand. I need to stretch a bit anyway, and besides, I'm still growing, you know, I dare to swear."

The blind man laughed at this. "That's you all over, Pancho. But welcome again, welcome, it's good to hear your voice again. We were only talking of you just the other day – Isn't that so, Carmen? – And how are things on don Roberto's ranch? Is our Cándido behaving himself? His good woman Laura would love to know, I'm sure."

"Cándido's behaviour is on a par with that mad dog of his when it's not chained down," grinned Pancho – which he changed at once into a hearty laugh, for the benefit of his blind friend. "But I keep a tight rein on him, you know, as one must, and he's doing well enough, I'm happy to say.

"All my compañeros send you their dearest regards and good wishes – "

"Oh, you mean Gerardo, and José and Emilio, hey?"

"The same, the very same. I almost forgot, but Julian too thinks fondly of you. Well, we all do, when it comes to that … And, uuy, you look fit and dapper, amigo, I must say – and I just did, hmm."

"Things are going well at present and God is good, my old friend. I guess I'm blessed," smiled Florencino, and the light of day was as a sparkle in his sight-starved eyes.

The everyday smells were full and thriving in his nostrils, the sounds around him gathered in, taken to acute-hearing ears to shape his thoughts.

"I can see you're busy enough here as usual," Pancho rough-voiced on with homely pleasantries, "like a city factory, so it is," as he glanced around inside the cluttered hut.

The floor was strewn with baskets and basket-making material, and there were earthenware vessels and tin boxes and crates of *Fanta* orange drink in small bottles – for his home also served as a local tienda.

"You carry on there with what you're doing, while we talk awhile, and I'll try not to get in the way, great lumbering beast that I am.

"But, ay que caray, how do you manage it, compadre, with all this stuff about? I'd get lost myself – and I've eyes to see with."

"Oh, but I have my *eyes*, Pancho," said the other coyly. "My Carmen here, for instance, is one of my eyes at least," and he spoke the truth, for the voice of a child gave sight to sound and made eyes of his ears.

"My wife Sofia helps a lot as well," he went on contentedly, "for she sees to many things for me. And I have my fingers and thumbs, with an eye on the end of each of them, if you follow my meaning. Sí, they're good for touching and feeling and *seeing*, as it were. Never fail me, I'm glad to say, whether I'm feeling silk or cotton or the bark of a tree – or the soft cheeks of my three little ones."

Florencino was not without a sense of humour, and went on: "My hands now … they come in pretty handy, hey!

"Now, Pancho, would you like a bottle of Fanta? I have some already cooling nicely in a bucket of well water. Well water, my friend, as cold as ice it is."

"No, gracias, Florencino, I'm fine, honest. But may I buy one for your Carmen? She works hard while the other kids are out at play."

"Did you hear that, muchacha? Our good friend Pancho wishes to treat you to a Fanta. What do you think to that, then? Muy bien, hey? You go and open one, and mind it's from the bucket and not the crate – Ah gracias, Pancho, muchas gracias," as he accepted a coin from the old ranchero.

Pancho was intrigued and impressed by the blind man's undoubted skill in basket weaving. Inside the hut he saw long thin strands of beige-yellow and pale green straw hung looped over a log cross-beam. Young Carmen brought out a fresh batch of already prepared bases for the baskets – and taking occasional sips at her bottled orange drink, a pleasurable treat.

The old man watched with interest as swift nimble fingers twisted and turned, stretched and weaved ; the basket Florencino was working on almost complete with its sides done.

"Carmen?"

"Sí, papá, here," as the child handed him a fresh basket base.

He snipped and cut, bent over the handle, gauging by touch the length required. *Snip! – Snip!* using a sharp machete. Folded in here, pressed down there – *Snip!* Bend. *Snip! – Snip!* That one done.

"Another, por favor …" he softly commanded.

The child passed over another basket, and she sorted out the different shades of straw strips at his feet. Pretty baskets festooned the space within, like Chinese lanterns. Filaments of light sliced through the roof thatching, danced in shimmering lines on the blind man's face. And insects hummed and whined about his head, his sweating face spotted with black flies.

Florencino paused in his work a moment, turned his face Pancho's way with unerring accuracy, and said:

"I remember you one time describing my daughters to me, old friend. You know, their features and how they looked to you. You said Estrella has a kind of snub nose, like her papá, while Carmen's is more pointed, like her mamá. Erendira has wide eyes, you told me, and Carmen's are more rounded. Carmen is taller than Erendira, but then she's a year older, and so on.

"But I must tell you, friend Pancho, that the three muchachas 'look' the same to me, if you follow me, even when I feel different shapes to their faces. I've known this all the time. The three of them are beautiful to me, and it'll always be so. Their beauty is not just in their shape, it is also in their voices and the way in which they touch their papá. It tells me all about them, everything I wish to know. My little ones are very real to me, though I've never seen them, as you see them …"

Old Pancho was always struck by the small man's serenity, witnessing it at this very moment, bringing on a reminding thought and letting it out:

"I once had three muchachas, a long time ago," he said huskily, a slight catch in his throat. "They lived like flowers, short but sweet."

"Sí, I remember you telling me once before. And you lost them too, poor souls – poor you!"

"Uuy, I can still picture their dear little faces, even after this space of time."

"That's so, that's so, I recall you telling me. And as I think on it – for I've never told you this before – but you're one of the few friends in my life I can put a face to – "

"The Lord love you, amigo!" exclaimed the old man, interrupting him, "but I'm an ugly old sinner, to be sure. If you had eyes to see with and you looked at me, why, I'm certain you'd wish yourself blind again – No disrespect intended, mind," as he stooped forward and laid a hand on the other's shoulder.

"You can give me a face, you say," Pancho went on, "and how is that then? The times I've known you, you've been blind."

"Well, the matter of it is this, you see, it's your voice I hear that gives me a face I can see," smiled Florencino. "You sound exactly like my old father when he was alive and thriving. So in my mind I can see him when you and me get talking.

"Mind you, Pancho, I don't find it easy to picture him in my head – I've near forgotten many faces since being blind – but in my dreams he's still as real as when he were alive. When I remember him as he was. After all these years his features are still fairly clear, because I always have him in my dreams.

"He was a fine man, and in a way you're keeping him alive for me. You have his self-same expressions and turns of speech. You have his laugh as well, and his very tone of voice."

"So," returned the old man, "are you thinking you're talking to your papá when we're gabbing together?"

"Oh, no!" laughed Florencino. "You're Pancho Ramírez, and there's no getting away from that. No, my friend, what I mean is, you're reminding me of him, my papá. And so I can put a face on you and know it. You're not offended, I hope, are you?"

"Hell, no!" rasped Pancho. "I'm surely old enough to be your father anyway. Do you speak to him when you see him in these dreams?"

"I can't say that I do, no, I don't think I do. But he speaks to me. And it's that picture of him, you understand, with a certain look on his face. For me to see that, being blind and all, is something very special, don't you think?"

The old ranchero gave a sigh of pleasure, a sigh of deep satisfaction. He was pleased over Florencino's openness, his honesty, and his confiding with him as a valued friend.

"There's another thing I wanted to say," went on Florencino. "You're a good compañero to me, Pancho. A caring sort of man, I should say, and I'll tell you why."

"You talk direct to me, to my face I mean. When I'm rabbiting on and suddenly ask you something, you're sure to be there talking to my face with your answer, or whatever. You'd sound different, you see, if your face was turned away."

"Hmm, that's strange …" mused the old man, "because you do the same thing. I could never think why it's so, on account that you can't see me, if you'll forgive me for saying it. I mean, you could still be listening to me whether your face is up at the rafters or down at your toes."

"That's true, that's true, you're right," smiled the other enthusiastically. "I don't have to 'look' because there's nothing for me to see anyhow. Sí, I suppose it's a point of politeness on my part. Especially with old friends like yourself, when I need to 'look' at your face, so to speak, when we're both rattling on – Ah, who's this now? My Erendira, I shouldn't be surprised," as Florencino's youngest came tripping up to him.

"Papá!" she shrilled, "Juani was kicking mud and stuff at me, and I'm all dirty now. Feel my frock, papá, it's all dirty!"

"Never mind, niña," he soothed her, laying a hand on her shoulder, "mamá will wash it later. You'll be in the tub tonight at any rate, and you can be first."

"How about some *Chiclets*?" said Pancho, with a beatific smile. "Would you fancy a packet of Chiclets for yourself, eh?"

"Sí, señor Pancho," the child returned shyly. "Muchas gracias."

"*De nada, niña*. A packet for each of your pals as well. That'll be how many of you?" as the old ranchero scanned the compound. "Can't keep count here, those muchachas are never still for a moment."

"There are – let me think now – ah sí, fourteen of them," said the tienda-keeper, Florencino, groping by his side for a carton of the chewing gum.

"It's to be one packet each, Erendira, claro? There you go, your papá's got them out ready for you, or will in a shake of a cat's tail … And here's the payment, amigo, quite correct I reckon," handing a fistful of coins to the blind man.

"Oye, there's too much here, I'm thinking, my friend."

"No, it's right I tell you," insisted Pancho. "Go on, take it, hombre, and no arguments, eh?"

"Well, I'll turn a blind eye on that," and Florencino gave him a mischievous grin.

The conversation continued:

"Tell me if you would, Florencino," the old man opened up once again, "does it not drive you crazy sometimes, seeing total blackness all the time, an endless night? Leastways, that's as I think on it."

"Oh, my blindness isn't as black as you paint it," said the other quietly. "I see colours oftentimes, but they're mostly a kind of bluish-grey, rather than black. It somehow seems to have a texture to it as well, like looking closely at a wall or a barn door, but in the dim light of late twilight.

"It's not that way all the time though, I have to admit. There are times when I might be upset, like if one of my muchachas is poorly, then I find myself in a darkness that can be frightening. At the other end of it though I can see a kind of light and colour.

"That's why I enjoy your company so much. Because you manage to light my way when you're around. Not exactly light itself, you must understand, but a sense of light – a lightening of things. Best if I call it a forgetting of the darkness. You make me forget my blindness, even when we're talking about it! You give me a 'light' that I can 'see' by. I feel or sense it, rather than actually see it."

There was a momentary silence between them. Then Pancho realised something which alarmingly dawned on him. It struck him that in not speaking, in that emptiness of silence, he was no longer existing as it were for his blind friend. Being silent, he might as well not be there at all. Silence has become distance. As far as Florencino was concerned, he thought, he had vanished, simply wasn't there anymore.

He hastily put this to rights at once and began to speak:

"I guess you won't have read a book, eh? Excuse my asking, I'm blunt at times, I know."

"I once felt a book – handled it, you know – and it was a nice thing to feel, though of course it would have been nicer to *read* it. Someone told me that it was a Bible, but I knew already it was a Bible, it had to be a Bible, hadn't it?

"Must be kind of wonderful to read a book. And speaking of which, I was once told on good authority, Pancho, that you are a reader of books. Is it not so?"

"Not so much these days, amigo," admitted the old ranchero a shade ruefully, "but sí, I was a great reader of books for a long time. Only good books, mind, from don Roberto's library – where else!

"In reading good books you learn much about others, but also about your own self, your own humanity ..."

"Sí, I expect you do," said with an air of wistfulness.

"Most people are quite ordinary, do ordinary everyday things, live ordinary lives ... but *humanity* itself is a wondrous and forceful entity."

"I expect it is, sí," said wistfully.

"But in saying that, in every human face there is a story, so books aren't everything."

"I agree with you there, Pancho," said the other, lightening up, "especially as I'm not *able* to read."

"But even without books, you're content enough, aren't you? You seem content to me, and always seemed so."

"Oh, I am, I am!"

"Ay que bueno. Contentment is a bonus in life, like a two-yolked egg, or a soft-seated saddle.

"And which reminds me to tell you, that I've brought *him* along, by the by."

"A saddle, is it?"

"A saddle, and a horse to go with it."

"Not ... Not – "

"Sí, amigo, Juanito's Chapulín."

"And you're going to take me riding on him?" asked Florencino eagerly, with the excitement of a child.

"I certainly am at that. Are you ready for it?"

"Oh, I'm ready alright. ¡Muchismo gracias! I've been looking forward to this for a long time," and the blind man was up from his stool in an instant.

"*Looking* forward, do you like that one, Pancho, hey?" he grinned, cleverly nudging the old man in the ribs.

"That's the spirit, compadre. We'll make a ranchero of you yet. Well, come on then, let's be off!"

And a gathering of youngsters industriously chewing away with good, strong, clean white teeth that have had little experience of sugar-tasting, stood and contentedly watched the two adults leave the hut.

40

Florencino's 'World'

They wended their way together to the wattled gate. Pancho untied the horses, and the kids came and gathered round, chattering like sparrows finding breadcrumbs.

The old ranchero led Florencino to the chestnut bay.

"He's an easygoing friendly fellow is our Chapulín, so you're going to be okay with him," said Pancho, holding the bay by his halter. "Now, amigo, you put your foot up here – I'll guide you, that's it. He's taller than your little burro, mind, so you jump high to mount him. Up you come!" and the ranchero bodily lifted the diminutive blind man with powerful arms and settled him securely in the saddle.

"Ay que bueno, Florencino, you're a born horseman, no word of a lie," grinned old Pancho. "The other foot needs to be in the stirrup though – I'll come round, so don't run off anywhere – Hold it, Chapulín! We're not off yet, you hasty creature," stumping round to the horse's right flank.

"Ah, you've already done it, I see, compadre, and I'm wasting time taking a walk – How did you manage that, then? A ranchero in the making, no doubt of it.

"Now hold them reins slackly like for the present and just relax, you've gone stiff as a post. There, that's better. Give me a moment to mount my Macha – Oye, muchachas, not too near or you'll get trampled on and only be good for dog food," as he shoo'd a passle of young ones away from the horses.

He had almost forgotten that he had an audience, and knew craftily that they knew, equally craftily, that they were only waiting and hoping for some mishap or other. Well, they'd get no satisfaction while he was in charge of matters.

Presently, the two riders set off along a track skirting the pueblito, at a steady walking pace, the youngsters running alongside and behind them, chittering like a flock of birds. Folk emerged from the adobe huts, curious to see what was going on – 'Pancho was in town', that was clear.

The old ranchero guided his mount through a flowered meadow by the river, Florencino on his left flank, a smile of pure delight on his face. The young ones following were soon outpaced and skittered on back to the pueblito, after madly waving farewell to the fast departing horsemen.

They rode through lush green meadowland, Florencino's ears attuned to a symphonic drone of insects in the balmy air, and wind-voiced grass sang too in its rustled, stirring movements.

He heard birdwings and birdsong, whistling and scuttering, here and over there and here again, insect life and birdlife busy about the springtime air.

He heard the pleasant jingle of snaffles and a squeaking of leather, a rhythmic swishing as the horse hooves ploughed through grass. Warm spring wind pushed gently into his face, and he could smell horse-sweat and saddle-leather, dust and pollen and bittersweet herbs. And something else besides ...

"I smell the river," he announced joyfully, "and something else too, like many flowers."

"That's blossom, we're coming in to Antonio's fruit orchard," Pancho informed him, and keeping a careful eye on Chapulín's progress. The bay was behaving admirably, no doubt enjoying the fuss, as his rider felt at his mane, continually stroking his long handsome neck. Florencino weighed no more than Chapulín's master Juan Ramos, so he was no burden at all.

They passed through the Ramos farmstead's sun-dappled orchards, into another meadow brightly peppered with wild peonies, then out on to open, dusty ground.

"We can speed up a bit, if you'd like to try it," suggested the old horseman. "It's pretty flat along this stretch."

"Lead the way," smiled the blind man, "and I'll follow," as the other broke Macha into an easy canter. Chapulín immediately took the hint and followed suit.

The horse's hooves kicked up dust, a wind playing hard against the riders' faces. Florencino felt a complete exhilaration with the forward movement.

"Oh my, Pancho!" he called over ecstatically, "I feel like I'm flying through the air."

"Crossing the river any moment, wait for it!"

The mounts crashed through water, hooves crunching rock and gravel, water cascading high to their withers, silver and rainbow hues in the sunlight.

On the opposite bank Pancho paused, then wheeled away and headed up the long slope of a hill scattered with maguey and cacti and thorn bush. The bright spring sun shone fully on them.

After a time the ranchero slowed to a halt at the rise of the hill, with its commanding view of the San Angelo valley and far beyond. Chapulín and Macha got their heads together and sniffed companionably at each other.

"We're overlooking the valley," Pancho told his friend. "I can see the pueblo over by the left, and the fields this side of the river … the Ramos place down there somewhere, which I can't see for that bit of woodland hiding it.

"And your pueblito, compadre, I see all of it in every detail – even your home. Glad to say it's still there and standing, or would it be sitting, hmm."

"The air smells different here, sharper, fresher …" noted the blind man, face angled toward an unseen sky. He levelled his face before forgotten hills and lost fields, sniffing with appreciation at good clean air, as Pancho himself was apt to do.

A short moment later Florencino's ears pricked up. "I can hear the music coming from the pueblo," he said in some wonder.

"Ay amigo, and it's my favourite tune," said the other, "*Sentimiento y Dolor*. God's greatest creation is Man, and Man's greatest creation is music, I like to believe."

"If the pueblo is down there, as you say, then we haven't ridden far. Yet I feel as if I've travelled a fair distance."

"Ah, we did circle round a bit," explained the ranchero.

Florencino again uncannily turned to face the other's way. "You know, Pancho," he went on, "you have stretched my little world by bringing me here. A new place for me, and with different sounds. Do you hear someone chopping wood down below us somewhere? Like a lazy woodpecker taking time boring a hole in a tree. Do you hear it, my friend?"

"I hear it, and I reckon it's coming from the Ramos farmstead – it'll be young Juanito, most likely as not."

Florencino appeared to be ruminating, thought Pancho, glancing over at him.

"It's a strange but interesting world we live in," the little man continued on. "You know, if we stopped our chatter and the wind should drop too, and there was a silence about us, then I'd be right back in my own little world again …"

"When you say *world*, just how big is this world?"

"Oh, only as far as my arms can reach out to touch things, I guess. Most of my world is inside of me – in my mind is what I mean. But my world does at times kind of expand. When the muchachas are calling and laughing by the riverside, say, it gives me a sense of space and distance. It's the same with that music we hear from the pueblo, giving more distance to my world, you might say.

"I know you like to describe things to me, Pancho, telling me of colours you see. You tell me what's happening around us, and I like that very much, because it widens my world, so to speak. But a lot of what you describe doesn't really mean all that much to me.

"Ah, you're tensing up, my friend, I can sense it. But listen, I'm hoping that I'm being open and honest with you, and maybe you'll understand what I'm getting at."

"Carry on, amigo," said Pancho quietly, tugging at one ear. "It's you I was thinking on, not myself, for I'd hate to disappoint you."

"I know that, and if anyone understands my condition, it is you. You show it in the way you speak to me.

"What I'm trying to say is this: You describe things you see, hopefully thinking I can see the same in my mind. So you work at it to be careful and accurate in what you're telling me. Of course I can't see what you point out so faithfully and in such detail, but I still get a picture – oh, indeed I do! – a blind man's picture of what you're trying to paint for me.

"I always take note when you put great store in describing the clouds and their shapes, the blue of the sky, the sharpness of stars at night. The real honest truth is that such things are barely known to me, because they're things of silence and great distance. They are things I can't ever hear or touch, do you see?"

"Why! ¡Újule!" gasped the old man suddenly in a flash of revelation. "The clouds and sky and stars, they're silent and untouchable for me too. I'd never considered that, I'd never thought of them in that way before."

"I've not offended you?"

"Not a bit of it. You've enlightened me in a way I'd never have guessed."

Pancho's blue eyes twinkled, and he felt somehow suddenly younger, and vastly pleased over what his friend had disclosed with such devastating force.

Florencino chatted on: "You have to remember that my world is very small. My real world is the one where I can feel and touch and smell. My wider world is shaped by sound. Far off sounds, like a coming thunderstorm – or that music floating up from the pueblo – these are the things that make my small world grow a bit bigger.

"I must confess, you do go to lots of trouble in telling me the colours of things, I know you do – like someone's new camisa, a flower, or a field at harvest time, and all that."

"Ay caray ..." mourned the old man, "so colour is wasted on you as well, is it?"

"No, not exactly ... that's not so, if the truth be known."

"Can you see colours, then?"

Florencino hesitated, thought a moment, then said, in slow deliberate tones: "I don't see colour as you do, I can't see colours you describe to me. In my *living* world, if I can call it that ..." and he paused again.

"Your conscious world, you mean? Is that what you're getting at?" Pancho prompted him.

"Sí, my friend, that's it exactly. My *conscious* world is dull and grey, with maybe a bit of blue in it at times. Everything is a kind of fading dark time grey and blue ...

"But in my dreams," and Florencino's voice rose in some excitement, "in my dreams I see many wonderful colours. Oh, Pancho, you cannot imagine, you wouldn't believe the kind of colours I experience in my dreams. I dream a lot, you know; blind people usually do, so I've been told. Anyway, I have these lovely colours before me in my dreams.

"Such shapes they have too. And I can *feel* them! I can actually feel their – ¿Como se llama? – their ..."

"Textures, is it? You mean textures?"

"That's it! That's it exactly." The little blind man was getting more worked up by the minute, fidgeting and shifting in his saddle. "Sí, I feel the texture of them, like feeling rough wood or warm rock – or the earth itself.

Solid they are, a solid substance I can touch or hold, and feel their weight and shape, their very being. And *see* it all in beautiful colours!

"Mind you," he lowered his voice, also coming back down from his height of ecstasy, "don't ask me to put a name to any of these colours, for I honestly couldn't tell you. If you say 'pink' I couldn't imagine the colour pink, because I don't know it, I can't remember it, I've only heard of it, for I've long forgotten it.

"The names aren't important at any rate, are they? What's in a name? as they say. You can't feed on the name *tortilla*, can you? It's my *seeing* these colours that gives me so much pleasure. That is what's important to me, you understand."

"Well, that's a relief to me, I can tell you. So how am I of use to you, then?" Pancho wanted to know.

The blind man chuckled, his small frame shaking in the saddle. When he finally got a hold of himself, he continued on:

"How are you of use to me? I'll tell you, my friend. When you speak to me, as you often have in the past and present times, you put me almost in a dream-like state – Oh, it's true I tell you! You give to my poor existence a richness – that's it! – a richness, I'll have you know.

"You bring out the colours from my dreams. You give to everything that rough texture I mentioned before. Not so much in the scenes you describe, or the colours you spend time and trouble over.

"No, my friend, it is all in your voice; the honest tone of it and, might I say, its sincerity, and in what you're saying to me.

"All of that brings a rich meaning to my life, that's worth more to me than all the pesos in Mexico."

Though Florencino was of slight build, so small of stature, almost like a child rather than an adult parent of three children, Pancho saw him, not physically but humanly – or, perhaps more correctly, psychologically. He saw him as a positive giant among men. He saw his blind friend as a veritable living saint.

Florencino enjoyed his ride out into the country. And the old ranchero, the regular horseman, he did, too.

PART EIGHT

41

Pancho's Abode

Francisco Medina Ramírez was a man of property. Assuredly, it was an extremely modest piece of property – but who quibbles over such matters in Mexico's heartland? Certainly not old Pancho. And it definitely was all his, he owned it outright, plus the modest plot of land it stood on.

Its exterior consisted of two walls of adobe brick, and two walls partly cane-stalked partly weather-boarded. With an outhouse – almost as large as his dwelling – adjoining at the rear side, where he stabled his white rawboned mare, Macha.

This solitary structure was set back from a winding goat track, and afforded a broad view of San Angelo valley's slightly curved length. The southern area was dominated by a steep sloped hill sensually carved by nature into the shape of a woman's breast, the illusion heightened by a long-derelict chapel standing at the summit like an erect nipple. It was this same hill where Pancho had taken his friend Florencino, when they roamed around on horseback.

A day or so after the ride with his blind companion, Pancho was 'at home'.

On this spring morning he gazed non-seeingly about his 'quarters'. Light, filtered through chinks in the cane-stalked walls, exposed the old man's only material wealth, or the lack of it.

On one side, before a smoke-blackened corner wall, stood a low stone hearth, a pile of silver-white ash cool in the bowl. Alongside the hearth, a half full sack of mouldy corn leaned against the wall, in company with a clay water jar, its top protected by a round plywood board with a corncob handle.

The opposite side was adorned with nothing more than a coarsely woven sarape and a straw sombrero, which had seen better days and now hung on a nail; and a wooden crate of dusty, undefinable junk. Above, at a normal man's height, was grouped a trio of earthenware pots, handles roped and hung on a meat-hook in the main log beam.

All of these things cast about the place an eerie luminosity.

There was no sign of knick-knacks or pictures or anything that could be termed superfluous, but on the slatted clapboard door was pasted long ago the front page of a newspaper, flyblown and parchment-brown with age. Now faded print told of the assassination of President Obregón and the dissolving of the *Confederación Regional de Obreros Mexicanos*, events that had occurred back in Pancho's early years.

The old ranchero began to hum to himself. An intuitive feeling had suddenly snatched at his senses.

He stepped out into the broad bright morning sunshine.

42

Passing Travellers

He was right, as he knew it would be so, steady gaze sweeping over distant terrain in a careful survey, then stopping sunwards at a distorted blob that could be taken for a lifeform approaching from the lower reaches of the hill.

Pancho thumbed his eye socket and looked again, fastening sea-blue eyes on a man astride the crupper of a lightly laden though fairly emaciated burro. With a youngish woman following on foot a few paces behind, half obscured by dust the donkey kicked up.

Nearer now, the skinny animal minced on awkward legs as it followed the stony goat track, stiffening its forequarters on a downward dip in shadow. Hooves clipped stones and milled the earthcrust, and the crust crumbled, turned to dust.

The creature jibbed to a sudden halt, straddled limbs trembling, directly in front of Pancho's property.

A friendly hand was raised in greeting to these strangers, sharp eyes casually taking in potware strung broadside on the beast, clattering tinnily by scraggy flanks.

Pancho watched with interest, as the stranger slid swiftly over the rump of his carrier in that manner peculiar to the Mexican peon or campesino, and wiped the palms of sweaty hands down patched pantaloons.

The woman – Pancho could now see that she was quite young, most likely the stranger's daughter, he readily assumed – the señorita took the rope rein without a word and quietly led the animal to the scant shade of a nearby scrub tree.

"*¡Buenos dias!*" barked out Pancho in his hoarsely toned morning voice, but with evident enthusiasm, one hand extended as he loped forward, and the other courteously lifting his sombrero clear from his head – a real token of respect in that sombrero-raising. And the man, face powdered with fine, orange-sienna dust, showed an open dirt-grimed palm.

"Sit yourself, please do – sí, right there," rasped Pancho, offering the dubious comfort of a matted cob of earth stuck up in the ground, foot stool high. While he himself squatted nimbly on his hunkers in the traditional stance of a ranchero – which the stranger immediately took him to be; he *had* to be, because of his cheerful disposition and open friendliness, so unlike the normally morose country peon.

A brief pregnant silence ensued, the two men slyly appraising each other, like dogs sniffing for clues or information of some sort.

"Tell me, hombre," Pancho began again, spade-size hand pulling at his moustache, and rocking on booted heels, "where are you come from and where do you go? I trust Saint Anthony is with you."

"By La Cruz del Palma, señor," the other returned briefly.

"Ah, La Cruz, eh? Ay que bueno, a real nice place to be sure – " He had never been there in his life. " – And where is it you go?"

"The town. The big town. San Stefan."

"¿Sí? San Stefan, is it? The big town," Pancho echoed in gruff, husky tones, "And San Stefan it'll be," gazing steadily into the man's coffee-brown eyes.

"The market, señor," the man expanded further.

"To be sure, the market. Hmm, que bueno," swishing a hand at an early squadron of morning attacking flies.

"I have pots to sell," the stranger resumed, indicating the laden donkey with a motion of one arm.

"So I see, and there they are," said Pancho. But he was staring at the woman. She's surely this hombre's daughter, he thought, though not with total conviction.

"Uuy, I'm forgetting my manners. Can I offer you a drink of water?" He patted his kneecaps, then rubbed a hand down one shin.

"Gracias, no, we have water."

Presently, the traveller politely coughed, to indicate further speech, kneading the thin stretch of muscle over his kneecaps. "We must be off," he said, and stood abruptly, wiping palms against his sides.

Pancho jumped instantly upright with alacrity. "You're on your way then, is it?" he choked out, an element of disbelief showing on his face, as if the stranger was there solely for his pleasure.

Moments later, the man took the rein from his partner's hand and led the burro down the track which wound away round the hill. The young woman followed submissively behind as before, her rather dainty feet picking their way carefully over sharp, loose rock.

Old Pancho regretfully watched them go, tugging at his moustache, a wreath of flies busy about him. The couple disappeared from his view behind a bluff.

Guess it's time for me to be off to don Roberto's, he decided, and wheeled resolutely on his heels, to saddle up the mare.

A dust-devil briefly swirled across the track, and insects buzzed busily in the fast warming air.

43

A Hog for Don Roberto

Birds called in the branches of a tree overhanging the Ramos homestead's tumbledown stable. Young Juan glanced up, seeing tatters of straw and lead-white stains of birdlime under the eaves, where a pair of starlings had set up a nest for this year.

The boy opened the sun-blistered stable doors and entered a woolly gloom, a nimbus of flies about his head. The air in the stable pulsed with swarms of seemingly maddened insects, and there was a sharp ammoniac reek of horse piss, always at its strongest in the morning.

Juan's booted feet ploughed through rank-smelling swathes of cornstraw and dollops of fresh manure, to his horse stamping skittishly in the roomy stall.

"Impatient today, hey, Chapulín, my handsome one," the boy murmured fondly, patting the horse's croup, and the animal whickered with pleasure and a spray of dust fell like a veil from the stall-top.

The horse was a fine-formed, toasted chestnut-brown bay, well-muscled and long-tailed, with alert, neatly pointed ears. A beast of superb strength and conformation, by its looks more of a racer than anything.

There was an undeniably appealing expression in its nut-coloured eyes, swinging its head to nuzzle the boy's shoulder. And why he should have named the horse *Chapulín*, meaning 'grasshopper', no one knew.

Chapulín gave his young master a 'Well, you're here at last and about time too!' sort of look, then blinked at sharp sunlight sluicing through the open stable doors.

Juan led him out from the ramshackle stable quarters, hooves plopping heavily on manure and piss-sodden ground straw, to the farmstead's tilt-cart parked at an angle like a pair of cannon, dripping rusty trace chains and sun-hot leather harness.

Dust-devils waltzed across the yard, and Chapulín tossed his head and twitched ears at pestiferous insects about him.

"Easy, my beauty," Juan commanded softly in his mount's ear. He would need some help to hitch him to the tilt-cart, and his eyes pinned on papá, who was quietly sitting on a wooden keg in the shade of a nearby open burro stall, busily twining strands of rope hemp, and apparently oblivious to a high, steady drone of flies in the stall.

"Papá, could you spare a moment, por favor?" Juan called to him, and don Antonio came straight over.

He tidied up a tangled knot in the trace chains, the links clinking with an oddly musical sound.

"Where are you off to then, Juanny?" he inquired in a low sonorous 'lay preacher's' voice. "The *hacienda*, no doubt."

"Sí, papá, don Roberto's," the boy replied, slipping a snaffle on Chapulín.

"Pancho's hide-out – workplace, I should say. You'll see Pancho?"

"Most likely, papá. He's bound to be there."

Don Antonio smiled on his only male offspring. He assisted in lifting the shaft, and they hitched the horse to the tilt-cart, while scrawny chickens pecked and grubbed at dirt dangerously close to the horse's hooves.

"I suppose you're taking the hog, is it?"

"Sí, papá, it's time I did, seeing as it's already paid for," dropping in the last linch-pin.

Papá watched Chapulín's pointed ears flick at tormenting flies. The don and his boy heard a bird warbling gaily to its mate somewhere off in the orchard.

Salté, Juan's big dog, came trotting to them. It sank to its knees in the dust and stretched its forelegs out, muzzle resting in a bowl of warm, aromatic dust.

The heat of the day raised fresh dung odour from the stable, and it drifted over to them. The dog sniffed at the pungent scent, and dust on his nose caused him to sneeze. He closed one eye, then the other, almost in slow or at least lazy motion.

Juan picked fussily at loose threads curling from the edge of an old saddle-cloth, as the homely lilting melody of *El siete legüas* floated towards them, through warm morning air from the pueblo across the river.

"I'll go and get the hog," said Juan, "Stay, Salté!" he commanded sharply, and he spun on his heels and strode off, leaving his father to patiently wait under growing, swelling heat.

The boy returned moments later, drubbing a hog with a stick. The beast's underbelly was caked with dirt, smelling abominably. It tried to turn and Juan whacked it one across the middle of its rough bristled back.

The man and the boy hoisted the hog into the tilt-cart, and the hog kicked up a mini-storm, thudding the cart bed with hind hooves, angrily snorting and snuffing in its outrage. Dung and dried mud fell from it, like fragments of clay pottery.

Juan quickly tied its rope halter to the seat stanchion. "There, you stink!" he snapped, and slammed down the tail-gate.

The boy was now seated on the cart and he loosely gathered the reins, while the dog at once led off. Juan gave a short curt command and Chapulín began to strain at the traces, nostrils flaring with effort and tossing his mane. The traces tautened and the cart shuddered and groaned, wheels creaking, axle rattling.

"Wait! *¡Un momento!* Just a moment!"

Mamá came ponderously along the path from the farmyard, puffing and listing slightly with the weight of a bulging string bag tucked like a huge turkey under one arm, and Juan brought the horse to a halt, turning in his seat.

"What is it, mamá?"

"Here, Juanito, take this," blew mamá, all of a fluster and quite out of breath with her exertions, "some fruit for the rancheros ... *Puff*... phew! Apples, last year's crop." (A fine example of the Mexican way of doing things at the last moment!)

Mamá patted her brow, mouth in an 'O' shape. She got back her breath and said, "They're scrubby and a bit hard I'd say, but they'll do I expect for those ruffian rancheros, tone down their rogueries, hey?"

"Put them in the back, mamá."

"What, as a gift for the hog! Have the hog get them behind your back!"

"Here, then," laughed Juan, and mamá dropped the bag between the boy's feet.

"If you see old Pancho, give him my regards. Off with you then, can't idle around here," ordered mamá, throwing out a hand as though it held a knout. "*¡Ándale!*"

"Okay, *hasta luego*. Ay-yah, Chapulín!"

Metal jingled, aged leather squeaked like a thing alive, wood creaked, and once more they were on their way.

A cock strutted and capered boldly before cart-and-horse, a hen and posse of chicks pattering after it. The dog, knowing exactly where it was going, turned at a fork in the track, enveloped in a haze of dust. Chapulín cheerfully followed, the cart grinding and rumbling and looking very likely as if it would crumble to pieces at any moment – every part of it seemed so loosely jointed.

Juan glanced backward as the tail-gate shook and the hog shivered, squealing indignantly and losing its footing. The wheels scraped and jarred over hummocks, ruts and bumps, rubble of stone and rock.

And the travelling party left behind a swirling trail of gold-washed dust caught by the sun.

PART NINE

44

Ruth and Julia go to Market

The Ramos girls Ruth and Julia, on their way to market in the pueblo, were beyond a wood surrounding the farmstead, treading a pebbled pathway along the edge of a gently sloping cornfield near the river.

Arriving at the river – at this time little more than a stream threading the bed by the opposite bank – the girls paused at a curve of a cutbank, to watch a group of women beating out washing in the ridged bottoms of wooden troughs.

The girls took their feet down earthen steps crudely carved out the cutbank. One of the women turned at that moment and smiled at them from a simple, bovine face.

Julia scooted across the gravelled riverbed, the child's vital energy not yet sapped by sweltering heat. Her flying braids flashed silver-blue in the incandescent sunlight. Ruth caught up with her.

In the clear blue sky the sun hung hard and unrelenting.

They entered scrub grass scorched brown and dull with dust. Julia stompingly followed an ants' trail, Ruth behind her and walking in the wake of her dust. Grasshoppers jumped on ahead of them in dry sapless grass, and the 'hoppers sounded like snapping twigs. The girls bypassed thickets of dusty thorn scrub, and at length arrived at the pueblo.

The pair passed along impenetrable walls of thorny bushes and pipe organ cacti lining a narrow by-lane, and at last approached the plaza itself, where the market almost covered its square ground.

There seemed a general air of gaiety about the market stalls. Waves of sunburnt, dark-eyed people chivvied and bunted among sunsplashed stalls, gesticulating expressively and conversing in soft, subdued, musical tones; exchanging sincere pleasantries with timeworn simplicity and naturalness.

These country-folk crowded around booths festooned with coloured streamers and flower garlands; they promenaded the dust-spumed square walk of the plaza – and the very dust in the air had a fragrance of its own, spiced with cinnamon and burned chillies.

The festive element was further reinforced by the Victrola gramophone, strategically situated in the doorway of a hut facing the plaza, the records playing their *corridos* and country *canciones*.

Here, then, was the true gritty essence, the very flesh, blood and bone of the land and of its people. Evidence enough in familiar smells of burros and horses tethered to posts here and there; a drove of goats dipping brown-beards to the dust of the ground, clipping across the plaza; hobbled pigs rolling in their own filth in the shade of clapboard and canvas booths. And crowing cocks, runabout mongrel dogs …and hordes of happy, exuberant youngsters.

Under the late morning Mexican sun, people were buying and selling, trading homemade wares; straw-woven baskets, grain and fruit, raw untreated goatskins stinking highly in the heat, and primitively patterned, thickly glazed pottery, bright with brazen colours against a sunstream light.

Smiling mostly, these country folk, women dominant among the crowds. Pressing and pushing and jostling, but in a gentle, civilised fashion. Smiling, as already noted, readily and broadly, murmuring socially to one another:

"*Con permiso*, with your permission …" said a jolly, broad-cheeked stout woman, carrying baskets upon baskets of flowers in full strong arms *and* on her head!

"*Sí*, yes, *pasale*," replied a little woman half the other's size, rather short-sightedly nosing into a heady bouquet of blossoms, and at the same time trying to get out of the stout woman's way.

"*Oye, don* Carlos, is it you!" called a smart ranchero with a thick dark moustache covering the lower half of a merry, good-natured face. "*¡Buenos dias!*"

"*¡Buenos dias! ¿Que paso, compadre?*" returned his friend, equally smartly turned out in buckskin shirt, striped *ranchero pantalones* tucked in León leather knee-length boots; and the two of them put heads together, chatting for all their worth, exchanging local news of note.

"Oh, *muy bien* – very good!" exclaimed someone.

"*Perdónome* – excuse me," murmured another. "*Gracias, señor.*"

"Esperanza! *¡Hola!*"
"Ah, *doña* Margarita, you'll never guess what I heard …"
"*¡Oye, compadre!*"
"Why, it's Frontino himself!"
"*Con permiso, por favor* …"
"*Pasale, señora* …"
"*Gracias, muchas gracias.*"
And so it went on all over the market.

45

Market Business

Thrilled to pieces with everything around them, Ruth and Julia sauntered joyously between stalls displaying pyramidal piles of tomatoes, onions and peppers, papayas and yellow mangoes and purple-hued guavas.

At one stall three pretty señoritas, dark, bold eyes flashing from laughing faces, busied themselves heating corncakes over braziers in astonishingly prodigious numbers.

"Look at that lot!" gasped Ruth.

At another stall hard by, melon and squash seeds were popping and dancing and roasting on griddles, giving off a tantalising sweet nutty aroma.

"Them seeds aren't liking the heat," noted Julia, a merry, satisfied look on her face.

Ruth stopped for a moment at a booth selling brightly coloured bolts of cotton prints, and she was unable to resist spading a hand under a length of material which had instantly caught her eye; plum-coloured cotton with slashes of powder blue and aquamarine – "Is that aquamarine or turquoise?" she asked the seller, pointing a finger.

And the two moved on between tiny stalls, carefully shunted along by a throng of humanity.

A muleteer entered the dusty square, leading a drove of mules laden with stickwood, golden brown under the brightness of the sun. A mule at the rear of this short caravan stopped itself. It blew heavily and noisily in the warm dusty air, then angled its knobbled hindlegs in the unmistakable stance of an animal about to defecate.

And it did indeed do so, agate eyes fixed on an illimitable point in space.

That done, the mule twitched its ears and clopped on, with a somewhat easier gait. Julia followed behind the beast, stepping over a smouldering monk-brown heap of dung.

Ruth's attention was taken by a little girl, skinny and bedraggled, chewing on a stick of sugar cane. The child wore one adult-sized shoe and she hobbled and gimped slantwise down the street; and it was that peculiar mode of movement which reminded Ruth of señor Ramírez – better known as Pancho – who walked about in a not dissimilar fashion.

The little girl, one foot in the oversized shoe, paused a moment at a corner, in order to gain equilibrium, though tilting like a keeling skittle, and disappeared from view.

The two girls approached a fruit-and-vegetable stall, and behind pyramids of fat, though slightly misshapen tomatoes, sat an old woman, with a face Indian-dark and creased as a prune.

She smiled at them, multi-wrinkled, displaying teeth small and stained, like unhusked rice grains.

"Fresh picked, as new flowers. Like you, my dear little blossoms," she said in warm, full round tones, indicating the fruit with flapping hands.

Ruth's cheeks flushed with pleasure, while Julia simply stared at the woman, innocent-eyed and respectfully angelic.

"How much for one kilo?" asked Ruth, pointing to the tomatoes.

The old woman seemed to deliberate, a closed expression on her face, then replied, opening up the 'market shopping' game, "Only eight *pesos*, my flower. Does that sound alright to you?" fondling a tomato perched on top of a pyramid stack.

Ruth did not respond immediately, but permitted herself a smile with that so-called elemental naivety of the young. There was no doubt in the woman's mind that this *muchacha* would purchase something or other, and her irrefragable conviction did not prevent her from pursuing the normal exercise of bantering sales talk, as much a necessity of social discourse, just as it was a materialistic effort in selling fruit.

And so the old woman and Ruth, and even Julia, all three wagged in spunky ebullience, in that not so extraordinary way commonly found in simple, age-old cultures.

"I can give you seven-fifty, señora."

"Oh, I couldn't possibly, my conscience wouldn't allow it. You would see me ruined, a poor old woman – but see how red and ripe they are, fresh-picked, as I said."

"They're *muy bonita*."

"Sí, aren't they? Like you, in fact …"

Ruth considered it no compliment to be compared to a big red tomato, pouting sulkily. She thought of a new tactical move.

"It's a busy market day, never known it to be as busy as this before."

"To be sure, my angel, you're right enough there, and *busy's* good for business. Business thrives on it, I honestly declare."

"Well, let me think now."

"Take your time, my lovely, I'm here for the whole day, I might add."

"Can I just feel one?"

"Sí, but of course, help yourself," and the woman's aged, gnarled hands fluttered with elaborate eloquence.

"My mamá says they should be firm."

"Firm and ripe, just so."

"Seven seventy-five," Julia spoke up, going the wrong way. Ruth pulled a face at her younger sister.

"Ah, you're such a pretty one," the old woman bubbled in her warm rolling voice. "Both of you in fact. So let's say seven pesos, hmm, how does that suit?"

"Six pesos, fifty *centavos*," Ruth countered.

The market woman laughed, sweetly and roundly like a young girl, and winking grandly, increasing the wrinkles. "Six pesos seventy-five."

"Muy bien, very good," Ruth agreed at once, "two kilos, por favor."

A slant of sunlight fell through a rip in the canvas awning of the stall, and Ruth shaded her eyes with one hand, as she watched the woman weigh the tomatoes on old-fashioned scales. Ruth leaned forward, able to smell the woman's breath of milky nuttiness, as if she had been chewing toasted pumpkin seeds.

"There, my flower," the woman declared, dropping the tomatoes into Ruth's open bag, and throwing in a small hand of chilli peppers as well, being a token of luck and goodwill, as usually practiced at these affairs.

The girls politely smiled, thanked the woman, and left the stall; into the light and warmth of the sun and the dust of the day, deciding to visit next a tienda by the plaza – to treat themselves to some toffies.

PART TEN

PART TEN

46

On the Ranch

The squarish figure of Pancho moved around in the gloom of a stable on don Roberto's hacienda. Pottering about and checking the horses, going from horse to horse with a swaying erratic gait, like a storm-tossed boat, as if his heavy chunkiness was too much for his short, bandy legs. Long arms hung loosely at his sides, fists slackly curled; and, as his massive torso listed to one side with a drop of one shoulder and a rise of the other, his arms swung in lazy arcs, slapping solid thighs.

In this manner of movement the old ranchero sauntered about, and as he did so he rattled amiably all the while to the simple stablehand, Julian.

"And there we were," he chummily tossed to the simpleton, not looking at him but throwing it over his shoulder in that rough, gritty, 'morning voice' tone, "and there we were in the dead of night and caught in a sudden downpour, searching out for that wily coyote, uuy.

"And bless me if Gerardo isn't sitting in the bushes with his own company, hmm.

"Well, two – no, three torchlights zeroed on him squatting there with his pants wrapped around his boots. *¡Chingada!*

"'Where's that animal, Gerardo?' we says to him. 'Where did it get to?'

"'What animal?'

"'That damned coyote we're after.'

"'Oh, that. Over there it must be,' calls over Gerardo, pointing as far from himself as possible.

"'Are you sure?' we says – that's me, Cándido and José – our lamps steady on him.

"'Why, of course I'm sure,' says Gerardo, a square of paper in one hand, 'I saw him, didn't I? As you lot see me!' which gave us a good laugh at

Gerardo's expense, the poor shy, put-upon creature – Pass the saddlecloth, Julian …

"What, it's not there? Now, I wonder where I left it, then? Where did I leave the damn thing? *Aay*, come to think on it, I must have left it by the roan gelding's.

"*¡Carajo!* Pancho! Are you getting so old these days that you can't remember where you've left things?"

"Sí, I'm talking to myself now, not you, and that's bad too. Come on, muchacho."

Pancho rambled on amicably, and the half-wit Julian, who was not entirely taking in what he was told, but docilely following the old man like a faithful dog.

Bronze blades of light cut through chinks in the stable walls, shining sharply on the flanks of a yearling mare. Pancho paused, running knowing eyes over the horse. He hunkered down on his haunches to inspect a mark on the mare's left fetlock, and as he did so his face hit a cobweb and he softly cursed.

"See that, Julian?" he growled. "She must have done that all by her little self, the creature, rubbed at herself with her own hoof, most likely. Strange though, it looks like a wasp's sting, I'd say," he remarked, with something like the assured authority of a Xenophon. "It'll be best I guess to rub in some of that – What's its name? – that special ointment of mine, hmm. But let her finish her feed first, and you can water her too, I expect," the poor-wit nodding acknowledgement.

"Well," Pancho resumed his tale, "one of us – I reckon it was José – he says, 'I think I smell a skunk or something hereabouts.'

"'No-o,' says Cándido – Or was it me? – 'No, José, you're mistaken, it's Gerardo you can smell, and doesn't he smell sweet!'

"*¡Por la Madre Santisma!* Did you hear that, Julian? 'It's Gerardo you can smell," and a great belly roar erupted from the old man, raising an arm blindly to pat the slow-wit on his shoulder and clouting a stable post instead, catching a splinter for his trouble.

Pancho stood and scratched an armpit, screwing eyes and nose and sniffing like a dog.

It felt close and stuffy in the stable. Ground straw stank of horse piss, droves of frenetic flies seemingly owned the air. Sweat popped on the old ranchero's brow, small beads of it hung on his eyebrows, runnels of it on the weathered seams of his face.

He crashed his way through ricks of cornstraw and sunworn saddlery, to get to a docktailed sorrel which had foaled only the day before.

His stumbling progress was checked by a familiar sound from beyond the paddock.

"Rider coming in," he grated succinctly. "That'll be José, I shouldn't wonder…"

47

José's Ride-in

Pancho made for the open stable doors, threshing through stooks of cornstalks, the weak-wit Julian right behind him and banging against a broken hand-plough, but following the old man like his shadow.

Brilliant light of the forenoon sun smacked them in the eyes, as they stepped out into the wide paddock – or corral.

The ranchero by the name of José – a lean, dark-faced individual – mounted on a dappled grey colt, rode into the sunflooded yard at a good clip, not being a one for slow cantering.

He reined abruptly before Pancho and Julian, swung from the saddle in one easy movement, letting go the reins of the halter for the tender-wit to grab.

"¡Hola!" he greeted them with a grin, showing ratty, tobacco-stained teeth. He swept off his sombrero and, with an eggyolk-yellow bandanna, swabbed sweat pouring from his face. "Hot one, isn't it just."

"Sí, sí. ¿Que paso? Did you ride over the ridge to check those bays?" Pancho asked at once.

José nodded, slapping dust from leather chaps. Then he released bit and snaffle from the foam flecked colt. Young Julian had managed to tear himself away from the old man, in order to remove saddle and cloth from the sweating horse. He unfastened the saddle girths, at the same time whispering 'sweet nothings' in the colt's ear, his habitual one-sided communication with animals.

Pancho set critical eyes on the colt's sweaty flanks. Splotches of yellowish foam dropped from its mouth and heaving belly. Clearly, all this was not much to his liking.

He hawked and spat in the dust at his feet. "You shouldn't have ridden him so hard in this heat," he mildly reprimanded the ranchero, "there's no future in it, hombre. Why ride him like that? You always do it. Uuy, what's your hurry, hmm?"

"I was fast losing time," José mumbled moodily by way of an excuse.

Turning to Julian and abruptly changing his tone, old Pancho said, "*Que bien*, muchacho, walk him up and down a little ways, but over in the shade at the back of the stable," he advised the lost-wit. "Walk him till that ticker of his slows down and the sweat dries on him, poor creature. Then give him a carrot for his trouble and feed him some meal, but not too much – do you hear? – or we'll have him sweating all over again."

Julian nodded knowingly, turned about and walked the colt on.

"Well, José, and don Roberto, where is he?" Pancho's sandpapery raspiness directed back at the ranchero, a glitter of anger still remaining in his eyes at the way the mount had been treated.

José, swarthy face closed – the lone silent hombre routine he always liked to portray – wiped travel sweat and dust away with a sweep of one arm. His fast ride-in had caused yard and chaff dust to rise in the air, and it hung almost motionless in a dry heat haze.

"The boss, he rode north with the others to the *barranca*," he informed the old man, now giving a sheepish look. "The fencing was in fact down, as we knew it would, along a fair stretch of the boundary line. That damned whirlwind of yesterday."

"Sí, they tend to do things like that. And the bays, did you lose them?"

"Thought we might have, but we rounded them up okay. Now the men are working on re-fencing that line."

"Don Roberto, out there sweating with the rancheros, eh? *¡Caracoles!* That's something, by all that's queer – But wait a moment, hombre, what are you doing back here?"

"To pass on a message to Tulia at the *casa*," face tight and closed once more.

"You best get on with it, then. You can *walk* over."

"I thought I saw a dustcloud back there from the pueblo way," said José, pushing back his sombrero and scratching at his scalp. "You can see it now, look, and coming this way," pleased over what he had earlier surmised.

"The Ramos waggon," guessed Pancho, keen eyes clapped on a distant moving object distorted by heat haze and dust. "It's the Ramos waggon right enough," he confirmed, "and if I'm not mistaken …"

"When do you make mistakes?" José dared to say.

"If I'm not mistaken, that'll be young Juanito driving …"

48

Juan Arrives

The old ranchero stood like a rock and waited for the tilt-cart to roll on in. And soon enough the boy Juan Ramos came into full view as he entered the dusty hacienda corral, the cart rumbling and clattering with the noise of a whole waggon train.

Chapulín, as if a contestant at a horse-show, trotted majestically with knees almost up to his withers, snaffle jingling like tiny silver bells. Not to be outdone, the dog Salté clipped in the lead with equally regal grace. While the hog in the back of the cart grunted and squealed furiously – furious at being so ill-treated, and not having enjoyed the ride worth a pig's trotter.

Juan pulled on the reins and gaily waved.

"Señor Ramírez! ¡Buenos dias!"

"My little compañero, buenos dias! How goes it with you?" Pancho roared with aggressive cheerfulness.

He doffed his sombrero in a salute, gazing on his young-timer friend with a wide grin; then scratched his backside and twisted his nose both at the same time.

Juan jumped down from the cart into thick dust and sand. José, being on hand, voluntarily took control of Chapulín, unharnessing him. Pancho shook the boy's hand, a gentle clasp in the customary manner of Mexican countryfolk, then embraced the youngster with massive arms.

Salté went bounding off across the corral to explore new terrain and sniff out rare new scents. A sudden dust-devil stormed frenziedly across the ground and the dog went chasing after it, for it to suddenly vanish as speedily as it had appeared, which mystified the animal.

Within moments José had Chapulín unharnessed. The cart teetered and fell back on its shaft ends, the hapless hog sent flying –

"Who said pigs couldn't fly!" Pancho promptly voiced, grin widening.

– and mamá's apples burst out from the bag, rolled round the hog's back and stopped at the tail-gate, like balls in a slot machine.

"That one's for don Roberto. He ordered it," Juan informed the old man, hooking his boot heel on the wheel hub of the cart.

"So I see, Juanito, and there it is. A hog for don Roberto. He likes his pork, you know," and Pancho extended a grin once more at the boy, like a wedge of orange.

He threw José a meaningful glance and called over with casual affability: "Before you go see Tulia, walk that beast and rub him down, amigo, then you can water and feed the fellow."

José went on, shrugging shoulders and muttering darkly that he knew the score and didn't need reminding.

"What shall I do with the hog?" enquired Juan.

"If I had my own way," replied the old ranchero, mirthful blue eyes resting on his young friend, "I'd bleed and gut it and get a good roasting fire going. *¡Caramba!* It's a month or more since I last teethed into pork."

"Well, not to worry, *amiguito*, José will presently take charge of the hog; the two should go nicely together, don't you think?"

"Which reminds me," Juan said shyly, "you've reminded me to tell you, mamá says that you're not to take too long when next you're invited for *comida*. The invite is open, as you ought to know, says mamá."

"Comida, eh? ¡Ay que bueno! I must hunt out my dinner jacket and dancing pumps – And, ay caray, you've reminded me too of something I have yet to do, damn near forgot it, old sinner that I am – You needn't take that too literally, amiguito.

"You see, I have to skin and gut a goat for him, for don Roberto. He'd skin me if I forgot, but you did remind me and the job's as good as done already, yet for all that I still need to skin and gut the damn thing. And kill it first, mind, mustn't forget that.

"Do you fancy helping me with it, hmm?"

"Sí, I can help, my pleasure," smiled Juan.

"Que bueno, my compañero, spoken like a true assistant for a sacrificial offering. Well, let's see if José is taking good care of your Chapulín first. Got him watered and fed and curried and rested up a bit. It's a long haul from your place with a waggon, a muchacho, and a hog…"

The old ranchero stumped off toward the main stable with jerking shoulders and slackly swinging arms.

49
Fixing a Goat I

They entered the welcome shade of the stable, and Pancho's eyes turned slate-blue in the semi-gloom.

Juan was pleased to see that Chapulín had his head deep in a crib, contentedly chomping away at corn straw, as used to the place as though he lived there. José stood nearby, a currycomb locked in his fist, watching the horse eat, and looking almost as if he'd love to join it.

"Comida with you, eh? The next time I'll come with a bigger appetite, to impress your mamá," Pancho went on urbanely. "Forget the dinner jacket and dancing shoes, go with hunger and an appetite. Best things I reckon to honour an invitation such as that.

"You know, Juanito, I was always hungry when I was about your age. One time the *policia* were chasing me down a street of a small town up north where I lived – only for a short spell, mind, I don't like towns and never did, not my style."

"The policia after *you*! What for?"

"Well, the fact of the matter was, I'd smashed the window of a casa belonging to the widow of a famous bullfighter – I forget his name – and she, the widow woman, uuy, she was mad as any bull could be."

"What happened to you?" the boy smiling all the while.

"Well now, I ran like a road-runner down that street – my guts groaning for grub, of any kind – and at the bottom of the street near the market-place, I spotted old don Fuente, who was also after me for stealing biscuits from his tienda. Hmm, they were in a barrel, you see, those nice scrunchy biscuits; and it stands to reason that if you're hungry enough and your peepers are level with a barrelful of biscuits – naturally, I followed my own inclination and snatched me a handful.

"And so don Fuente and the policia were after my tail. I nipped through a little alleyway into the marketplace and stopped at a fruit stall. Coming at me from one side were the policia, panting by now no doubt with their heavy carbines, and coming at me from the other was old Fuente, face all red and raging, uuy."

"So what did you do?"

"What could I do?" grinned Pancho villainously, "*Que va,* Juanito, my guts still growled. I grabbed myself a good hand of fruit from the stall!"

Julian made an appearance, tramping in in the gloom, tripping over a rush broom.

"Aha, Julian, and what are you up to, eh? Up to no good, I'll wager. Go and get the goat from the pen, por favor."

"The goat, señor?"

"Sí, the goat, you little tender burrito – for the don's dinner, I don't doubt. And tie it to the block, while I put an edge to my skinning knife."

"Ah, sí, the goat ..."

"Hmm, he catches on real quick, that one, can't keep up with him," as Pancho looked around him in search of the grinding stone, nose twitching as if about to smell it out.

He found the stone – where it was always kept and from where it had never moved – all ready for immediate use clamped on the side of Gerardo's smallish carpenter's bench. He slipped his knife from its sheaf, and with the pad of his thumb felt its dull edge.

Then he set to with the task, Juan cranking the handle for him. The wheel whirred and whined, and sparks shot from it. Flies whined too, huge horseflies in a band of light where the sun cut into the stable.

"Did you know," began Juan conversationally, "that Carmelita in the pueblo is going to have a baby?" his arm yanking the grinding stone handle.

"Is she now?" returned the old man. "And who might the father be, I'd like to know," stopping a moment to test the cutting edge of his knife with his thumb. "No one seems to know that, by all accounts."

Juan continued winding the handle, not wanting to break off now that he had fallen into a steady rhythm.

Pancho again put blade to stone, while Juan kept a wary eye on sparks flying from the stone, scattering over crisp, dry straw at their feet.

Pancho again put blade to thumb.

"They say it might be that Cesar fellow," Juan said in a whispering 'gossipy' tone. "Cesar could be the father, people reckon. I remember – "

"Why are you turning that handle, amiguito?" asked the old man with a grin.

"Oh, are you done?" and the boy stopped at once, feeling slightly foolish.

"Well, a few more turns, then," and Pancho leaned over the stone, Juan resumed cranking the handle, sparks flying and the stone whining as if in torment.

" – I remember mamá saying that she had long suspected Cesar," Juan continued, back to the thread of his thoughts, winding arm finding its rhythm once more, "but I guessed it might be so a long time back – don't know why exactly …"

Pancho lowered his head to one side and spat, then said: "You could be right, my compañero, and your mamá too, of course."

He leaned closer to the boy and the whetting stone, the brims of their sombreros touching. Juan could smell the other's breath, and it reminded him of warm goat's milk.

"We'll know soon enough, I shouldn't wonder," the old man went on. "It'll come out in the end – including the babe," wiping grinding dust off the knife blade with two fingers and sheaving it.

Juan dropped an aching arm, and it dangled loosely at his side as though it didn't belong to him.

Pancho turned and made for the open stable door. "You've got the little fellow, eh?" he grated, listing over on bandy legs towards Julian.

The goat, loudly bleating as if acutely aware of its fate, was hitched to a wood-chopping block, a thick tree stump in the corral, charred by the sun, hacked and scarred by axe and machete.

The old ranchero spat into his palms, rubbed them briskly, glancing sidelong at Juan with a humorous glitter in his eyes.

"Let's get started then," he rumbled. "Julian, go and fetch the pump and the buckets, por favor," and the youth hurried off again, managing not to trip or bump into some obstacle.

Pancho had in the meantime grabbed the goat by its hind-legs and twisted the animal to the ground. He knelt before it, admiring its size. Julian presently returned, carrying two metal pails and an ordinary bicycle pump – 'What was the bicycle pump for?' Juan must have wondered.

The limp-wit Julian planted himself in what he assumed his duly appointed place, directly behind Pancho.

"No, round here if you please, muchacho," the old man chipped him, above a high desperate bleating of the goat. "Come round here, I say, and grab them forelegs – Juanito, you hold him here, por favor, hard and tight – that's it!" and Pancho let go of the hind-legs.

He held the goat by its jaw over the stump and put the smaller of the buckets under it. Then he unsheaved the knife, blade glinting, sharp and deadly, and swiftly slashed the animal's throat, cutting through its pulsing jugular vein.

The beast's tongue slipped out at the side of its mouth and its eyes rolled, showing waxy white.

"It's still crying, señor," trilled Julian, in a high-pitched girlish voice.

"Sí, they never can shut up, even when their head's half-hanging off," returned Pancho with a savage grin.

His face then became all at once quite serious as the animal's lifeblood spurted out; rich, thick and smoking-crimson, into the bucket. It dripped sluggishly now like hot molasses from the long gash in the neck.

The goat of a sudden appeared to shrink somewhat in size.

"The pump, Julian. ¡Újule, muchacho! Where's the pump I asked you for?"

50

Fixing a Goat II

The dull-wit stablehand retrieved the bicycle pump and passed it quickly to Pancho, who then pushed the nozzle end a little way up the goat's anus. Juan looked on in silent amusement, as the old man pumped away with the air plunger.

"Fatten him up again, you see, hmm, so we can more easily skin him," Pancho explained with a deadpan face.

'So that's what the bicycle pump was for,' Juan smiled to himself.

The goat did indeed swell up like an inflated toy animal. Pancho pushed the point of his knife into the throat and cut all the way down to the testicles, a sound not unlike that of a zipper being unfastened. He then incised along each leg to the fetlock joint; and Juan, with his own knife - (The Swiss army knife he had been given as a Christmas gift) – began cutting away the hide closed around the skull.

Julian simply stood poised to one side with a knife in his hand, as though ready if in case the goat should decide to run off.

The dog Salté came and poked an inquisitive snout in the bucket of blood.

"Hey, you!" and Juan cracked him one on the haunch.

"This shouldn't take too long, eh?" said Pancho with a genial grin, giving the boy a gentle dig in the ribs with his elbow.

All the same, it was taking far longer than he originally anticipated. Juan took note of a large mesquite tree nearby, with a broken lower branch which he saw as ideal, so suggested the goat be hung there to ease and speed up the operation. The old man readily agreed with that, smiling somewhat ruefully; why hadn't he thought of the idea?

Julian again sloped off to find some rope, and they soon had the goat strung up by its neck from the tree branch, the carcass now accessible from all sides.

Pancho began stripping the hide with the point of his knife, while Julian took over to pull and knuckle, almost tearing at the skin.

"Go at it carefully, Julian, if you please," advised the old man.

The boy observed a mist of tiny gnats around the goat's white gleaming skull, where its eyes boggled grotesquely, tongue protruding stiffly between its teeth.

"I think we're getting there – or somewhere," said Pancho with a beam, breathing heavily through nose and mouth. Sweat cut channels in the dust on his face, and there were dark stains spreading from his armpits.

Said Juan, "What's that thudding sound I keep hearing?"

Pancho fastened eyes on the boy. "Thudding sound?"

Thud!

" – Ah, that'll be José. He's over by the other side of the stable, practicing his knife-throwing skills. I'd rather he did that than set fire to something, which is also in his style. If ever don Roberto gives him the push, uuy, José will straightway go join a circus … as a knife-thrower."

He went on: "José is a man of great ambition, the lone and not-so-silent hombre – Oye, José!" he shouted over in a voice fit to rattle the timbers of the stable, "what's your target?"

"A picture of your namesake, Pancho Villa," called back the response. "Already got his nose and two ears."

"Only *two* ears? Can't you do better than that? Anyway, it's as well he isn't still around, he'd make a handsome stuffed taco of you."

"It's quiet round here otherwise," observed Juan. "Where're the others?"

Thud!

"Hmm, well, after the fencing job, Cándido and Gerardo were supposed to head on to the railroad depot with some army cavalry mounts to be sent on south to Mexico City. They'll be back soon, I expect, won't want to hang about. Then the peace and quiet will take the highroad to hell, no doubt.

"As for Emilio, our fat friend is flat-out fast asleep on a bed of straw in the haybarn. Spent too long at that fencing job."

He turned a twinkling blue eye on Juan. "And he got up too early this afternoon."

"But it's still morning."

Thud!

"Perdónome, I meant *yesterday* afternoon – Uuy, speak of the devil's disciples, here they are now," as two dusty rancheros rode at an easy canter into the main corral.

He called over to them: "I knew it, the devil's own disciples, and how long have you been back here?"

"Ever since we arrived," returned Cándido, tipping a cock-eyed wink at his fellow rider.

The two rancheros dismounted, tied their horses to corral posts, and came over to the 'goat crew'.

Gerardo was limping badly, or perhaps exaggeratedly – one couldn't tell with the lifelong devoted hypochondriac.

"Oye, Gerardo," rasped the old man, "you're limping, I see."

"I know I'm limping," grumbled the hapless horseman.

"Got a stone in one of your boots, is it?"

"He maybe has several of them," grinned Cándido cheerily. "But no, some great heavy chestnut stallion – you'll know the one I mean, I'm sure – took it into its head to back-kick and hit Gerardo on the shin. Could have been much worse had he not worn his chaps.

"Hurts badly, doesn't it, amigo?" smiling unpityingly, even joyously at his partner.

Grunted Pancho irritably, "I wasn't asking you, queer-eyes."

"Ah, Pancho, I know you always think highly of me."

"Sí, like a clogged cog in a rusty wheel."

"You see, I knew it!"

Thud!

"What was that?"

"Gerardo's leg dropping off, I shouldn't wonder," grinned Pancho, regaining equability. "Now where are you hopping-along to?"

"To the casa," grumped Gerardo, "see if Tulia has anything worth eating. Seems an age since we broke our fast."

"Me, too," Cándido said, joining the other. "A double breakfast is what my guts are asking for, I'm fair starving – " - *Thud!* - " – What the hell is that?"

"Not another leg dropping off?" grinned young Juan cheekily.

"Juanito! ¡Hola! Didn't see you there, hiding behind our Julian. How's the family?"

"Fine and well."

"Are you coming?" grouched Gerardo. "Hola, Juanito, good to see you. Must excuse, got to see Tulia," and off he went, with a most pronounced war hero limp that was impressive to witness.

"Let's get back to the job in hand, amiguito," said Pancho soberly, giving the goat carcass a thump.

Juan stood back now to watch, ready to be entertained by bubbles of banter sure to spill from the old ranchero – and he was not disappointed!

"Ease up there a bit, Julian," Pancho started up. "Do it right, and right first time, if you will. Go at it carefully, muchacho, if you please."

"With your permission, señor, I'm doing well."

"Sí, my tenderfoot, as well as you were another time, as I recall. Do you remember that chicken Tulia wanted us to fix for the pot?"

"Sí, señor, I chopped its head off, I did."

"You did indeed, and the headless chicken went tearing off, running about all over the place. 'Catch that chicken!' I shouted at you."

"Si, senor, I remember," smiled the simpleton sweetly.

The old man turned to Juan, and went on:

"Do you know what he did, Juanny? You wouldn't credit it but he went to pick up the head and gave it to me."

"It was part of the chicken, señor."

"While the headless chicken had disappeared somewhere round the corner!"

"I soon found it, señor."

"Sí, you did, though it was a bit too late as it happened, for Tulia had witnessed the entire circus performance, dammit!"

"She said words I couldn't understand, señor."

"I know, I know, and I'm not surprised. She was giving me a right rollicking, that's what Tulia was doing – You're still not pulling right, that way a bit, that's better."

"Look! Look at its fat belly."

"Uuy, you'd think he was a she and in the family way."

"It was the pump that did it," said Julian with unconscious wit, flashing a smile at Juan.

"The air is still in there, is it? That's its guts, you sad-saddled burrito!"

"Whew! It stinks well enough, señor."

"Aha, and I thought it was you."

"I stink? Like a goat?"

"No, like a sewer — Ay que caray, I reckon we're getting there," and Pancho's breath came in dry, sharp gasps as he fisted at the join of hide to flesh.

He paused a moment to wipe his hand against the bark of the tree, then wiped at sweat dripping from his brow.

The inane chatter between these two — as one would only hear in country parts — carried on apace:

"Just look at the coat on him, señor!"

"It's a damn sight more than what I've got."

"Well, he's losing his."

"Which is what happened to me, I lost mine — You're at it again! Why don't you pull more to the side there, you plank!"

"That's what I am doing, señor."

"Just as I thought. Pull *down*, you twisted taco!" In more tender tones he added: "As experience will tell you, the more you do it right the more you do it well."

"Señor, where's its tail?"

"Still between its legs, I shouldn't wonder."

"I see it — thought it had dropped off."

"Listen to this one, Juanito — Are you pulling down as I asked you to?"

"Sí, I am pulling down …down."

"It doesn't seem like it. Damned thing must be stitched or glued on."

"Coming off, señor, bit by bit …"

"Ay que bueno, so it is, here we go!" exulted Pancho presently. "It's coming now, coming off," and with one last pulling rip the hide was clear from the carcass.

Julian hung it carefully on the end of another branch, as though it were his own best sheepskin jacket — an item which of course he didn't own.

"Well, that broke the back of it, though as yet it's only skinned. Juanito, give an eye to where the bucket stands," Pancho warned, and instantly split the belly from top to bottom with a slashing sweep of the knife.

Balloon-like purplish-blue intestines spewed out, warm and steaming and odoriferous, sliding as a whole entity into the bucket. There was a faint squeak as the bulbous mass separated from the rib cage cavity and rolled out to fill the bucket to overflowing. The old man lopped off the yellow-green bulb that was the bile duct and threw it to the dog.

"There, Salté," he grated, "a bitter lemon for you."

Wraiths of flies appeared as if from nowhere and settled like soot spots on the innards in the bucket. Splashes of blood in the dust oxidised to black with exposure to the air, and flies held a hearty 'convention' there as well.

"Alright, Julian, we'll cut him down and you can take him to the kitchen scullery or outhouse – or wherever. Tulia can take over from there."

"Do you fancy an apple?" offered Juan, remembering the bag of fruit he had left in the tilt-cart, and the old ranchero's merry blue eyes turned on the boy.

"A nice plump red one for me, amiguito, if you have one – and if not, I'll have a banana. Aha, only kidding, don't mind me," leading the way to the cart.

They were presently hunkered on their heels by the cart, scrunching into their apples, disinterestedly eyeing Julian shambling across the sunblasted yard, with a bucket of congealing blood in one hand and a bucket of entrails in the other – and the goat strung over his back.

And it seemed to Pancho – invariably on the lookout for a touch of humour – he could see plainly enough that it appeared as though the goat had just taken a flying leap to mount Julian … !

PART ELEVEN

PART ELEVEN

51

Call for a Patera

"Doña María!"

The high piercing child's voice split the air of the Ramos homestead. Mamá immediately dropped what she had been doing under the smoky kitchen lean-to, and came rushing out into the brilliant light and heat of a near noon sun, hastily wiping hands on her apron.

"Doña María-a-a!"

"*¡Chihuahuas!* What is it, Angel?" she asked of a double-dimple-faced boy who suddenly materialised in front of her, panting like a puppy, little face glistening with perspiration, streams of it filling his dimples.

"Doña María, you must come quickly!" he gasped breathlessly. "Carmelita is about to have her baby and you'd better come quickly."

Mamá sighed, not with relief but with some satisfaction. She was the *patera* – or midwife – for the pueblo, and knew that it was the girl's first baby. No doubt she was panicking before her time, thought mamá, as young first-time mothers are apt to do.

All the same it was prudent to make certain.

"Are the contractions regular?" she enquired with keen interest.

The child of a mere six or seven summers gaped at her, a puzzled look on his upturned face.

"*Con-contraptions?*" and Angel's deep dimples shot from one part of each cheek to the other.

"*¡Mi madre!*" mamá cried, slapping a hand to her forehead, "they send me a slip of a muchacho who knows nothing of these things!"

"Pepe should have come," piped Angel, "but I was sent instead. Pepe has a bad leg, you know. Anyway, Carmelita's having a baby. Might be a litter of them, going by the size of her belly. She's as big as – "

"Pssht! That's enough, muchacho."

"Señora Pozas says for don Antonio to come, too," added Angel.

Señora Pozas was the pregnant girl's mother.

"Ah, of course he must. Well, you know where he is, go to him then and tell him. ¡Ándale!" and little Angel sprinted off to don Antonio's sanctuary.

The request for don Antonio to attend the event, or at least to be on hand and available, was natural enough, because he was the locally acknowledged *rezandero* – or layman preacher – to give services for the dying or for difficult deliveries.

"Angel!" mamá called from the kitchen, swiftly setting things in order about the cooking range. "Angel, run on back now and say we're on our way."

There then followed a feverish spate of activity which instantly dispelled the normal quietude of the near-noontime hour.

Angel shot off like a little jackrabbit, mamá arranged and rearranged black earthenware pots on the fire, at the same time attempting to wrap her *rebozo* about her. Don Antonio was now there, standing like a post, twiddling anxious thumbs, not knowing what to do or say, simply standing there and waiting for some measure of order to emerge from this momentary – hardly unpredictable – confusing chaos.

"Cristina! Ruth!"

The parrot on the porch screamed and clawed at the bars of its cage, don Antonio turning to scowl at it, and Cristina came running from one of the rooms.

"You see to the pots here, por favor. We have to go to the pueblo, me and your papá."

"Carmelita, mamá? Is it Carmelita's time?"

"Sí, sí… Now where is Julia – and Ruth?"

"Carmelita having a baby," breathed Cristina wonderingly, "and she's younger than me …"

"Are we ready, María?" enquired don Antonio in the background, in the politest tone he could muster.

"Where in heaven is that little – *Papacito*, you don't have your prayer book. Where have you left it?"

"I'll get it, papá, it's on the dresser."

A new voice, it was Ruth, suddenly appearing as if from nowhere.

"Ah, Rutí, there you are, muchacha. The chicken, child, it'll soon be ready."

"Sí, mamá, I know."

"Put it where the cats can't get at it, you hear? And find Julia, she can shell the corn, which ought to keep her out of mischief while we're away."

"Where are you off to, mamá?"

"Never you mind."

"Is it Carmelita? Is – "

"Ought we to take a candle?"

"Merciful heavens, papacito! The girl's not on her deathbed – we all sincerely hope – she's ready to have her baby … and we hope there as well."

"Now, I'll need this soap, and clean towels and the rest of it," mumbled mamá, addressing herself and no one else, plunging hands deep into a box of fresh linen.

And at that point the farmstead's tilt-cart rumbled into the courtyard.

"Juanito's back, *tambien*," muttered mamá with evident relief, stuffing towels and other odd 'necessities' into a string bag. "Juan and Cristina can take charge here – Julia-a! JULIA-A!"

"Didn't she go to Florencino's, mamá?"

"Of course –" A brief smile broke out on her flushed face; a slightly embarrassed smile - "Well, at least now we know where she is – Juanito! Juanito, we're off, me and papá to the pueblo. Carmelita's time has come, it would seem," as mamá soaked a hand-towel in cold water and dropped it in a plastic bag.

"I'll take you, then," the boy offered, leaping from the cart.

The parrot squawked noisily and Juan's dog Salté barked at it.

"No, son, Chapulín will be tired. We can walk, papá and me, we have two legs each for it. Won't take us such a while, at any rate – if we don't dawdle."

"Would you shut him up," said don Antonio, referring to Salté's powerful doggy lungs.

"It's the parrot, papá."

"It's the dog, please quieten him."

"Where's Cristina gotten to now? …Ah, she's here. Cristina, you'll see to the fire. And Ruth, don't forget the chicken, my pet. Juanito, your Chapulín looks all in and dry; must be he needs a drink, wouldn't you say?

"Well, come along, papacíto, I have to deliver a new baby today, not celebrate its second birthday."

And mamá was off with purposeful strides, the alacrity of which amazed and amused those she left behind.

52

Four Females in a Room

"You go on, María, and I'll be with you later," don Antonio told his worthy wife at the door of a chapel in the pueblo precinct. "I'll pray to the saints for an easy birth…"

He entered the stone chapel, sombrero in his hands, fingers toying with the narrow leather band of the crown.

It was still and quiet and peaceful in the small, modest, and very old chapel; with a smell of mustiness and mice and stale incense in the cool air. Outside sounds were muffled, unable to seep through the thick stone walls. Dappled scallops of golden light played on a dark, flag-stoned floor, winging in from a dusty cupola above.

Don Antonio crossed himself and moved silently toward a humble side altar which was devoted to the saints. He lit two candles of rich yellow beeswax, and burned a little incense of lavender and rosemary.

He signed the cross toward an alabaster figurine of his saint, San Antonio, then knelt on knees and prayed in soft murmurings for a time.

Doña María had in the meantime reached the far side of the pueblo, freely perspiring under a broiling noonday sun. She arrived at the simple adobe home of the Pozas family, a small group milling curiously but quietly at the cane door of the hut, shuffling their feet in the dust. They moved aside deferentially to allow a passageway for doña María, the men removing straw sombreros as a mark of respect.

"Go right in, doña María, por favor – for they won't allow me in there on any account," said a voice, and mamá recognised señor Pozas. Who was not working in the fields on this day and would not be for the next three days, as it was considered unlucky for the coming infant.

María nodded acknowledgment with a faint air of dignity and without saying a word. She stepped into the hut, and at once took charge of the situation.

The girl Carmelita, a pretty creature of delicate build and with wide, almost Asiatic slanting eyes, lay sweating heavily on a petate on the hardtrodden dirt floor, her mother squatting by her side, repeatedly patting the girl's hand as if that would give some comfort. The mother was equally of fragile build, though more scrawny and without softness; more life-worn, evident enough in a thin, harsh-lined face.

The one-room hut was low-pitched and divided by a large heavy blanket nailed at two edges to a rafter. There were no windows. And in the centre of this partitioned room where the girl lay, a loop of thick rope hung nailed to the rafters, its lower end a few feet above a wooden stool.

It was relatively cool in the room, as adobe dwellings usually are, though it soon began to warm with the body heat of the females.

The moment María entered the hut, señora Pozas jumped to her feet, wringing hands and spluttering out a torrent of barely coherent words in her obvious distress.

María's first concern right now was to examine the pregnant girl, who didn't look in the least pretty in these circumstances, with pain-shrunken cheeks indrawn, dirty perspiration from her exertions streaming from her.

"Ooo, doña María!" cried the woman, face distraught, "she's been having the pains most of the morning – But where have you been, doña María? We've been waiting for you to come."

"Hot water, señora, hurry it now!" María ordered. "I have soap and nice clean towels, too."

"I was told Pepe was sent to you this morning. Oh, doña María, what has taken you so long?"

"I haven't seen Pepe today – hot water now, ándale!"

"That Pepe! What a fool! An idiot he is! – Oh, my poor little Carmelita!"

"The water, señora, quickly if you will, and I shall light a candle," for it was dark and murky in the room.

"Sí, we have it already!" exclaimed señora Pozas. "It's boiling now – on the fire in the yard. Juanita is helping, the good soul. Juanita-a! Juanita-a!" and the near-hysterical woman scurried to a kitchen lean-to at the rear.

Doña María found a stub of cheap wax candle and lit it, sticking it in its own wax on the hard-beaten earth floor. The flickering yellow light managed to dispel at least some of the gloom, making the room appear almost cosy.

She felt the girl's pulse, which was racing a little, smiling warmly and reassuringly into her face. Then set to task, picking out the towel she had soaked in water, and placing it tenderly on the girl's hot feverish brow.

"We must have you up and walking, Carmelita," said María softly, as though comforting a child who has just suffered a nightmare. "It doesn't do to lie here like this. Movement is the thing, to get you on the way. Here, let me help you up."

"The water, doña María, we have the water," señora Pozas said, returning from the yard, and she appeared to Maria less upset now that she had something to do and with supportive assistance at hand.

She and her neighbour, the woman named Juanita, carried in a large steaming pot of water and tin basins.

Doña María knew Juanita as a homely, sensible, friendly sort, and immediately warmed to the woman as one of equal footing. Juanita smelled of the field; of cornstalks and alfalfa, of countrysweat and small livestock.

Carmelita was now up on her feet, swaying slightly, held firm by María.

"Is she to stand on the stool, then, and hold tight to the rope?" asked the girl's mother.

"Not that method, no, Carmelita must first be walked up and down a bit, to loosen up," advised María in no-nonsense tones.

"Oh, is she a mare, then?" expostulated señora Pozas with biting native wit.

María and the woman Juanita glanced at each other, trying to restrain a smile.

53

Doña María Delivers

"The contractions have gone on far too long for my liking, and she's a frail little thing," María explained.

"Is my muchacha in danger, then – Put the water down there, Juanita, gracias."

"She'll be all right," María assured her, "she has spirit and that counts for much in matters such as this."

"Well, bless the saints for that. But, doña María, my poor muchacha, she's been asking – she's been wanting chocolate. Chocolate!"

"Then give her some by all means, we can't have her infant to be born marked, can we?" (Such was the belief of countryfolk, if a woman in labour did not get her wants or unusual fancies.)

Señora Pozas looked embarrassed, and María understood at once.

"Here, Juanita," she said, taking a purse from apron pocket and snapping it open to snatch out a coin, "get yourself over to the tienda and buy two bars, ándale!"

Juanita fled like one possessed.

"Help me walk Carmelita," went on María, "it is for her own good, you'll see."

The woman readily complied, and the young expectant girl was made to walk within the confines of the hut, María murmuring encouragements, even at times throwing out silly jokes to put the other at her ease – and the mother, too.

Don Antonio then came in silently and unobtrusively. His great height seemed incongruously giant-like in the low-ceilinged hut, and he stooped with a decided humble air.

His nose twitched at the chilli sharp scent of female sweat. He flicked large, expressive eyes over to mamá and solemnly nodded, then crept like a thief to the other side of the partition. Mamá heard a soft thud as her layman preacher husband sank to his knees on the close-packed earthen floor. He smelled of melted bee's wax and incense.

A genteel cough to clear his throat, and don Antonio was once again off into prayer-mode. A sound of raised voices from outside came to him. What is happening out there? he must have wondered, for he knew full well what was happening *inside*.

Carmelita was allowed to lay down again, legs drawn up and spread wide. She's so narrow-hipped, observed María, glancing at the girl's thin frame.

A strong contraction came on, gripped the girl like an iron fist. She gasped and gulped for air, mouth open like a round black hole.

"Take it easy, muchacha," María soothed her, pressing gently down on the girl's glabrous, distended stomach. "Don't breathe in like that. Try and relax and take little breaths. Sí, I know it is hard for you, my poor petal.

"Push with yourself as I press …"

"Ooooh!" moaned the girl.

Juanita returned, holding up a large candy bar, as if presenting it as a votive gift or peace offering. María wagged a negative head at her, letting the other know that it was now of no consequence and much too late.

"Push now, muchacha," urged María. "Push hard!"

"I can't! I can't!" rebelled the girl with a wail.

"All right, alright. Rest a moment. You rest just for a moment. That's it, there's plenty of time. Now, take deep breaths. Deep …slow …breaths."

"She's puffing like a locomotive," complained señora Pozas.

María and Juanita again exchanged suppressed amused glances.

"Relax, Carmelita, you're doing fine for the moment."

"She seems so tensed up!" cried the mother.

"Am I going to die?" asked Carmelita in a little girl's voice.

"You're just fine. I can see that you're fine. Now, can you start up again? Easily does it, gently like, but push … you must push. That's more like it, strain all you want, because you're pushing well and hard, which is good."

"She's fair worn out!" moaned the mother.

"Well, it's hard work, as we know, but she's got spirit," smiled María with utter confidence in her conviction, "and that'll help matters, I'm thinking … Push … Rest a bit, pause a moment. Sí, you can stop for a short while …"

"Will it take much longer?" wanted to know señora Pozas, anxiously wringing nerve-charged hands. "It was easy for me when I had Carmelita. Two or three strains and she popped out like a cork from a bottle; well, so it felt like at the time."

"Oh, just look at my child now!"

"We can start up once more, Carmelita. Begin again and push, push with all your might. Because your time is almost on you, my brave little one –

"Juanita, hold a wrist, but gently. Sí, we're getting there, or somewhere!" – Voicing the very same sentiment Pancho had uttered at the fixing of the goat.

Then, without warning, though María may have suspected as much, the birth bag broke, with a dreadful scream emitting from the girl in labour. A steaming torrent of blooded fluid fell from her and filled the air with a fetid, stupefying odour.

"The towels, Juanita! There!"

Don Antonio behind the screen stopped praying in mid-sentence, and a soft murmur like a rush of wind arose from the small crowd outside.

"Oh, God in Heaven!" cried señora Pozas.

"Now we're well on our way," María said with an air of calm assurance, one arm lost between the girl's pulsating legs.

The atmosphere in the room was warm and humid, with an almost animal rankness about it. Flies flew in, torturing the thick reeking confines of the room.

"We are almost there, muchacha."

"Oh, the pain! I can't stand it!"

"Bear down, my precious …"

"Oh, mamá! Mamá-a!"

"I'm here, darling!" an ecstatic look on the mother's previously troubled face.

"I think it's coming!" Juanita burst out joyously. "Look there, see!"

"But of course, what else did you expect," smiled María, with a touch of triumph.

This poor child has surely suffered enough, thought María, helpless to alleviate her pain. The sharp stabbing pains Carmelita felt turned to a burning kind of torture, spreading to other parts of her body. She could barely gasp for air as she struggled weakly. The burning pain hurt her back, set her ears hotly ringing, arms and legs throbbing. The burning sensation then ceased, to be replaced by the sharp cutting pains once again.

"Oh – my – God! I want to die!"

"Oh, my Carmelita …"

"There, there, my poor sweet thing."

"I see its head. Do you see its head?"

"I want to die! – To die …"

"The baby! The baby, the baby! Oh, it's beautiful!"

"A lovely creature," smiled María happily.

"A girl! It's a girl! Well I never. Oh, the saints be praised!"

"Well done, Carmelita. Let's clean things up a bit, Juanita …"

'Well' thought María with some relief, 'a worrisome delivery to be sure, but a successful one nonetheless.'

A short while later, the young mother saw for herself the newborn infant – wrapped in a swaddling cloth, actually María's best towel – and with all the pain and suffering now gone and near fast forgotten, she unequivocally burst into tears of ineffable joy.

PART TWELVE

PART TWELVE

54

Towards Silence and a Scorpion

Pancho was riding his white rawboned mare Macha, returning from the northern boundary, after inspecting where the fence repairing had been carried out, and presently brought his mount to a halt by the closed hotness of a gully.

He gazed around him under a midday sky and hot-tempered air. No one about, the area was devoid of any active life. Not that he expected anyone would be about, not in this isolated wasteland patch.

Dismounting, he stretched stiffly, feeling his age on this day, maybe because of the stifling heat. Macha lowered her head where she stood, to crop a tussock of dry coarse grass.

The old ranchero absently trod in a powder of sienna dust, fully catching the probing noon sunlight, then stopped his meaningless meandering and hunkered down on heels.

He could feel the unrelenting heat on him, feel it drawing out sweat from his pores, slowly draining his body of energy and the will to move.

The old man screwed up his seamed dark brown face against the hard sunlight and watched a lone hawk – or was it an eagle? - too far to tell for sure – on the wing. Watched it soar up in a clear empty sky, watched it describe a perfect circle across that immanent sky. Then it speared the eye of the sun and disappeared, and he saw it no more. He had seen plenty in his time, and under exactly the same sort of circumstance and condition.

It *was* a hawk, that was a hawk, he was now reasonably certain, not that it mattered a wingless flea, and he shrugged off the inane thought.

Pancho sat perfectly propped on his heels over a stretch of time, and he could smell the dust and hot stones, faintly aromatic …

And there was something else, something else beside the ubiquitous dust, the growing heat …

Silence.

The harsh landscape was still and quiet – no droning of insects, no sighing or stirring of wind – sagely and mysteriously silent. And dead as Ishmael's plain.

At this present moment the look on the old man's face was of an uncharacteristic brooding sadness. It was as if he were entirely alone in this large tract of land. He was, if anything, a volubly social creature, often in need of the company of his fellow man. But at times he also needed his 'space', and so now he could also afford the time.

What had brought on that sense of sadness in him?

He crinkled sea-blue eyes and wrinkled his nose, sniffing warm dry air. Without thought, he threw a sudden scowl at the baking sun, as though he had only at this moment discovered its tormenting, sap-stilling heat.

All the same, he did at least appreciate its hot dusty scent. He always did 'have-a-nose' for the seasons' smells and scents – and silences.

He breathed in the stony silence through his nose and mouth and every pore of his skin, and his whole being became a silence. Even the fine sienna dust which settled softly on the ground, was fed by silence; a silence serene, pure and perfect.

The rocks around him – light-coloured angular humps resembling fresh butchered joints of veal – stood loose but still in the heat, enveloped in their own silence.

Time.

Old Pancho had long ago realised the value of time, his own time that is, as the American Henry David Thoreau had once intimated in one of his famous essays, which Pancho had read.

Time for one's self, to think and to contemplate and to get a perspective on things that matter. Or, deliciously, not to think at all, but simply and unconsciously enjoy the land's naked beauty around him.

Time past.

It was a curious thing, the realisation brokenly dawning on him, that the death of his three little daughters so long back in his personal history – So there was the reason for that short spate of brooding silence! It was so long ago. And yet now it didn't seem all that long ago at all. In fact, his whole early life seemed so near when thinking about it, the details of those times becoming clearer in his mind as he was growing steadily older.

Purely out of curiosity – the innate probing, searching curiosity that had helped forge his humanity – the old ranchero, with the toe of his booted foot, dislodged an interesting looking rock in front of him, stimulated by sheer inquisitiveness.

And there – he would have won a wager straight off, were he but a betting man – there in a damp hollow, ready to attack or repel or to defend itself, was crouched a largish amber-polished scorpion.

He knew the creature would be there under that rock, his instinct spot on.

The scorpion's pointed distal end was arched, thrumming, over its back in a threatening posture, claws trembling, slightly vibrating.

"¡Hola, amigo!" the old man mouthed in a soft murmur. "Did I disturb you?" admiring the colour of the creature, and its courageous stance.

He carefully rolled the rock back to its original position.

"¡Hasta luego, amigo!" he bid it farewell.

Pancho continued gazing at the rocks, felt the heat they contained and smelled the dust on them. Pockmarks were holes of shadow, and the holes were like eyes that stared blankly at him, the earth and the sky.

Colours changed with the play of light, warm desert colours; he saw dun and ochre and orange, burnt sienna and vermilion. He became fully aware of the rocks, their intrinsic beauty and mystery and dynamic shapes.

The old man was at one with the rocks and in harmony, and the harmony encompassed all rocks, the birds in the sky, the mountains and valleys … all things that mattered on earth. This was how he felt in that deep silence, and many moments passed without real conscious thought.

He remained in this immovable rocklike state, locked in silence and heat, gazing ahead at the sun-swept gold-washed rangelands, like a melancholy Marius haunting the ruins of Carthage …

Without warning, a hot searing wind rose in the west, dust and grit riding the wind.

Pancho at once looked up. He felt the wind hot and hard against his face, as he raised himself to his feet at last. He lowered his eyes, resting them on a small thorn tree miraculously growing from a crack in the solid, stony ground.

His eyes flicked from the thorn tree, and he shook himself from his brooding reverie, or whatever it might have been.

A further surprise jolted his senses, eyes round and large with disbelief. For there, some hundred paces ahead in a heat shimmer, was the barely distinct form of a human figure, though he could see now that it was somewhat of a stunted, gnarled appearance, trotting with short rapid steps over a hardpan flat.

It was dressed in filthy dusty rags, back bent forward against the wind and the weight of a large bundle of what appeared to be driftwood.

It was as if this gnome-like creature had suddenly sprung out from the very bowels of the earth.

55

Meeting Up With Santo

Pancho glued eyes in amazement on the apparition agilely skipping across the flat, windflown dust swirling around it.

The figure came nearer, and all at once Pancho smiled with relief, for he recognised who it was – Santo, the pueblo's oldest citizen.

"Oye, Santo!" he called over huskily. "¿Que paso, hombre?"

"You! It's you!" returned the man agedly, twisting his dark, wizened face sideways under his load of stickwood, brushwood, and some rare jetsam. "What is it? What's the matter?"

"Why nothing, you old stump," laughed Pancho, in naturally companionable good humour once again. "But what are you doing out here? Ah, that's it, I see well enough what you're about," glancing at the other's load. "It's a hot one, isn't it just. Ay que caray, the only thing growing out here is this damned infernal heat."

"You noticed, is it? He-he!" chuckled the ancient, and he stopped and waited for the other to join him, all the while bouncing up and down on knotted limbs, as if he couldn't bring himself to a positive standstill.

"Well, how goes it, compadre?" Pancho pleasantly enquired, gazing cheerfully into the old one's black beady eyes; like a cock's, hard and glintingly cunning. The face was a mesh of fine brown wrinkles, and he was toothless – except for one small lower grinder, dark as tobacco.

"Muy bien, very good, if you must know. But where's your horse?" and the oldie followed Pancho's nod. "Hum, in the gully, is it? And you're here, why? What are you up to, hey?" voiced the old one with some acerbity, sniffing disapprovingly severe looks at the other, shrivelled form stiff with suspicion.

"Nothing, you old stick. Just back from a bout of fence repairing – which my compañeros carried out."

"Don't see any fencing around here," said Santo with a sly, cynical look on his walnut-wrinkled face.

"Up at the northern boundary. Don Roberto's land, you lame coyote."

At that moment the wind died down of a sudden; the air became still again, hot and choked with dust.

"The wind has dropped."

"Sí, as it must," quipped the ancient.

"Strange weather …"

"It's a sign, that's what it is, he-he!"

Santo then jumped to something that was more in his interest: "Well, do you have a drop of mezcal to share? I'm afire with thirst."

"No, my friend, afraid not."

"Not a drop? Of anything? Tequila, pulque?"

"All I have is spit and sweat, which you're welcome to."

"Hah! That's bad, that's real bad, that is. Hell, I'm afire, see you!"

Santo spat his own spit, still skipping nimbly with the cumbersome load of collected wood strapped to his back, wholly incapable of staying motionless, even for a moment, moving about on his feet in a half jogging fashion.

"Tell me, Santo, what goes on in the pueblo, for I know you as a nosy old rooter and get in everywhere, usually where you're not supposed to be."

"That's me! That's me to a turn, he-he! Because I'm sharp on the uptake, I am, and never miss a trick," giving a crafty, old man's wink.

He poked a twig of a finger at dust in the corner of one eye, and winked again with the other eye, rather slyly, as if there was something of note to impart.

"Ah hum, you know the Pozas muchacha – what's her name? – the skinny one … Carmelita?"

"Sí, I know who you mean."

"Well, she'll drop today, if she hasn't already done so, you mark my words."

"Now how can you say that?" laughed Pancho.

"I just said it, you heard me say it, he-he!"

"But how can you know, eh?"

"When you've lived as long as I have, you get wise to things."

"You don't get wise, haven't got it in you; you get more nosy, poking into people's affairs."

"That's me! You got it! And I'll tell you something else, my fancy horseman, I know who seeded her, too."

This was thrown out with malignant glee, hopping with agility on one foot to the other with utter restlessness. There was cunning and craftiness in every nook and cranny of his not-so-senile brain.

"We all know that," Pancho countered, which took a bit of fire out of the old one.

Pancho pondered on what this gnarled old figure of a man might have been like in his years of prime, how totally different a person he must have been in those times.

"Well, old friend, your early life was illustrious, by any standards, or so I've been told," he said conversationally, "fighting during those Revolutionary days, eh?"

"Not fighting as such, Pancho," responded the other. "I was a courier, you see, for General Villa – sí, *Pancho Villa*, the man himself."

Old Santo changed his tone and attitude, his whole demeanour, as he talked on of his early life:

"I travelled a lot as a courier, as you'd expect, up and down the country. If I wasn't riding a fast pony, it was the railroad. The boxcars, with Villa's *soldaderas* and their mounts. North, to Zacatecas and Gomez Palacio, and back down south, to Mexico City itself ..."

He spat in the dust at his feet, ready to fire more guns – and even stood himself still at last, in accord with his reliving of earlier momentous times:

"That was when General Villa and Zapata occupied the city with their troops. A different Mexico City then, by the by, more like a wild frontier town. It was a dangerous, crazy time, with nothing properly settled, you understand. Until Carranza came back with his own army.

"Lucky for me, I was riding hard to Torreon when Villa and Zapata quit the city. What damned turmoil that was! What chaos! But, like I said, I was out of it, thank God.

"All in all," he tacked on as a finale, "I was damned lucky to have survived every bit of those troubled times."

"Well, I'm on my way now, I am," said Santo abruptly with a grimace, now reverting to his normal, present day irascible old man personae. "Out of my way there! Let a man pass, will you? All this open space around here and you have to park your damned hide right in front of me. I'll see you when I see you and not a moment before.

"I'm off! I'm off *pronto* and you can't stop me, he-he-he!"

And at last, like a fully wound clockwork motor, old Santo's restless movements propelled him forward, and off he went at that half-trot peculiar to the Mexican peons, who customarily travel in that same manner, even with a load – usually with a load – on their backs.

"*¡Vamónos Santo! ¡Adiós Pancho!*" he called over his shoulder.

"*¡Adiós, hombre, adiós!*" and Pancho watched him go with a helpless grin on his face.

He lifted his sombrero and scratched a sunsweat scalp, reddish hair standing upright like a stiff scrubbing brush. He hawked and spat on the hot rock of the flat, then took himself to the gully to mount his Macha.

The old ranchero gently urged on the mare, and she snorted and sneezed with the stinging dust. She kicked up heels and set off across the hardpan flat at a near hurried walk, hooves clopping-clipping hollowly on the rock.

While old Santo soon became a blurred dark smudge in the shimmering distance; appearing, as Pancho saw it, not unlike a worker ant carrying a dead fly.

PART THIRTEEN

56

A Sick Child

Using a square piece of cardboard, doña María Ramos wafted a draught at her new-laid woodfire, and the smoke grew and mushroomed up around her. She glanced over at the rough wooden table where the family usually ate their meals, assuring herself that little Julia was still there.

The child had shown herself quiet and subdued these last few days, as if her well-known spirit had deserted her, and mamá wondered at it. There was something amiss, though what it might be she could not fathom; she only suspected that the little one was sickening for something.

Julia was sat on a long bench by the table, industriously drawing with a pencil. She liked to draw, and seemed fairly competent at it. The colouring book that sister Ruth had bought for her at Christmas time had long since been filled in, each page neat, clean and correct. Now, she created her own pictures, drawing flowers or animals on a pad of cartridge paper.

The child's evident artistic flair – her new raw talent – had come quite naturally, as is generally the case with those of an innate creative bent. No one had taught her to draw with such precision and sure accuracy of eye. Finding an outlet for this precocious ability had become her major preoccupation in recent times, spontaneous ideas and ambitions developing on a daily basis.

Mamá glanced over again, as Julia raised her head from her task, and on her small oval face was a look as sweet as spring blossom. Mamá smiled, but the little girl was not looking at her; that serene expression seemed intent on something far away, staring at whatever it was in an abstracted manner.

Mamá returned to her work, hand-scooping beans into a black pot, throwing coriander stalks and parsley into her stockpot, and picking mouse droppings from a bag of rice.

When she happened to glance over once more a short time later, Julia had her head resting on the table-top, arms splayed out before her. And mamá, with acute maternal instinct, sensed something was indeed wrong with her this time. She dropped everything at once, and was soon by her child's side.

"Julia? My good angel, *mi muchachita?*"

The girl languidly lifted her head. She was drenched in perspiration, her face in a hot flush. Her little frame began to shake.

"Mamá," she barely whispered, "I don't feel well …"

Mamá lifted the sick child, held the little one in her arms and carried her across the courtyard, calling: "Cristina? Cristina!"

She took Julia to her room, hurriedly undressed the child and put her to bed, covering her with a light blanket. Cristina came rushing in then.

"Mamá? What is it? What's the matter?"

"Julia's poorly, a kind of fever it must be. Go to the well, I need cold water – and some clean towels, fetch both the small and large ones. Hurry it, ándale!" and Cristina dashed from the room.

When Cristina returned with the towels and a pail of clean, cold well water, she found mamá sitting on the edge of the bed, resting the back of her hand against the child's fevered brow. Mamá then set to with what she felt was necessary for the situation, Cristina helping as best she could. The child shivered spasmodically, eyes closed, face taut, and softly moaning.

Mamá wiped her face with a dampened towel, then her hot body and limbs. She gently dried the tenderling with a large, soft-fleeced towel, covered her with a sheet and blanket. After these exertions it was Julia who became exhausted. She soon fell into a restless, troubled sleep.

A time later, as mamá pushed a loose strand of hair away from her brow, she eyed her eldest daughter as though weighing up how much trust she could place in her.

"Cristina," she said, touching the girl's shoulder, "you stay with her. I need to collect some herbs for that fever. Keep wiping her face, if she starts sweating again. Don't give her anything to eat, not that she would want it, I'm sure. If she wakes and is thirsty, a little water will do, and she's to sip it slowly.

"Now, I must be off, and don't know how long I'll be, but I shall be back as soon as I can, do you hear, my pet?"

Mamá went over the nearby countryside, scouring the earth in a search for the curative herbs and alleviative medicinal wild plants she needed to use in order to save her little girl's life. The child's life was indeed in danger, she knew from experience, and much depended on what she might find. If she could only get the fever down, to ultimately break it. If it raged on at its present rate without some form of alleviation, the child will surely be near death's door by morning, she feared.

So mamá searched the land about for the precious herbs and plants.

57

An Old Friend Calls

Cristina attended to Julia's immediate needs in the sickroom – sibling Ruth had moved to Cristina's room for the time being – and spent nearly all her hours there. When the invalid child slept, she slept a little too, on a stool, with her back resting against the wall.

She did not in the least mind this nursing duty, it made her forget for a while her own morass of melancholy. As so often happens with life's travails, it put Cristina's personal misery over her failed love-life in a different light, able to see it from a new and somewhat healthier perspective.

Whenever mamá or anyone else came in, Cristina would whisper the latest development, then step out into the courtyard for a spell of fresh air and a look at daylight, or the night sky, depending on what time it was.

One morning mamá heard horse hooves clattering in the outer yard, and guessed it would be Pancho. When he stomped into view mamá greeted him with a strained look on her face, and he knew at once that something was amiss. The place was far too quiet for a start, he thought with foreboding.

"Well, María," he gravelled, "I can tell there's something up. What is it? And where's the little one? Where is my sweet rose-flower? Has something happened to Julia?"

Mamá wrung her hands, said, "She's in bed, taken sick with fever."

"Fever, is it? Is she bad, then?" and the old man's weathered face turned pale.

"Stricken fairly badly, it would seem. I'm so afraid she might not pull through and I'm near out of my mind, I'm sure," returned mamá in a tremulous voice, a tear rolling down one broad cheek.

In response to this Pancho did a most unusual thing: he removed his sombrero and held it in his hands, blunt fingers fidgeting with the brim. It was a direct indication that something was seriously the matter in the affairs of loved ones.

"We can get a doctor from San Stefan," he suggested kindly.

"No, my dear, a doctor wouldn't come all the way out here, not a town doctor."

"Why, I could go and fetch him myself. Set off this moment and be back with him by sunset. Sí, that's no problem."

"No, Francisco, it wouldn't do. A town doctor would never make such a journey. Besides, what could a doctor do for my niña that I'm not already doing myself? No, it is in the Hands of God, and God is merciful, I know. The fever must run its course, and it depends a lot too on Julia's own inner strength and spirit, bless her."

Pancho seemed to spend a deal of time gazing down at the toes of his boots.

Then, at last, he said, in a mumbled, low, humble voice, "Do you think – can I go and see her, María? Only a moment, mind, and I shan't disturb her, I promise you that."

"She's sleeping at present," sighed mamá, "but you can go and take a look in at her."

Pancho crept in the manner of a thief, slowly and stealthily across the sunlit yard to Julia's room, his boots creaking, and cursing his own clumsiness. With his sombrero still in hand he appeared now like a latecomer creeping into a church service.

He spoke to Cristina for a few moments at the threshold of the sickroom. She went on to confer with mamá, while Pancho entered the room alone, with a deeply anxious expression.

Julia was sleeping lightly, or so it appeared to the old man, his throat constricting as he gazed at her pale, thin-looking face. And as he stooped over to kiss her wan cheek, he could smell her little girl's smell, of warm milk and flowers and clean fresh air.

The child must have sensed a different presence in the room, or more likely her nostrils caught the pungency of man-sweat, cornstraw and horse-dung.

She stirred slightly, opened her eyes, big and rounded and languid.

"P-Pancho …" she whispered hoarsely, a ghost of a smile on her pallid lips.

He took her small hand in his large rough one, and said, "My spring-flower, my little button-nosed beauty… Rest easy, niña… rest easy now, there… there…"

"Am I going to Heaven, Pancho?" she quavered, her small white hand trapped in his great fist.

"We are all going there eventually, my poppy, us good ones, that is."

"I know, but will I be going soon?"

"Why no, not as I think on. You see, you haven't got a ticket, and first off you must have a ticket to get there."

"Have you got your ticket, Pancho?"

"Uuy, I reckon I can go there without a ticket, on account of my age, you understand. Hmm, I've been asked to, but I flatly refused their offer, so there's an end to it. At least for the present, it is. No rush yet, you see, even for me."

This brought a smile to the child's wan face, a small sad smile that cut the old man to the quick; his eyes glistened and he was unable to utter a sound for a moment.

"'… The winter is past … The flowers appear on the earth; the time of the singing of birds is come …'" he quoted quietly. "As it says in the Bible. The joy of life shall be yours for a long time yet, my sweet precious. God willing, of course, and God will, I'm certain of it. And these sufferings, well, they'll be all forgotten in no time.

"Now, I must be getting on back to the ranch," he said a while later, having recovered his composure. "You continue resting, my flower. Cristina will make you some lemon-grass tea, with lots of sugar to give you energy. I'll call again soon to see how you are …"

As he stooped again to kiss her, again she breathed on him her 'sweet warm milk and blossom' smell. And this second time, it was that singular, though universal smell of a young child that triggered a memory in him; sharp and clear, though acutely painful. He was reminded of the passing of his own three little muchachas, now so far distant in time. The memory however, forcefully brought it to the present.

'How odd a thing it is,' ran his thoughts on leaving the sickroom, 'how smells can awaken and evoke memories'.

58

Julia's Nadir

Julia stoically suffered her burning, bone-aching, black-fired fever.

One time, she began to feel 'pins-and-needles' prickling her little hot body; experiencing a peculiar sensation of growing smaller and ever smaller. Diminishing until she felt as merely a tiny dot in a far distance. She seemed to feel ten times her body weight, falling heavily into illimitable black space.

There would then occur a swift return to her normal size, the 'pins-and-needles' now thrusting outwards, her body growing larger, expanding to a massive bloating. Her real self was somehow detached, and observing the physical sensation with the same detachment. What was that form on the bed if it was not herself? Cut off from her 'other' self, and longing to be joined to it.

This tormenting hallucinatory process repeated itself over and over, wearing her down. Until, finally, she fell asleep from sheer exhaustion.

Later on still, in her fevered state the child was having vivid and not altogether unpleasant dreams. In these dreams she played with her friends of long standing, familiar faces of her childhood.

On awakening however, with the dreams still fresh and clear in her mind, Julia discovered a disturbing anomaly. In her mind's eye she scanned the faces of these 'friends'.

She recognised not a single one of them. They were absolute strangers to her, had never seen them before in her life – except in these recent dreams, when they had seemed so familiar, so well-known to her there.

Then one morning, awakening from a thankfully refreshing sleep and feeling better in herself, she came to a happy answer concerning the strange playfellows she only knew in dreams. Her quick intelligence found a satisfying solution to this strange enigma.

Julia had been dreaming *someone else's* dream!

Someone else. That must be what it had been. That was the simple and reasonable answer. Some total stranger from far away, maybe in another State, probably a little girl just like herself.

These thoughts soon tired her, and she presently dropped into a deep and *dreamless* sleep.

Another time, she lay in bed with head propped against a pile of pillows, staring muzzily at a framed picture hanging on the opposite wall. The painting depicted the Virgin of Guadalupe in robes of startling electric blue, stood beneath a heavily foliaged tree. Around the robed figure sat a group of children, from different regions of the country. In the foreground was a dark-haired girl, a sash across her chest, in the colours of the national flag.

This girl in the picture reminded Julia of her sister Ruth. The girl looked remarkably like Ruth in every detail of her face. Julia stared at her *sister*, as though willing the two-dimensional form to speak to her in her present pain.

And in her pain Julia began to cry, a silent, self-pitying weeping. Warm tears rolled on the softness of her facial features, cooling down in their journey over the cheeks. They were salt and sweet tears, like morning dew on a coastal plant, like the tears of every child that cries.

Presently, the crying ceased and her tears dried, minute salt crystals clinging to the fine hairs on her face.

She ignored the picture, instead, stared long and hard at bumps and cracks in the whitewashed walls. Her fevered imaginings created faces of creatures in the rough contours of the wall. Julia looked next at the bedsheet covering her body, at undulating snowy hills with curvaceous shapes and shadows.

Then she glanced up and saw Cristina, who had quietly crept in a few moments before, and thinking that her little sister was asleep. Cristina was sitting on a stool, straight and still as a sphinx, also staring, staring at another blank, whitewashed wall.

What can she see on the wall? wondered the child. Can she see the faces I saw?

Julia sniffed, caught the dry spicy scent of laurel leaves, the tree itself standing guard outside the window of her room. She heard the phonograph music lilting over from the pueblo, and a steady high whine of a fly caught in a web in a corner of the room.

Her eyes drooped stickily, dusk and gloom enveloped the child.

Then darkness descended.

Julia slept.

Without a single movement of her form she slept on.

59

Pancho Calls Again

Pancho rode in on the following day, hurrying anxiously into the inner courtyard. He found mamá sitting on a stool under the kitchen lean-to. She was pounding herbs in a stone mortar, in readiness for a brew of infusions to alleviate Julia's sore throat and aching limbs.

Again, the old ranchero removed his sombrero, a gesture not unnoticed by mamá and slightly amused by it – she knew it cost him a great deal to make such an act.

"How is she, María?" he enquired at once in high-hoped tones. "Is she any better? Can I see her?"

"Her temperature's still high," mamá informed him, "but we're managing to get a little food down her at least, for which she'll soon feel the benefit, I'm rightly thinking.

"It is a matter of time, I suppose. She's awake at present. Cristina is with her. Go on, go and see her, but don't excite her, Francisco, she is not strong enough to take it," and the old man was off like a shot to the sick child's room.

Cristina, sitting at the bedside, was attempting to get a dish of milk gruel down the poor child's sensitive throat. Pancho waited until she had been fed, twisting the brim of his sombrero with agitated, nerve-stressed fingers. Cristina might have felt some compassion for him, except that he looked at that moment rather comical with his reddish hair sticking up at all angles, as if from an electric shock.

Then he went to her and Cristina left him with her patient.

The old man sat himself gingerly on the side of the bed, smiling on the child. She glanced with almost sparkling eyes at his ridiculous stand of hair, and, guessing what might be amusing the child, he stroked his head from back to front to smooth down his unruly crop, much improving his general appearance.

They talked softly for a while of small, inconsequential matters of interest to them both, without any feelings of discomfort on either side. He touched her pale cheek with the rough pad of his forefinger, stroked her cheek as gently as he could, just as he would with a newly-born foal; and the male roughness of his finger was somehow reassuring to the child.

At one point, he said to her:

"What might your favourite colour be?"

"Red," responded Julia without hesitation.

"Well, that's interesting, hmm. So, red it is. Ay que bueno, for I kind of thought it might be red.

"Red like the *bandillero* flower, or the ripe flesh of a watermelon – or a setting sun. Also, red is a sign of danger, did you know? No? No! But that's only thought by grownups and then they're from foreign lands. Not surprising then that you didn't know…

"Red is a symbol of luck among the Chinese people, and a symbol for bravery. You're being very brave, I can see that plainly enough.

"Sí, my little muchachita, red is definitely your colour."

"Now, my daisy-dove," he said a short time later, "you need to sleep some more, to get your strength back. I'll come visit you again soon. And bring along a red bandanna which I'm hoping friend Cándido will sell to me, to pass on to you as a small gift, and you can then let everyone see that your colour is red."

The old ranchero left the sickroom, with his usual exaggerated tip-toeing carefulness.

Julia's pain-glazed eyes fastened on a criss-cross of thatching above her head. She thought she saw a mouse, but it was in fact a bird, after straw to make a nest.

A heavy drowsiness came over her. Her eyelids flickered, and dropped. With an effort she opened her eyes. She needed to see the thatching, because it was familiar to her and comforting.

The sleepiness took over once more, heavier than before, and she involuntarily closed her eyes.

She was soon into a dream.

Less than an hour later, the sick child awoke with a start, her fevered body wet with perspiration.

60

A Crisis is Over

"And how is she today, María?" asked Pancho the following day.

Mamá's eyes glistened. "Our niña is better," she said with a tired smile. "Her fever broke not long after you left, and she's a lot better, thank God. She's sleeping at the moment, poor little thing, and needs to rest a bit more to get back her energy."

"Ah, the Lord and the Saints be praised!" quavered the old man in a cracked voice. "Didn't I say she'll pull through alright, María? Did I not tell you so? I knew it all along, for that little muchachita has resilience, she has spirit, as I've often said. And she has your blood in her, which puts a cork on failure of any kind.

"Ay que bueno, what wonderful news, eh? Couldn't be any more amazing. She's going to be okay and well out of danger now, to be sure. ¡Újule! wait till I tell my compañeros about it," he went bubbling on, and practically dancing on the spot. "They'll be right pleased – they have asked about her every day: Cándido and Gerardo and Emilio – even José! And Tulia, of course, and young Julian too. They've all been concerned – frantic actually, if I may so put it – but certainly most concerned, constantly asking about our favourite little muchachita.

"Ay que caray, springtime is no time for a young one to end her time on this blessed earth, and - ¡Uuy! the mare by the stable, Macha, she's not tethered. I've just this moment remembered – not much wrong with me, is there? Not right away, at least.

"But Macha now, I left her by your stable door, I did, distinctly remember that. And will she wander off? As certain as nuts is hard! A regular Marco Polo traveller is that mare of mine.

"Perdónome, María, while I just slip her rein to your hammock-tree …" and he turned abruptly with head down, hurrying out of the courtyard as though being chased by a pack of rabid dogs.

Out of an odd feeling of curiosity, feminine intuition no doubt came into play here, mamá went over to the wall at right angles to her kitchen. There was a hole where brick and stone had worked loose.

She peeped through this aperture into the outer yard, her mind already decided on what she might discover under her investigative nose.

The old ranchero was standing before the stable door, with his back to her.

His shoulders heaved, she noted, and he was making strange sounds. A rough hand came up to wipe his face, body trembling and shaking like an old tree in a gale.

Mamá understood at once, turned away and left him to it.

61

Convalescence

When Julia recovered sufficiently to quit her sickbed, and got a little stronger, she was allowed to wander about, though she was still weak and wobbly on her legs.

A day or two passed, before she was able to take a slow amble on her own down to the river. Along the pathway which led to the river she slowly moved on unsteady, hesitant legs.

But what a beautiful day! Such light there was, the light of day, a glorious sunbright colour-filled springday. Such an abundance of shapes and shadows in the undergrowth: tender tendrils twirling around lobed and toothed leaves; corollas and cups of flowerheads reaching out on milk-papped sap-trapped stems and stalks to light and air and prying insects.

The little one stared at all around her with wondrous eyes, as if seeing it for the first time. It was for her a fantastic transformation.

From the child's eyes – from a fresh outlook of things for someone who had been so very close to death itself – for Julia it was all so deliciously marvellous.

She didn't mind the whining and buzzing of winged insects about her; in fact, in some peculiar way they were a kind of comfort, a reassuring presence of a familiar life.

That went also to the birdcalling, in the air and in among the branches of nearby beefwood trees. And the sound of the old wind-up phonograph, repeatedly playing some favourite *corrido* – might it be Pancho's favourite? *Sentimiento y Dolor?* – At any rate, to Julia it was like the sweetest music ever in her ears. Thrillingly, she was conscious too of the song of breezes sweeping gently in along the valley floor.

It was the child's 'artist's eye' that was seeing everything around her; an artist's perception of the many and varied colours and textures of her physical world.

How sharp and diamond clear things appeared. The sun shone on the grey adobe walls of dwellings in the pueblo across the way; looking like delicate pastry, those dusty walls, and the roof thatching of cornstraw becoming honey-glazed in the light, and faded red roof tiles like curled clumps of marzipan. Skeins of cloud in the high sky like a stir of cream in that deep bowl blue.

That was how she saw it all.

Beyond the pueblo boundaries on one side, a group of young-timers had the task of taking care of a herd of lemon-eyed goats. Handsome beasts, buttermilk-yellow and gingerbread-brown, busily cropping what they could over rugged stony terrain. The young ones saw Julia and knowing her, gaily waved, and she lifted a hand in timorous, solemn acknowledgement of their greeting.

The air was thick with herb and flower scents, with pollen and dust and warm spring sunlight. Even the very ground Julia now trod on, seemed somehow made of the stuff of childish fantasy. A wasteland of cornstraw and stone became a mosaic pattern of fawn and henna and ochre. The dirt on it sparkling as gold-dust in this daytime hour. The grass shining like quartz-and-crystal or finely spun sugar.

Ahead of Julia in the near distance a line of five *milperos* worked a furrow in a field. Stooped to their labours altogether as one, stretching erect at one moment, then bending again in unison, like clockwork soldiers working at a military drill. Over in the same field was a donkey, smoky-grey and biscuit-coloured, copiously pissing in a furrow; a gushing sunsplashed cataract, like clear golden honey spilling from a honeypot.

Quick as a wink, a bird picked a strand of straw in its beak, glanced up and around in rapid nervous nods, and down went its head again, snapped another straw. Several times it did this, then away it flew, a bewhiskered bird, to build a nest someplace.

And again, there was birdsound, clear and mellifluous around her; and again, the long familiar music from the old Victrola phonograph in the pueblo. Young corn swished and sighed, as a spring-wind blew and breathed over the land.

It was as if the good earth was smiling on the child, mellow and serene and tender; familiar yet quite different here on this day, in some kind of mystical magical way …for Julia it was utterly enchanting.

Charming and refreshing, under a warm, gentle sunflow on this particularly special life-loving mature spring day.

THE
SEQUEL

BOOK III

AUTUMN

PART FOURTEEN

62

Harvesting Season

Autumn arrived. The twilight of the seasons. The slow creeping in of decay. Dead-leaf brown the earth in a solemn mood of these autumn saffron days.

But first, it was the harvest.

The land had given up its bounty and now lay in a torpor of exhaustion. It was the time for the grain and pod, the husk and chaff and heavy fruit. The time of pomegranate sunrises and purple-plum sunsets. The earth breathed its autumnal mists, rolling over the lowlands, thick as woodsmoke along the winding river near the Ramos farmstead. A great sea of grass ran lush through the orchard grounds, swirling around the lower trunks of fruit trees, wavering with a damp and moody breeze. And the wind performed a balletic dance through falling leaves.

Between two dawns a day is done and a day is to do, and campesinos came out from their adobe homes and wet their bare feet in morning dew, as they took the measure of long autumn grass, that won't grow anymore this year.

The Ramos orchard was hazy with morning mist, the grass glistening with a heavy dew. The dew shone silver in the early light. Thick, grey-hued clouds slugged ponderously overhead, fat and low in the sky this day, and appearing as if resting on the hilltops. The morning face of the low-slung eastern sun beamed anew through gaps in the slow-moving clouds.

It set the scene, it fashioned the light and moved the day.

Who can hear the sound of movement when flesh of fruit ripen in their singular spheres? For it was getting picked by the women and children. Each opulent peach or apricot was carefully cupped in a square of tissue paper and placed on layers of dry straw set in baskets and crates.

Treble-voiced the calls and cries of kids, energy-wasting their youngsterhood in play and in picking fruit. Under a massive cloud-stacked sky.

A child called from across the river, and her keen young nose twitched at the smell of the river and of ripe-harvested orchard fruit. And a river wind blew at the women's rebozos and tugged at their skirts, and attacked the late flowers scattered about meadow and field.

Mamá was busy in a lower meadow near the river, building a fire-pit and hearth from a pile of riverstones. She did this every year at autumn time. Each passing year the stones would get kicked around by boys and many thrown back in the river.

During the harvesting, mamá cooked for the entire pueblito, and they ate all their meals out in the open, under typically mixed weather skies. In recent times she was ably assisted by Cándido's wife, Laura – the girl with a slight cast in one eye, so compatibly a bride for that young ranchero, cross-eyed Cándido.

Laura was tripping along now toward her friend, carrying in her arms many of the spare largest pots she was able to scrounge, steal or borrow from the people of the pueblito.

"I have them, María!" she called over gaily.

"*Tambien*," smiled mamá. "You can put them on this flat rock here. Handy, isn't it? Like a table. How do you like my 'kitchen' then, hey?"

"Oh my, María! Look at the firewood you have there. Who collected that lot?"

"My Juanito – and Pancho helped a bit too, after I'd twisted his arm. But it's only enough for one day, would you believe. Here, let me help you with those pans. You're like a circus juggler, our Laura."

"Well, María," laughed the young woman, "I always reckon I have three pairs of hands at home, so why shouldn't I use them here?"

"And three sets of eyes to watch over your Cándido, too, when he's at home and up to mischief."

"Oh my, you're so right! How did you know?" Laura giggled like a schoolgirl.

As already mentioned, Laura had a slight cast in one eye; which was why, some people often said – particularly the pueblito folk – why she and the young ranchero Cándido married; they were a truly well-fitted pair. All the same, this was not the case by any means, because Cándido had fallen for her from a distance, and had no inkling initially that she had this small defect. It did not in the least detract from her natural womanly beauty.

On the contrary, if anything it rather enhanced her general good looks. Most especially when she smiled, which was often, for Laura was a fun-loving, life-loving female. When she smiled her eyes sparkled and danced, and her whole face was at once lovely and charming and quite appealing. The slight cast gave one a yearning to look longer into the delight and sweetness – not to say, a certain mystery – so plainly evident in those eyes.

Laura possessed an otherworldly beauty; just as Cándido, queer-eyed though he may be, was still nevertheless handsome in a rough and rural sort of way, and strongly attractive to the fair sex. Laura always kept a close eye on him when the opposite sex were around, or rather, kept a wary eye on females that happened to be around Cándido.

"If you'll get the fire going I'll just nip down to the river," said mamá, wiping hands on a cloth. "An insect bit me on my little toe and it stings like fury. If I dip my foot in cold water, maybe the sting will lessen some."

"Okay, María, I'll see to things. You get on. I wondered why you seemed to be hop-hopping along a bit there."

Mamá set off, bare sturdy feet treading carefully on living grass. She reached a line of old willow trees and instantly caught the smell of the river, its clean running water smell, its earthy root and weed smell. It reminded her of many things in her life. The autumn wildflowers and late grass were as lush and familiar to her now as they had been in autumns of her younger days.

The water was dark and deep here, and so she plonked herself on the bank, allowing her feet to sink coolly into the slowly swirling body of it. The pain of the sting in her toe began to deaden, bringing her blessed relief.

"¡Oye, doña María!" called someone from behind a bush opposite, "Fiesta time, is it?" which was rightly ignored as if not heard.

The coolwater river ran silently by old willows, brooding and minding its own business. Running quietly, with somewhere to go, carrying its mysteries away along its length. In its broad bends and backwaters, mamá could see the river's bed of coloured pebbled stones. Pure clear water, inviting for hot, sore feet or dry parched lips – or insect stings.

She gazed on wildflowers carpeting the bank opposite. A river-wind spread to embrace the flowers, causing them to nod and sway. And mamá was aware of a general movement, as a valley windsong stirred the earth and the stuff of life on it; birdwing and leafscrape, sinking stone and dancing dust, slow and fast life, life abundant still.

Doña María heard a cheerful piping of voices of youngsters; and saw, on the other side, a frail little chit of a girl running awkwardly through tall grass on thin, chopstick legs.

The child stopped a moment, glanced quizzically across the short expanse of water, and saw who it was watching. She waved, and María smiled warmly, waving back at her.

63

Pancho Ready to Harvest

A few fields further downriver on mamá's left, Pancho was crashing about. He too was heading for the river.

He noted a bundle of babies coddled on a sarape under the shade of a tree. Looking in on them, he saw one of the younglings curl a tiny fist, which seemed to the old man like a sleeping nightflower. A girl no more than six years old was taking care of these babes, slowly fanning flies off them with a small sheet of cardboard.

The girl glanced up, gave the ranchero a shy smile. My God! he thought, that smile was almost *maternal*.

There were other youngsters around, he could see, playing among themselves. These tumbling toddlers, he knew, were the seeds of earlier seasons, with seasons yet to grow.

He stumped on, storming through bush of russet-burned leafage, his boots crushing brown brittle undergrowth, until he neared a rash of large willows down by the river.

The clouds above rode by, below the blue and into it, and more came on, banking into one mighty mass and blotting out a greater part of the blue.

And there was the river before him, wide at this stretch, shallow-banked and silvery in the light upon it. He hunkered down on his haunches ranchero-style, handscooped and drank the clear cool water. Then he raised himself and stared at the water as though mesmerized. Was he perhaps looking for a sign from the old Aztec goddess of rivers, the one named Chalchiuhtlicue? While in the stone-cobbled shallows the language of the river became guttural and voluble, its meaning not as clear as its flowing waters.

The sun suddenly cut through a break in the clouds. Bejewelled and gem-stoned now the rocks in the shallows, shaped by a thousand million years of rushing waters, flashing rainbow hues under the sun's light.

The old man felt satisfied with life, it was good to be alive, gave him a deal of contentment; no, for Pancho it could not have been better. And being satisfied he turned resolutely on his heels, ready to set himself to work on the harvesting.

He was overtaken by two scruffy, scratched-kneed boys running, hands held tight to the shaft of a fully-laden handcart, fruit jolting off, bouncing and rolling in overgrown grass.

The two rapscallions glanced behind them, saw who it was they had just overtaken, and laughed with delight.

The old man smiled warmly back at them. 'The little rapscallions!' – That was his term for them.

64

Life Among the Harvesters

"Look at me, Pancho, I'm at the top of the ladder!" called down a girlish voice. It was mamá's middle daughter, Ruth. "And at the top of the tree as well," she went on with triumph.

"Ay, Rutí, they say the best and ripest fruit are the ones at the top of the tree. But be careful you don't fall off that ladder, muchacha, or you'll know about it. The falling is fine in itself, you might say a thrilling thing, whizzing freely through empty space like that. Only, it's the meeting with the ground afterwards which spoils it all."

"I'll be careful," cried Ruth, and lifted an arm peach-reached high, and her nimble fingers danced, plucked and caught from branch to bough. The luscious ripe-ready globes were later laid like fragile eggs in *tule* reed trays and baskets.

The old man craned his neck, beaming up at Ruth, her lips moist with peach juice. "It's the hand of labour that will turn the day," he murmured, more to himself than to the girl, at the same time that keen nose of his catching the tang of wholesome, ripened fruit.

Presently, mamá came steaming up, a dark look on her frowning face, as if as a threat to an unsuspecting individual, someone like Pancho perhaps.

"Perdónome, don't let me interrupt you," she said with heavy sarcasm, "as I can see you're worked off your feet watching the fruit trees grow."

She stopped and stood in the tall grass, four-square set and akimbo'd, ignoring a confusion of kids running about loaded baskets of fruit nearby. Several of the pueblito women gathered around her, smelling of cornstraw, bruised grass and fruit pulp. They eagerly anticipated what could prove a nice little storm brewing here.

"Ah, María, my own peach-pie," Pancho smiled innocently at her. "It is said, did you know, in the language of flowers, that peach blossom means 'I am your captive'," and threw a wicked wink at the women scattered about her.

"Ha! Is that so?" returned mamá, timber-faced. "But this isn't springtime, Pancho Ramírez, not when we're harvesting our peaches."

"My little tormentor, I was only picking a titbit for you from my – from my erudite knowledge."

"Ha! Were you now? And I am your captive, then? Is that it?" the surrounding women slyly smiling at this sally.

"I'm afraid to say that you're not, regretfully, for you're the one who got away."

"¡Chihuahuas! A lucky escape!" which prompted the women to explode into laughter.

Pancho was undeterred. "And it is also said that when 'the bloom is off the peach – " he pressed on, but was interrupted, as –

"You're not getting any younger!" – Laura quickly tossed in for him, coming up behind his back.

"You've got it, that's right," he agreed.

"Meaning who exactly?" mamá demanded to know, again with a dark and storm-warning countenance.

"Why, Methuselah's daughter, I shouldn't wonder," replied Pancho readily, adroitly slipping himself out of that possible scrape.

One of the women in the small crowd stepped aside, arms crossed tight as a new knot in a bootlace, eyeing one of her brood heading for the river, running through the sunsmacked windpushed meadow.

"Don't you go near the river where the willows are, my little cricket," she called shrilly. "The water's deep where the willows at and there are strong currents besides. You fall in and drown yourself to death, and I'll heat your bottom for you, understand? ¿Claro?"

"Rufino's playing there, mamá," piped the 'little cricket', his hair unruly and peppered with grass-seed.

"He's three years older than you are, and besides, Rufino has as many wits about him as you could count on one hand. Now, the warning's made, so you just take heed," and the woman turned then, almost fell into the arms of Rufino's own mother, who was standing there with a face like thunder.

"Her tongue runs faster than her thinking, and at the wrong moment she'll say the wrong thing," mamá muttered to her friend Laura, as dryly and saltily as a year-old tear.

Meanwhile, Rufino's mother smiled acidly at the crossed-armed woman.

"He may be a bit backward at times, my muchacho, but he was at least born in wedlock," she shot back in a molten fury, obviously rattled as far as mamá could tell.

The other tightened her arms even more in an effort to control the crimsoning of her face, a hot flicker of scorn in her eyes, and the women around her trying hard not to show their sniggers.

The arms-crossed woman had a dark smudge lined along her top lip – as Pancho saw it, like a well cultivated moustache any male would be proud to tote. He noticed, too, her bare arms clenched tight to her tense-stiffened body, a clear signal of her contempt. As for Rufino's mother, well, he thought, any words of apology would have to be chiselled out of that one.

A short time later, Laura's eldest girl, Sofia of five years, came tripping up.

"Mamá! Mamá!" cried the child wailingly, "Hilario was touching my bosom!"

"He was?" said Laura, glancing quickly at mamá, but she had turned her head to hide an amused smile on her face. "Where exactly did he touch you? Show me."

"It was over there, mamá, it was behind the cart over there."

"No, I mean where on you that he touched."

"Here, mamá," piped Sofia, holding her little tummy. "He was looking for my button, he said, so he could press my button, he said. And then he was touching my tipples."

"He was?"

"Sí, mamá, here and here," pointing at her small heaving chest.

"Why, that dirty little scoundrel! I'll touch his backside when I see him. I'll make him smart, so I will!"

At this, mamá couldn't help darting an amused glance at Laura.

Little Sofia sniffed, and said, "When you smart him, mamá, can I watch?"

Laura was about to answer, but suddenly decided to tack toward a different direction. "Have you taken those empty baskets back to the apple orchard, yet?"

"Sí – No, mamá," admitted the child.

"Well, you take them there this very moment, or I'll be smarting you too, and so hard you'll not sit for a week," and Sofia scooted off in a bird-wink.

Laura looked at mamá and Pancho, and the three of them burst into a bellow of laughter, so loud that heads were turning in the next field.

Above them came clouds, and these clouds came on like herds of huge white cattle, cropping the blue of the sky.

There were roistering cries of boys, kicking hoof-scuffed stones on a goat-tracked hillock above a hay meadow.

Smartly turned out gusts of wind went skirmishing through the fruit trees, where more kids, when they should have been working, were frolicking under leaf and bough, and they were as gay as the fruit was ripe on the wind-savaged upper branches.

65

A Trio of Note

Comida time and a welcome break from work for the harvesters. The people of the pueblito ranged themselves in scattered groups about the meadowfield, in which burned the communal cookfire. Mamá was in among them, like a general looking over his troops. They helped themselves to the food, passing hot dishes to one another, laughing and gossiping as countryfolk will when they get together.

The men pushed their machetes into the ground to polish the blades. And the young ones ran wild and joyously with indefatigable energy. The phonograph in the pueblo played, its music carried on the backs of hills and valley winds.

Pancho squatted next to his blind friend, Florencino, on his own patch in a corner of the meadow, where he was crafting large straw baskets to load the fruit in.

Presently, they were joined by the young cross-eyed ranchero, Cándido.

"You were up on the ranch yesterday, is it?" asked the old man.

"That's right, and came here this morning, as you can see," returned Cándido matter-of-factly.

"Everything okay there is it? They're managing without you?"

"Just about. José has a bad cough and gave up smoking a couple of days back. Now, he's as mean as a cat with its tail caught in a gate. Gerardo's got a sore – a boil, or something – on his backside, right where it hurts most, and sits his saddle like a man with his pants afire. Emilio, well, he fell asleep on his mount the other afternoon, and the horse clopped on and ended up on the railtrack, where it fell asleep as well, no doubt.

"Then along comes the 3.42 express, hooting like mad. He got clear just in time, according to the fellow at the junction, who saw it all. Had Emilio not cleared the track in time, he would have been plastered all over the front of that steam-engine like tomato salsa – though he would also have got a free ride all the way down to Mexico City.

"He's stayed wide awake ever since. Has nightmares over it, so he tells me. 'But you're not sleeping, so how come the nightmares?' He has them all the time, he says, day or night, stark wide awake."

Pancho pursed his lips. "I wondered how he has these nightmares when he's not even sleeping."

"You can have nightmares during the day and be fully awake," Florencino put in diffidently. "I know I sometimes have them."

"Oh, you mean frights in general," pursued Pancho, "which I suffer from too when I see Cándido's face first thing of a morning – frightful!"

There were no more 'affabilities'; rather the opposite as the atmosphere became almost frosty. Cándido, touchy about his looks, felt bitten to the bone over the old man's cruel comment, considering it singularly lacking in truth or tact.

"Well, well, look at this!" declared mamá, appearing suddenly from behind the three men. "Two villains and an innocent squashed in-between. Don't you listen to these two rogues, Florencino, else you'll give yourself a bad name, I'll be bound.

"I don't *see* much of my old friends these days, doña María," smiled the blind man pleasantly.

"'I don't *see* much …'" repeated Pancho, chuckling. "Ah, hermano, you ought to be on stage or the wireless. You're missing your true vocation – Ay, María, what a look you're giving me. She's giving me one of those looks, Florencino, you know what I mean? That can melt steel."

"No, really, María, you're like one of them peaches everyone's a-picking of," he continued with open urbanity.

"I don't trust your compliments, Pancho, so out with it! What exactly are you implying, hey?"

Sunlight was kind to mamá's face, gilding the broad cheeks, making something of a handsome woman of her. And there was a definite spark of merriment in those dark eyes of hers.

"Hmm, well," began the old man, without even a safety harness of caution, "you're soft and downy on the outside, and rich with flesh that's fit to burst. But in the middle you're stone-hearted, just as a peach is."

"Ha! I knew it!" exclaimed mamá, as the others laughed.

"He's teasing you, doña María," smiled Florencino, coming to the rescue, thinking kindly that these two – Pancho and doña María – were kindred spirits, "and he's only teasing you because he likes you."

"You mean he's only teasing me because he likes *to*!" slammed back mamá, a certain knowing look apparent on her face. "And why aren't any of you eating, I'd like to know? Too busy drinking tequila, are we?" her mildly perspiring face flecked with tiny midges, glued there to the moisture.

"Do you see us drinking tequila – or mezcal, or anything?" Pancho was again plunging in with zeal, totally disregarding a safety-net of caution.

"No, not unless you're hiding it," retorted María in cracked ice tones.

Pancho glanced at his horseman compañero, Cándido, winked a merry blue eye, and said:

"Go and get us some grub, amigo; for me, yourself, and our friend here, Florencino. There's a good fellow. Pronto, now!"

"Go and get your own food!" blistered out mamá. "And you get some for Florencino while you're at it. ¡Chihuahuas! It's help yourself here, I'll have you know. Everyone helps themselves."

"Sí, I know, you're right," grinned the old man, "and I'm helping myself to Cándido's hospitality."

This last little witticism had the blind man Florencino stitched up with merriment for a considerable length of time. While Pancho scraped up an almost seraphic kind of smile, totally unsuited to his swarthy, bandit-looking face.

66

Picking and Packing

The autumn days ran on in a serene way, like the quietness of ripening fruit or slowly growing grass. Each day the workers awoke and walked the silver-spangled dawntide dewfall, bare brown toes kicking late-year wrinkled, dry beige leaves.

The youngsters with cheeks blush-bloomed as the peaches they picked and put away. And the full-fleshed fruits hung lushly; awaiting the touch of fingers, the bite of teeth, the taste of tongue, in this earthtime season.

After the stone-centred fruits were picked and packed, the men came along with their machetes to cut back the branches of the trees, in readiness for the next year's growth.

Two boys – the same two who ran with a hand-cart – collected stickwood for the communal cookfire stockpile.

The women and children then made a start on apple-picking. Some were sent scattered far and wide in search of more brushwood, or anything useful to burn, for doña María's cooking-fire. She set great store in having sufficient and more in stock.

Mamá and friend Laura continued cooking the meals for everyone each busy day. It was well appreciated by the pueblito folk, knowing there was no one better than these two culinary mistresses.

Young Juan, mamá's only boy, and Pancho were kept occupied loading the farmstead's buckboard tilt-cart, Juan's chestnut horse Chapulín between the shafts. They made endless trips to the nearest highway, where the produce was reloaded onto waiting trucks going to towns in the region.

Said the old ranchero on one run, which he considered one run too many:

"What say we just carry on down to Vera Cruz, Juanito, and jump on a ship bound for China? It'll be easier out there, I'm reckoning, than this slave labour we're presently involved with. What say you, amiguito?"

"I'm game for it," grinned the boy. "I fancy a cruise on a ship, and China would be an interesting place to visit."

"What! And leave your Chapulín here in the old country!"

They plodded on with their load, their imaginations nonetheless running riot …

Meanwhile, back at the 'hive-of-industry', everybody worked cheerfully enough about the sunlapped fruit trees. The orchard grounds were densely populated with bird-beak battered, juice-sluiced windfall fruits.

The evening came on and another day marched west into the fiery glow of a blood-orange sun, broadening as it sank beyond the western hills.

67

Cornfield Conversations I

By mid-October the harvesters had moved on into the cornfields. The women wore their hardcloth aprons, frayed and patched and dusty. About their heads they wore the ubiquitous grey-blue rebozo, tilted over the brow to protect them from the low sun's still strong light.

A rush of children boiled into the cornfields, their faces showing excitement, eyes as black and round as little beetles.

Old Pancho gazed into his field of standing corn, a cross-hatched print of shadow and gold and smoky yellow. He set to work with a will.

While the women worked on collecting corncobs in their husks, the old man and a few of the youngsters concentrated on picking the beans growing in rows between the high cornstalks. His thick blunt fingers deftly plucked at the long green beans, dropping them by the fistful into a gunnysack which he kept dragging up by his side.

The women joked and laughed quietly among themselves, and the little ones whispered and giggled and played hide-and-seek games. Pancho was conscious of bird calls, the morning hum of winged insects, and the phonograph playing popular corridos in the pueblo, its tinny sound filtering through the stands of corn, spreading along the valley. He was hoping they would put on his favourite record: *Sentimiento y Dolor*.

And a gentle, mild-autumn wind caressed the contours of the land.

Pancho worked peacefully and methodically. It seemed to him like another world here below the golden frazzled leaves of corn. A miniature shadowed forest of straight stemmed stalks, dust-dark and blue-green. Grasshoppers churred their dry-rasped yellow wings, and flies buzzed as they constantly moved from one spot to another in investigative fervour.

Ants scurried briskly and easily over the rough terrain of topsoil. And shiny-cloaked beetles mosey'd unhurriedly along dry, biscuit-crumb soil.

The earth pulsed with its heavy growth, and the mild, pleasant heat pushed upward to the old man's loins. His knees sank into this earthsea, sails of leaves ready furled on corn-masts, and his quick fingers reaped the earthtide reward of gentle green.

He reached a threesome of women, and they were not aware that he was there among them, near enough for them to smell him, but well hidden.

It is strange, he mused thoughtfully, how the autumn harvest time affected some folk. How the intimacies of human nature came out, particularly among the women. And especially when they imagined they were alone and without the company of men.

It had never before occurred to the old man how differently the women talked when among themselves.

'Ay que caray,' he thought, 'they're much worse than we are,' meaning his own male sex.

He could not help but hear their revealing female chatter:

"Do you know what my Manuel wanted me to do the other night?" began one of them. "You wouldn't credit it but he asked me to bend over. Not like as in prayer, oh no, but to bend right over with my bottom in the air.

"'What do you take me for,' I said, 'a bitch dog?' If you want to do that sort of thing,' I said to him, 'you can cut along to the burro stall and try it on the mare, for you'll not be trying it on me, I'll have you know, oh no!' I told him straight. I did indeed."

"So what happened?" enquired another.

"Wouldn't speak to me for hours on end, which suited me fine."

"Mostly quiet as a meadow mouse, is my Guillermo," said the third one of this small group. "I sometimes wonder what makes him tick, I really do. It's like he's forever low on his batteries or something. Mind you though, if a man were to cross him, then things would happen alright, believe you me. He can get sparked up when he wants to, can my Guillermo. But as I say most of the time he's a bit low on his batteries, bless him."

"Your Guillermo," tittered the woman next to her, "he sounds more like a motor car."

"Hush, you!" admonished her friend. "Did I ask for your opinion?"

"Well, I'm glad old Pancho is here helping us," went on the first speaker. "It's good to have a real man around to keep us in order, tee-hee!"

"That man's nothing more than a *pistolero*, did you know. A regular *guerrillero* – a bandit!"

The first speaker considered his so-called rascality a mere whiffle of a dust-devil. "No," she said, "Pancho is as softhearted as they come. And he's a real marvel with the kids. They love him to bits, they do."

"Well, say what you like but he gave me the come-on the other day when no one else was around. You know what I mean, a wink of the eye and all that."

Listening in, the old reprobate immediately fancied that he could detect a potent sexuality exuding from himself. But it was of course a mere fancy – the pungency of horse and stable predominated as per usual.

"Don't you believe it. Dust in his eye is what his problem was. A wink and come-on? – Ha! Anyway, he's old enough to be your father and all."

"I bet he was some kind of an adventurer in his younger days."

"Certainly not a Casanova."

"What do you mean, an adventurer?"

"Well, you know, always one for the women and that sort of thing."

"I told you, he was no Casanova."

"Want a wink from him, is it?"

"More than that, I'd say!"

The females erupted into coarse laughter at this, and a grin spread wide and wolfishly on the old man's swarthy, suncracked face.

'Well, at least they're talking about me,' he thought, reassured, 'there must be something in that.'

So he cocked his ear some more with mounting interest:

The third woman – whom the old ranchero knew well, with a face like a codfish and a voice that could crack granite – was ready with a sniper shot:

"If you think Pancho is one for the señoritas, then I'm a pickled chilli," causing the others to hoot over that kind sally.

The old man, well hidden as heretofore among cornstalks three rows away, grinned a Mephistophelian sort of grin.

All the same, the comment from fish-face had, as it were, swiped the salsa off his taco.

"Speaking of which," one of the threesome opened up again, "My Mariano has taken to eating pickled chillies of late. And they're not cheap, either, pickled chillies. At any rate, he can't get enough – "

"Just like mine! He can't get enough, so he keeps telling me."

"Tee-hee-hee!"

"Shush, you! And wash your mouth out."

" – can't get enough of them pickled chillies, he can't. The only trouble is, apart from them being dear to buy, they give him wind something dreadful.

"At nighttime especially, he breaks wind like a damn burro. Loud enough to wake the whole pueblito, everyone no doubt imagining that a thunderstorm is about to break.

"I tell you straight, no word of a lie, one of these fine nights he'll lift the thatching off the roof," which caused another storm of vulgar laughter.

The women's idle chitchat and murmurings faded, and the noises of the land returned to the old man's ears, as he went on with his picking and sacking the beans.

And joyfully ruminating without reservation a certain newfound pride over what he'd overheard, as though he had won a prize for some special achievement.

68

Cornfield Conversations II

Afternoon came on and the old man was still hard at it bean-picking. He could now overhear two boys whispering a couple of rows away; and again, they too were quite unaware of Pancho's near presence.

"Oye, Alberto, how many beans have you got?"

"I'm not counting. Do you think I'm counting them? What's the point of counting them! Just filling my bag, I am."

"Okay, how much have you got, then?"

"About half a bag, I reckon."

"Half a bag already! Have you been taking them from out my sack and putting them in yours?"

"Do you want a fist in your face or something? No, I haven't taken any from your sack. Why should I want to do that anyway?"

"Well, señor Ramírez – you know, old Pancho – says he's going to give four packets of Chiclets to the first one with a full sack."

"Is that what he said?"

"That's what he said. As true as I'm here, he told us all. You mustn't have been there."

A brief pause, then:

"Alberto!"

"¿Sí?"

"If you empty your half-sack into mine, then we'll soon have a full one, and we can get four packets of Chiclets which we can share, hey?"

"Ah no, gracias. I don't trust you."

Another, longer pause, then:

"But you can empty yours into mine. I can trust myself."

"Forget it, Alberto, I'll pick my own beans and fill my own sack is what I'll do, and do it faster."

"Well, please yourself …"

Pancho straightened up for a moment, hands pressing at his lower aching back. He glanced around him, saw rebozo-clad heads bobbing up and others dropping as the women worked on either side of him. In the bobbing and ducking of their heads in the separate rows in the bright sunlight, they appeared to him as a swinging string of beads loosely strung with gaps in them.

He bobbed down too and continued on. His spatula workman's hand groped and snatched on, stripping each line of growth of its bounty.

Hearing voices once more, over to his right, he stayed down and paused a moment. A couple of the young ones, he recognised. He listened to them as he carried on with his picking:

"Show me then, Rosaría."

"You promise you won't tell if I do?"

"I promise. I already told you so, didn't I? Come on, before someone comes, let me see it."

"A moment …"

A brief silence, except for a slight rustle of material. Pancho held his breath.

"Oh, Rosaría, it's just a slit! Why, my own sister has one of them."

"All us muchachas have a slit there. Are you *loco* or what? What did you expect to see, anyway?"

"Well, I thought … I thought you might have a hole."

"A hole!" came the exclamation.

"Sí, you know, a nice round hole."

"Well, it's a slit and there's an end to it. Now show me yours. You did promise, remember?"

"Okay. Wait a moment …"

And a moment passed.

"Ayí, Felipe!" laughed a little girl's voice.

"What? What's wrong then?" asked a little boy's voice, one still feeling cheated and hard done by.

"Why ask about a hole when you have something so tiny! I've never seen anything so small, not even a little baby worm!"

Pancho put a hand to his mouth in order to suppress the laughter welling up in his chest.

And the air thrummed with a heavy drone of insects. Also in the air were bird notes and dust motes. Through the dusty hours long of the harvest days, the music played in the pueblo, sounding cheerily over the valley, the fields, and the nearby hills. It was as though the Earth itself were singing, joyful in its autumn fill of food, its seed and pod and shell, the sap-and-salt of the living land.

And Mexico's music was the music that lights a world. Its scent is of dust and flowers and livestock; its people fashioned, as it would seem, from the clay of music and song, and numerous in their progeny in this fast-growing many-peopled happy land.

PART FIFTEEN

PART FIFTEEN

69

A Fire and A Death

"Señor Ramírez!"

The high piercing child's voice split the air of the pumpkin field where Pancho was at present working. The old man glanced up into the brilliant light of a mid-morn sun, a huge pumpkin in his hands.

"¡Oye, señor!"

"Uuy! What is it, Angel? What's the matter?" he asked of a small, dimple-faced boy who suddenly materialised before him; panting like a puppy, face glistening with perspiration, streams of it filling his dimples.

"Señor Ramírez, you must come quickly!" he breathlessly spluttered. "Your hut is on fire, señor!"

"¡Újule!" and Pancho dropped the pumpkin.

He began to run, leaping over piles of pumpkins in his path.

"Is it bad, Angel?" he panted between his teeth, as the little one tried to keep up with him. "How bad is it?"

"Very bad, señor," burst out the youngster. "Blazing up to the sky it is!" and Angel's deep dimples shot from one part of each cheek to the other.

Pancho soon reached the end of the field. He crashed through a stand of *carrizos* and ploughed across the river like a gunboat. Up a hillside he ran and along a winding goat track to his old home. The hut was thoroughly well ablaze with nary a hope of saving any of it.

The old man pushed his way through a small crowd of onlookers, and quickly stepped back from the heat and smoke. He watched miserably as his modest little home, and the few precious possessions contained therein, all, all of it burning to the ground.

The stable at the rear was also totally destroyed. He thanked God that his white rawboned mare, Macha, was safely stabled over on the Ramos farmstead.

He felt utterly crushed, lost; at a loss to what he should do about it, but there was nothing he could do, that was plainly, painfully clear. He was like a bird with a broken wing.

Is this some kind of omen? he wondered darkly, watching the roof beams finally collapsing, sending fresh flames and sparks soaring up in the air.

He remained there in the same position, hardly moving a muscle, until the hut was merely a smouldering heap of ashes.

A while later someone was riding a chestnut colt along the goat track, Pancho recognising him as one of the men who worked for his longtime ranchero friend, don Fernando. This man worked for that same don Fernando from whom Cándido and José had won a stable in a poker game – not long after the time when José had negligently burned down a stable on don Roberto's ranch, and which had to be replaced.

"Victor, hola!" Pancho greeted him almost with a grimace, unable to put on a proper smile at present. "¿Que paso, amigo?"

The man reined his colt but remained seated in the saddle, staring at a black, smouldering ruin before him.

"It's a sad business, Pancho," he said without preamble but ready to console the other.

"Ah, que caray, these things happen," the old man responded philosophically. "I expect I'll find someplace somewhere to rest my head of a night, even if it's but a stable," perhaps inferring here the stable that was won in a game of cards.

The man Victor was a trifle confused. "No, no, I mean about poor old don Fernando," he said, his confusion replaced by a look of concern.

"Don Fernando? What about him? He's alright isn't he, Victor?"

"Why, he's dead, Pancho. Died only yesterday it was. So he did, and quite sudden like. His heart gave up on him was the doc's verdict. So you didn't know about it, then?"

"No, I didn't …" breathed the old man, stupefied with this fresh calamity.

Misfortunes seem to be the order of the day, he mused miserably, heaving a sigh as if all the world's cares had suddenly fallen upon his shoulders.

Although he now sorely grieved over the death of his long-held friend, the old man could not but inadvertently feel a sudden guilty satisfaction in being alive himself. But in the same vein, also more aware of his own mortality.

All the same he was feeling too kind of raw and tired. So bone-achingly tired it almost hurt.

He moved his legs for the first time in a while, gave a jerky kick outward with one foot, bending his knee. And did the same with the other foot. He had stood in one position far too long and needed to reactivate his blood circulation. Or perhaps he unconsciously kicked out to ascertain the fact he was himself still alive – alive and kicking, as it were, as he would himself have put it.

He realised that the ranchero Victor was still there, loosely holding the reins of his mount, his attitude expectant and still concerned.

"Why didn't anyone tell me?" he asked the rider heavy-heartedly.

"Word was sent to don Roberto. We thought you'd know soon enough."

"I've been working the Ramos fields, harvesting, you see – And the funeral? When's the funeral, or is that over and done with as well?"

"Oh, that'll be day after tomorrow, I do believe. Eleven-o-clock. San Juan church."

"Another damned omen," the old ranchero mumbled. "Ay que caray, man wonders why and for what, and God decides who."

"What's that, Pancho?"

"I said he was a good friend of mine, don Fernando was …"

"Of course. Everyone knew it. Written in stone, you might say. You two go a long way back, to be sure. Most folk know of your close ties with him, I do bless his soul – " the ranchero Victor crossed himself, hitting his face twice with the slack of his reins.

"Well, Pancho," he went on in a lighter tone, "the son-in-law gets the ranch, so everyone believes and I'm not surprised. Sí, the land, the property, the livestock – every damn thing!"

"I suppose so…" Pancho morosely mauled his moustache with one hand.

"Well, and what happened here, hermano?" pointing at the smouldering fire debris of the old man's home.

"Oh, just burning up a whole load of rubbish," replied Pancho, now wishing to make light of it.

"It's a bad business about the poor boss." The ranchero gave a polite nod, said, "I'll be on my way then. ¡Adiós!" giving a respectful farewell salute.

The rider dug heels into the colt's flanks and set off at a fast jolting trot. Pancho watched him disappear beyond a bluff, and continued to brood.

'So don Fernando's own world is gone forever,' and because of it the old man felt that his world was now sadly diminished, smaller in every way.

He stared at the remains of what was once his own humble home, but without actually seeing it, not fully taking it in right at present, his mind in a dark whirl and quite elsewhere.

70

A Sympathetic Soul and an Invitation

Later, still at the fire disaster site, kicking at cinders in hope of finding he knew not what, Pancho cheered up but only slightly when he saw doña María Ramos hove into sight, puffing along the goat track.

When she reached the old man she laid a comforting hand on his shoulder. Her sympathetic eyes travelled to his lined face, measuring the depth of her friend's evident misery, then up at the brash blue of sky and back again to the old man.

It is all part of the human condition, she was thinking, not consciously but with feminine intuitiveness.

"Little Angel told me about it – the fire – but couldn't say how it had happened. Would you know by any chance?" she quietly asked him.

"Hmm ... I think I remember smashing a tequila bottle by the woodpile the other day ... " Pancho paused a moment, a bleak smile on his troubled face. "You know how it is," he carried on. "A shard of glass and the sun burning down, a wisp of straw underneath. It wouldn't take long for a fire to flare up," he ended, with a despondent look.

"Never mind, never you mind. It's happened and that's it. There's an end to it and nothing can change it now."

María again put a hand on his shoulder and gently squeezed. He faced her squarely, an expression on his weathered, aged features that spoke volumes. "You can stay with us, for as long as you like," she assured him warmly, with repeated pats on his shoulder. "You can have your old room by the cornstore."

"Our house is your house, you know that, dear soul."

"Ay, María, I thank you gladly. But I'm not so much bothered about this," pointing to his wrecked home. "No, it's don Fernando I'm thinking on. He's dead, you see," gazing back at her with seemingly unseeing eyes.

"Dead! Don Fernando! You don't mean - ?"

María looked at the smoking heap of ashes with horror, her arms already rising to describe a cross.

"Ah, no!" said Pancho hurriedly, realising what she was thinking.

He managed to squeeze out a smile from a too taut face. "He died just yesterday. A heart attack, according to Victor – you know Victor – who told me not ten minutes ago."

"You mean to say you've only just found out about don Fernando?"

"Not ten minutes ago."

"Oh my dear Francisco, it's no wonder you're so upset, doubly so with this burnt mess here that was your home. Everything in it totally destroyed, you can see. Then getting more bad news on top of that. Oh, I am so very sorry – sorry for poor old don Fernando, and sorry for you too."

Pancho rubbed at his jaw. "It seems all the old ones are dying off of a sudden. Wasn't so long ago when Santo gave up the ghost," he said despondently.

"Oh my dear, old Santo was pushing ninety at least, if not more. It was well past his time."

"It'll be my turn too soon enough, I shouldn't wonder," he next remarked in a hard, brittle tone.

"Ha! Such stuff and nonsense!" María returned at once with heat. "You? Ha! Don't talk silly, and stop feeling sorry for yourself. ¡Chihuahuas! It's this burnt out old home of yours, and the news of don Fernando's passing on, one bad thing after another and in short order as well.

"That's what's making you so low. It'll pass, dear soul, I can promise you that. You'll be living with us, Francisco, and probably outlive us all, just to spite us, you rascal, you!" she rammed into him, in an effort to cheer him up.

Doña María decided to try a different tactic:

"Do you believe you've led a good life? An honest answer now, Francisco, if you would," she said with appealing chirpiness.

"Good in what way, María, for it has many grades and meanings."

"I suppose I mean being honest with others and caring for others."

"Uuy, you can answer that better than me," the old man nearly smiled.

"Ha! I thought you'd say that. What I really want to know is, *how* you have led a good life – if such is the case, it goes without saying. What do you think about it, deep down in yourself."

"Again I say, my serious minded orchid, you know me better than most, so you tell me. You suspect there are flaws in me, am I right?"

"Certainly you have flaws, many of them, but then most everybody has flaws."

"Sí, María, it's part of our human make-up I guess, warts and wrinkles and wrong-doing. We are all capable of it, we're all at it, some more than others."

Old Pancho glanced skyward, saw what he thought looked like a buzzard silently sailing in the thermals.

He went on: "So, my dove, you want that I assess my own flaws, is it? Or count them, if that is possible, eh?

"No, we need to be who we are, and know our own identity, be it good or bad or a bit of both, which is usually the case.

"But the main thing all in all, the main matter is to be happy, and it doesn't take much to be happy, enjoy the simple pleasures of life, no great effort needed there. As long as we can be open to others, share their problems along with your own.

"What we experience, how we relate to the many obstacles and contradictions thrown our way … That, María, is how life is and always will be, though I don't have to tell you something you already well know. At any rate, once we accept it as a fact, take life on its own terms, then we are on sure tracks to any-which-way: Satisfaction, contentment … sí, and happiness itself."

Doña María, having listened to her old friend with empathy, with quiet, patient passivity, now felt that she should say something. She did:

"You're not happy about your home burning to the ground – sorry for sounding cruel and crude – and you are not happy over losing your friend Fernando. That, I can understand, but – "

"We are not meant to be happy all the waking hours," Pancho interrupted her, "because it doesn't work that way. Sí, María, you are correct there. I must confess I've lost a fair deal the notion of happiness. I suppose in good time I'll get over losing my home, my old hide-out, eventually come to terms with it – as I think just may be happening right now.

"And instead of grieving over Fernando's passing, I ought to be ready to grieve over everyone, because we too are destined to go the same way – it's a matter of timing.

"I accept these basic truths, and by and by in time I'll no doubt regain that sense of balance, and once again enjoy life as one must. Enjoy a kick of coffee or tequila … and be happy in the process."

The old man was inclined to think that it was so.

"Happy as Epicurus," he concluded.

"Epic-Epicurus? Another one of your ranchero friends?"

"No, my flower, Epicurus was an ancient Greek philosopher." (Don Roberto's library had a lot to answer for, old Pancho was thinking)

"Ah, I see …" María smiled a mischievous smile, amused by this, twinkling her eyes at him. "This Ep-Epicurus, would he be some relation of yours? Some old ancestor?"

Which put a decided halt to their little insightful confabulation.

Doña María now thought it time to move on to more practical matters, thinking of accommodation for the ranchero. She hesitated a moment, as something else occurred to her mind.

Once more, she patted him on the shoulder with affection, and said:

"Look, dear friend, soon I'll be off to town for the *Day of the Dead*. I didn't go last year, but now there's no excuse. I'm taking the little ones with me, Ruth and Julia. We'll be staying with my sister Esperanza and her husband Juan. Now then, you are coming with us. No 'ifs' or 'buts' about it either. It'll do you good to come, a nice change for you.

"Look you, Francisco Ramírez, you'll be around to reach a hundred years. Eventually, they would have to beat you to death with a big stick!

"Come on, cease your moping and let's go home, shall we? Your new home with us. We can put you up with us no problem … and put up with you easily enough as well. ¡Ándale!

PART SIXTEEN

PART SIXTEEN

71

Juan and Esperanza's Casa

So Pancho found himself once again – twice in the same year! – yet again in the town of San Stefan, this time in the company of mamá and the girls. They settled in easily in the house of Juan and Esperanza.

It was a large, rambling building, with a maze or warren of interconnected rooms; some large and long and high-ceilinged, practically furniture-free, except for the odd chest of drawers here and a truckle-bed or two somewhere else; and not a few tiny rooms, cramped and cluttered as a townhouse pantry.

The place was a happy household; carefree and chaotic, noisy and untidy; invariably teeming with young humanity; Esperanza's own brood of four – or was it five, for old Pancho lost count – and their friends from the immediate neighbourhood, plus cousins that always popped in, bringing along their friends, too.

There seemed nothing more entertaining than a houseful of happy children, as the round-cheeked youngsters ran riot in the rooms, and there was no such thing as privacy – or peace and quiet. Doña María's younger sister, Esperanza, a large-sized, red-faced, jolly woman, would not have it any other way.

It was in truth a typical Mexican family home.

Without adults in attendance to marshal order and discipline, in many of the rooms the kids seemed wild. The girls, particularly, were constantly shrieking and laughing. Their games kept them joyously occupied and doing no harm, as Pancho could plainly see. But what an almighty din they made! However, he was not complaining.

For the old man it was something of a tonic and a welcome change for his bruised spirits. These family divertissements reminded him ruefully that once in past time he, too, had had a family.

Here, in this town dwelling, he flourished and soon became his old cheerful self again. ('Ha, Chihuahuas,' doña María had earlier thought, before their arrival in town, 'where was his fire, his wit, his vigour?')

The children sensed a happiness he felt being among them, and this they exploited and tormented him to the fullest possible degree. It was mamá however who dominated the entire roost, Esperanza playing the secondary, submissive role of a younger sister once more – doña María stamping down hard on anyone who dared to overstep the mark. In all fairness to mamá's 'methods', the kids knuckled under to this new regime with equanimity.

The husband Juan, a mild-mannered easy-going fellow – half the size of his bounteous beauty of a wife – was out of it most of the time, working long hours as a clerk at the local post office, spending his evenings playing dominoes with his cronies at the corner cantina. He drank very little during his time in the cantina, a couple bottles of beer at the most, and was more than eager to play and interact with his offspring in the relatively short periods he was at home. Usually, these appearances were at meal-times before the minors were shooed off to their beds.

On the morning of his first day in town Pancho was up early, as was his habit, taking a short constitutional in the stone-flagged courtyard. He had left María in the kitchen, her rightful domain, bustling about there, teaching the eldest girl Erendira how to make a proper *salsa*, from a recipe of her own concoction, and extolling the merits of *epazote* and oregano for the savouring of other dishes.

Two or three scrawny hens clucked with scant enthusiasm, chipping away with their beaks but getting short shrift from a yard paved with solid flagstones.

There, also in the courtyard, he saw Esperanza, fat but fit, and full of chuckling laughter. She stood at a deep stone sink, up to her armpits in soapsuds, thrashing clothes against a ridged washboard.

"Imelda, I shan't tell you again!" giggled that good lady. "Get from out of there or I'll be warming your backside for you – and that's a promise!"

The old man looked around the empty yard with some mystification, hitching up an eyebrow questioningly.

"Oh, Pancho! Buenos dias. Did the kids wake you this morning?" she asked gaily, her plump face shining with the joy of morning, her spirits carefree and lightsome.

"I'm thinking of selling them for butcher's meat, my lot. What do you think to that, then? *Butcher's meat,* I tell you!" she went on happily, podgy arms plunging into soapy water and dragging up a dripping of shirts and 'smalls'.

Then:

"I SAID I'M THINKING OF SELLING THEM FOR BUTCHER'S MEAT!" Esperanza boomed at the top of her voice, which caused Pancho to nearly jump out of his skin at the suddenness and loudness of it.

"Imelda! You'll cop it, I tell you. Stop that at once. Oh! Come on out this minute!"

The old man watched as Esperanza's generous skirts took weird shapes in their folds. And a young one popped out her head, face flushed and hair dishevelled. She sprang from under her mother's voluminous skirt and darted away, disappearing into the kitchen or someplace, a long shriek on her lips.

Esperanza chuckled on, shaking her head at the old ranchero, as much as to say, there is nothing to be done, you simply can't stop their mischief.

He dawdled and chatted with this immensely cheerful soul for a spell, then continued on at his walking exercise, boots loudly clacking about the length of the yard.

He happened to notice a cat lying by the side of a wooden crate in a far corner of the yard. A tawny tomcat, thickly furred and well-nourished. Too fat for a yard-cat, he conjectured, must be a pampered pet.

What really attracted his attention was the animal's curious behaviour, lying there on its side in a strangely stiff posture, white-socked paws pelting out at thin air.

He went to investigate further, to satisfy his curiosity.

The feline creature stared, eyes bulging and almost popping from their sockets. It stiffened further, evidently giving up a straining struggle, then stilled. It was quite dead. It happened in only a moment. Must have choked to death on a fur-ball, he guessed, gazing down on its thick fur coat, and at the unfortunate creature's glazed, large-marbled eyes.

And at the very moment it expired, when the last of its precious air was spent, all the dogs in the neighbourhood set up a clamour of whining and howling. The old man was amazed that the dogs should know an animal in their vicinity had died at that precise moment. Even the insects knew, for already there was an influx of horseflies and bluebottles buzzing and hovering and settling on the rich, furry, fresh carcass.

How had they known? He pulled furiously at his moustache, gloomy thoughts returning to him for a short while.

Later, in the afternoon, Pancho was again in the yard. It was unusually quiet and empty. Then, beyond the high wall, there came a little boy's shout, and a sudden uproar of schoolyardish sounds, a free-for-all backstreet violence of noise. Piled on further from outside with the harsh braying of a burro, barking of dogs, and yard cocks crowing up their craws.

Town life! It only needed for –

Church bells began to ring, several churches at it. Town life!

His attention was taken by the sight of two boys who had suddenly materialised, as they are apt to do, noted the old man.

The twosome stood staring at him with interest. One boy nudged the other and said, within hearing distance:

"See that hombre, that's Pancho."

"Who?"

"Pancho! Pancho Villa. He's a bandit!"

"Him?" rudely pointing.

"Sí, of course him. A bandit, he is."

"A real bandit?"

"Would I lie to you!"

And the young ones didn't seem to care, or were perhaps childishly unaware, that this rough looking ranchero type was hearing every word they were spouting, so freely, so touchingly naively.

"There's a Pancho Limón lives on our street," announced the second boy. "He's a Pancho too, see!"

"Pah! Not like him," another pointed finger directed at the old man. "He kills hombres, he does, because he's *Pancho Villa*."

"Pancho Limón, who lives on our street, he kills as well ... he kills chickens."

The old ranchero backed away, turned his face, a wide grin creasing his swarthy, '*banditry*' face.

He returned indoors.

After an exploration of the premises in its entirety, Pancho discovered and decided to take advantage of a useful townhouse utility – a shower room – a dank, cellar-like place he'd found located at the lower rear end of this whimsically structured property.

He recognised the shower as such, although he had never in his life taken one. Now was his opportunity to do so.

Dust-motes danced in a narrow band of light cutting through a small, one-paned window positioned high up the wall facing him.

Shortly, he set himself to showering, feeling all of a sudden 'the modern town man'. And soon found that it ran only cold water, his heavyset figure jumping and jigging under a sharp, stinging spray of mountain-ice water.

Without a by-your-leave, a clutch of kids scooted into the room, probably in hopes of hiding from their playmates – it sounded like there was yet another crowd of young ones out in the yard, clamouring to get into the house.

The kids already in, and in the shower-room at that, stopped dead in their tracks.

"Ooo!" they cried as a single voice, utter astonishment stitched to their little rosy faces.

They stared, transfixed in amazement and disbelief at this hairy, soapsud-clad, broad-backed old man, stark white-bellied mother naked, in the throes of hopping about, crouching and cringing under the cutting cold darts of water shooting from the showerhead.

The absurd, grotesque sight was really too much for the education of young and innocent eyes. Which did not stop two or three from bursting into fits of the giggles.

Old Pancho was now aware that he was not alone, that he had company of sorts. Turning round his red-wet head, he glared fierce-eyed at them, horribly rolled his eyes at them, roaring like a lion.

The little ones scattered like a startled flock of starlings, childish rips of laughter ringing in the empty rooms.

Pancho's very first shower!

72

A Reunion

One day Pancho was exploring once again the central plaza area. He ambled across the *jardín*, where warblers and orioles and other such songbirds flew and chittered noisily about thick laurel trees.

A sudden surprise confronted the old ranchero, for there before him, sitting on an iron bench and sketching the *parroquia* yet again, was his English friend, Matt Conners, whom he had first met in the wintertime.

He crept up behind the young man, clapped a hand on his shoulder, and said, trying to disguise his voice:

"¡Oye, gringo! You have two pesos for me? I have *beeg* family for to feed, señor."

"Pancho! Bloody hellfire, it's Pancho!" exclaimed Conners, jumping up with a delighted grin on his pale, English face. "It's bloody good to see you, me old matey! How are you keeping? *¿Que paso, amigo?*" breaking at the last into his usual atrocious Spanish.

"Muy bien. And you, my English man friend, are you well?" returned the Mexican, shaking the other's hand.

"Great, just great! Couldn't be better. Here, sit down. Oh hells bells but it's good to see you, Pancho. And it's nice to be back in Mexico. I missed all this, y'know."

"Ah, so you have been some place else, is it?"

"Yes, the States. America, Pancho, the good old US of A. My visa ran out end of February and I was forced to quit the country sharpish. So I went to the States, to a friend of mine in San Francisco."

"Bueno …Ay que bueno," beamed the old man.

"Hell, yes! But oh my, it's smashing to see my Mexican friend, too," as the young Englishman impulsively took Pancho's hand to shake once more.

"What unbelievable good luck I had back then," Conners resumed with enthusiasm. "I managed to get a lift from here in San Stefan, all the bloody way to Sacramento – Over two thousand miles, Pancho! The long way, y'see, which I'll explain in a minute.

"I met up with a couple of American girls, art students from the Instituto. One of them – Charla, she's called – was beating around in a big yellow Ford truck, and she offered to take me as far as Sacramento – in California."

"Sí, I know that."

"Of course. Anyway, it took us six days, and what a trip it was. We travelled up as far as Ciudad Juarez and across the Rio Grande – Sorry, you call it Rio Bravo, right?"

"But that's opposite El Paso," the old ranchero interjected. "Lower corner of Texas country."

"Yes, the long way round, y'see, as I mentioned. Maybe I should now explain. Charla wanted to get into Sacramento by the back door, sort of, because her old truck needed relicensing. So we took the long scenic route.

"I'm glad it turned out that way. Only, at the El Paso border the yanks wouldn't allow me in, into the country I mean, because I didn't have a valid visa. Thought I'd get through on the strength of my return air ticket to England. The buggers stopped me there, with only the river to cross to reach the United States.

"It was as well those American girls were with me, or God knows what I'd have done. They could cross over, y'see, and they promised to stick with me. We stayed overnight in Juarez, in the hope of me getting a visa at the Yankee consulate in the morning."

Conners smiled wickedly, continued on: "You know, Pancho, the three of us checked into one *single* room in a downtown hotel, and the desk-clerk never batted an eye. We were pretty skint at the time – "

"Skint? What is that?"

"Short of cash, little money, and could only afford the one room. Proved an interesting night …

"Next morning I got my visa, after many long bloody hours waiting. I should have worn a suit and tie, look respectable, you know what I mean? When you're in jeans and scruffs you don't get much attention paid you, leastways, not the right kind.

"Anyway, we were in Texas at last, the western tip of it, and we drove clear across New Mexico and into Arizona. Charla went out of her way to show me the wonders of the Grand Canyon and Hoover Dam – Oh, and we slept under the stars one night at the Gila River Indian Reservation, without permission, though managed to keep our scalps!

"We moved on to Nevada, and Charla kindly took us to Las Vegas, a place I'd long wanted to see. All glitter and glitz and blazing neon up and down the main boulevard.

"And guess what, Pancho, I won over a thousand dollars on the bloody slot machines! Which is why I'm back in Mexico, here in San Stefan for another round – as long as the brass lasts out."

"Brass? What is brass?"

"Money, pesos in plenty."

"You could live here for years with all those dollars, my friend," grinned the old Mexican, happy for his English companion's good fortune. He allowed the other to babble on, missing only odd words and phrases.

"We drove on from Vegas to the edge of Death Valley in California. Should we cross it? we each thought. And we did. It was alright, we had plenty of petrol and water – and bottled beer!

"Then we were back into Nevada once more, up the high Sierra Nevada mountain range, up as far as Lake Tahoe. On along Highway 50 – what was the old Pony Express Trail, apparently – and down into Sacramento.

"The minute we hit Sacramento the cops pulled in Charla for her out-of-date license plate, and they booked her, the rotten sods! Well, my friends picked me up there, after a nervous phone call, and I spent a few luxurious months in San Francisco. Touring around a bit, but painting and drawing mostly.

"Because of the Vegas win, amigo, I flew back into Mexico, after getting my visa in Los Angeles and flying from there. And now, here I am in dear San Stefan, meeting old friends, and I've been rabbiting on to you like a ruddy football commentator."

The young Englishman smiled blissfully at his Mexican companion, said, "Are you staying long in town, Pancho?"

"I'll be here a short while, sí. I have come to town for the Day of the Dead."

"Wow! I've heard of that. Well, good. Then we can have a few nights out, hey? Share a jar or two, toss off a few tequilas?"

The old ranchero broadly grinned. "Los Dos Durangos bar, is it?" he said.

73

Dia de los Muertos

On the afternoon of the first day in November, the people of the town began preparing for or making their pilgrimage to the cemetery, to pay respects to the dead and departed, their *muertitos*.

They came in quietly but with open hearts, for this was not a sad or solemn occasion; it was not a time to mourn, or for grief or morbid lament. This was simply a kind of vigil or devotional, a remembrance, a communion with those who were gone, by being present on this *dia de los muertos*.

They brought food and flowers and candles. They came in warm clothing and brought blankets with them, for their vigil would most likely last on into the next day, November 2nd, the actual Day of the Dead.

The gloom-stricken aspect of the cemetery didn't bother anyone, not in the least; it wasn't seen or sensed but unconsciously accorded respect and not a little reverence.

The townsfolk filed in an orderly manner through wide open gates of the cemetery grounds, spreading out along pebbled pathways, passing irregular lines and a helter-skelter of headstones and gravesites. Kids played about these headstones, in a somewhat subdued and decorous kind of way.

Mamá arrived in the early evening with the girls, accompanied by old Pancho. Earlier that day mamá had wandered over the town marketplace, where numerous small stalls sold cakes and sweetmeats, of a different sort than usual. Made with pastry or sponge-cake, pastillage and sugar candy, shaped or decorated in a similar manner. That is, in the form of *calvaleras* or skulls, or iced over and painted with lined drawings of skulls. Folk bought them by the score to be offered to their dead. It wasn't considered morbid to any degree, or insulting in any way. It was for those still alive, representative of an integral aspect of the country's cultural heritage.

Mamá settled herself fussily at the foot of her mother's grave. She tidied around her space, uprooting weeds and throwing them to one side. Then she began arranging and rearranging her many bags and baskets of foodstuffs and bunches of flowers.

Ruth and Julia chattered between themselves, and Pancho stared around, taking in the scene. The cemetery grounds appeared unkempt and scratty, was his view of it. He also took in the fact that he was the only male person there, apart from a scampering of small boys.

People went on by mamá's little group, loaded with bags and boxes under their arms. Lines of old trees, along one side of the cemetery walls, threw sinister shadows across the graves. And out of a symphony of dead leaf-sound came a wind's adagio of prolonged and saddened sighing, mutely harmonious with the orange and lilac glow of the setting autumn sunfire.

Mamá placed her flowers about the grave of her parent, and the girls quietened, clasping hands and lowering their heads. Pancho sat gazing at a black globule of a long-legged spider, stilting from behind an overturned earthenware urn. It soon vanished.

Mamá softly prayed for a length of time.

The sun had set and dusk was coming in. Votive candles were lit all over the place. Soft murmurings were heard from end to end of the cemetery grounds. The myriad lights, bobbing and wavering in a sea of growing darkness, appeared as a single living entity. Moths flitted and scribbled out their erratic flightways in the fast falling dusk.

The girls became restless after a time, no doubt bored because nothing of interest was happening.

"Can we go take a wander round, mamá?" politely asked Ruth.

"Acapulco, is it? Tampico?"

"We don't want to sit about, mamá."

"Muy bien, that's fine, but stay together, mind. Julia, let Rutí keep a hold of your hand. Don't wander off too far. Stay in the grounds here, stay where I can still see you – "

"¡Ayí, mamá!"

"Okay, you know what I mean, show your faces now and then. Come straight back when you feel hungry. Off you go then, ándale."

The two girls were off in a flurry, happy for the freedom just granted, leaving mamá and Pancho sitting on their own.

As the two free spirits melted away into the crowds, mamá manoeuvred into a more comfortable position, and said:

"Do you remember the birthday party we had for Ruth's eighth? I baked a nice cream cake with candles on it." The old man smiled at the memory of it. "And when she blew out the candles you dunked her face in the cream piping on top of the cake. You remember, rascal-face?"

"Ay well, it was because of your Antonio. It was Antonio who put me up to it. Told me himself to do that. Said it was the regular custom of the family, and that I could do the honours."

"It was the same time when you danced on our big kitchen table. You got up there, head full of mezcal, and started stomping over that table of ours. Like a big bear drunk on honey, that was you. And my little niña says, 'Mamá, what's he doing up there?' So I told her straight, I said, 'Why, my little sweetie, he's stamping on the flies to kill them dead.'"

"Sí, María," ruefully grinned the old ranchero. "I'd sure had a skinful that time and no mistake." He leaned toward mamá at his side. "It was your Antonio, you know, who was throwing mezcal down my throat, like there was no *mañana*," causing a spluttering of incredulity at his side.

Though she would never admit it, except to herself, mamá was always held in awe of Pancho's powerful life-force, his irrepressible personality. She saw clearly that he seemed to be losing it of late – because of his recent misfortunes – and ardently hoped that he would, given a space more of time, he would reinvigorate himself and be once more the old Pancho she admired so much ... even loved, in a chastely, sisterly way.

He was at this moment gazing up at a now black velvet night sky, at the immutable eternity of blacksky, from where diamond-sharp eyes of stars glared and glittered back at him.

A SHORT INTERLUDE

74

Summer Tales I

It was a fairly hot day, naturally enough, it being smack in the middle of summer, and high noon at that.

The rancheros were comfortably squatting in the shade of the main stable's double doors. Only Emilio was deep inside the stable, having a *siesta*. The men had already eaten, silent and passive for the moment, allowing things to digest, or to simmer, or to brood upon.

Cándido glanced over at Gerardo, who was absorbed in plaiting strips of leather.

"My God, but you're ugly, Gerardo!" he suddenly shot out.

"You only just noticed?" whipped in José maliciously, holding up a fat, freshly rolled *cigarro* as though it were a marshal's baton.

"Hang on! Hold on, Gerardo," roared Pancho. "Don't you rush off in a huff. Come back here, I say. Sit yourself down, that's it, amigo, and listen to what I have to tell these two puppy turds."

Gerardo regained his squatting position in the semi-circle of horsemen.

Began Pancho, glaring at the two 'mean streaks':

"You are what you are, and you are what you are right in here – " tapping his skull with a heavy loaded forefinger. "Each of us is what we are in our mind, in our brain. Physical attributes or looks count for handfuls of dust. Everything depends on what we are in our heads."

The old man's expression turned inwards with strong thoughts, and went on:

"Before my father died, for a twelve-month before he passed away, my papá did not recognise me, his own son. Nor did he know my brothers. Worst still, he failed to recognise the one woman in his life – my mamá! – after a lifetime together, since their early youth, in fact.

"He had lost his mind, his brain diseased, you see, and didn't even know himself. So the father I'd known, loved and respected all my own young life ... he had gone. There, physically, but as good as gone.

"Now, I come to my point:

"Gerardo here, no matter how he looks on the outside, physical attributes or physical defects – what you will, whatever to speak of.

"Well, the fact of the matter is this: I don't think I have ever known such a decent fellow, such a kindly soul, who would do anything for anyone without reward or thanks. Inside of him, in his head, is the manly beauty of a saint.

"There now, I have said my piece," and the old ranchero started to fumble and fold a horse blanket, as something to do with his hands.

Cándido glanced lowly-eyed at José, said, "Did you manage to separate that foal from the mare, José?"

"Sí, I did, eventually. Took some doing, mind. All's well now, I guess," he responded, head down.

He finger-pinched the end of his 'smoke', putting it in the top pocket of his *camisa*. Guiltily feeling that he somehow did not deserve a nice fat cigarro. Not at present at any rate. He was for the moment looking the definition of iniquity, the epitome of insignificance, a complete nonentity.

Gerardo, back plaiting his pieces of leather, had a strangely beatific, saintly smile on his rubbery face. He was, it seemed to old Pancho, almost handsome-looking at that moment, in a rough, rugged way.

Then young Juan made an appearance, loping lithely in like a lean lion. "I've just seen don Roberto's hog he bought this morning. My God, but it was an ugly-looking beast. You've never seen the like – What? Why are you all laughing?"

"Didn't you know, Juanito," put in José wholesomely, "that hogs are really quite beautiful creatures."

"Sí," clocked in Cándido, "you can ask any sow."

Juan shrugged, stepped into the stable, to look in on his mount.

75

Cemetery Conversations I

Meanwhile, jumping forward to autumn, returning to November 2nd and the Day of the Dead...

Said doña María presently, "I saw some sombreros in a shop by the *mercado* this morning."

"Hmm?"

"Good strong material they were, real nice and smart I thought. Light tan and mid tan, from fawn to dark brown – such a selection. Any one of them would suit you a treat."

"I'd like to buy you one for your birthday next year. You do have a birthday next year, don't you?"

"My dear María, we all have a birthday – and usually once a year."

"Ha! I know it, but you don't, do you? You once told me that your birthday falls on the twenty-ninth of February, so you can only celebrate it every four years. You said so yourself, Francisco, making you now – what will it be? – making you only sixteen or seventeen at the most!"

"Ah, María, who celebrates birthdays at our time of life, eh?" old Pancho expostulated.

"*Our* time of life, you say! Speak for yourself, you old rascal, you."

"Okay, at *my* time of life, then. Anyway, if you try to keep count of your passing days, your life becomes something of an arithmetic problem. No, we mostly want to forget birthdays, in my case assuredly so," he reflected somewhat soberly.

"That's true enough, I suppose," smiled María. "At any event, I'm going to buy one of those nice smart sombreros for you next year. Such quality material, strong, sturdy – a bit like you - the shopkeeper told me so."

"The shopkeeper told *you* that I was strong and sturdy?"

"I'll ignore that."

"And I know what you're going to ask next," grinned the old ranchero.

"So, you can read my mind, can you? Ha, that'll be the day."

"True enough, for a man could never read a woman's mind, not in a thousand years. But he could easily predict a change of mind, which women often do."

"Brazen stuff and nonsense! Well, go on, what am I going to ask you?"

"'A large size, is it?'"

María laughed, punching him in the arm.

"Ah, my dear one, don't be hard on me, be gentle with me, for I am a very sensitive fellow, I'll have you know."

At this astonishingly ludicrous remark, María gave him such a quelling look, that he felt impelled to rephrase it: "What I mean is, I *could* be sensitive if I was *allowed* to be."

While the timeless black void above them raised more stars to shine upon the land. The night-earth dreamed its darkness, and dreamed too of dawn. The hand of this late autumn season turned of its own free will, turned uncounted along the wheels of its own slow-clocked time.

Of a sudden, María made a motion to raise herself, a spare bunch of flowers in her hand. "My uncle is buried here somewhere," she said softly, "and I'm going to look around for his grave. I have some idea where he's resting. Will you be alright here?"

"Sí, sí," returned Pancho, also getting to his feet. "I'll take a turn around the grounds, get my motor muscles moving."

"Then let's not leave our stuff here to be pinched – Here, you take this … and this one as well," handing him bags and a blanket. "Come back to this spot so we don't lose the muchachas," and mamá immediately set off, seeing her way by the light of numerous flickering candles about her.

Pancho ambled along narrow pathways, feeling on his face the breath of Yoalli Ehecatl, the Toltec night wind.

He stopped a moment, gazing at the gravestones illumined by candlelight. There under the grass and stone, he acknowledged musingly, lay the bones of humanity, soil of their own corrupt flesh. And these long dead slowly turned in the earth, to rise again in the guise of grass and flowers.

Generations of people devoured by time and the soil of the land. Sisters and brothers, sons and daughters, mothers and fathers, family and friends, bone-scattered and resting in eternity.

The old man walked on in slow-time.

'Here lies a carpenter,' his imagination stirring, 'his father, and his father's father.'

'Here lies a child who died of fever, and her mother, and her mother's mother.'

'A metal-worker perhaps rests here, a tiller of the soil there. Here maybe lies a basket-weaver or a potter, a miller or a fruit-grower, a fruit-seller. There lies a street-cleaner and a stone-mason – and their wives – a blacksmith and a baker, a shoe and sandal-maker – along with their wives and children, too.

And a candle-maker and a rope-maker, a saddler and a rodeo-rider; all manner of craftsmen, their wives and young ones, and all the people they ever knew among their generations. All they had known and experienced in their lifetime, individual memories locked in eternity, drifting now endlessly with the winds of the land. Lying now in silence in a dominion of darkness, deep beneath the turf and hidden from the turmoil and clamour of the living world.

Such were the old man's thoughts in the dying of this day.

76

Cemetery Conversations II

Doña María presently returned and settled herself by the side of the old ranchero, her mind dwelling on her friend.

"You've got your thinking face on," she opened up. "What are you thinking about?"

"Uuy, María, nothing at all, to be honest. My mind was a blank, as it fancies going that way at odd times." He sniffed a little, as though to say 'So there you have it, now kindly leave off, *por favor*.'

María was not to be fobbed off with that. "Do you think that now you're maybe getting on a bit in years," she pressed relentlessly, "you have to face the consequences of such?"

"What, you mean getting forgetful and that sort of caper? Senior failings, I think they call them – the psychologists, that is."

"Sí, I suppose that's what I'm on about."

Around them now there seemed a restful bluish tinge; on the people and in the air, extending over the cemetery whole. It was as if outdoors were indoors, like you'd see in a cinema or a theatre. It gave off a mystical though comfortable sense of ease.

A few paces to one side of María and Pancho, a family of five or six folk were sitting happily in a tight group, tucking into semi-hot food they had brought in baskets. Savoury aromas drifted over, María trying to identify them, fried tomatoes and chillies predominating.

"You know, María, it's strange but I can remember things from the distant past – in every small detail and clear as broad daylight – yet I forget what I was doing only moments ago."

"Ha! So you're saddled with that sort of problem, are you?"

"What problem is that, my dove?"

Which earned him a sharp elbow jab in the ribs.

"There's not much wrong with you, even though you are a furry-faced fossil, you aging specimen, you!"

Returned Pancho with a grin, "Like Gerardo once told me, 'I've got all my facts – my faculties'."

"Is that a fact!"

"Ay que caray, woman, don't the pair of us start at it. And as for the dead and departed," - waving a hand at headstones dotted about them – "there is one great thankful consolation in being dead …"

"Sí, I'm all ears and waiting."

"Well, the fact of the matter is, you *don't know* that you're dead. You never know that you're dead when you are dead."

"Some consolation, I must say," dryly replied María. "As I see it, if you're dead then you're as dead as dead can be, with not a spark of anything in you. Even you, Pancho, if you were dead, you old firecracker. Heaven forbid that as well."

"No, my flower, it's those left behind alive who have to suffer and pick up the pieces …while you are comfortably and wholly unknowingly …dead as a hitching-post."

She glanced at him with amused affection, said, "Dead, whichever way you look at it – I wonder where my muchachas are, for I can't see them," changing the subject.

"I see them. They're heading back, it looks like. No, I tell a lie, something else has caught their interest – But they're still in view. I'll keep an eye on them."

"The eyes of a hawk are what you've got. I can't see as far as you can."

A restful silence fell between them for a spell.

Pancho made an abrupt movement. He sat up stiff straight with long arms extended, as though ready to embrace an approaching loved one, or maybe about to begin a speech; he was certainly ready, as María acutely surmised, to spout off something or other:

"'…Those who live many years should rejoice in them all; yet let them remember that the days of darkness will be many.' That, María, my precious, comes from *Ecclesiastes*."

"Sí, I know that, I'm not a heathen."

"No, of course you're not. You are an angel, a perfect angel."

"Ha! So flattery is seemingly rearing its ugly head, is it?"

"No, my honeypot, it is sex that does that."

"Shush, you! Just remember where you are and have some respect for the dead."

"Oh, I do. I respect the fact that it's them and not me."

"Not you what?"

"Not me that is dead. Not at this present time at all events."

"Well, mind you stay that way, there are enough dead bodies in here as it is."

"Sí, leastwise, that's what you generally find in a place such as this. They wouldn't be altogether *out of place* here, I'm thinking," hazarding a knowing grin, which earned another sharp elbow dig in the ribs.

Pancho rumbled on: "Life seems so short, you know, when you have lived well."

"How do you live well?"

"By always having the right views on life, and the right attitude – "

"Ha! I like that one! Going by all the untruths you come out with, it's to be hoped for your sake that you have a good memory, that's all I can say."

" – and to take the rough with the not so rough."

"Anything else, clever know-all old mule?"

"Sí, cultivating… having good friends… like you."

"I shorten your life then, is that it?" taking him to task once again, his ribs by now beginning to get sore.

María continued on, soberly faced: "You are content with life then, are you, Francisco?"

"I'd be an ungrateful idiot if I were not."

"Out of interest, have you any regrets to speak of?"

The old ranchero reflected a moment, seriously considering this, then said, "I dare say I would have liked the experience of being bored with a life of luxury."

"You! Bored with luxury!" laughed María. "Luxury, and you! Oh my, may the saints preserve me!" twinkling her eyes at him.

"A figure of speech, my flower, a slight slip of the tongue; opened my mouth and those nonsense words flew out. You'll forgive me, I know, for I am normally quite harmless, as surely you must agree."

"You're harmless enough but hardly normal."

They lapsed once again into a momentary silence.

Broken by the old man, who couldn't help himself if he tried.

"When I was a kid," he started up afresh, "I always wanted to grow old in life's travels, but didn't realise how rough and rocky the journey could sometimes be."

"At least you've travelled well, still have a good head of hair, your sight keen as a hawk's, and your hearing too is sound."

"*Perdónome?*"

"I said – never mind …Oh, you're joking me again, is it?"

María had not yet finished with him. "Your heart now, how is your heart?"

"Ah, permanently reserved for a certain person."

"I see …but how is it healthwise?"

"Healthwise? Well, apart from the occasional heartache, the sometimes heartbreaks, it's fine, I do declare in true honesty." He bent his head to her. "It doesn't beat, by the by, as regular hearts should, especially when I am with a certain person. No, *újule*, it *thuds* like galloping hoofs."

"Ha!"

"Old age, eh, María? Not that *you* have anything to do with it – at this moment in time."

She looked at him mock-coyly, said, "I thank you for that, señor."

"But thinking seriously on it, though. I was in this here town in the winter, around the Feast of Candelaria, it was – Oh, you know about that, of course." He smiled deprecatingly, and María loved him for it. "Well, anyway, on the autobus coming here I got speaking with a real old ranchero, long retired as you'd expect.

"I said to him, 'How old are you?'

"'Have a guess,' he says.

"And I look at him and weigh him up, and made my guess: 'Ninety-two?'

"'Hell no, hombre,' he spits back, mightily offended it would seem. 'You're way off the line.'

"'Well, how old are you, then?'

"And he says, 'I'm ninety-one!'"

María softly chuckled at this.

"And to think I was only out by one year, but he appeared mortified that I'd given him an extra year."

Pancho continued on in similar vein: "I then asked the old fellow, 'How long do you reckon you've got left?' You know what he told me? He said, 'I aim to squeeze a lot more rather than a bit more out of life yet. I was a bad one when in my prime, so the Good lord won't want my company until the last possible moment.'

"That's exactly what I intend to do as well, María, to squeeze a bit more out of life, or a lot more if possible."

"Well, the Good Lord won't be anxious to see your hide soon, either," smiled María.

She gave him a speculative look. "How old are you, Francisco?"

"Uuy, here she is with her melting eyes! I'm not saying, and will ignore your guesses, too."

"I could guess, and accurately as well no doubt, but I shan't say anything – or tell you my age either."

"Fair enough, my young fair petal. With you I wouldn't dare hazard a guess – too hazardous by far, I'm thinking. Hmm."

"Glad you think so – Ah, at last, my precious muchachas are back. You can be on your best behaviour, Francisco Ramírez, or I shall disown you."

"I give you my word of honour, and my word is my bond."

"Oh, listen to it! Chihuahuas!"

Little Julia was first to reach them, tense with excitement. The child could barely wait to gush out what she had seen.

"Mamá!" she began breathlessly. "Mamá, at the bottom end there – you see? – we found lots and lots of bones. Human bones!"

"Including skulls, mamá," Ruth joined in. "Scattered about all over, like – like litter."

Their mother gave a look at the old man, as though seeking an answer, some explanation.

"Sí, sí," mumbled Pancho quietly, "after a time the coffins are dug up and thrown aside. To make room for fresh ones. It has always been the way," he ended lamely.

"Fancy you knowing that. I never knew that sort of thing went on here." Mamá was shocked at this revelation.

"You see, María, some of these graves are centuries old, with no one left to care for them, all of them dying off, too."

"All the same, it doesn't seem right. It's not dignified. In fact it's downright disgraceful – scandalous! It is not right by any means."

"At any rate, I don't suppose it bothers the dead none – "

"Pancho! ¡Por favor! ¡Chihuahuas!"

The old ranchero went on, almost wearily, certainly warily: "You've got to see it this way, María – and you too, Rutí, Julia. Listen to me, dear hearts, the spirits of these long-dead are long gone …to another place, you maybe know where.

"This cemetery is but an 'autobus-station' waiting-room. Only their bones remain here … There is no spiritual substance in old bones."

He continued on measuredly: "The past existence of those now departed are as treasured memories in those who still live. You are here – all these folk around are here – to honour their passing …and bones don't come into it."

To put matters straight and to finalise at last his pedantic outburst, he gave the three females a winning sympathetic smile.

PART SEVENTEEN

77

Our Lady of Guadalupe

It was a fiesta day in San Stefan. The town was noted for its colourful and exuberant fiestas, and this one was no exception. In front of the parroquia and along the entire street on that side of the plaza, elaborate scaffolding had been hastily erected in readiness for a fireworks display scheduled for later in the evening.

Flags and bunting flew and flapped bravely in the autumn wind which swept over the open square. People were coming in from the surrounding countryside and from nearby pueblos, filling every available space in an already crowded plaza. Two bands played boisterously and simultaneously at opposite ends of the lower plaza, with the sun shining brightly on tuba and trumpet, and booming drums resounding over the whole township.

Here, a little boy was wailing, having just lost his balloon in the wind, and a harassed mother tried to console him with a stick of sugarcane; to no avail, for the child would have none of it.

There, an underfed pickpocket deftly snatched a fat wallet conveniently protruding from the rear pants pocket of a corpulent merchant type; and the merchant happened to have a look of smugness on his overfat face, but for how much longer would the smugness last, an observer might wonder.

Presently, a loud cheer went up and heads turned, as the town mayor appeared on the balcony of the main municipal building, surrounded by his minions, like a shoal of scavenger fish around a small whale – for the mayor, also, was barely the lower size of obese. This top official, though decidedly over-plump, was of small stature but of monumental pride. He waved grandiloquently to what he imagined his adoring masses.

Meanwhile, Pancho was in a cantina facing the jardín, with his English friend Matt Conners, playing dominoes of all things and downing tequilas, the pair of them, one after the other in quick succession, as though time were of the essence.

A grand pageant was about to commence at the parroquia. The massive double doors of the church were swung open, and out was carried the focus point with all due pomp and dignity: A portable dais on which stood a life-size alabaster figure of Our Lady of Guadalupe.

The dais was smothered in fresh flowers, the whole structure held by two long poles, hoisted on the shoulders of eight highly privileged bearers with appropriately solemn and important visages.

At length the procession began to move, followed by groups of schoolchildren, pouring out from the open church entrance; boys in blue knickerbockers or pantaloons, girls wearing long white frocks with frilly hems and other adornments, and flowers in their hair. Lined up in ranks of four abreast, their young-formed features glowing with pride and excitement. They carried banners and flags, ribbons and rosaries, and bouquets of crepe flowers in green, white and red, the colours of Mexico's national flag.

Nearby, as the onlookers, proud parents looked on with glistening wide-alive eyes, frantically searching out and waving to their little ones:

"There's Teresa!" cried one exultant mother. "Oh, no, it's not! But how like Teresa, that one – Ah, there she is, our Teresa, there I see her. Look! Behind that big boy – Teresa-a-a!"

Next came the boys' brigade with its own brass band. And troops of boy scouts and girl guides in khaki and brown uniforms, militarily spruced up with toggles and tassels and proficiency badges.

Several bands were now playing in the plaza; a discordant, bombastic crescendo, as ensembles played different tunes all at the same time, each competing for dominance of loudness with cheeky exuberance. But who cared? The people loved every moment of it; the music and the noise, the bustle and colour, the very atmosphere of which they themselves were creating by simply being there.

The crowds roared their approval, fought among themselves in order to obtain a better view of the revered alabaster statue stiffly swinging from one side to the other. The mayor looked on beneficently, his officials widely smiling as they basked in their leader's glory.

The procession wended waveringly to the lower end of the plaza, where a cantina was situated, right on the corner. It was the same cantina wherein the old ranchero was downing drinks. He heard a tumultuous roaring increase in volume, and decided to get off his backside and go take a look by the western-style half swing-doors of the cantina.

The bands blared and brayed on and the buildings shook, while folk drank in this festive feast with smiles of satisfaction.

Then something untoward happened of a sudden. The left lead man of the bearers, with their heavy, cumbersome burden, stumbled in a pot-hole, and he dropped at once to his knees.

The dais swivelled to an alarming angle.

The man tried to rise, as the other bearers continued on forward with the momentum. The hapless fellow's foot was entangled in the long robe he was wearing.

"Our Lady!" cried someone. "She's toppling!"

A gasp from the crowds came like a roar of wind, a look of horror on every face.

"She's falling off!" warned a voice in the crowd.

"She's going! ¡La Señora!" yelled another.

The figure, so life-sized, was at that moment precariously balanced on the flower bedecked dais, only the flowers holding the Good lady for a brief second more. Over She went, falling from the dais.

And landing, horizontally and perfectly and quite fortuitously, into the outstretched long arms of Pancho. He caught Her neatly and held Her tight and safe.

The crowds gave one massive sigh of relief.

"He caught Our Lady!" bawled a rotund shopkeeper, face ruddy and slick with sweat, pushing his way through the throng.

"She's saved!" cried a pockmarked metal lamp-worker, waving work-worn hands.

"Oh, praise be!" voiced a vulpine-visaged old woman, addressing her companion, an equally unprepossessing pinch-cheeked woman.

"That man! He has Her!" shouted a big-nosed, wall-eyed fellow.

"He saved the Virgin!" shrieked an ecstatic woman standing next to the wall-eyed man.

"A miracle from Heaven!" wept a wen-faced lady dressed in black, tears of joy running down her cheeks.

A murmuration of praise swayed, swelled and swept over the people, right around the plaza.

'Well, the good Lord love me,' thought Pancho, holding the sacred statue firmly to his chest, 'at last I have a woman in my arms, and it's my luck she's made of plaster – or is it alabaster?' At all events he made a 'I'm punch-pleased with that little action' face.

He carefully swung the figure down and rested it base-side on the pavement. People shot into view, slapped him on the back and shook his hand, praising his brilliant handling of the situation. Fresh murmurings arose from behind them.

"Make way there, por favor!" snapped an official in an officious manner.

"Stand aside for the mayor!" called out another council-man.

The portly presence of the leading person in town, bouncing in his patent-leather shoes, sprang forward with a wide smile splitting his fat face. He approached this ranchero-type fellow with short rapid mincing steps, as if his trousers were too tight for comfort. He halted directly in front of Pancho, who still held one arm protectively around the waist of the precious alabaster figure.

"Fantastic! I saw every bit of it!" the mayor beamed expansively. "Saw it with my own eyes, as neatly done as anything I have ever seen. Well done, dear fellow! Well done indeed! You must tell me your name," pumping Pancho's hand with agitated enthusiasm.

Behind the mayor now stood a phalanx of *aficionados*, there ready to protect him from the heaving press of humanity filling this end of the plaza. Beyond the tight bunching of officials and spectators, more murmurings sang through the air, passing from mouth to mouth:

"Who is he?" asked a coarse-faced man with thick sideburns obscuring his cheeks.

"Who knows? But the mayor is talking to him this very moment," said a red-faced woman, gesticulating with one arm as though conducting an orchestra.

"Does anyone know the fellow?" asked an old man in tremulous tones.

"Who is that with the mayor, then? Is that him?" wanted to know a dark-faced man with large gapped teeth.

"Sí," someone answered him. "He's the one who saved Our Lady from getting smashed to pieces. That's him alright."

"Who is this hombre, anyway?" snapped a sharp-face señora with a tight prim mouth.

"Why, I know him," said a seasoned regular of '*Los Dos Durangos*' Bar. "I recognised him straight off. He's that ranchero from out of town. Pancho, they call him."

"His name's Pancho!" cried a gaunt-faced man with craggy brows and the eyes of a dead fish.

"*Pah-noh!*" earnestly uttered a dark, gnarled gnome of a man with a cleft palate. He tried once again: "*Pan-co!*"

And the cry went up, loudly and more articulately. The name spread right around the plaza, like a river in spate.

The town mayor conferred further with this citizen hero:

"It was a splendid turn, my good fellow, and I shall personally see to it that you are rewarded accordingly. I'll have you declared the freedom of this town. You can depend on it. How does that strike you, hey?"

Pancho, incongruously, still stood with the statue by his side, with one arm now resting on its shoulder, like a caring husband out in town with his wife. He kept scanning the faces in the milling mob around him, in the hope of seeing his drinking partner, Conners. The young Englishman, however, was still inside the cantina, drunk beyond redemption, near slumped under the table, fast asleep.

Meantime, the stumble-footed bearer who had slipped in a pot-hole and fallen from grace, as it were, had wisely made his self scarce and slipped in among the crowds. Later, he would drink himself into a stupor on tequila, never to live down the shame of what he had done on this day.

The other bearers, who had stood around for a time, also shamefacedly, got themselves together, and with a voluntary extra man they relieved Pancho of his alabaster acquaintance and repositioned it securely in its original place.

The pageant continued amid enthusiastic cheering of the multitude.

The mayor put an arm around Pancho and led him off to his upstairs office, where they could carry on watching the spectacle in the plaza, through double French windows before the balcony. And fortify themselves by sharing a bottle of champagne at the same time.

They had to get there first. "Make way there por favor for the mayor and señor Pancho," said an official, prodding and pushing importantly through the throng. "By your leave, por favor, and allow the mayor to pass," heaving a way through bystanders.

"How is the hombre who fell, your honour?" asked Pancho. "It was an accident, you know, and – "

"To hell with that dolt!" the mayor cut in indignantly. "I'll have him sweeping the streets for a year, that one! Indeed I will. You mark my words, you can depend on it – This way, my good fellow …"

'No point in pursuing this any further,' thought the old man. 'Besides, it is no hardship in sweeping a street. Was it not, only this last winter, when I was doing exactly that? Sweeping a street, by thunder! Right here in this town. I bet this fat one here at my side doesn't know that …"

Shortly after, when the mayor of San Stefan once again stepped out on to the balcony of the municipal building, he had Pancho on one arm. The crowds went wild with delight at the sight of this hero.

The old ranchero looked down on a sea of upturned smiling faces, and diffidently scratched his nose, then poked a finger in his ear and wiggled it some, and finally took an all-absorbing interest in the toes of his boots.

While the bands played on …

78

Escape to the Countryside

Soon after noon, when the hysteria of the pageantry in town began to ease off, Pancho somehow managed to escape the possessive clutches of his honour the mayor. He bought himself a half-dozen savoury filled tacos and a handful of hot chillies from a street food-vendor.

Catching a cruising taxi along the same street, he ordered the driver to take him out of town. Anywhere would do, he said, as long as it was out of town and in the blessed peace and tranquillity of the countryside.

Some ten minutes later a green and pleasant spot was found, remote and quiet, a short distance along a minor dirt-road. The old ranchero got out here, asking the driver to return to this place to pick him up at a certain time, and not a minute before.

He settled himself comfortably under the shade of a beefwood tree, contentedly munching his way through the six stuffed tacos. A few paces in front of him ran a narrow stream, burbling softly by. The grass was almost rich-green and fairly thick here where he half lay, back resting against the trunk of the tree and shaded by its solid branches.

There was a decided particularity that he noticed about this place, that it somehow appeared strangely familiar. Had he visited here before? No, he certainly had not. He couldn't possibly have even seen this place before, the very idea was quite absurd.

And yet, that compelling déjà vu element was strong enough to almost convince him otherwise. At all events he was happy to spend time now in what he felt an ideal – an idyllic! – location.

After the *al fresco* meal, the old man once again settled down, making himself comfortable and composed, his keenly acute ears catching the calling cries of birds on the wing, in flight above him.

Sí, this is muy bien, he reckoned, smiling to himself with satisfaction.

He breathed in deeply, smelled the clear, fresh, open air with relish, and the grass too around him smelled wholesome, no doubt because here it was free of dust. The bark of the tree he was pushing his back against, that also seemed to exude a pleasant odour similar to something he couldn't quite identify – possibly liquorice? Well, something like it, not that it mattered any, ay que caray.

With sombrero lowered over his eyes he took a short siesta. Sleeping off the effects of this morning's tequila and champagne, as well as the rare excitement of events which had come his way. The old man rested well in a state of regenerative repose, waking up just less than an hour before the appointed time of the taxi's return.

In this peaceful, still and quiet, near full hour, Pancho reflected on his life and where it had taken him.

He was in the late autumn of his days, he knew by the feelings in his bones; and a long lifetime of memories surged and eddied in his still-active still-young mind.

The sweetest of these remembrances, in marvellous clarity of detail, were the earliest ones. He saw his mamá's large flashing eyes with their characteristic glint of humour, of which he had inherited a great deal; and he could smell her smell, a peculiar blend of maguey honey and cedar-smoke and goat's milk. The long-held memory was so real to him at this moment that he sniffed, an involuntary action, causing a sharp pang of nostalgia to thrill and jolt his heart.

Pancho had from the very beginning developed a healthy attitude in his approach to life, able to deal with its myriad vicissitudes. From as far back as his wild youthful days as a *charro* – the cowboy of Mexico – he had always known how best to cope with life and achieve a fulfilling existence. It was as simple a formula as anyone could ever imagine.

Life was to be grasped by the throat, every dear moment of it, he had reasoned. You were born, you lived, and then you died. It was as basic as that. There was no need of a higher purpose in things for man, and no point in searching for some eternal truth, though he often did, all the same.

Man was after all merely an animal; a reasoning, resourceful, intelligent being, but an animal nevertheless. That is how he looked at it.

He gave thought to the people he had known and who had passed through his life, a procession of them six decades long. Although he had never kept in touch with many of them in any way, he at most maintained the memories. And with these people, scores of whom became his friends, he had had the knack of bringing out the best in *them*, and because of this they had enriched his life, as he had theirs.

What did it matter that he had not governed a state, or led a squadron of cavalry into battle, or composed a symphony or built a church? What did it matter he owned only one pair of boots and a ranchero's sombrero? All the great men of history, he knew (don Roberto's library had a lot to answer for!), these men had had their day on the stage of life, and were now gone, bones and dust, text in a history book – even though many had helped shape the nations of the world and left long-lasting legacies of improvements for mankind.

But what about the masses of people down the long years past, who never got a mention and were hardly mourned except by family and friends, who went the same way, the way of all flesh?

Our thoughts and memories of life, where do they go after death? The old man pondered on this. When flesh leaves the bone and blood dries as dust, do lifetime thoughts untwine and float off into a long dark journey, unravelling through the vastness of the universe, reaching back to the beginning of time? Is that what happens? Old Pancho would have loved to know what was, so to say, impossible truths forever locked away.

He gazed about him, at this dear land, remembering its bloody history. The rolling rugged hills told of strife and hardship, some of which he had experienced. The lonely landscape, sparse and severe, seemed to speak to him in its hieroglyphics of ravines and gullies and *arroyos*, understanding that well enough. The dust of Mexico he had known all his life. In its windshifting movements, from plain to hill and mountain, through centuries of time, it had settled intermittently on the faces of Maya and *mestizo*, on priests and *peons*, on all the people in Mexican history.

Enough! Enough of this. The old man wanted to think of pleasant things, of his own personal happier times. Like this last summer ...

Firstly, he considered his compañeros, and others that he knew. There was squint-eyed surrealist Cándido, the teller of bizarre, tall tales; Cándido, with a smile to charm the frocks off females, or so the young man fancied.

Ugly Gerardo, generally accident-prone and a devoted hypochondriac; but a cracking carpenter, a competent craftsman. Less so as a horseman.

Introspective, closed-faced José, the self-styled *'lone silent hombre'*; also, a bit of a firebrand, almost a serial pyromaniac. He was in love with fire.

Buck-toothed Emilio, corpulent and somewhat of a somnambulist, who could sleep standing-up, sometimes with one eye wide open; his devotionals were decidedly related to slumber. He loved to always catch up on his sleep.

The young halfwit Julian, caring stable-hand, simple soul of the stables, and general roped-in servant and dogsbody to the others.

Lastly – on the ranch – Tulia, don Roberto's cook/housekeeper, also counsellor, helpmeet and dear friend to Julian and to the rancheros.

Pancho's thoughts now sprang to this summer now gone; when young Juan Ramos had joined the rancheros on don Roberto's hacienda for the whole summer period; when he, Pancho, was summoned to a distant town to meet an accommodating fair señorita; when José found an abandoned baby, and when a lone bitch coyote led Juan and the old ranchero to a horse trapped in quicksand.

…When the boy Juan suddenly fell ill a long distance from the ranch, and spent two days and a night in an isolated, empty pig-pen, almost dying of heat exhaustion and dehydration; to be eventually rescued and given succour by Pancho, Cándido and José.

When José inadvertently burnt down a stable, and Gerardo, skilfully carpenter-wise, organised the building of another, won in a poker game on a rival horse ranch.

When Pancho and his ranchero *compañeros* stopped a foursome of ruthless escaped convicts terrorising a small pueblo.

When don Roberto's 600-strength herd of longhorns stampeded, and when old Pancho saved the president of Mexico from an assassin's bullet, catching one himself in consequence.

Sí, those summer months proved eventful enough, mused the old man. Those long, hot, wind-whipped, dust-peppered summer days …

Sí, happy times too, without a doubt, a smile now forming on his face, as swiftly passing thoughts turned pleasurably to *a touch of the late summer…*

THE LONG INTERLUDE

79

Summer Tales II

*I*t was a little after a noontide blast of sun on a mid-week day, and the men squatted or sat on straw bales within the entranceway of the main, sun-polished stable. The poor-wit Julian was somewhere deeper in the stable's gloom, grooming a grey.

A young obnoxious wind came on, sweeping and blustering between the stables and across the corral ...till it met with a great high banked wall of heat, and was instantly annihilated.

"They say now that Lavinia in the pueblo is going to have a baby," cited Cándido, opening up the usual idle chatter, "and we've yet to know who the father might be," glancing a telling look over at José.

"Don't look at me!" retorted that put-upon-soul.

Poked in Pancho: "Well, José, you do have a guilty kind of look on your face."

"That's because," began Emilio, with a face like a red balloon, and smouldering like a fumarole, "because he snatched up the last tortilla – just when I was reaching for it."

Young Juan joined in: "There're tortillas still under that towel in Tulia's basket."

"Ah, thank you, Juanny," said the fat man, letting himself off the boil.

"And so there are," noted Pancho, "and so there you have it," springing energetically to his feet. "Pass me the basket, Juanito, I'll dish them out ... Hmm, sí, two for me, one for you, Gerardo, two more for me – "

"What the - !"

"Only teasing you, Emilio. Simmer down now. You're welcome to the lot, we're quite done," passing the basket to the supposedly starveling fat man.

Said Cándido: "You eat well enough anyway," addressing the old man.

"Has the con-constitution too of a steam locomotive," gave out Gerardo in grudging tones. Even he was replete, not only with the normal ranchero fare, but also a good morning's harvesting of nose-pickings.

"You are what you eat," put in Pancho.

"Then you're a steam locomotive," cracked Cándido cheerily. He gazed squinting back at the old man.

Another sudden wayward wind waged war on the ranch. It howled and hooted between the slatboard timbers of the stable walls, blowing dust and grit which scraped against the wood like rough sandpaper. The view from the entranceway was lost in a swirling mist of dust and sand.

"The wind's getting up again," observed someone.

"It's getting my back up with its infernal noise," complained someone else.

"And look what the wind's bringing in ..." said the observer.

It was Tulia making an appearance. The men gave astonished glances at her. To them it seemed positively indecent for Tulia to be so far away from her kitchen habitat.

Tulia, don Roberto's esteemed and treasured cook/housekeeper. Who possessed a particularity known to everyone. She had two most distinctive *moods*. Tulia had a good *mood* and she had a bad *mood*, with no shading deviations between the two. Luckily for everybody, most of the time she reposed satisfactorily in her good mood.

At this present moment however, that small portion which was not anywhere near 'good mood' mode was undeniably showing its forbidding face.

"Hola, Tulia," the old ranchero greeted her somewhat cautiously. "Anything we can do for you?"

The cook, short and stout, stood with hands aggressively on ample hips, glaring at the rancheros.

"One of you bandits has taken a knife from my kitchen," she charged in at once. "A fine butcher's knife it is, bone-handled, stainless steel blade. One of my best knives!"

Everyone turned faces automatically and questioningly at José.

"Don't look at me!" bleated the blame-blighted fellow.

"It's just that you've got a sort of guilty look on your face, hombre," Pancho told him in fruity tones.

"Can't help how I look – "

"I concur there," crowed Cándido, playing his comedic role.

" – I haven't taken Tulia's knife, or anyone else's knife. I got my own knife. You know I've got my own knife."

José cat-footed one way, and cat-footed back again in agitation, giving scant credence to his denial of guilt. "*¡Caramba!*" he exploded. "You need a full-time lawyer around here, for your own good and safety. For your own sense of honour!" he added for full measure, thinking that honour was indeed at stake here.

"Hold on a moment," piped Juan. "I think I know where – Salté! . . SALTÉ! Here, you scruffy thieving hell-hound! Here! Heel!"

The dog trotted from behind a wall of straw bales, with a purely innocent and polite look of enquiry stamped on his hoary face. He carried between his jaws what looked like a bone. With a six-inch steel blade appending from one end of it.

"Our Salté sure has a snout for snaffling things that aren't his," remarked Pancho dryly. "Give him a bone, Tulia, if you can spare one," he grinned. "You can make a fair swap with Salté I daresay, as long as it's a bone. Salté does enjoy a nice chew on a bone – I do myself, to be honest. More natural for a dog, though."

Thus, an almost instant declaration of war was averted.

II

José, Gerardo and Emilio were at it hammer-and-chisel, being argumentative, probably pressured by an exceptionally hot sun on this particular summer day – in the main stable, firing shells of scorn and abuse at one another.

Cándido came to the rescue: "Hold it! Hold on!" he cried, almost desperately. "Our Juanito has a story to tell us. Haven't you, Juanny?"

"Have I?" asked the young one in surprise. Taking in his friend's peculiar look of pleading, he said, "Sí, I do, I do. I'd forgotten," giving a cheeky boy's grin of mischief.

"Not an unhappy story?" wanted to know Emilio.

Juan nodded a negative nod.

"Got a happy ending, then?"

The boy wagged his head in the affirmative.

"It's about a – "

"One moment!" José gushed in like a torrent of scalding water. "I've lost my tobacco pouch. I can't find my tobacco pouch. Has anyone seen my tobacco pouch?"

José's precious pouch, cleverly crafted from a young bull's scrotum, treasured like a valuable heirloom.

"Is that what you're looking for?" said Pancho, indicating an untidy heap of hound-dog splayed out at Juan's feet. Something suspiciously like a tobacco pouch was snugly nestled between the dog's fore-paws. Salté was licking it with evident satisfaction.

"Damn *perro!*" snapped José, snatching back his prized possession, giving Salte a look fit to set his fur aflame.

"When José loses his temper," pursued Pancho, "you must give him a day or two to find it again."

"It's about," Juan proceeded at last, "about a short swordsman, the shortest swordsman in the world. And one day, as he was practicing cuts and thrusts and parries and whatnot …he happened to accidently slice himself in half – "

"Half a swordsman is better than none."

"Shut it, Cándido – Carry on, Juanito."

"Then there was a knock on the door, and he managed to open the door. 'It's me!' said a voice, 'your other half. Can I come in and join you?' They got together again, the two halves of him, but he was still the shortest swordsman in the world … "

A momentary silence, broken by Gerardo: "Is that it then?" he gruffed aggrievedly. "I can't catch the full con-connection of that one."

"No, just the *half* of it," dead-panned Juan.

"I expect he was always doing that sort of thing," guessed Pancho, "and was maybe once the *tallest* swordsman in the world."

"Sí," grinned the boy, "that's the *long* and *short* of it, in a manner of speaking."

The old man leaned his broad back to the warm, warped weather-boarding of the stable wall, eyes fastened on a dust-devil which of a sudden whisked itself across the open space of doorway.

He turned to Juan and said, "Tell them about the butcher's shop, *amiguito.*"

"The butcher's shop? – Ah, sí." Juan cast a speculative eye on the rancheros ranged around him. "Some hombre went into town and entered a butcher's shop. 'Is this a butcher's shop?' he asked. And the man inside, wearing a butcher's apron, said it certainly was a butcher's shop, pointing an arm to meat carcasses hanging everywhere. 'So,' said this hombre, 'how much are your butchers?'"

"And he didn't get that from a comic," declared Pancho. "He made it up himself – didn't you, Juanito?"

"What town was this and why did – "

"Oh button it, Gerardo, go saw a plank of wood or something."

Cándido dropped down his usual calling card: "My uncle in Querétaro—"

"Oh, not him again!" groused Gerardo.

" – My uncle in Querétaro," Cándido carried on coolly, "was friends with a butcher, whose shop was on the street corner where my uncle lived. This butcher had a crooked leg. Well, not exactly crooked, he had one leg longer than the other."

"So," put in Pancho, "he had one leg *shorter* than the other."

"If you put it like that, sí, but he definitely had one leg longer than the other. Anyway, this butcher naturally walked with a limp."

"He would if he had one leg shorter or one leg longer than the other."

"Am I doing penance here? Can I get on?"

"Nobody's stopping you, impatient pup!"

"I think you told me this before," Juan joined in. "Wasn't he the one with that funny nickname? – What is it now? – 'Hop-Hop Pecan Pedro'."

"Something like that," Pancho barged in, "for I heard this story, too. He was better known, by the by, for an unusual reputation."

"What was that, then?" asked José, lighting up a cigarro.

"Well, as I heard it, he offered to sell his mother to the Devil, but the fact was, his mother was already the Devil's own daughter, so such a sale couldn't go through."

"Who told you that?" Cándido demanded to know.

"Why, you did, you sorry-eyed burrito."

"Ah, sí, so I did. What I didn't tell you is that this crooked-leg butcher was also known as 'the crooked centavo', on account of his dealings with customers, which were crooked one way or another."

"He *short*-changed them, you mean?"

José began to tie on his favourite eggyolk-yellow bandanna.

"Where do you think you're going?" asked Pancho.

"I don't think, I know."

"I know you don't think," cut in Cándido.

"So, where're you off to, then?" again questioned the old man.

"To the pueblito."

"Ah, bueno. Give my regards to Teresa."

"Who the hell is Teresa?"

"You're not going to the top end, I take it?"

"The top end?"

"Sí, hombre, the red light district."

"What's that? Now you're kidding me. I'm only going to ride over to the tienda for tobacco. I'm clean out of smokes."

Said Cándido, "While you're there, José, get me a couple of square hen's eggs, a cold can of steam, and some of those chilli toffees ..."

"Oh, listen to this madman," grumped Gerardo.

"... And a kilo of chest-pain tablets for our Gerardo, the suppository kind, they're the best."

"The *suppository* kind, what's that?" enquired Pancho, smiling.

"You know, the kind you shove up your – "

"Ah, I've got you now. Bueno. I'll have some too, José, banana flavoured will do very nicely."

"Everybody's loco round here," sneered José.

Old Pancho squared already four-squared chunky shoulders, mischievous blue eyes glancing upward at cobwebbed rafters, as if his thoughts hung there ready to be plucked and processed.

"Now," he rumbled amiably, eyes dropped to a lower level, "I wonder where our Julian has go to ... Julian? – JULIAN!"

"¿Señor?" The simpleton stablehand's head peeped out at the side of a stall.

"Come out with your hands up! Ah, that's flushed you out. Did you worm that roan like I asked you to?"

"Sí, señor," fluted Julian melodiously in his high, girl's voice. "I wormed the roan, like you asked me to."

"Then why has it still got a miserable Gerardo-type face?"

"*¿Perdónome?*" gruffed Gerardo, greatly offended.

"Keep your spurs a-jingly, Gerardo, only testing to see if you're awake."

"You want I should worm the roan again, señor?" the youth asked politely.

"No, muchacho, best not, it'll do I guess. I would say, in fine, that it'll do just as it is. You worm it once more and the damn horse might break into a Spanish tap-dance or something."

"¿Perdónome?" queried Julian in puzzlement.

"In any case, time itself will sort it, I dare say. But you can walk it round the corral a couple of turns, maybe that should improve its expression."

"Maybe," began José – still hanging around – began somewhat coyly, indicative of a witticism about to bloom, "maybe Gerardo should take a turn or two walking the corral, to improve *his* expression, like."

"You still here, hombre?" said Pancho pointedly.

"Clonk him one, Gerardo, why don't you?" advised Emilio.

"God's thunder, you still awake too," grinned the old ranchero.

Meantime, José chose to ignore the fat one's remark. He wished only at this present time to revert to his true role of the 'lone silent hombre'. He tried to light the short stub-end of a roll-up cigarro, evidence enough to denote a diminished supply of tobacco, and time he ought to head for the tienda in the pueblo and restock his supply.

And, as happened time after time, the swarthy smoker nearly set alight both his moustache and the long hairs sprouting from his nostrils. The pyrotechnician par excellence, thought old Pancho, watching with wicked delight.

"I thought you said that you were off to the pueblo for more fuel?" he purred.

III

It was one of those not-quite-right days when hot, weird winds suddenly sprang up to make their presence known. One such at this present time, a rogue raider, swooped down on don Roberto's stable area. It buffeted open several stable doors, running riot and ransacking the stables, lifting straw and chaff. It keened and moaned, riding the rafters, clearing out cobwebs and accumulated dust in its wake, pushing out stable end doors, to begin next on the corrals. It made the horses – those stabled and not out grazing the rangeland – made them skittery, jumpy; hoofs kicking in agitation at the stalls, which only increased the general din. All of this in a moment, then it ceased altogether. The 'rogue raider' died.

The rancheros were occupied in the task of sorting out equipment and junk in the saddle-room. The equipment was mainly old and worn, not yet condemned as junk, whereas stuff designated 'junk' was undoubtedly that and should have been thrown out long ago.

As well as the rancheros and the paraphernalia of equestrian equipment and accoutrements, the air too was charged with the smell of ancient dust and mouldy leather. An additional odour when Pancho, at one moment, caught a hefty whiff of acrid sweat emanating from Emilio's armpits; strong enough to taste, powerful enough to water one's eyes or put a mouse to sleep, he reckoned.

The men's voices rose and fell with muffled tones in the tight confines of the saddlery. A superfluity of idiocy and confusion reigned, as they messed and kicked about a scurf of straw and smelly substances littering the floor.

PANCHO: "Think on, Emilio, the world is more than all the seasons. If you wish for patience there is no harm in waiting for it – We can get rid of this old saddle, it's seen more seasons than a century."

EMILIO: "No, don't throw it away, I can still make use of it."

CÁNDIDO: "What as, a museum exhibit?"

JOSÉ: "Who's a museum exhibit? Who said that?"

PANCHO: "Uuy, words can hurt more than a knife cut, eh?"

EMILIO: "God's sake, dump that, it stinks. It's rotten."

JOSÉ: "So would you be, penned in here for donkey's years."

CÁNDIDO: "I reckon Emilio stinks stronger than that."

JOSÉ: "Emilio's not saying anything."

PANCHO: "Even a fool is wise if he can keep his mouth shut – Sí, amigo, you can sling that little lot you've got there. Make room."

EMILIO: "Anyway, as I said to that no-good waste-of-air Alonso, I said we have our standards, we do, our sense of right from wrong. I mean, you'd never hit a woman, would you?"

PANCHO: "You asking me? Well, I'd have to remove my sombrero first ... then think about it – We can keep that halter, hermano."

JOSÉ: "Probably? I'd say he probably would, no problem."

PANCHO: "In life the probable is always possible. At all events I know who I *would* hit."

CÁNDIDO (smiling): "He's looking at you, José."

JOSÉ: "That's as may be, makes no odds, means nothing. Wouldn't you say, Pancho? Or maybe you would."

PANCHO: "I never argue with myself ...in case I could be wrong."

EMILIO: "Can we get rid of this?"

PANCHO: "Leave José alone, I can still get some juice out of him."

CÁNDIDO: "As juicy as a toasted taco."

EMILIO: "Okay, sorry, José."

JOSÉ: "You will be, you fat whale. You great gob of grease. Buck-toothed hippo, slobby lump of lard!" – José was content enough in mouthing off inspired damnable remarks against the fat man, much in the mode of a decrepit though still functioning boiler letting off steam - "Now, shove over, there's hardly room to move in here."

PANCHO: "I must say, our Emilio is smelling pleasant today, which makes a change. A regular *Sterculius*."

CÁNDIDO: "Ster – who or what the devil is that?"

PANCHO: "Sterculius, as I said. He was the ancient Roman god of manure." (Don Roberto's library having much to answer to again)

CÁNDIDO: "Caramba, a god of horse-shit, what next!"

"Right, hermanos, that'll do it, I reckon," suddenly announced old Pancho. "Out to the corral with you, we're neglecting our horses…"

The bright blue of sky welcomed the horsemen, the heat and light smacking them in the face, as each made a move towards a mount.

"Where's Gerardo?" asked Cándido, fiddling with a tangle of reins.

"He's coming …"

Gerardo came galumphing into the corral, an uncharacteristic smile on his rubbery face.

"You're looking chipper," commented Cándido unctuously.

Pancho noticed too and knew why it was so. "It was that day off he had yesterday – A good day off, eh, Gerardo?"

The happy man sat himself on the corral fencing, exuding good health and well-being. "That's right," he agreed.

He went on: "You'll never guess who I met up with in the pueblo," his ugly, mobile face radiating happiness.

"Your good wife?" guessed Pancho.

"Doctor Gómez, that's who! Doctor Gómez was there, and we got to talking about things."

"I would never guess what you might possibly talk about," grinned the old man.

The doctor in question was in fact a veterinary surgeon, dealing mostly with cattle and horses. Everybody knew that he was a vet. But for some obscure and unaccountable reason, Gerardo always took him for a general family physician, and had had many a serious consultation with him.

"My hypochondria, he told me, my hypochondria (he loved the word) isn't as bad as it used to be. That's what he told me …"

"Was he in that old crate of a motor-car of his?" wanted to know Emilio.

"Of course, of course, he needs it for his rounds."

Said Pancho, "I don't think much to a motor-car or autobus, but I do believe in a lot of *horse-power*."

"You've got hypochondria, you say, Gerardo?" asked Cándido, bringing back the original topic.

The chronic hypochondriac put on a sombre look, to fit in with what he earnestly believed an extremely rare type of ailment.

"Oh, sí," he admitted emphatically, "I had it real bad, he said, Doctor Gómez did. But now he tells me that things are easing up a bit, at least he's hoping so, he tells me," carving his face into a vacuous grin, like some dumb primate.

Said Pancho, "Now it's José with a medical condition. Piles, I think he said…"

José was indeed suffering from that particularly painful ailment. The old man watched with interest as Jose struggled with a different kind of problem with a 'difficult' horse.

The old ranchero leaned toward Cándido, and candidly interpolated: "There are those that do and there are those that don't; and of those that don't, most of them can't. Uuy, I can't see our José ever mounting that there hot-tempered rascally-minded piece of horseflesh, not in his present condition. Can you?"

The young man replied, "You recall me saying only earlier that nothing but trouble would come of this."

"I don't recall you saying anything of the kind – earlier. Or earlier on still."

"Ah well, look on here …"

José had given up with the 'awkward' horse and passed its halter on to Julian to sort out.

Young Juan came on the scene, leading his chestnut bay, Chapulín. "I'm taking a ride," he announced, leaping into the saddle. "Keep Salté here with you, por favor."

"Stay, Salté! Heel!" commanded Gerardo, in a ludicrously loud ringmaster's bellow.

"So, Gerardo, you have actually got this hypochondria thing," crowed Cándido, throwing a cock-eyed wink at old Pancho.

"I know what you're thinking," returned Gerardo gaily. "No worries, hombre, it's not catching, you see. It's not con-contagious."

"No, it wouldn't be," put in Pancho, "you'll want to keep it all to yourself."

Gerardo opened his mouth to say more, catching a large horsefly, which he almost swallowed. He fussily spluttered and spat it out. It looked to Pancho not unlike a wet raisin.

"You were saying . . ? Or about to," the old man prompted dryly.

"Oh sí, I also saw Alfredo Gonzalez in the pueblo, who I hadn't seen in a long while. He'd spent some time working up Chihuahua way – You remember Alfredo Gonzalez, don't you, Pancho?"

"Uuy, Alfredo Gonzalez, who once called you 'The Handsome Prince'. Isn't that what he said?"

"I guess so," replied Gerardo unguardedly.

"Hmm. Alfredo Gonzalez. I remember he'd been taking out a certain señorita – Marlena, that was her name – courting her for nigh on seventeen years. Might have been longer. And this Marlena got fed up waiting in the end, and asked Alfredo was it not time for them to get hitched at last …"

"Didn't know that," grated Gerardo.

Cándido cut in: "What did he say to that, this Alfredo hombre?"

Pancho paused. Like an actor who knows that silence is as dramatic as any a line, then swanned into his finale:

"He said it was all very well for them to wed … but who would bother to have them now."

"Always has to have the last word," moaned José in a lowly tone, leaning against a post, too wary of sitting down.

"You see, hermanos," the old man pattered on, "people are as they are. People are people, and there's no changing them – "

"That's interesting," carped Cándido, "I never knew that."

"Tape your mouth and listen up ... People are much the same right around the world. They have their faults, their virtues; make the same mistakes; do things the wrong way, the right way, any way they care for."

Pancho breathed in, holding his chest, let it out, and fired on: "But there is one thing that people tend to forget. We are all destined to die – "

"I never knew that either," added Cándido with mock-candour.

"Shut it, muchacho ...And in life give it little head-space."

Said Cándido, "I shall live forever, or hope to."

"Sí, exactly! It's the young ones who think they're going to last forever, think they are indestructible, imagine life like eternity, which is why they can be so foolish and careless and so damned reckless at times. There is something they don't think about, never enters their empty thoughtless skulls. Time marches on. Life is short. It's only through maturity, common-sense and maybe experience too, that you realise just how short life can be, and how fast time moves on.

"A wasted hour is a mistake you can forgive, a wasted day is just gross criminal negligence."

"There's nothing we can do about it, then, wouldn't you say?" supplied José, tentatively caressing his backside with a careful hand.

"Only this, amigo, always be aware of what you do with your days. You are part of humanity, so think too of others and not only yourself. Share your humanity and by doing that you're putting quality in your own life and in the lives of others."

The old ranchero stopped a moment, gazed paternally at his compañeros. "Look at our Cándido here, such a normal, soberly sensible soul. And José, riotous and noisy, talk the stalks off a cornfield."

"And me?" asked Gerardo guardedly.

"Sí, Gerardo, the fittest, the most handsome hombre that ever rode a horse – Sí, I'm coming to Emilio ... Our active, energetic, wide-awake whirlwind of a fellow."

"What about you, Pancho?" pushed José.

"What about me?"

"Maybe you can tell him, Cándido. I'm right out of words."

"A loud-mouthed braggart, a know-it-all know-nothing." Cándido coughed a pause, trying hard to knock up a further embellishment: "A fast-talking machine with everlasting batteries."

"Anything else?"

"Sí, one sure talent, that of dishing out the orders."

"Well," returned Pancho, after a fulsome hawk and spit, "there is something else about people. Something I've noticed in my travels through life, you understand …"

"Go on, we're not stopping you."

"People can be such blatant liars, don't you reckon?"

"Always has to have the last word," darkly muttered José.

"Sí, hermano!" laughed the old man.

Those long, fun-filled summer days of summer tales, with a touch of sun and dust on everything, on everyone.

This was, as old Pancho stated … *just a touch of summer.*

PART EIGHTEEN

80

A Grand Display I

Pancho's taxi arrived from the town, not quite at the time ordered, for the driver was the best part of half-an-hour late for his pick-up fare.

He stepped from his vehicle, a sorrowful and almost abject look on his face, holding hands together as though in supplication.

"A thousand apologies, señor!" he cried.

"That's okay," grinned the old ranchero, "the extra time was well spent – at least you remembered to come."

"San Stefan, señor, it was so busy! *I* was so busy. Ayí, mi madre, that señora Gabriella – *doña* Gabriella! – she kept me well past her usual time. 'Take me here,' now 'Take me other-where, to so-and-so'. Ayí, there was no end to it. I do apologise, señor Pancho."

The taxi-driver looked keenly at the old man. "It is you, hey? *The* señor Pancho? I knew it! What a carry-on, what a to-do this day has proved. The town has gone mad – no other way to describe it. And you, señor Pancho, you are practically considered a saint, if folk are to be believed. Still, in any case … at any rate, I mean to say it is an honour to serve you, and I'm happy that you chose my cab service. Vastly honoured, to be sure …"

"Well, are we to be off then, or shall we stay here and gossip like a couple of market women, eh?"

"I apologise again, perdónome, señor Pancho. Please to step this way – Oh! Ayí! Look at that! What's that?" The driver stood transfixed.

"What's what? Where?"

"There, señor, in the sky!"

"Ah sí, bueno, I see what you mean."

"Is it a plague of locusts? It looks like a plague of locusts, a dark cloud of them, I've never seen such before."

The old man gently smiled. "Look closer, as they come nearer, they're not locusts, amigo."

"Not locusts, you say? Then what must they be?"

"The Spirits of the Dead, my friend, that's what we see there in the sky. A bit late this year, I figure, but they come around the *Dia de los Muertos*."

"The Day of the Dead, of course! Spirits of the Dead …"

"Or, to be more practical… *butterflies*."

"Butterflies, of course! I recognise them now as such. Butterflies in their thousands, tens of thousands! Never seen so many!"

"Maybe many millions," murmured old Pancho.

The old man and his taxi-driver stood respectfully silent, gazing in rapt wonder at the sight of clouds of migratory Monarch butterflies fluttering now over their heads, like large confetti, like coloured snowflakes.

"Señor Pancho, is it not a wondrous sight? A truly wonderful thing for us to witness out here, just the two of us, and no one else around to feast on this miracle in the sky."

"Sí, a beautiful natural wonder, uuy …"

"But where have they come from?"

"The mountains of the south. What they call the mountains in the clouds."

"And where is it they go?"

"To the far reaches of Canada."

"Canada! You would hardly believe it. Such a long journey … such fragile creatures, too. You wouldn't credit it, would you?"

"It's true enough, and a one way only trip it is for them."

"Ayí, look at them, they're dropping from the sky!"

Many of the gorgeous insect creatures, with their wings of magenta and saffron, black outlined like miniature cathedral windows, began to settle and rest awhile about the two men, alighting on Pancho's sombrero, on his shoulders, on his clothing, even on his boots.

He was delighted. He was full of a joy that seemed unearthly and rather heavenly. And the heavens had opened up over this fortunate pair.

Millions more of these mighty Monarch butterflies continued on with their long, arduous flight to the far-flung northern regions of North America.

"I shall never forget this day, señor Pancho. Never …"

The taxi-driver's eyes were moist with emotion. Pancho, too, was visibly moved by this rare and exotic spectacle of nature, feeling humble one moment, uplifted the next.

It was a lovely, God-given, mind-expanding experience, not ever to be forgotten – as it was also to the driver of a taxi motor vehicle.

"Ayí, what a day it has been today, señor."

Old Pancho again smiled his gentle smile.

"And it is not yet over ..."

81

A Grand Display II

On that same day, in the evening, Pancho went along to see the fireworks display, taking mamá and the girls Ruth and Julia with him. They were not to watch the pyrotechnic spectacle among the crowds, as it happened, but to view the whole extravaganza from the vantage point of the balcony of the mayoral office at the municipal building.

The crowds once more roared when the mayor with Pancho in tow showed themselves to the townsfolk. The mayor appeared almost comical in full evening dress. The dark evening suit was marred by an inordinate length of the coat-tails, on one so short in stature, making him look somewhat similar to a well-nourished penguin.

The girl Ruth however was overawed by the regal-like company she found herself in, especially the obsequious attentions paid her by the mayor's two teenage sons. Julia was simply thrilled to pieces with everything and enjoying herself immensely.

Mamá was at first a little bemused by it all, not feeling comfortable until a short time later, when she fell in conversation with the Mayor's good wife, the pair of them discussing the merits of various culinary herbs.

Pancho of course took it in his stride, not one to stand on ceremony, and happily accustomed to his newfound celebrity status.

The mayor took hold of the old man's elbow, guided him to one side, so as to converse with him in private.

"This afternoon," he began in a confidential manner, and speaking in a harsh and peculiarly metallic voice, like a man with dodgy lungs, or so Pancho thought, but in fact his normal speech pattern. "Early this afternoon I made a special telephone call to Mexico City, and actually got through to the President's Press Secretary, without any bother at all – How marvellous is the telephone!

"And it wasn't too long before the Secretary was able to put me on to *el presidente de Mexíco* himself! I was deeply honoured, to say the least, to be talking with the President.

"'Mr. Mayor,' he says to me, the President, he says 'this Pancho fellow, is he by any chance señor Francisco Medina Ramírez to whom you are referring?'

"'The very same, your Excellency,' I assured him.

"'Mr. Mayor,' he continues on, 'I want a report on the remarkable incident of this morning. A full report, you understand, to be dealt with the utmost expediency.'"

The mayor became expansive, a hand gently coddling the old ranchero's shoulder; and again, Pancho listened to the other's curiously hollow, metallic tone of voice:

"This paints a perfectly auspicious picture for my political future – and of this town, also. It happened on my patch, during my tenure here, the … the saving of Our Lady of Guadalupe."

The high official kneaded Pancho's shoulder for emphasise, said, "I could very well earn a further term in office. And it is all thanks to you, my dear friend," with a final friendly slap on the shoulder.

Pancho stared back at him with some bemusement.

After that little confabulation, they began to chat as the best of friends, the pair of them swapping jokes and ribald anecdotes like cantina habitues, and occasionally glancing down at the plaza crowds …

Three men stood in a corner of the plaza side-on with the municipal building: a know-it-all municipal clerk, a shy and diffident book-seller, and an argumentative-type with an apoplexy-red face.

"That's him," said know-it-all, "that's *the* Pancho."

"What 'Pancho' is that?" wanted to know the argumentative one in belligerent tones.

"Why, the same Pancho that took an assassin's bullet while protecting our president. That's who I'm talking about, and there he is in person up on that balcony with the mayor."

"When was this attempt on the president's life?"

"It happened just near the tail-end of summer."

"Ah, sí, and the president shot this Pancho hombre."

"The president didn't shoot anyone."

"But he must have," force-fed argument-face, "I read of it at the time, I remember that much."

"This Pancho fellow was indeed shot," politely interjected the third party shyly and diffidently. "He was shot in the shoulder only, and so survived … or so I was led to believe," he ended apologetically, as if he were himself responsible for the shooting.

"He was shot dead, I tell you, that's someone else up there," insisted the second party with utter conviction, bristling with indignation and bursting for an argument.

"The assassin was shot dead," said know-it-all, knowingly, "a moment before he wounded the Pancho fellow. And I can tell you for why I know … *I was there*! I was with our president's entourage, during his visits to the northern states. Only this last summer it was."

"How can that be when he was in Vera Cruz at that time?"

"He was never in the south then. The president was in Guanajuato and Durango, then on to Chihuahua – or was it Sonora? At least at first he was in Guanajuato, because *we* were there. *I* was there. Only, I didn't go any further north – stayed in Guanajuato."

"So, who shot the president?"

"No one shot the president, damn it! An attempt was made, that's all."

"Okay then, why did the president shoot this Pancho?"

"Oh, I give up!" cried the clerk in frustration.

Elsewhere, practically everywhere, eyes were by this time on the jardín, where strings of coloured lights gave a festive glow to proceedings, rather like a Christmas fantasy scene. It was dark enough now for the lights to show their true colourful effects.

The parroquia bells rang the hour and an expectant hush fell on the dense crowd in the plaza. All that could be heard were the many birds settling for evening roosting in laurel trees, chapping and chittering in the dark evergreen leafage.

The grand fireworks display began with a double bang, as two cannons fired together from the twin belfries high up the church edifice. Instantly, five thousand or more roosting birds rose as one from the trees in the jardín, flapping wildly away in alarm into the darkening sky. The sound of those ten thousand or so wings was like a thunderous wash of ocean waves crashing onto a shore.

Then: a cracking, splintering crash of multiple rockets shot up into the eveningsky, squadron after squadron, exploding at their zenith into vibrant rainbow colours, showering down through a cloud of smoke. Followed by more explosions, of Catherine wheels and elaborate fireworks fixed to giant scaffolding, and set spinning and tossing, spewing out galaxies of coloured sparks.

More rockets were fired from the two belfries, soaring into rust-orange smoke and bursting into a novae of brilliant suns; the townsfolk and the countryfolk, especially, thrilled to the bangs and crackling of it all. And particularly before the massive church frontage, there was a continuous susurration of '*Oh!*'s and '*Ah!*'s.

There was in the air about the crowded plaza, a pungent stink of cordite, mingling with the more familiar smells of candy floss and steaming chillies and griddle-baked goodies, as street food-vendors pressed among the people. The crowds thickened in places, squashed up cheek by jowl, but with all eyes and attention focused on the display.

The dazzling, noisy, colourful show ran on unabated: Stars and a shimmering of bright spangled lights, bursts and flares of bottle-green and wonderful feathered tailings of iridescent green, like a great host of quetzal birds in flight. Purls of purple and saffron-yellow lights cascading down with sparks of brilliant diamonds, to be lost at street level in cordite smoke.

Explosive belching of crimson and sapphire and bolt-lightning-blue; huge falls of sulphurous silver and wildfire-red; flumes and flashes of turquoise and fountain streamers of blood-red, of royal blue and lemon-orange; popping and booming, cracking and barking – an incandescent starstorm of noise and colour.

The youngsters among this mass of humanity had for long moments forgotten a need for a stick of candy, or to go and have a wee. Their upturned faces scanned the sky with fascination, as the magnificently extravagant display went on with its noise and excitement, its smoke and eye-aching brilliant colours.

82

A Famous Bar

When the entertaining fireworks display finally came to a close and people began to move about more freely, many of them dispersing to vanish in the side streets, Pancho sent the girls back to Juan and Esperanza's house in the care of a mayoral official, who took his duties seriously.

The old ranchero escorted mamá through the crowds, heading for Los Dos Durango's Bar.

The place was already heaving with revellers when they arrived, the noise level increasing with their alcohol-induced shouting and laughter. The old man gazed about him, or at least tried to; the air seemed so thick and heavy with cigarette smoke, he reckoned you could just about cut bricks out of it, and said as much to María at his side.

What a place! Chattiness was the game here; chattiness, drinking and maybe dancing too later on. Pancho was to his surprise welcomed with cheers and open arms. Folks rose to their feet to grandly applaud the town's hero. Doña María was treated like a prima donna and could not help blushing crimson with embarrassment for the first twenty minutes or so.

The proprietor, don Tito, an openly warm sort, came forward and shook the old ranchero eagerly by the hand, while others at the same time were slapping him on the back.

Pancho had already taken a liking to this don Tito, whose volubility it seemed was of the nonstop over-exuberant kind. Don Tito was a caricature or comic character; and yet, not one to be taken too lightly, for he was an astute businessman and certainly a competent host.

He was a tiny man – like a boy – but full of vim and spirit; cheerful, garrulous, friendly. Perfect attributes for his post, alive with ebullient good humour. His large luminous brown eyes showed susceptibility to excitability. He was, even for one so small of statue, a massive personality.

Don Tito at once ordered chilled champagne, to be presented in a silver bucket with lots of ice, and with his compliments – he was in fact honoured to be Pancho's host and told him so. Room was made for the ranchero and doña María at the best table, directly facing a small stage. The noise soon increased a few decibels more.

The Englishman Matt Conners was there, long blond hair dishevelled, and appearing a trifle hungover from the morning's drinking session. Yet that could be put to rights, he averred, muttering something about the hair of the dog and that the night was young – would Pancho like a double?

The bar's resident musician Marlowe and his quartet were there too, banging out lively jazz pieces, with hardly a pause between each number. Marlowe was evidently on top form – a glass and a half-bottle of brandy rested on the piano top, between two flaring candles – and Pancho thought it rather exhilarating, enjoying what was to him a wholly new musical sound.

At regular intervals throughout the evening revelry he stopped his foot-tapping under the table and, unable to resist further, he plucked María from her seat, to dance between the tables. When this happened everyone clapped in time to the beat, urging him on in staying up with his short, plump partner, who danced exceedingly gracefully.

At one point a huge pizza-like savoury as big as a waggon wheel was brought in, perfectly fitting a deal table on which it lay, carried by four aproned señoritas from the kitchen. This enterprising *pièce de résistance* was preceded by the proprietor don Tito, who headed straight for Pancho's table.

On this special night don Tito was dapperly attired in a fine pin-striped suit, which he considered fitting for this occasion. It was of no concern to anyone, least of all to don Tito himself, that the trouser legs of his suit ended a good hand up from his ankles. Visitors to Mexico (and there were many American tourists here in the bar) quickly caught on to the notion of wearing anything one liked, no matter how inappropriate or bizarre. So it was that no one batted an eye at the strange attire of Benji, who was as usual propping the bar and gabbing with Gabriel the bartender. Benji was dressed this night in his old Korean War battle fatigues, chest ablaze with rows of genuinely earned campaign ribbons.

"I thought you were doing Lawrence of Arabia, Benji," said Conners, nursing a shot glass of tequila, "or was that last night?"

"Last night, my friend," replied Benji, gently smiling, "I was a Bedouin chieftain. *Salaam aleikum!*"

Meanwhile, don Tito fussed about the giant pizza on the deal table. "The culinary delight here is for you, Pancho, on the house," he declared expansively, "and for your guest too, it goes without saying," making a polite bow to María. Her red face deepened even more.

The deal table was placed before the old ranchero, and one of the kitchen girls began to cut a few large wedges from this unusual creation.

Later, there came the chief cook of the establishment, a roly-poly of a woman in whites – rumour had it that she was in fact don Tito's wife – and bearing in podgy arms a substantially sized iced cake, tastefully decorated with miniature sombreros in tinted pastillage. She lowered the cake on the main table, and with hands now free blew Pancho an audacious kiss, then curtsied before María, whose face seemed to be on fire.

"But it's not my birthday!" protested the old man with a laugh.

"It is for the event, my esteemed friend," announced don Tito, without doubt totally enamoured of his guest's celebratory status. "The event of this morning which has made you famous and the talk of the town. This is a supreme honour for me in having you sitting right here in my humble establishment."

There was a whole carnival of fun and bonhomie in those dark, dancing eyes of his; that happy host look, as joyous, contented, tequila-tanked tourist-types joshed and jittered about the crowded tables. It was said that one could always rely on don Tito for creating the kind of slap-happy carouse, which in this instance appealed to Pancho's own sense of fun.

Moreover, nor did he believe – this child-sized Peruvian host – in skimping when it came to treats for his customers, although he preferred the more cultured term – 'clientèle'.

Pancho watched with amusement as don Tito now tripped pigeon-toed over to a table on his left, saw that all was as it should be, and crossed to another table, jabbering jovially to anyone and sundry.

Benji eventually wandered over to the table where food was passed around. Around him in the candlelight laughing faces told of their happy and celebratory mood.

"I must congratulate you, Pancho my friend," he smiled, thumping the Mexican's back, "not only for your heroic action of this morning, but also your good taste in women. First, it was Our Lady of Guadalupe, and tonight it's our lady of field and meadow here, for I can see she's a country gal," with Pancho nodding but not fully understanding the other's words.

Nor did doña María understand what the American eccentric had said, which was probably just as well – she had enough to cope with in this strange company.

"Sí, amigo, gracias," was the old man's stock answer.

Moments later something singular, something quite odd occurred. It was after Marlowe and his group had finished playing a hot jazz number … There was a lull in the table-talk …A hush fell upon all in the room. Ears were cocked and listening …

To the sound of horses' hooves hollowly hitting the cobblestones in the street outside.

"It's the Seventh Cavalry, boys!" cried Benji, breaking the near quietness.

83

Rancheros Reunion

Matt Conners rushed outdoors to investigate, a few others following. The setup outside in the lamp-lit street could not have been more choreographically pleasing, at least to the eyes of idle onlookers crowding the narrow sidewalks; watching with interest as a fivesome of mounted rancheros in perfect line abreast, walked their steeds in sedate fashion. Preceded by a ragged line of *policia*, chattering among themselves in excitable tones. Behind the horsemen was another bunching of the town's police force, along with a solitary slow-moving police truck – the very same one old Pancho had been thrown in after a night of drunken revelry (at Los Dos Durangos!) back in the wintertime.

The Englishman Conners soon returned with excitement showing on his face. "You won't believe it!" he bubbled. "The police are out there, but they're not the ones riding horses."

"What's happening, friend?" enquired Benji.

"I've just seen the meanest looking bunch of desperadoes you're ever likely to find anywhere – except maybe in a Western film." Conners turned to the old man with open admiration sparkling his eyes. "Guess what, Pancho, they're coming in to see you! Tying up their horses to lamp-posts and car fenders."

"What about those cops?" asked Benji. "What are they up to?"

"Oh, they seem friendly enough, acting as escorts or guides or so it appears."

Conners eyes lit up once again. "Look!" he cried, pointing to the main doorway, "Here they are, Mexican bandits, coming in now!"

And with spurs jingling and boot-heels ringing on the flag-stoned floor, four unshaven, dust-smothered horsemen slouched insolently into the crowded, smoke-filled bar-room. People stepped aside as the riders moved forward, walking wide-legged – for they were horsemen after all. They brought in with them a smell of the stable and of rangeland dust.

Pancho got to his feet, his jaw almost in two pieces as he recognised his ranchero companions.

"¡*Viva* Pancho!" cried the first one, cross-eyed Cándido. "¡*Viva* Pancho Ramírez!"

"¡*A-Ahua!*" came the Mexican cry from José.

"¡*Ay-ay-ay-ayii!*" ran out the ranchero's call from Emilio, showing his horse teeth to great advantage.

"¡*Drrrrh!*" sounded Gerardo, fluttering his tongue behind teeth in an effort to consolidate a true macho image.

Pancho joyfully gave a Mexican abrazo to each of his trusted *compañeros*, with hearty back-slapping and '¡*Ay que bueno!*'s.

"What the devil, Cándido," he gravelled huskily, quite emotionally taken. "What's brought you lot into town?"

"We've come to bask in the glory of your newfound fame," grinned the young man, "which is known right across the State by now."

"Oh my!" gushed Gerardo, gazing around at an unfamiliar scene.

Gerardo was under the illusion that everyone was admiring him, he being one of the celebrated rancheros, and he modestly blushed. The cruel truth of it however, was that these people were more likely staring at his striking ugliness. Not realising this even remotely, Gerardo continued to blush modestly, adjusting his bandanna which had somehow become awry.

The rancheros then noticed doña María sitting at the main table, and they whipped off their sombreros and made a respectful bow to her. María rose from her seat with stately dignity, her cheeks back to their normal colour. She blessed each of them in turn, made the sign of the cross, and kissed them on the brow. The foreign tourists in the bar watched this moving ritual with fascination.

Don Tito, always attuned to the atmosphere of his own place, told Marlowe and his musicians to make an early night of it. He sent a runner cum errand boy named Gonzalez to a cantina across the street, with orders to bring over a mariachi band which was playing there.

This is going to be a proper Mexican night, the proprietor decided and to hell with these gringo tourists. He thumped a tall American on the chest and declared:

"A Mexican night this is, my good sir!" nodding and gesticulating with emotive energy.

"But you ain't Mexican, Tito," returned the American with a grin, "you goddamn Peruvian pecan nut!"

"Ah, sí, that is true, but Mexico has adopted me, and I've adopted Mexico. So there, you big Yankee tree-trunk!"

Spying Gabriel at his regular spot behind the bar counter, don Tito called to him imperatively:

"Bartender! Sí, I do mean you, Gabriel, don't look so surprised. Four tequilas *pronto por favor* for these thirsty ranchero fellows – doubles, of course! – and do hurry it, Gabriel!" Then the little man dashed outside to see if the mariachi players were on their way.

"I hear the policia are out there," Pancho was saying to Cándido. "You're not in any kind of trouble, are you?"

"No, no, amigo, it's no problem. At first they wouldn't allow us to ride into town. After we told them that we were working companions of Pancho Ramírez and had come to see him, well, they became sweet as honey and falling over themselves at being accommodating. They escorted us in and showed us the way to this place."

Cándido glanced around, squint eyes filled with amusement. "This is some weird kind of cantina," he opined, "but I like it all the same." And he did too, gazing interestedly at the mainly American tourist types, many of whom of female gender which was of special interest, though the whole crowd appeared unfamiliarly attired.

"It's a gringo's bar – for tourists and students," explained the old man. "They are fine people; uuy, they sure made me welcome here, and that first time when I came here early in the year.

"Ah, look what we have coming in, *hermano* …" as the mariachi players strolled in, already starting up with their instruments and singing voices.

Gerardo, in some response, felt compelled to run an encore of his Mexican greeting.

"Is Gerardo okay, or what is it?" asked Pancho, amazed at the ranchero's unusual extrovert behaviour.

"He's been like that all day," Cándido chipped in with a grin. "Can't you see? He's happy, and it's not often you find our Gerardo in a happy mood.

"By the by, don Roberto wanted to come but sends apologies as he's tied up with business matters, as you'd expect. Roberto and Jorge would have come along too, only they're still at the horse-fair in San Luis Potosi."

"Señor Pancho!" burst out don Tito, hustling his customers in order to reach his honoured guest. "My boy Gonzalez is helping bring the horses into the courtyard, where they'll be safe and not get hit by an *autobus* or a truck. Town life you know has its drawbacks and dangers, one of which is motorised traffic – a scourge on this very ancient town. Your young man out there is already tethering – Is that the term? – tethering them to the balustrade posts. Fine handsome horses they are too."

The old man shot a quick enquiring glance at Cándido, and growled, "Who is that then, muchacho?"

"Why, who do you think, Julian of course," laughed Candido.

"Julian! Here in San Stefan! Well, I'll be a two-legged coyote! Tell him to come on in, for God's sake."

"He won't come in here, Pancho," said José, smoking a regular cigarette given him by some American. "I can bet my boots on it. Much too shy to venture in here."

"He will need something to eat, surely," put in doña María concernedly.

"Take him some food and drink, then," the old ranchero ordered. "Here, a bit of this gringo grub will do."

"Don't you be worrying yourself, señor Pancho," soothed don Tito, the ever attentive proprietor, shoving himself in view, "it's already being taken care of. In fact, my friend – " - here he gave a conspiratorial wink – " – one of my little *señoritas* has taken a fancy to him and will be his slave for the rest of this night."

With such a clutter of clientele around him, don Tito was more than eager to rattle and gabble on, hardly able to catch his breath:

"Ah, bless me, it is marvellous how I arrange these matters just so – And sí, señor Pancho and gentlemen rancheros, the horses themselves will also be fed and watered, as soon as my runner boy is ready. I shall send him off for fodder in a moment, and he'll be back in a flash. I suggest you be seated here and enjoy yourselves – Please move along there for these friends of señor Pancho, that's it, *gracias* – Do you like my mariachis? Yes, I also think they're good – Sit, please, I implore you – That is perfect and yes, *bueno, bueno* – Oye, Gabriel! Four, no, five more tequilas as quick as quick, my man. Ah, these tequila-drinking rancheros, they keep you busy, I must confess ... Well friends, how is the music? Any special requests? Only say the word and I will arrange it for you in no time ... Ah yes, señor Pancho, *Sentimiento y Dolor* it shall be. I expect they should know that one. I'll see what can be done this very moment – " One of the kitchen girls came running up to him, urgently whispering in his ear. "Please excuse me but duty calls it seems and I am required elsewhere. I need to be two, three don Titos – Yes, Conchita, I shall go this instant, and who started this little problem in the kitchen, hey? That's what I want to know, and I intend to get to the bottom of it - *¡Carambas!* as they say in local circles," and don Tito trotted off to his trouble-shooting tasks.

"What was all that about?" asked Cándido of no one in particular, casting a cockeye at the small departing figure.

The glorious festive evening wound on with endless drinking and laughter. Even Gerardo seemed as gay as a goose that had laid a golden egg. He downed his tequilas with verve and aplomb, under supposedly admiring eyes of several American female art students from the local *Instituto*.

There was don Tito, happy as a lark, dapper and diminutive; his penknife-trim, slight frame needling through between tables, bouncing along on childlike tiny feet – clad in black patent leather dancing shoes – tip-toeing now as he peered over the shoulders of large-sized overgrown Americans.

Don Tito listened for a short spell with approving consideration, to his guests' inane chatter, nodding now at something he thought most profound, snatching keen eyes and ears of interest off one and focusing on to another, like a metronome clocking data, not missing a beat, whether it be music or conversation.

The drinks were coming fast and plentiful:

"Here, down this, pal."

"Is this what you ordered?"

"Can't recall, but it don't matter."

"How many have I had? What a dumb question!"

"You can play that one again – I say! – I say?"

"I'll have another, sure."

"You just had another."

"So what, I'll have *another*."

The hilarity and the revelry were ever constant, ever on the increase.

"Come on, Pancho," pressed the Englishman Conners a time later. "Get up on that table and dance where everybody can see you."

"That is it," poked in don Tito, materialising like a small genie. "As señor Pancho told me himself not so long ago, if you want to live life to the full … then you must live it exactly so."

"Go ahead," urged José, smiling a wicked smile, "make a fool of yourself."

"That's the ticket," said someone, of the foreign crowd. "Here, clear this table, you guys. Grab your drinks and take away the candles, somebody."

And somebody did. Pancho needed no prompting. He clambered onto the rough wooden table, put out a hand to heave his partner, María, up after him.

The mariachi players swung once more into a Mexican flavoured swing tune. The two dancers began their routine on the table-top, amid wild cheering and clapping. The rancheros banged fists on the wood, boot heels clacking like castanets on the flag-stoned floor.

"What marvellous nimbleness," said Conners, more to himself than to anyone who might be listening. No one would have heard him anyhow with the volume of noise issuing from both mariachis and the crowd. "What incredible deftness, for a bow-legged, barrel-chested horseman."

"Go on, Pancho!" encouraged a voice in the smoke-choked room, "give it some stick, old feller!"

The old ranchero's face was ecstatic as his boots crashed down on the thick solid table. Doña María pluckily kept pace with him, her face almost serene. While Pancho's working compañeros now slid into ranchero mode by thumping their thighs, slapping their leather chaps.

"Steady there, Pancho!" someone warned, as he gave a queer lurch and twist to his body.

"God's sake, he's going over!" cried another voice in alarm.

The old man was indeed keeling over.

He fell heavily on one knee, crunched up, with a hand holding hard to his chest, a look of anguished pain on his face, wet with sweat.

The old ranchero toppled over like a dead weight onto a bench and rolled over again to land hard and awkwardly on the stone floor.

84

Time to Leave

"He's hurt himself!" came the first cry out of a momentary hush.

"What happened to him?"

"He's drunk, can't you see!"

"He's *borracho*! Drunk!" declared Gerardo, rising from his seat.

"No, it's not that," called out doña María, who knew better, who realised at once that this was clearly a more serious matter.

Then Benji barged forward and took over. "Out of the way, fellers," he ordered gruffly. "Make some room for him, goddammit! Let him breathe, stand back there and let me get to him. I'm a medic – or used to be. Stand back, you apes!"

Benji had in truth worked as an army medic in the Korean War, and knew what he must do here.

"Help me!" María opened up. "Help me down, for heaven's sake!" she cried with a desperate air, and Cándido threw up arms to steady her down off the table.

He turned at that moment and found himself face to face with the simpleton Julian. The mild-wit was quietly weeping.

"What's wrong, Julian? What's up with you, what is it?"

"Señor Cándido, it is the end," declared the youth in a flat tone.

"The end? The end of what?"

Julian stared at his ranchero friend with fright in his eyes, and said, "The end of *everything*, señor …"

Old Pancho was at the other side of the table, lying inert on the floor. One hand was crooked like a claw and there was a peculiar grimace on a now ash-grey face.

"He's assuredly overdone himself," said María, hurrying round to him. "Done some serious mischief, it looks like, the poor soul."

"I reckon you're right, señora, and could be more serious than you think," said Benji soberly, and sober he was, as sober as he had ever been in a long time. "I guess he's suffered a stroke, and it just may repeat itself."

"We must get him home at once," said María, wringing hands in agitation, "to my sister's casa – not far from here – and telephone for a doctor. At once!" she said again, feeling that everything would be alright if only they could have him safely at Esperanza's casa.

"Of course, señora, don't you worry, it'll be done as quickly as possible," Benji assured her.

He was kneeling by Pancho's side, glancing at the faces around him, and recognising the young Englishman, Conners. "Matt, old buddy, is don Tito about? Can you go get the guy?"

"I'm here! I'm coming!" called the bar owner from the rear of a mass of people pressing by the table. "Let me through, please!"

The mariachi band had of course ceased playing and an altogether different atmosphere pervaded the room.

"Don Tito, we must get Pancho home quickly to this señora's – It's María, isn't it? – to María's sister's house, and call a doc for him." Benji spoke in low urgent tones to the proprietor, also on his knees by the other's elbow. "In the courtyard, that door leading to your wine cellar – "

"Yes! Yes?"

"It's off its hinges I noticed. I need that door to use as a stretcher. Do you read me?"

"Clearly, I understand. To use my door as a stretcher, that is a good idea."

"And blankets, my friend, I want some blankets – and a pillow too. Send one of your girls to fetch the stuff, and please hurry it!" He saw Conners standing over them. "Matt, here, I want a word with you."

"A door and some blankets and a pillow, double pronto. I am gone already," said don Tito, getting to his feet and scampering off to the courtyard area.

"Matt, Pancho here has suffered a heart attack, I'm certain of it, which is bad news, real bad, buddy," Benji informed Conners in a hurried whisper. "We need to – Look, can you stand back there, you guys, and give us some space, damn it!" he shouted at the press of bodies behind him.

He turned to face the Englishman. "We need to get him out of here fast and take him home, which isn't far according to the Mexican lady. This old man is gonna need lots of peace and quiet and rest, I reckon. As soon as the 'stretcher' arrives, along with blankets."

"Hey, Gabriel!" he called over, spotting the bartender hovering close by. "I'll want some assistance pretty soon. Maybe these ranchero guys who are friends of his. Pick yourself a sturdy lifting team, okay pal?"

"Right," responded Gabriel, large eyes rolling, and understanding the situation at once, requiring promptitude. "I'm with you, or will be after I talk to these cowboys," and he began explaining to Pancho's fellow rancheros.

Space was made for don Tito and half his catering staff as they struggled to manoeuvre a door through the main entryway. Gerardo and Emilio stepped forward and took over the task from the staff. Cándido and José soon joined them to assist.

While this was going on, María held the old ranchero's crooked hand, gently stroking it, desperately trying to get a grip on her feelings. The old man was fully conscious but unable to speak. His one good eye was fixed on her with that familiar twinkling amusement, as if he wanted to say, "So here I am on the floor and not for the first time, but don't mind me for I'll be up again in a moment, you'll see."

"Stand aside, please," said don Tito, with his helpers steering the door to where old Pancho lay.

"Push that damn table to one side," ordered Benji. "Did you get the blankets? – Right, that's swell. Put them there for now. Two on the door first, spread them, okay – "

"A pillow too I have," said don Tito, his face lined with concern. "Here, Margarita, the pillow, gracias. There, a pillow for the poor fellow's head."

"Thanks, Tito, you're doing alright," Benji praised him. "Matt, Gabriel, we've got to lift him on to the stretcher, in one swift swing. Easy does it, let's co-ordinate our movements. Okay, guys, gather round him – You take that side, mister – Hold him … so …okay now, lift up! Over, fellers, that's it. The blankets – Excuse us, María, you wait this side, there's a honey. Don Tito, I want Cándido and Emilio at the front, and you – José, is it? – at the back with the good-looking guy (meaning Gerardo). The others can help when and where needed. Try not to jerk, we slide up gently in one easy fluid motion. And we go! Lift! Easy with it now and up we come, steady. Great stuff. Let's move on out."

The door on which Pancho lay was hoisted onto the shoulders of the four chosen bearers, his companeros, with a good half-dozen willing hands about them. The stretcher was borne out of the bar, into the courtyard, through the large, carriage-way double-doors, and into the street. The door stretcher was pointed in the direction of the plaza, the bearers setting off toward the parroquia.

85

A Second Procession

So! There it was. On this day in the town of San Stefan there happened to be two processions, though this latter one was not without its oddities; rather strange and unconventional, eccentric if not entirely crazy.

With doña María hurriedly leading the way along the lamp-lit street, the bier-like object directly behind her, followed by nearly fifty half-drunk revellers who were however soberly subdued by this time.

Los Dos Durangos was practically empty, save for the cook and a couple of kitchen-hands. The bar was totally deserted, the candles on the tables burning low and guttering one by one. The rancheros' horses were still 'stabled' in the cluttered courtyard, faithful Julian attending to them.

María kept turning round, as though afraid that this cortege might turn and wander off somewhere. A curious cortege ever to be seen, with its followers. The long scraggled line of humanity stitched its way along a narrow, semi-illumined street, quietly and funereally.

A fair distance past the parroquia, María said, "Can anyone run on ahead to warn my sister?" which stopped the procession. 'Who are all those people?' she wondered, gazing back at the extended procession.

"Of course, doña María," said don Tito, hovering nearby. "The boy Gonzalez can go. Gonzalez! Are you there, muchacho?"

"Sí, señor," came a prompt reply from a stringy youth, who quickly ran up to the stretcher.

"Did you hear what doña María said, to go on to her sister's house?"

"I didn't hear that, señor," the youth replied, "but I can easily run on to the señora's house – Where does your sister live, señora?"

"*Cielito Lindo*," said María in a tremulous voice. "One street on past the post office on the right. My sister is at number twenty-three, on the left as you go down – Oh, and the doctor!" she suddenly realised. "Don Tito, the muchacho can also go to the doctor's house, as it's on the same street."

"Did you hear that, muchacho?"

"Sí, señor," replied the youth.

"On the other side from my sister's casa," said María, almost getting a little flustered. "I think it's number thirty-four – But my sister can show you."

"Have you got that, muchacho?"

"Sí, señor."

"You must ask the doctor to wait at number twenty-three. Off you go, pronto."

The youth sprinted away down the street.

"Well, that is that for the present," said don Tito with satisfaction. "He's living up to his name is that one, our *Speedy Gonzalez*," and the procession once again proceeded on its way.

No one had noticed a slight movement on the moving door.

"It's now nothing but s-sackcloth and ashes …It's all of a p-piece," slurred the old man quietly to himself. "It is the Judgment no less …I asked for it but n-never saw it coming …" he uttered, in a seemingly faraway voice, heard by no one.

The right half of his face was twisted, distorting his features. A curve of his lips made him appear about to snarl or grimace; and there was no more that special light, that twinkling good-humour, showing in those blue eyes of his.

The old ranchero, barely conscious and a little confused, wondered if his sombrero was still on his head. The notion that he was without it weighed heavily upon him, yet he need not have stressed himself, for the 'permanent fixture' was still just so.

People in the street, on learning who it was stretched out on the mobile door, and remembering him saving Our Lady of Guadalupe figure only this morning, these townsfolk tagged on to the procession as it wended its way.

Doña María couldn't resist glancing back every few paces, to assure herself that they were still following her. She was amazed at how long the procession had grown. And more people were joining them, coming in hurried droves from the plaza area and adjacent streets.

When they reached the turning into the side street named Cielito Lindo, María once more halted the proceedings.

"I think Francisco is trying to say something," she said apologetically. "I'm certain he is. A moment, please," and stooped to the old man, as the door was obligingly lowered a foot to help the matter.

His face remained the same with the lopsided twist to it, but seemed not as pronounced as earlier, María fancied.

"Too m-many… damned omens, María," he managed to get out in a mangled, gravelled voice.

María strained her senses, hardly able to understand what he was trying to say. "What are you telling me, Francisco?"

"Damned o-omens, María…"

Mumbled and muttered and barely comprehended though his words were, it struck María that these might be the last words she was ever to hear from the lips of this dear old friend.

Old Pancho was at last carried into the house of Juan and Esperanza, carefully lifted off the door stretcher and put in a proper bed in his own small guestroom.

The doctor was already there at the house. He shooed everyone out of the room, and immediately began to examine his new patient.

86

The Waiting Game

Outside in the street were now well over a hundred townsfolk, patiently waiting for the doctor's report, which had been promised them in order to hold down growing consternation and turmoil existing out there in the packed street.

At one stage doña María's sister Esperanza came outdoors to ask the crowd to quieten a little, although in fact they were hardly making any noise at all; it was simply their sheer numbers, filling the entire side street.

The Ramos girls, Ruth and Julia, had managed without their aunty knowing to manoeuvre out behind her, dressed in their nightclothes.

Julia spotted a familiar face at the front edge of this large gathering blocking the street. It was Cándido, and she ran to him.

"Cándido," she opened up breathlessly, "what is wrong with Pancho?"

"Why, he's been taken poorly," bending to the child, mustering a sympathetic smile.

"I know he is poorly. So is that it, then?"

"What do you mean, flower?"

"Well, Pancho is ill, sí?"

"Sí, he's ill."

"That's alright then. He won't be going anywhere, because he hasn't got a ticket," she explained to him seriously.

"Going anywhere? Ticket?"

In a small voice she said, "When I was ill in the springtime, I asked – "

"Ah, sí, I understand." The young ranchero understood only too well, and a tight, heavy sensation gripped his throat.

"You are right, Julia," he carried on, "as far as I know Pancho has no ticket to go anywhere …"

Behind Cándido stood his ranchero compatriots, in a strictly sombre, subdued mood.

Gerardo had put on his diagnostician mantle, wondering whether his friend Pancho's present condition was a temporary ailment or not, or – God forbid! – it might be of a chronic nature, like his own back problem which was indeed that way inclined.

A moment later he began scratching his large, rubbery comedian's nose, feeling somewhat unwell himself, clearly suffering the effects of the drink, food and excitement of the evening. Maybe *he* should see a doctor, was his sudden thought. His ugly face in the dim streetlight partially disturbed some of the townspeople, taking him for a villain or desperado.

Emilio's fat flubbered form was like a barrier against the people pushing and pressing towards him and José. He shifted his bulk, took a firmer stance.

You won't get past me, he was thinking.

He yawned widely, large teeth gleaming yellowy under the street lighting. Deprived of sleep for such a long number of hours, the fat man was beginning to feel that he hadn't slept for a week.

José was on a different wavelength altogether. His mind seemed in some kind of mental turmoil. He knew at last that he no longer wished to play his accustomed role of *'the lone silent hombre'*. No, not anymore. He began to realise that it somehow didn't synch with the way present things were turning out – or might turn out.

A sudden surge to enjoy and make the most of life ran through his whole mean, lean frame.

He turned to Emilio by his side.

"What do you reckon, hermano?"

"About what?" The fat man, too, was in his own dreamworld.

"This business …old Pancho."

Emilio roused himself. "Oh, he'll pull through alright. Strong as a stallion is that old man, in spite of his age."

He held a hand to his chin, fingered the folds of fat flesh, and deliberated. He was wondering when old Pancho would be 'in harness' again, the thought raising his spirits.

Brightening of a sudden, like sunshine filtering out from behind a cloud, he announced in cheerful cadences, "What he needs more than anything is plenty of rest and quiet and sleep – "

"That's what the *norteamericano* said," murmured José.

" – Sí, so he did. I have always maintained – as you well know – always maintained that a fair and solid helping of rest, quiet and sleep does you a power of good. It's like recharging your batteries. Believe me, hermano, I stand by it with great faith."

In thinking of these thoughts, so dear to his psyche, Emilio of a sudden felt pooped, wound-down, worn out, and more than ready for some rest. His one overriding desire right now, was to fall into sweet slumber, as sound as a stone. He could sleep standing up, as he had done many times in the past.

José nodded absently. With reluctance, though powerfully drawn to it, he returned to his own troubled thoughts. His carefully acquired and stored hardheartedness was beginning to dissolve and melt away. He felt utterly lost, helpless, and even afraid; of what he was afraid, he couldn't put a name to, were he to be asked.

There was a growing uncomfortable tightening in his chest, an unusual constriction in his throat – Had he perhaps knocked back a tequila too many in that gringo cantina?

Minutes ticked on inexorably as the street crowd waited. Among them and no less desperate to hear news of whatever kind, were Pancho's ranchero friends and *compadres*. The simpleton Julian, left with the men's mounts at don Tito's famous establishment, sensed instinctively that all was not well, had sensed it long back, and accepting it now with profound sadness.

87

Juan Ramos

Back on the Ramos farmstead, out in the quiet countryside on this dark moonless night, the boy Juan was asleep in his room. The air was utterly still, with none of the normal night noises. The night was silent and serene as untouched silk and full of an ineluctable mystery.

Juan usually slept soundly, but of a sudden he awoke with a start. He couldn't fathom what it was that had caused him to come wide awake. Had he experienced a bad dream? He couldn't recall.

The night was still silent. He sat up in bed and stared into the blank black void of darkness, sweating slightly on his brow, and he wondered why that was so. The night air was cool, his room was cool. The slight perspiration soon dried on him.

Well, he couldn't sleep, he knew that much, at least not for a while.

He slid out from his bed and pulled on shirt, pants and boots, quietly and unhurriedly. The dog Salté rose too, hound jaws wide in a cavernous yawn.

The boy and canine companion stalked softly across the courtyard, out past the stable, following a track leading to the river. Salté trotted on ahead, leading the way as was his usual habit. Seeing their way by starlight.

This night-time wandering was natural enough for them; they'd done it many times before. On this occasion however, Juan was driven by some compelling force.

The boy soon reached the river, a slow winding band of quicksilver reflecting the light of innumerable stars in the blacksky. He stopped at the river's grassy bank. For a while he stood at the riverbank, a hand absently fondling Salté's big hairy skull.

To young Juan the darksky seemed mysterious and awesome this night, much like a few times before during his time spent this last summer on don Roberto's ranch. He smiled, thinking of the old ranchero and friend Pancho, and the others: Cándido, Gerardo, José, Emilio …and Julian.

It was so unearthly quiet and still everywhere around him. There was no wind. There was no sudden scutter of a fieldmouse or a soft swoosh of an owl in flight. To his mind it was as though the world had stopped and held its breath.

The only real things about him were normal enough, like the silvery lane of the river's length, cactus and carrizos silhouetted by starlight. And a sweet homely earth smell; its soil and grass and stone. A musk odour of settled dust on the cooled ground, and the night perfume of rock herbs, strong and sensuous in the stillness of this night.

His gazing took him at last to the real earthnight: its night sky. Such a number of stars in the heavens. He marvelled as they glittered in celestial glory, twinkling and colouring, as if beckoning him; urging him to reach out to them, daring him to grasp them as one would grasp diamonds on black velvet cloth.

Suddenly, there was a fine arc of light in the sky as a shooting star sped across the high, silent darkness into oblivion. Then there was another! And yet another.

A shower of meteors silently exploding in the vastness above him. He had seen plenty of those, with the rancheros only this last summer, knew exactly what they meant to the simple people of the land.

It was at this moment that Juan realised what had impelled him to come here. He had forgotten something of importance, and even now could not remember what it was. Why had the night walk failed to jolt his memory? What was it, something of consequence, he knew that much, but what? It'll come to him eventually, so he relaxed his troubled mind.

At least he had seen the display of shooting stars.

Salté cast dog-devotional eyes at his trusty master, as if wanting something, which to Juan was not in the least out of the ordinary.

"You want to go back to bed, do you, lazybones?" he smiled. "Come on, then…"

The pair loped back, like two night predators on the prowl, following alongside a field of farrowed earth.

Of a sudden, a spectacular shooting-star streaked across the sky, brightly prominent and long-tailed.

But the boy had his head down and never saw it.

EPILOGUE

EPILOGUE

I

It was spring again.

Three years had gone by since the passing away of the old ranchero Pancho Ramírez. In that time there had been only a few changes in the valley of San Angelo. The pueblo now boasted electricity in several of the humble adobe dwellings, though on the nearby Ramos homestead they still burned their old-fashioned kerosene lamps and oil lanterns.

Doña María – better known as mamá – had fulfilled a long-held promise to travel all the way to Mexico City and visit with another younger sister and family in their noisy ground-floor apartment off *Insurgentes Sur.*

Her sister lived in quite different circumstances, and had an indoor kitchen with an electric cooker, which mamá totally distrusted, and not to say disapproved of. While staying with this family branch she had one time nearly lost a hand when experimenting with an electric food mixer.

The horrendous nonstop noise and traffic of city life unnerved and proved far too much for her to tolerate with any equanimity. In short, she had hated every hour of it and returned north to the blessed countryside as soon as she was decently able to, without showing offence to her sister, vowing never to go there again. Let her sister come up north, she had told everyone.

Don Antonio had purchased at great expense a new generator to pump water from the well. These days he seemed to spend an inordinate amount of time standing guard, so to say, over this valuable piece of machinery as it loudly chugged and rumbled in its workings. He obviously intended to fully protect his investment. He fiddled and faffed about this new-fangled machine, and often listened to its wayward murmurings as a doctor would listen to a patient's irregular heartbeat. He did try not to tinker and interfere with it, tried very earnestly to resist his obsessional hankerings.

The eldest of the family, Cristina, was wed at last, to her mother's relief and satisfaction – on two counts, for the girl had married well two years last June to Jorge, the youngest son of don Roberto, the *haciendado*. Cristina was blissfully happy, her whole temperament changed almost out of all recognition, thus did married life admirably suit her. Helped to a considerable degree by the fact that the marital home was built near the old casa at don Roberto's expense. Cristina ensured that every room was daily inundated with fresh-cut flowers, her mamá in the permanent role of nurserywoman.

Ruth, now a precocious teenager, had grown tall like her papá, and was considered stunningly beautiful by everybody. All the young bucks from the pueblo and beyond would hang around the farmstead in hopes of catching a glimpse of this rare beauty.

And now that Cristina had flown the nest to attend to her own home, Ruth spent more time helping her mamá about the ancient, smoky cooking-range under the kitchen lean-to, and other sundry chores. Her culinary skills, baking in particular, had improved beyond everyone's expectation, including her own.

Each day as she worked with a will about the kitchen yard, she cheerfully sang or gossiped and was an enormous source of pleasure for her mamá.

Young Julia had come along in great strides with her drawing, and was now producing quite competent artwork. Two years back her teacher had encouraged the girl to try the medium of watercolours. Much to the family's astonishment, Julia proved just as adept at painting. She positively flourished, evidently possessing a natural talent for the medium.

She was not one would say a prodigy, but considering her artistic isolation, Julia had made remarkable progress in her skills. No one had taught her, the girl's techniques came about through trial and error, acquired by accident or experiment, or even sometimes by luck.

Julia had managed to develop a style that was entirely her own, of wonderful artistic merit. She was never afraid to put brush to paper, such was her abundant confidence. Her bold bright strokes of colour lent an air of vivacity and splendour to her paintings of ordinary everyday scenes and landscapes.

She would wander off through the valley, her board and pad and paintbox tucked under one arm, and spend almost an entire day sketching and painting. Always aware of the changing light, always managing to capture the spirit and essence of anything she saw that inspired her.

Juan, now in late-teenage, was a strapping good-looking youth. He too had grown tall, was well-proportioned; and had such a look of drive and intelligence, assets of which gave him a commanding presence. This was recognised by don Roberto, who had readily taken him under his wing as a potential ranch foreman.

He had already gained the respect of the rancheros – namely Cándido, Gerardo, José and Emilio – and these men willingly accepted the young man's natural authority and leadership. All he had learned from old Pancho he put to use on the ranch, the road ahead appearing clear for a full managerial position. Part of his time, notwithstanding, was still spent in helping papá around the farmlands; the rest was utilized in don Roberto's extensive stabling and horse-training activities, in readiness for sales mainly to the military authorities and the *federales*. He even took advantage of don Roberto's extensive library of interesting books – just as old Pancho did in his time.

II

One clear bright day in mid-spring, mamá was as usual enveloped in woodsmoke under the kitchen lean-to. At one moment she turned, sensing the presence of someone other than Ruth, who was sitting at the big family table, shucking corn.

There, coming into the yard, was a boy. A stranger, for mamá had never seen him before. He was short and stockily-built, more like chunkily-built. Mamá was instantly aware of his barefootedness, his clothes ragged and dusty. On his head rested, what mamá considered, a deplorably tattered straw sombrero with a gaping hole in the crown. But it was not this that piqued mamá's growing curiosity, it was something else.

The boy had reddish hair, thick and spiky.

And blue eyes.

Cornflower blue!

As he stepped forward, staggering slightly, as if he had been drinking, don Antonio emerged from his room. He looked enquiringly at this scruffy apparition, who merely gave him a polite glance and continued on to mamá. Ruth stopped her shucking of corn and stared large-eyed at him.

"Buenas tardes, muchacho," mamá opened up first, wiping hands on a cloth.

"Buenas tardes, señora," he greeted her, in a peculiarly rough, grating, older person's voice. "Doña María Ramos, is it?" he asked politely, removing his sombrero and making a small gentlemanly bow to her, the sun gleaming on his thatch of ginger-red hair, turning it gold.

"¿Sí?" mamá murmured tensely, her curiosity fully aroused.

"Señora, por favor, I heard that you could help me. You see, I am looking for señor Ramírez, and heard you might tell me where he is. Señor Francisco Medina Ramírez, that's his given name, señora. Could you tell me where I can find him? They said that you would know, señora …"

Mamá and don Antonio looked at each other with pained expressions.

"Please, muchacho," said don Antonio quietly, touching the boy's shoulder, "sit yourself, here by the table."

The boy obediently sat on a bench by the table, glancing at Ruth sitting opposite, but gazing steadily and earnestly at mamá with his startling blue eyes.

"Muchacho," went on don Antonio in a gentle tone, and the boy turned his eyes on him, "why are you looking for señor Ramírez?"

"Uuy, he is my uncle, señor," said the boy, with that same unusual deep-throated manly quality of voice.

Don Antonio held his shoulder again and said, slowly and gravely:

"My dear young soul, your uncle, señor Ramírez is no more, passed away nearly three years ago – "

"Passed away?"

"He died, my child, in San Stefan, at the time of the big fiesta – "

The boy did not hear the last portion of don Antonio's words. He slumped over the table in a dead faint. Mamá went to him at once.

"Ruth! Some pillows, from your room, quickly now!"

The girl returned within seconds with two fat pillows off her own bed. Mamá and don Antonio laid the boy out on the bench, head resting on the pillows.

"Oh, mama!" exclaimed Ruth of a sudden. "Look!" pointing at the boy's feet.

Apart from being dirty, his feet were cut, bruised and bleeding.

"Some towels, Rutí!" shot out mamá with urgency, "and I'll get some warm water. Papacíto, go and get me bandages if you will from the second drawer," and don Antonio stalked off on long legs to do his wife's bidding.

A short time later, after mamá had cleaned and bandaged the boy's injured feet, she took the opportunity while he was still unconscious to remove his ragged *camisa* and also wash his body. Ruth found one of Juan's old but clean shirts he'd grown out of, and this was put on the recumbent figure.

"This muchacho is fairly exhausted," said mama with feeling, "and goodness knows where he has travelled from, but some distance I'd wager – and on foot as well, it looks like. At any rate I shouldn't be surprised."

The young stranger came round to full consciousness. He sat up startled.

"It's alright, muchacho," mamá said sweetly, as though soothing a small child. "You're very tired and dropped off to sleep. I bet you might be hungry too, aren't you? When did you last eat?"

The boy gazed at her with vivid blue eyes, felt assured, and said:

"Yesterday, señora – I – I stole a *tamale* from a basket somewhere in – I can't remember the place."

"That's alright, it's not important, don't fret yourself. I'll give you something nice and light to start off with – Ruth, the *sopa*! – Would you like some chicken sopa? I'm sure you would. With warm tortillas. Wait one moment, dear soul."

Mamá managed to tear herself away and began bustling about the kitchen, Ruth helping her with the food preparation, by warming a small pile of tortillas.

The boy turned and smiled at don Antonio, who had sat himself on the end of the bench. It was a charming boy's smile. Ruth and mamá saw it – it caught the girl like a jolt of electricity. Glancing at each other, they too smiled.

"He's got beautiful blue eyes, mamá, don't you think?" whispered the girl, and breathed a deep and happy sigh, while mamá looked at her with a hint of amusement.

"Where have you come from, my child?" asked don Antonio, and mamá's ears were pricked and listening like radar scanners.

"Sonora, señor."

"You look as though you've walked it, all the way from there to here," don Antonio smiled gently at him.

"Mostly, señor. I got an autobus to Chihuahua. At the bus station in Chihuahua I was going to get another autobus, but two men set about me. They beat me, señor, and stole my money, every bit of it, ay que caray. I had to walk the rest of the way."

"You *walked* from Chihuahua to San Angelo?" gasped mamá, unable to resist butting in.

"Two men beat you?" agonised Ruth.

"Oh, you poor little soul!" mamá gasped again.

After hearing this appalling tale, two females could not get to him fast enough with their gifts of sustenance.

"Here, muchacho, get this down you," urged mamá, now broadly smiling, placing a bowl of soup before the boy. "Slowly, mind, or you'll choke – "

She turned to Ruth, throwing up her arms – "Nothing but a tamale since yesterday!"

The boy set to on delicious smelling chicken soup, everyone watching with a mixture of intentness, satisfaction, and not a little sympathy.

It was as if the young fellow had not eaten for a week, completely ignoring mamá's advice to eat slowly. He ate like a starved dog.

III

Ruth was soon regarding the young stranger with a singular fascination. What a lovely head of hair under that awful hat, she thought, like red gold. And such expressive blue eyes, she had never seen the like before, except for old Pancho, though his had been paler, she reckoned. When he speaks, oh that voice of his! He's not bad-looking either. In fact, when he smiles –

And the boy glanced her way at the precise moment the thought ran in her head, and smiled at her. Ruth was devastated. She felt faint and kind of wobbly on her feet, her girlish mind topsy-turvy with new emotions.

She parked herself down on a stool opposite him, blushing like a hothouse rose. He concerned himself with the matter in hand, as he rolled a tortilla and stuffed half of it in his mouth, eating mightily and wolfishly.

Mamá was dying for more information, to learn of his history, but could see how hungry the boy was, and dare not as yet interrupt him. When he was halfway through the bowl of soup, however, she could contain herself no longer. She next did something no member of the family had seen in a long age.

She sat herself down at the table.

Mamá placed her homely figure by Ruth's side, and leaning forward so that her ample bosom spread over the tabletop, said somewhat breathlessly:

"Muchacho, you haven't told us your name."

"Francisco, señora," and the boy got to his feet and made a small polite bow to her, much in the manner of a ranchero, which charmed mamá and Ruth. "Francisco Cruz Ramírez," and he sat down again, dipped his face to the bowl of soup.

"Well, bless him!" declared mamá, flabbergasted and unable to pursue anything else for the present moment.

"I'm surprised you did not know of your uncle's death," said don Antonio, taking over. "He was a good and dear friend of our family, by the by."

"I would not have come, señor," said the boy, "if I'd have known that. ¡Újule! I wouldn't have come."

"It was in many of the newspapers at the time," continued don Antonio. "The man who saved the President's life, and the statue of the Virgin – he died that very same day he saved Our Lady of Guadalupe. Our old friend, Pancho Ramírez ..."

"*Pancho* Ramirez?"

The boy stopped eating, casting a quizzical look at the solemn man next to him. "I did hear of that, sí. ¡Ay que caray! But I didn't know it was my own uncle. ¡Uuy! So it was my uncle Francisco and I never caught on to that," he went on in his peculiarly mature voice tone.

Mamá and Ruth again exchanged looks, this time of incredulity and astonishment.

"Did you leave your mamá and papá to come here in search of your uncle?" mamá managed to get out.

"No, señora, my mother died two years back. It was poison in her blood from a rat bite, and she died of it." – Mamá and Ruth looked at each other with anguish in their eyes – "And my papá, he left a long time ago, to work in *Estados Unidos* – the United States. He went to California to work in the orange groves and such. Hmm. And he never came back."

"Didn't your papá write to you or send money to your family?" asked mamá.

"Not as I know of, señora. You see, I heard a time ago from someone who went to work in California – "

"Ruth, the *chicharrones*, they'll be ready, *ándale* – Sorry, Francisco."

" – and this man said that my papá was in prison and would be in there for a very long time. I don't know what he'd done, señora, but the *norteamericanos* put him in prison. He was a good man, my papá, so I don't know what had happened."

"Was this in California?" asked don Antonio.

"Ay sí, señor, on an island somewhere, or so I was told. Hmm. A place called Alcatraz."

"Good grief!"

Don Antonio put a hand to his mouth and coughed. A cough of some significance, or so interpreted by mamá. Maybe he had heard of the place, she conjectured, and of its bad reputation too, no doubt.

"Have you no brothers or sisters?" asked Ruth, coming over from the kitchen range, carrying a platter of hot food.

"Here are some chicharrones," smiled mamá, taking the smoking platter from Ruth and placing it before the boy. "I hope you like chicharrones."

"Sí, señora, I like them very much, gracias," gulped the boy, not knowing who to look at first. He took a hot chicharrone and crunched into it. "I have an older sister – " he went on in a mumble, his mouth full.

"Let's give him time to eat, hey?"

" – who is married and lives someplace in Guadalajara. But I've only seen her once since she got married. She never comes up to Sonora, never visited.

"I have a brother as well," he carried on, "a lot older than me and my sister. He went away to work in Texas before my mamá died. He came back twice I think the first year, then I never saw him again. He used to send money, but that stopped as well."

So he lost his mamá, and his papá too, it would appear, mamá thought to herself. He must miss them dreadfully, surely. She remembered what old Pancho had said three years ago at the San Stefan cemetery on The Day of the Dead: 'The past existence of those now departed are as treasured memories in those who still live'.

"Who looked after you then, Francisco?" asked mamá, at last venturing to say his name, and desperately wanting to take the boy and hug him warmly in her motherly arms. "An aunt or an uncle, was it?"

"No, señora, I mostly looked after myself." – Ruth and mamá exchanged mournful looks at this disclosure – "But I worked for a time on a cattle ranch."

A dreamy aspect invaded his features, as he went on:

"There was an old man by the name of Jesús, who was a cattleman, and he was a good friend to me for a long time. Hmm. I kind of looked on him as an uncle – and best friend as well. Uuy, he took care of me better than anyone did …"

Ruth sensed another tragedy about to be related.

"And he is no longer a friend?" she asked in a small, compassionate voice.

"Oh, Jesús died," the boy stated flatly, eyes flashing at the girl like blue lightning. His head went down once more to the food. "He died last month. And that was when I decided to go and try looking for my real uncle. I knew he was ranching or something like around these parts."

Then the boy of a sudden lost his appetite to eat.

No one said anything on hearing this further travail, no one dared or could not say anything; there was really nothing that could be said.

IV

One late afternoon a week later, mamá's face was flushed as she worked on the finishing touches to *comida*.

"It's ready!" she called from the firesmoke. "Sit yourselves, quickly now, ándale!"

"Where is papá?" asked Julia.

"Sit, my little *niña*, or should I put my hand to you?"

"Ay, mamá, I wish you wouldn't call me that, I'm a big girl now," Julia complained, pouting her lips.

Mamá laughed. "You will always be my little baby," she said, "so you do as you are told   Juanito, go and get your papá   Ah, he's coming …"

Juan rose from his seat anyway, to place a sarape over the parrot's cage, to stop the bird from 'heckling' everybody at the table.

"Please sit yourself, Francisco," beamed mamá with matronly warmth. "There you go," the boy no longer regarded as a stranger but as a member of the family.

"Oh, *guacamole!*" enthused Julia, eyes popping. "I love guacamole, mamá!"

She turned to the boy. "Do you like guacamole, Francisco?" in a rather coy tone of voice.

"Ay sí, Julia, and more than one portion every time."

"Mamá makes the best guacamole in the State, don't you, mamá?"

"Are you sitting, as I ordered, little chatterbox?"

"I'm sure she does, Julia," responded Francisco with a smile.

The family sat in silence as don Antonio intoned a brief prayer of grace. They crossed themselves with their usual hurried motions, and set to on the food displayed on the table before them.

"…Then this cattleman was bragging about how many bowls of beans he could eat," Francisco was saying to Juan a short time into the meal, "and he says to my friend, old Jesús, 'That's four bowls I've had already'. And Jesús says, 'Ah, hombre, I've eaten two so far.'

"'Ha! You'll never catch up with me,' says this cattleman. 'Well,' says Jesús, giving us a wink, 'I'm about ready for the next lot,' giving a quick wink this time at the cook, who comes staggering over lugging a ten-litre pot of beans, which he puts before Jesús. Hmm.

"Straightways, old Jesús starts dipping in this huge pot with a folded tortilla, and the cattleman just stares at him.

"'What's this, then?' he says, with a face like he'd been slapped.

"'Well, hombre, like I said, that's two lots I've had,' Jesús tells him, 'and as you can see for yourself I am now making inroads on the third, and will soon catch you up anyhow,'" and Francisco broke into a hearty roar of laughter, slapping Juan on the shoulder.

"What was it like living in Sonora?" asked Ruth attentively.

"Always hot and dusty, Rutí. Sonora is not too bad a place to grow up in; that is, if you're a cactus."

Which put amused smiles on the faces of Ruth and Juan – and even elicited a curl of don Antonio's lips.

"I made some more pictures today, Francisco," said Julia sweetly. "Would you like to see them? I'll get them to show you – "

"Sit!" commanded mamá, as the girl was about to rise. "You can show Francisco after comida, there's plenty of time. He's busy eating as you can see – What's the matter now, I thought you liked guacamole?"

"I do, mamá, and it's lovely."

"Well get into it then and stop your dawdling." Mamá turned to the boy, her smile broad and happy, and said, with sure confidence in her culinary skills, "How is the guacamole, Francisco?"

"I'll show you my pictures after comida," slipped in Julia.

"*Ay que rico*, doña María, this is excellent," replied the boy, blue eyes on mamá.

"Oh! Oh – gracias!" flustered the female cook. She turned abruptly to lose herself in the smoke of the kitchen fire, tears suddenly springing to her eyes. Caused no doubt by the boy's complimentary remark, which she had heard uttered a few times in the not too distant past.

"So tell me, Julia, what have you been drawing today?" Francisco asked the girl, his charming smile encompassing both her and Ruth.

"I went to the pueblito, to draw Florencino making his baskets – he is blind, you know. I think my pictures turned out very well."

"Even though you're saying so yourself," Ruth could not resist putting in, giving Francisco a shy, beautiful smile to compete with his own.

"How old are you?" she asked him tenderly. "You haven't told us."

"No, you haven't," said Julia. "Is it a secret or what? I bet you're older than Juan, are you?"

"It's no secret. I'm fifteen," smiled the boy. "I was fifteen sometime in February."

"*Sometime* in February?" queried Ruth. "Why do you say that? Don't you know exactly when?"

"Ay well, you see, my birthday is on the twenty-ninth."

"Gracious me!" exclaimed mamá, having listened in to this conversation. "It's the same as Pancho's – your uncle, I mean, Francisco. His birthday fell on the same date. ¡Chihuahuas!"

"Oh, Francisco, poor you," Ruth sympathised. "You have your birthday only every four years. That's awful!"

"It's alright," Francisco brushed it off with a grin, "for I dare swear I am surely a year older every year, if I may so say."

"Still, never mind – I hope you're going to have some of my corncakes which I baked myself," smiled Ruth, her lovely face colouring.

She was as quick as a whiplash in presenting a platter of perfectly baked pale-gold corncakes.

"I will go to our stable door!" mamá ejaculated. "Rutí, my pet, they must be the best corncakes I've seen in a long while. Aren't they so, papacito?"

"They are indeed," said don Antonio in quiet tones. "Our girl is a perfect angel," smiling down on his favourite one.

"Gracias, mamá, gracias, papá," and Ruth's radiantly happy face flushed again rosewise with pleasure and pride.

"I will try one for sure, Ruth, maybe even two or three or four, eh?" Francisco gently teased her, reaching out to help himself.

"Ay, Francisco, I must say you're a good eater, and it's what I like to see in a young man," said mamá, bouncing on her toes and heels before the hearth, her broad face beaming.

The dog Salté was also quite taken up with the young newcomer. Though he was now old and grey and slow in his movements, he tried to act like a frisky puppy to gain the boy's attention. The great hound ambled up to him this moment and licked his hand.

"Who's a big soft mutt, then, eh?" said Francisco fondly, chucking the creature under his jaw. "Why, ay que bueno, you really are a soft beast, to be sure. But a good dog all the same. As good as a *Paracho* guitar, you might say. Uuy, I wouldn't lie to you on that score, you can depend on it," now knuckling the top of its scruffy-haired skull.

Both mamá and Juan heard this, and glanced at each other with an almost pained expression on their faces. Such had been heard before this day.

V

Late spring brought snowy cloud and a few small showers of rain, boosting the growth of things on the earth. Fragrant cotton-white apple blossom was caught by breezes, petals floating and dancing on air, to settle on the ground like snowflakes.

Sounds had shape and colour, and a smell had bite and flavour, as the spring turned inexorably on its course, under a hot blue blaze of light.

"Come on, Francisco!" said Juan on a sudden impulse one fine fresh morning, "I'll show you along the river way. We can go as far as *Sancho's Elbow*," and the two boys rose from their seats at the family table and set off across the sunslapped yard.

"Are you coming, Salté?" called Juan over his shoulder.

The dog was now fast ailing, cataracts beginning to form in his old grey-green eyes. In these present times he spent the better part of each day sleeping.

Salté got slowly and painfully to his feet, tottered a few steps with heavy tread. Then his rear-end collapsed and he sat there on his haunches, tongue lolling and panting away, trying to drag himself along.

Juan came to him, squatted by his old faithful canine friend.

"Alright, old fellow, you stay here and rest up," he said softly, tugging gently at one of his floppy ragged ears. Salté raised his grizzled head and licked his master's face.

He watched the two boys lope away like a pair of panthers, blinking at flies and sunlight, too tired and weary to snap at the tormenting insects. Even his scentscape had narrowed down to uninteresting, uninspiring levels. He dropped his muzzle into the dust, drooped one eye, then the other.

A short time later Salté made one more effort to rise. He slowly half-dragged his large body beyond Chapulín's stable, beyond the smelly wasteland patch, into an area of thick undergrowth.

Deep in the scrub and foliage of this undergrowth was a shallow hollow. Salté had obviously been here many times before, for it was almost carpeted with his hair and fur.

Awkwardly and somewhat hesitantly, he described a couple of circles in his turning, finally settling into a sleeping position, slack jaw propped on his fore-paws.

His moist though dust-covered nose, that organ still sensitive to rooting out the faintest of scents, caught now familiar smells of his surrounds; familiar and reassuring, but all the same, at this present moment, of no immediate or particular interest – he was past all that.

Once more he drooped one eye closed, then the other. Peacefully.

It was the last light of a day he was ever to see again.

VI

"I'm hot and dusty," said Juan. "Let's walk in the river to cool off."

The boys waded along the shallow riverbed, raising their feet in the manner of spatulas and splashing each other like a pair of toddler tearaways.

"¡Ay que caray! ¡Újule! ¡Uuy!" laughed Francisco, "I'm getting wet through," and Juan threw an odd glance at his companion, struck by the phrasing of his words.

The younger boy bent to pick up a pebble, oval shaped and smooth, yellow and black in colour, like the markings of a huge bumble-bee. He examined it for a moment, dried and polished it on the arm of his shirt. He felt its warmth and smoothness and well-curved shape.

"Hmm. *Muy bonita*, eh?" he said, raspingly.

"Like a gemstone," smiled Juan.

"Uuy, life shapes all things, is it, eh?"

Then the stone suddenly lost its charm and appeal, and Francisco shied it at a thin tree trunk ahead of them, and – *Clunk!* – as it hit dead centre.

A daredevil of a dust-devil danced over the ground before them.

"¡Újule! Did you see that, Juanny?" enthused Francisco with inordinate pleasure. "I wasn't expecting to see one here. We get them often enough in Sonora."

"I saw plenty one summer on don Roberto's ranch. Not as many as you in Sonora, I don't suppose. A lot of desert where you come from, hey?"

"Sí, sí, a dry, parched land – all of the northwest is like that. After saying that, there are odd pockets of grassland, and even some woodland. In the hilly parts there's more greenery, because of the rain those hills get. Hmm .

"But mostly desert, as you say … Lots of lizards and grasshoppers, plenty of snakes and scorpions, too."

The younger boy pointed to a thick growth of pipe organ cacti lining part of the outskirt of the pueblo beyond the river.

"See that stuff there, Juan?"

"Organ cactus. Make good solid walls. Big things, aren't they?"

Francisco smiled, a shade smugly. "Uuy, they're tiny compared to the cactus growing in Sonora."

"Sí, the – what's its name - ?"

"Saguaro. Giants! They grow really tall, thick and heavy, weigh many hundreds of kilos. Hold a lot of water, they do, store it, like, I'm bound to say – And I wouldn't lie to you," the boy grinned.

"They're the ones with arms, leastwise they look much like arms."

"That's so. The Saguaro. Only found in the Sonoran desert – No, I tell a lie, *perdónome* – they also grow over a great part of Arizona."

"North America."

"Sí, sí… but it was *all* Mexico at one time, you know, that Arizona state – and Texas, too."

Juan agreed there, because he'd often heard old Pancho Ramírez relating pieces of Mexico's past history.

The youngsters could hear bird-fluting sounds. And music coming from the ancient wind-up Victrola phonograph in the pueblo, playing traditional *corridos* and folk ballads, usually through the daylight hours.

"That music from the pueblo, hear it?" said Francisco. "That tune …I like it."

Said Juan, "Gets played ten times a day, that one."

"I know it, the tune – *Sentimiento y Dolor* – I always liked that one …"

Which left Juan a trifled unsettled, knowing of someone who had loved that very same tune.

VII

At a stand of carrizos by the riverbank, Juan cut a long thick stick with his Swiss army knife and gave it to his friend. He then fashioned himself a stick and they sauntered on along a trackway.

"Sometimes there are dog-packs around here," Juan cautioned his companion. "There are two things you can do if you ever come up with them. Either threaten them with your stick, which works well enough in these parts, or bend down as if you're about to pick a rock to chuck at them."

The newcomer grinned, explaining that that is exactly what they do in Sonora. "Without a doubt, the dog is a cowardly creature at the best of times, and will back off if given half a chance, I always find – But don't get them cornered anywhere, they'll fight then, alright."

Later, they reached a sharp bend in the river's course.

"This is what we call Sancho's Elbow," Juan explained. "It's where your uncle used to take me fishing when I was smaller. Over on that side, see, where the water is deep."

"Ay que bueno, a lovely spot for fishing, to be sure. Hmm," returned his companion. "And a lovely pastime, it would seem," he went on in an ironic tone, "for a ranchero!"

They ambled on, slashing their carrizo sticks at long lush grass at the river's bank. Soon, they came to a broad and straight stretch of trackway. On the left of it ran the river, on the opposite side were fields of growing corn and alfalfa, and small, sheltered wooded areas.

"Now here, Francisco," said Juan, pointing up the track with his stick, "here is where your uncle first taught me to ride a horse. I had a real terrific buckskin mare, a three-year-old, only fifteen hands. A lovely creature," he sighed, "but was forever down with one ailment after another. She never reached five years, and it near broke me when we had to put her down.

"*Estrellita*, I called her … That same year papá and Pancho – your uncle – came into our yard leading a tall, well-proportioned chestnut bay. It was of course Chapulín. Oh, what a handsome devil is Chapulín – and fast!"

"¡Újule! I know it. The best I've seen in a long while, and I've seen plenty of good fast horses up in Sonora, and no mistake."

"Hey! Did you see that in the trees? Over there, look!"

"What was it, Juan? What have I missed?"

"The ravens. I just saw the ravens in that tree."

"Ravens?"

"That's right, an adult male and its mate. They've lived here in the valley ever since I was knee-high to the grass there. Not *those* ravens, I shouldn't think, but certainly the same family of them. This is their territory. Egg-stealers they are, that pair especially, forever raiding the nests around here.

"It's a wonder we still have other birds in this valley. Your uncle knew of them. It was Pancho who told me of their existence. He used to call them the 'black bandits', because of their stealing habits."

"I thought the raven was a scavenger bird," said Francisco.

"They're that as well, but those two specialise in stealing eggs. They take hens' eggs too, given half the chance, so they are not popular in the pueblo – Oh, there is one of them! Do you see it?"

"Ah, sí, taking off to somewhere, a special raid maybe. Ay que bueno, it looks a magnificent bird in flight …"

"Well, time to head back, I guess. We can come again mañana – early."

Responded Francisco, with a smile: "I look forward to it. It's an early dawn that kills the night."

The two boys moved on, retracing their steps.

VIII

Night time. No moon. Stars like city lights glittering and winking in the vast heavens.

Juan and Francisco, on a warm night excursion, strode to the river, swishing their sticks at long grass and weeds. They made themselves comfortable at the riverbank, grandstand seats for the spectacle in the sky.

"In Sonora this'll be scorpion time," the younger one opened up, in his unusual sandpapery, older person's voice.

"It's like that here as well. Come out at night, to hunt I suppose."

"And *get* hunted, Juanny. In Sonora, at any rate. We have big-eared bats that come out from hiding to hunt scorpions."

"Not to eat them, surely?"

"Sí, sí, amigo, juicy and good for them."

"But the venom, such powerful stuff."

"Uuy, these kind of bats are – what's the name? – they are immune to a scorpion's poison. Only creature that is immune, by the by. Every species to their likes and dislikes, as the saying has it. Hmm …"

They gazed up at the brilliant array of stars in companionable silence for a spell.

"You know," Francisco was up and running once again, "where I come from the land is so empty, empty of people, I mean – plenty of wildlife though, if you know where to look for it. Keep your eyes peeled and look carefully, as they say.

"But there are no cities in Sonora, no big towns. So no lights to spoil the view of nightsky stars. Over the desert lands for instance, the starlight is tremendous. Uuy, you have never seen so many stars. The sky is so clear when there are no town lights interfering, and the same goes for moonlight. On nights there's no moon showing, not a sliver, you can look up at those bright stars, and it's as if you could just reach up and pluck yourself a star like picking fruit …"

"Every star we see is in fact a sun, that much I do know."

"Sí, I know it too …But it makes you wonder, don't you think, that each out there – each a sun – well, uuy, may have planets as well."

"I expect so," agreed Juan. "It would be possible, I guess. Hard to detect, though, because they won't be a light like a star is. And you only see the light of a star, and not the star itself."

"Sí, okay, but just imagine, Juanny, billions of planets! Millions at least like our Earth. ¡Újule!"

"I expect so, sí," repeated Juan, trying hard to take in such preposterous phenomena, essentially because he believed that they could not ever be detected.

Francisco changed course. He wanted to tell his friend more about where he came from.

"Up in Sonora we have peregrines, you know, the peregrine falcon."

"And the falcon?"

"Same thing, in a manner of speaking."

"A real predator bird," enthused Juan keenly. "Do you see many of them?"

"Only when you're looking," the boy's blue eyes glinting with mischief.

"¿Que?"

"Only kidding you. No, you see a good few, you might say. Uuy, a good few more, to be honest."

"Tell me more about them. How do they hunt?"

"Sí, I could tell you, I do suppose …"

Francisco hesitated deliberately, a cheeky grin working its way on his schoolboyish features. He liked to tease.

Juan was having none of it.

"Well, tell me then, I'd like to know."

"Sí, of course you do. They usually only prey on other birds. They go for smaller birds, as you'd guess. The peregrine kills with its beak, by the way, not with its claws."

"As the eagle does – with its claws, I mean."

"Sí, amigo, and the hawk too. The peregrine falcon tries to catch its prey in flight, which is not that easy, even though the falcon is damn fast in flight. Hmm, believe you me. The fastest bird of all birds, I'd dare to say – when attacking, that is."

"Just think, Juanny, their '*comida*' flying in the air …"

"So that is how it does it, uses its beak. Never realised that."

"Mind you, I wouldn't in all honesty say that's so. The thing is, you see, it doesn't always catch prey in that manner – in flight.

"No-o, we know birds can be stupid, which is why we say 'bird-brain' of anyone not so bright. Instead, as nature itself comes into the matter, it is *instinct* that's taught them clever tricks. Many of them as I've seen hunted in pairs. Ay caray, makes it easier all round.

"I've seen them and watched them, time after time, and so successful they are too, hunting in pairs. But then they squabble – I take it that's the word – they squabble over the 'kill'. Uuy, wonderful to watch though."

"I've never seen a falcon, except a picture in a book," confessed Juan, a shade envious of the other.

"We have eagles too in our region."

"That is a handsome bird; we have them as well, but you don't see many."

"Ah, to be sure, the eagle, the royalty of the skies – Oye, Juan, feel that wind? A warm wind, eh? Must be God's breath on us …"

Francisco's blue eyes sparkled, almost indigo in the night light.

Said Juan: "We had better be getting back, I have certain chores to do."

"Ay que caray, Time has no patience, waits for no one, and must always run on. If only Time would drift as time should – Ah! Did you see that mouse? There! The little rascal, eh? Muy bien. Now the tiny fellow is gone, just like that …"

The two set off for home.

And Juan was beginning to sense in his young friend a deep and sensitive reverence for all living creatures.

IX

One early evening young Francisco wandered alone down to the river. He hunkered down on his heels by the water's edge and removed his battered straw sombrero. The lowering sun fell fully on his head of ginger-red hair, which shone like molten gold.

He cupped a hand and scooped water to drink. Then he splashed water over his face, most of it hitting his shirt front. It would soon dry, he knew. He shook his head as a dog would, to remove the excess water, and slapped the sombrero back on his scalp – he always felt naked if he was not wearing his sombrero.

Getting to his feet he gazed over at the far distant slate-blue peaks of mountains thrusting into the lighter blue of sky. The swelling sun was descending into a glowing flow of orange and magenta.

The boy's attention was suddenly taken by something not thirty paces away in front of him, and his eyes widened in open astonishment. On the opposite bank of the river was a man mounted on a horse.

The rider was – as Francisco could plainly see – a most distinguished-looking white-haired elderly gentleman. He was dressed in the immaculate and resplendent uniform of a master *charro*, sitting straight-backed on a magnificent velvet-black stallion with a long, red-ribboned tail. The horse and rider appeared so extraordinarily handsome, debonair and almost otherworldly that the boy could not but be visibly impressed and moved by the sight.

With superb control the white-haired *caballero* halted his mount and held it square on four legs at the very edge of the bank on its opposite side.

The old gentleman spoke first, in a deep and commanding, resonant voice which easily carried over to the boy's ears.

"I can take it, muchacho, that you must be Francisco Cruz Ramírez," and it was a statement rather than a question.

"Sí, señor," replied the boy, his astonishment now knowing no bounds, as he stared at this marvellous apparition before him.

"Still staying with the Ramos family, I presume."

Again, a statement of fact, already known.

"Sí, señor," in a low, gravelled tone.

"Tell me, muchacho," went on the distinguished caballero in rich, rolling, friendly cadences, "can you ride a horse?"

"Sí, señor. In Sonora where I come from I was never off the back of a horse."

"Splendid! I thought as much, and what you have said is what I needed to hear. Well, that is decided as far as I am concerned," smiled the gentleman, his words for himself as much as for the boy.

He continued on: "You can work for me on my ranch, if that idea suits. Does the offer appeal to you by any chance, young man? What do you say?"

"Sí, señor!" grinned Francisco with delight and wonder.

"Good, good! It is settled then. You can start next week if you like. An opportunity for you to see a new delivery of horses to be trained.

"I tell you right away, young fellow, you will live in my house as one of the family, till you come of age – hopefully, if all goes well."

The old gentleman moved on to more immediate matters:

"Do not forget to bring your gear, whatever you may have. If you don't have anything, other than those rag-ripped *pantalones* and that disreputable hat sitting on your head, then you need not give it any further thought. I shall ensure that you are taken care of. My sons will kit you out nicely and properly, and there is a spare saddle I think you will like.

"We shall make a ranchero of you, muchacho, if I am not mistaken. That is the idea in the main. Well, how is that to your liking, hey? What do you say?"

"Señor, I don't know how to thank you," the boy burbled happily, removing his sombrero as a mark of respect, and revealing his thatch of hair in all its reddish glory, and which momentarily startled the old *haciendado*. "I am very grateful, señor, to be sure I am."

"I am certain you are. But of course, as you surely realise, you have to prove your worth to me first of all, though I am equally certain that you won't disappoint me on that score."

The ranch-owner changed the subject:

"You see, muchacho, I knew your uncle well. We were firm friends for many long years … We shared many tribulations, and many good times, too, I am happy to say."

He gave a heavy, emotion-loaded sigh. "Your uncle never got the decent breaks he really deserved," he went on, studying the boy's features with great interest, no doubt making comparisons in his mind. "However, for all that he lived a full and contented life. I shall make every effort to see that you get the breaks, muchacho, and hope you turn out in life as good a man as my dear late friend, Pancho."

The haciendado gazed keenly at the boy, now with an unmistakable amused look on his aristocratic countenance.

"You will most likely be working with Pancho's old team. Juan Ramos is their immediate superior, and holds a tight rein on them – he has to! Do you know them, by the by?"

"Uuy, I can't say as I do, no, señor."

"You will know Cándido, surely."

"Ah, sí, I have heard Cándido mentioned."

"Apart from Cándido, there is also José, Gerardo, Emilio … and our wayward Julian."

"Never heard of them, señor."

"Well, you will get to know them all in good time," which was said in a somewhat ironic tone.

"Sí, señor."

After a long strained pause, the old man and the boy staring keenly at each other, in an effort to know what the other might be thinking, the caballero continued:

"Well, I must leave you for the present. Young Juanito can tell you or show you the way to my spread. In the meantime, I will have one of my saddle-horses sent to you – maybe Juanito can do that for you – so you can ride to work, my boy.

"I expect to see you there next week on the Monday, by noon at the latest, okay? Until then, I bid you *adiós*!"

"Adiós, señor, and a thousand thanks!"

With cool precision the old charro rider backed his mount in four short rapid paces, wheeled round, set silver-rowelled spurs to the horse's flanks, and began to trot off.

A moment later the rider brought his stallion to a halt and swung round in the saddle. He turned his mount round, to face the boy standing stock still on the far bank.

"By the by, muchacho," he called over conversationally, "I do not for a moment think you would mind at all if we addressed you as … Pancho?"

The boy could not help but laugh at this, slapping his thighs like a seasoned ranchero.

"¡Señor!" he shouted back with glee. "In Sonora everybody called me that."

"Did they now?" smiled the old man. "Bueno … Pancho it is. See you soon."

"But you, señor, I don't know your name!"

The rider brought his mount a little further to the river bank's edge, again with that fancy dressage style of manoeuvre.

He laughed with hearty cheer, calling over: "Forgive me my deplorable manners, young *Pancho*, but I simply assumed that you already knew," sweeping his sombrero regally from his head and describing a salutation in the air, and announcing:

"I am Zedillo. That is who I am. Roberto Arías Zedillo."

"Ay que caray, señor, but I have heard of you. You are well known in Sonora among the cattlemen. You are famous, señor!"

"Famous, or perhaps notorious better fits the description," the old man smiled grandly, like a senator. "One of the two, depending on who says it. But you, little Pancho, you can call me … don Roberto."

Don Roberto!

And don Roberto swung round once more and rode on in equestrian splendour, the black stallion kicking up dust. The boy stared after him, his chest full with barely constrained emotion.

He turned and headed back for the homestead, broke into an easy trot, eager to be back to tell Ruth and the rest of the Ramos family of his extraordinary good fortune.

Young Pancho could not have felt happier in life's situation in which he now found himself, a new and hopeful, promising condition.

He had found himself a *patrón*. Or rather, to be more accurate, a *patrón* had found him.

And his pounding feet stirred up the dust, the dust like gold in the setting sun's rays. In the air the dust motes whirled and danced in their erratic, microscopic orbits, to eventually settle on late spring wildflowers and the like.

AN AFTERWORD

The literary character *Pancho* is a survivor. From 1978 in Mexico, where he was first created, he moved on from the novel "The Scorpion's Last Day" – which was later aborted – to the narrative prose poem "From Dust To Flowers: A Day In The Life Of Rural Mexico", to the eponymous novels of 2016 and this recent publication : "PANCHO II".

The old ranchero rode through four separate manuscripts, over four decades, to emerge once again for the interested reader.

DON ERIC CARROLL 2018